# LORD OF WAR: BLACK ANGEL

A Medieval Romance

**By Kathryn Le Veque**

Printed by Dragonblade Publishing in the United States of America

To my husband, Rob

# LORD OF WAR: BLACK ANGEL
*A Medieval Romance Novel*
By Kathryn Le Veque

**De Russe Family Tree (Generations between 1313 A.D. and 1457 A.D.)**

*Succession of the male de Russe line:*
Brandt b. 1313 *(Known as the Black Angel, born in Exeter, only son*

*of Aramis de Russe)*

Aramis b. 1357 *(Mother was a de Nerra, bringing the bloodlines of*

*the great mercenary Braxton de Nerra into the de Russe bloodlines)*

Trenton b. 1390

Brandt b. 1428 *(Second son of Trenton, younger brother is Martin*

*de Russe, father of Patrick and Nicolas – eldest brother, not*

*mentioned in* The Dark One: Dark Knight, *is the heir to the dukedom*

*of Exeter)*

Gaston* b. 1457 (Son of Brandt, known as The Dark One)


Trenton b. 1487

*  Maternal great-great-great grandfather was Braxton de Nerra,
mercenary commander


*Author's Note:*

*The storyline involves the Battle of Poitier and for the most part,
the locations and events leading up to the battle are historically
accurate. If you are interested in Medieval warfare, it makes*

9

*interesting reading. There is a future(real) Duke of Exeter during this time, but he was only four years old and not yet the Duke of Exeter at the time of Poitiers. I have given the Dukedom to the House of de Russe during this period in time and for the purposes of the fictional story.*

# ENGLAND

*In dreams we grasp at finite bits of reality, premonitions of what may come to pass. In dreams we are all witches, straining to see what the future holds.*
*~ Anonymous Poet, circa. 13th century*

# CHAPTER ONE

*She'd had the dream before. She was standing on the edge of a meadow, looking at a massive castle in the distance, partially obscured by sheets of driving rain. In spite of the weather, smoke rose in ribbons over the damaged battlements.*

*Overhead, the sky was the color of pewter with fat, angry clouds, but upon earth, the field was flooded from the unforgiving rain that had been falling for days, perhaps weeks, mayhap even months. It was difficult to know. It seemed as if it had been raining forever.*

*A great battle had concluded upon the field and there was a sea of bodies strewn about, like pieces of driftwood upon an endless muddy sea. Her heart was in her throat as she observed the scene, her breathing coming in panicked little gasps. Something was here for her, something she loved so desperately that she couldn't think of anything else. The feelings were so strong that they overwhelmed her, blinding her to her own safety as she plunged into the sea of death, searching, looking for something she wasn't quite sure of yet could feel it more strong in her heart than anything.*

*... her heart....*

She awoke in a cold sweat.

***

*London, 1356 A.D.*
*Reign of Edward III*

It smelled like death.

Chargers bearing great and bloody knights clip-clopped wearily along the street leading from the great wharf along the Thames followed by equally weary men-at-arms who had seen perhaps one too many battles. They were exhausted, beaten, bloodied and doomed by the depression that often infects those who have witnessed much strife.

They collectively expelled a stench that smelled like death. The Lady Ellowyn de Nerra ignored the stench for the most part as she watched the great army of the Duke of Exeter disembark their sea-scarred *cogs.* They filtered up from the wharfs along the Thames, a great rolling tide of humanity that brought about the reality and carnage the Black Prince's war in France had delivered to England.

Ellowyn wasn't observing the downtrodden army because she was curious. She was looking for someone, the great duke who had taken command of eight hundred of her father's retainers. Although she'd never actually seen the man whose warrior skills were legendary, she'd heard much about him from her father as well as others. He was a warrior whose name struck fear into the hearts of both English and French alike, a name so awesome that to even whisper it was as if to mention the Devil himself. Men did not take the name of Brandt de Russe lightly. The French even had a name for him; *L'Ange noir,* they whispered fearfully. *The Black Angel.* The most powerful knight in the arsenal of the Black Prince, the Black Angel brought the Apocalypse with him wherever he went.

The Duke's army was kicking up clouds of dust in the already dirty city of London. They were heading for the training grounds about a mile west of the Tower of London, the mammoth structure that loomed over to the east from where Ellowyn was standing. She could just see the black spires of the White Tower reaching to the sky. However, her attention was on the army as it rumbled past, turning to the escort of soldiers she had brought with her from her father's seat of Erith Castle. These men had remained behind while others went on to fight with the Black Prince, but they knew de Russe on sight.

"Do you see him yet?" Ellowyn asked the soldier standing to her right.

The man, seasoned and blind in one eye, shook his head as his one good eye skimmed the returning troops. "Not yet, my lady," he replied, "but make no mistake. You will know de Russe when you see him."

Ellowyn looked at him queerly. "How is that possible when I have never met the man?"

The soldier wriggled his bushy eyebrows. "Because he is the biggest man alive and he wears armor with great spikes blooming from the shoulders. Some say he drinks the blood of his victims and hangs their innards over his shoulders. That is why they call him the God of War; in battle, the man has no equal."

Ellowyn thought on that a moment before returning her attention to the men shuffling past her. There were so many of them and she was beginning to get impatient.

"Well," she sighed. "I wish the man would hurry along. We must return home soon or father will drag himself from his sick bed like Lazarus rising from the dead and hunt us down."

The old blind sergeant fought off a smile. "Your father is a determined man, my lady," he said, thinking that Deston de Nerra's head-strong daughter was far more determined than her father ever was. "But I doubt he... by Jesus and Mary, *there* he is. Do you see him, my lady?"

The sergeant's excited tone had Ellowyn's head bobbing to catch a glimpse, although she was not entirely sure what, exactly, she was straining to catch a glimpse *of.*

"Who?" she demanded. "Is it de Russe?"

The sergeant grasped her shoulder, gently turning her towards the wharf where the gentle waters flowed and the boats bobbed about like corks. He was pointing down to the water's edge in the distance.

"There," he said, some satisfaction in his voice. "He is standing at the edge of the ship with the big black charger behind him. See him now?"

Ellowyn did. Even at a distance, she could see an enormous man in heavy layers of protection, plate armor intermingled with mail. The man was standing at the mouth of the gangway as the last of the soldiers disembarked the cog, and she began to walk in his direction.

The contingent of escort soldiers moved to follow but it was made difficult by the fact that Ellowyn was a small woman and able to dodge around people much more easily than a gang of well-armed men. The sergeant struggled to keep sight of the petite young woman with the deliciously curvy figure, a marvel of womanhood that brought suitors from all corners of the kingdom seeking a glimpse of her glory. With her buttock-length golden red hair and almond-shaped green eyes, she was an unearthly beauty. But she was also stubborn, opinionated, intelligent and determined, a combination that tended to shake even the most staunch of admirers.

"My lady?" the sergeant called to her as she began to lose herself in the crowed. "You must wait for us, my lady!"

Ellowyn heard his words but she ignored them. She was nearing the ships and resolved to speak with de Russe, as instructed by her father. She had a message to deliver and was determined to be done with it so they could return to the cool green fields of Cumbria. She'd been on the road for weeks and was longing for home.

She wound her way through the crowds standing along the smelly wharf, dodging soldiers and wagons as they off loaded, until she finally came to the edge of the water. Being rather short, she had to stand on one of the many tarred logs that were sunk deep into the shore, logs that the big ships would anchor on to so they wouldn't drift back out into the river.

Over the heads of others, she could see an enormous warrior standing with his equally enormous charger, watching the last of the men trickle off the boat. She jumped off the anchor log as her

16

escort struggled to catch up to her. She made haste for the knight with the well-worn armor.

"My lord?" she called, gathering up her heavy skirts so she wouldn't drag them through a huge puddle of horse urine. "My lord, are you de Russe?"

The warrior was speaking with another man in used and dented armor. He heard Ellowyn approach because he turned to look at her. He was without his helm, his cropped hair as black as night and square-jawed, chiseled features holding a handsome edge. However, his eyes were the most noticeable, smoke-colored and intense beneath intelligently arched brows. His gaze lingered on Ellowyn a moment before, without answering, turning back to the conversation at hand.

The man had completely ignored her. Struggling not to become incensed, Ellowyn came up beside him and tried again.

"My lord?" she said politely. "Are you the Duke?"

The man acted as if he hadn't heard her. He continued talking to the knight next to him. Coming to understand now that he was deliberately ignoring her, Ellowyn's patience began to fracture.

"My lord de Russe?" she didn't sound so polite. "If you would kindly address me, I would be grateful."

The knight did nothing more than turn a calculated back to her. Ellowyn found herself staring at the backside of the most enormous man she had ever seen. She was perhaps a little over five feet in height, but the knight with his back to her was easily three times her size and well over a foot taller. Standing next to him, her head came to his sternum at the most, and the circumferences of the fists resting upon his hips were nearly as large as her head. She took a moment to inspect the man, but his tremendous size did nothing to deter her rising irritation.

"My lord," she said shortly, reaching out to thump him on his mailed arm. "I require your attention."

He didn't respond. He continued to focus on the man beside him. Infuriated, Ellowyn walked around him and thrust herself in between the two men. Her angry face scowled into his dark eyes.

"You will not ignore me," she commanded. "I have come on behalf of...."

The colossal knight cut her off. "Be gone, wench," he rumbled. "Although you are pleasing to the eye, I have no use for you."

Ellowyn's mouth popped open in outrage. "You will not speak to me as if I am a common trollop," she fired back. "I have business with you."

The knight did nothing more than reach out and push her away. He'd really only meant to brush her aside but with his strength and her diminutive size, he ended up knocking her onto her arse.

Ellowyn ended up in the puddle of urine she had tried so hard to avoid and she bolted up, muddied and dirty, and pushed her way between the men with more determination than before. When the knight wouldn't look at her, she hammered a fist against his dented breastplate.

"Touch me again and you shall suffer the consequences," she hissed. "My name is Ellowyn de Nerra and you have eight hundred of my father's men under your command. My father has sent me with a message for you."

That got his attention. The warrior looked at her, perhaps more closely this time, although his stone-like expression didn't register as much.

"You are de Nerra's daughter?" he asked.

Ellowyn was so angry that she was shaking. "I am," she seethed, "and when I tell my father how you have shown me such disrespect, he will cease all ties with you, I am sure."

The warrior could see how furious she was. "Lady Ellowyn, had you told me who you were at the first, I would not have had cause to cast you aside," he said in a deep, rumbling voice. "You did not identify yourself."

"And this is how you treat every woman who does not identify herself? Are you so grand and glorious that you feel yourself head and heart above the rest of the world?"

He didn't rise to her anger, although he had to admit, it had been a long time since he had faced such fury. No one dared show him any emotion other than blind obedience, but this small and quite beautiful woman was different. She had much courage. Her anger threatened to bring a smile to his impassive lips, but he fought it.

"I thought you were a whore," he said bluntly. "What message does your father have for me?"

If she had been outraged before, his forthright reply set her to fuming. Her delicately arched eyebrows flew up.

"Do I *look* like a whore?" she nearly shouted.

He felt that odd urge to smile again. "Nay, my lady, you do not," he thought perhaps he'd better make some attempt to ease her before she exploded in all directions. "As I said, you did not identify yourself and...."

She waved a sharp hand at him. "Bite your tongue," she barked. "Listen to me and listen well. My father wants all of his men rested and ready to return to Erith Castle immediately. He expects a full accounting of how many men he has lost and expectations as to when he can expect monetary or manpower compensation for those losses. I am staying at Grey's Inn on Holborn Road and you will have all of my father's men delivered to me tomorrow at dawn. If you delay, I shall return home and tell him of your utter lack of respect for him and his directives. Is this in any way unclear?"

It had been years since he had been intimidated or fearful, but looking down into that beautiful red face, he realized that not only was he intimidated, he was contrite. He really was. Shocked, and somewhat amused at himself, he simply nodded his head.

"It is, my lady."

"Do you have anything more slanderous or offensive to say to me?"

"Nay, my lady."

"Then I bid you good day."

With that, she turned around and hustled off, dodging errant soldiers and beasts of burden. The warrior just stood there and watched her storm off, eventually surrounded by her escort who had, throughout the exchange, simply stood by in shock as their lady raged at a man three times her size.

More than that, she was raging at the deadly and legendary Duke of Exeter, Brandt de Russe. There was no one living in recent memory that had managed to do such a thing and emerged unscathed. Brandt reached up and scratched his head as if the entire circumstance had confused him.

"*That* was de Nerra's daughter?" he turned back to the knight standing next to him. "I did not even know he had one."

Sir Dylan de Lara lifted his dark eyebrows, catching a glimpse of the well-dressed woman as she faded down the avenue.

"He does indeed," he replied. "His son and heir committed himself to the Benedictines some time ago, a sincere shame because from what I heard, the man had the makings of a great knight. But he lives in a monastery somewhere in Lincolnshire while de Nerra's only other child is the lady you just met."

Brandt digested the information. "With that courage, she would make a fine knight herself," he muttered, scratching at his neck because his mail was chafing badly. "I do believe I have just been threatened. "

"I concur."

"Then I suppose I should do as I have been instructed and have her father's five hundred and sixty-two men waiting for her at Gray's Inn come dawn."

"That might be wise."

He stopped scratching his neck and pulled at the mail irritably. "Perhaps I should simply take them over to the inn tonight and be done with it. I shall let her worry about how she is going to house and feed over six hundred exhausted men."

"I am not entirely sure that is fair to the men."

De Russe was at the end of his part in the discussion. He mounted his massive warhorse, scarred and muscular, and spurred the animal up the avenue where the hordes of men had gone.

De Lara watched him go, thinking that perhaps he should follow. He was, after all, the man's second in command, a position that few men could hold simply because de Russe did not allow anyone, man or woman, to get close to him. He had known Dylan and his twin, Alex, for a few years and they all had much the same brooding, intense and courageous personalities. In that respect, they could tolerate each other. It was enough to keep them bonded.

Mounting his big bay stallion, Dylan spurred the edgy horse off the *cog* and followed de Russe's trail, heading into the heart of London.

## CHAPTER TWO

Grey's Inn was a popular place on the northern outskirts of London, a busy establishment with a very large main room and plenty of bodies to fill it. Now that the sun had set, it was full of the rabble of the city seeking shelter and comfort for the night.

Ellowyn sat in front of the big window near the front door. Her escort sat at tables surrounding her, for she would not let them sit with her. She wanted to sit by herself and enjoy her meal in private. Presented with boiled beef, turnips and carrots, she had quite a feast.

Wrapped up against the chill air snaking between the slats of the window, she unwittingly found herself in conversation in spite of her desire to remain alone. The head of her escort, seated at the table next to her, had mentioned something to his colleagues about de Russe, a comment that had fired up Ellowyn. Now the old soldier found himself easing a woman who was fairly quick to temper. He'd made what he considered a fairly innocent comment and she flared.

"Nay," Ellowyn snapped. "*You* do not understand. I care not of the man or his reputation. What he did was... was inexcusable."

"I am not excusing him, my lady," he insisted calmly. "But in fairness, de Russe is a wealthy and powerful man. I am sure he has women approach him by the dozens. He simply thought you were one of the rabble."

Ellowyn made a face, her lips twisted and her nose wrinkled, something her father called the 'pickle snuff'. She'd been doing it since infancy and it was an expression she never outgrew. It was comical and animated, displaying her vast displeasure at something.

"That is an insulting presumption," she said flatly. "You are intimating I look like a... a trollop."

"I am not, my lady."

She turned her back on him, obviously. "I will not speak to you any longer," she sniffed, returning to her food. "You defend de Russe."

The old soldier was trying not to smile, for Lady Ellowyn was feisty to the point of comedy.

"I do not, my lady," he said steadily, casting a glance at his smirking companions. "I was simply attempting to ease your anger."

"You did not ease it," she said, still facing away from him. "'You have only made it worse. Now you are making me speak to you when I swore that I would not. Go away and leave me alone."

The old soldier stood up from the table, biting his lip to keep from grinning. "We will not be far if you need us, my lady."

"Go far away," she sniffed. "Go sleep in the stables. I do not want to see you again until morning. Now, see what you have made me do? I am speaking to you again when I swore that I would not. Go away from me *now*."

She growled and smacked the table angrily. The old soldier and his three companions vacated her presence lest she see them all laughing at her. They wound their way through the tables and bodies of the crowded room, filled with smoke and loud men. They wouldn't go too far, for they would not leave their lady without protection. But with the mood she was in this eve, the old soldier truly pitied the man who might try to accost her. He would come away missing an eye.

So they hovered near the stairs that led to the second floor of the inn, a rickety set of slats that were in need of repair. The de Nerra escort tried to hide from her view but within minutes she spied them, lingering in the shadows, and her eyes widened with outrage. She pointed the knife she was using for her bread at them, silent words of threat implied, so the lot of them ducked away and went out the back of the establishment. They would head around to the front so they could watch her from the street.

Ellowyn watched her escort disappear into the back of the inn, satisfied they were finally leaving her alone. She had spent far too much time with them already and they were annoying her. Like dogs, the followed her around eagerly and she wanted no part of it.

23

At least, not tonight. Tonight, she simply wanted to be left alone to eat and rest before they began their trip home tomorrow.

Her solitude was not to be. No sooner had her escort vacated the noisy establishment than an unwelcome visitor appeared. Ellowyn smelled him before she even saw him, the scent of blood and sweat and disgust enveloping her like a fog.

"My sweet and lovely lady," a man in well-worn chainmail plopped down in the chair opposite her. "Pray, are you traveling alone?"

Ellowyn frowned and pushed back from the table, eyeing the man. He was a knight, not particularly young, with a ragged haircut and ratty beard. He was unattractive and rather big. She tried not to let her irritation turn to fear.

"I did not ask for your company, sir," she said. "If you would please leave me alone, I would be grateful."

The man merely smiled, showing his green-tinged teeth. "You should not be alone," he said. "You are far too beautiful. There is no knowing what manner of rabble will try to molest you. You must have protection."

"I *have* protection," she said, waving the knife in her hand in a dismissive gesture. "Be gone before my protection returns and you are in serious danger."

The man laughed. "Your escort went outside," he gestured lazily towards the rear of the tavern. "I saw them myself. I have been watching you, sweetling. You are a very fine woman."

He was tapping his head as if very clever and Ellowyn was starting to feel some apprehension. She could sense his unsavory intentions and sought to think of a way out of the situation that would not end with her screaming for help. She was coming to seriously regret sending her escort away.

"I am not speaking of my escort," she said, bluffing. "They are not all of the protection I have and you would be wise to leave immediately."

"Is that so?" the knight seemed interested. "Where is the rest of your protection, then?"

*You had better make this good*, she told herself. Her bluff was getting bigger and bigger. "My husband is expected at any moment," she said the first thing that came to mind. "Leave now and I will not tell him that you have seriously annoyed me. Stay one moment longer and I will make sure he punishes you."

The knight laughed again, boldly reaching for her wine cup and taking a big gulp. "If you are indeed married, then your husband is a fool for leaving you alone. He does not deserve you."

Ellowyn did the only thing she could do. She stood up, moving away from the table. The knight jumped up and grabbed her arm, causing her to take the knife she had been holding most of the evening and stab him in the hand with it. It was purely a reflexive action, infused with fear and fury. As she saw it, she was defending herself from an attack and had no qualms about using a weapon. That is, until she saw the look in the knight's face.

She was coming to think that stabbing him in the hand had been a very, very bad idea.

# CHAPTER THREE

"I do not have any preference where you bed them down," de Russe was dismounting his big charger, pulling off his helm and propping it on his saddle. He was weary, and his weariness was translating into snappish behavior. "Bed them down in the street for all I care. These are de Nerra's men and no longer my problem. Let his daughter worry about them."

Dylan de Lara cocked a droll eyebrow at the man as he headed towards the front door of Grey's Inn. "I thought we decided that it was not fair to the men."

"I changed my mind."

Dylan merely shrugged. The entry to the inn was a crowded entry with those waiting for room to enter, now scattering as de Russe approached. Even if they didn't know who de Russe was, it didn't matter, for there was no man in England with de Russe's size and implied temperament. With two words, he could make one feel as if Hell itself was approaching. With two words, he could strike fear into the heart of anyone within earshot.

Most people within a reasonable radius of Grey's Inn heard him snap at de Lara, a rumbling baritone that pierced the air like thunder. Brandt was fumbling with his heavy mail gauntlets as he reached the door to the inn, shoving it open with an armored elbow. He was looking for a particularly young woman, determined to dump five hundred and sixty-two worn and weary men on her doorstep. He couldn't be bothered by them anymore but, more than that, he couldn't be bothered with *her*. In hindsight, he hadn't liked the way she had ordered him around earlier. She had offended him, and he wanted to be done with the whole messy business.

The warm, stale air of the inn hit him like a slap in the face as he entered. It smelled like burnt meat and unwashed bodies. He had a perfect view of the entire room from where he stood, his hawk-like gaze scanning the area for either the barkeep or the woman in question. It didn't matter who he saw first, for the message would be the same – all five hundred and sixty-two men delivered as ordered.

It was a crowded place and badly lit. He hadn't taken five steps into the tavern when someone grabbed his wrist. With an intolerant expression that only Brandt de Russe could adequately deliver, he looked to his left and was surprised to see the very woman he sought clutching his arm. It was Ellowyn de Nerra in the flesh and, for a split second, Brandt allowed himself to appreciate the sight of a truly beautiful woman. He just couldn't help himself, realizing she was far more beautiful with the second encounter. But his momentary appreciation vanished and before he could open his mouth, Ellowyn spoke.

"Sweetheart, I am so glad you have arrived," she said, through clenched teeth he was sure. "This... this knight has been harassing me and will not leave me alone. Perhaps your mere presence will cause him to flee in fear."

She said it rather dramatically and, for a moment, Brandt was both puzzled and stumped. But then he tore his quizzical gaze from the lady's somewhat desperate features and noticed a heavily armored man standing a few feet away with a bloodied hand. The knight pointed an accusing finger at Ellowyn.

"Is this your wife?" he demanded. "She *stabbed* me, the little cow. She has injured me."

"I told you to go away," Ellowyn shot back. "Had you not grabbed me, I would not have had to defend myself."

"I did not hurt you!"

"But you grabbed me!" Ellowyn accused. "I never, at any time, gave you permission to touch me. Now that my husband is here, you had better run for your life. Go, now, before he becomes enraged."

There was a huge amount of conversation going on involving Brandt that he was not directly a part of. He simply stood there as Lady Ellowyn and some foolish knight shouted at each other. More than that, Lady Ellowyn was sucking him into something he had nothing to do with. Just as she had threatened him earlier, now she was in another confrontation with some other warrior.

Perhaps it was habit with her, being aggressive with men she did not know. Brandt thought it all rather odd, and rather ridiculous.

The knight, perhaps rightfully fearful of the lady's sincerely enormous husband, took a few steps back but did not leave. He held up his bloodied hand for all to see.

"Your wife has injured my hand," he nearly shouted at Brandt. "I demand compensation."

That seemed to snap Brandt out of his stunned silence. "Compensation?" he repeated, distain in his tone. "Compensation for what?"

The knight jabbed a finger at Ellowyn. "Because of... of her, I may not ever be able to hold a sword again. This is my sword hand."

Brandt cocked a dark eyebrow. "I see," he said, feeling Ellowyn as she clutched his wrist. "What did you have in mind?"

The knight seemed to lose some of his aggression, looking between Ellowyn and Brandt. "Well," he said after a moment. "One hundred crowns ought to do nicely, I think. That would keep me comfortable while I recover."

Brandt's eyebrows shot up. "One hundred crowns?" he echoed. Then he removed Ellowyn's hands from his wrist and extended them towards the knight. "Take her instead. You can sell her to the highest bidder and regain your compensation. Or you can simply have her work it off, for I am not paying you one hundred gold crowns."

Both the knight and Ellowyn looked at him, shocked. Before the knight could reply, Ellowyn yanked her hands out of Brandt's grasp.

"He cannot sell me," she raged. "How dare you suggest such a thing."

Brandt realized he was fighting off a grin as he faced off against a yet again very angry Ellowyn de Nerra. He'd never seen her any other way and wasn't hard pressed to admit he found it entertaining.

"I can do anything I wish," he told her. "I am your husband, am I not? I am not paying that man one hundred gold crowns, so he can take you instead. Perhaps next time you will think twice before assaulting a man."

Ellowyn's beautiful face turned shades of red. "You...," she seethed, backing away from both Brandt and the knight. "You... you *barbarian*. You beast! I will not let you do this, do you hear? You have no right."

Brandt bit his lip to keep from grinning, for he'd never in his life seen anyone so angry. "I have every right. If I want to sell you, I will. You have been far too much trouble since the moment I met you so perhaps this will teach you a lesson. You will be his problem now, not mine."

Ellowyn had backed into the table that contained the remains of her meal. Infuriated beyond reason, she grabbed the first thing she could reach and hurled it at Brandt's head. The wooden wine cup went sailing through the air, barely missing him. As he bobbed out of the way, Ellowyn picked up the nearly empty pitcher of wine and slung it at the knight, hitting him squarely in the chest. Wine sprayed everywhere, but there was no time to wipe it away, because now the fork was flying at them and the remains of the bread. Whatever Ellowyn could get her hands on when flying at Brandt and, if she thought about it, the bloodied knight. But mostly at Brandt; she was singling him out for a particular brand of hatred at the moment and he was going to feel her wrath.

Brandt couldn't help the grin on his lips now. Lady Ellowyn was having a full-fledged tantrum and he ducked a platter as he made his way over to her. The closer he got, the more furious she became. By the time he reached her, she was trying to throw a stool but he yanked it out of her hands. Bending at the waist, he tossed her up onto his shoulder and headed for the door.

"Call my wife a cow again and you forfeit your life," he made a point of making eye contact with the foolish knight. "Consider the fact that you retain your life this night the only compensation you shall receive from me."

The knight didn't say a word, watching rather wide-eyed as Brandt carted the snarling lady out of the inn. The last he saw, the big man had planted a trencher-sized hand on her bottom, causing her to howl. They could hear her howling once or twice more outside.

Ellowyn was howling because his swat bloody well hurt. She was not only in tantrum mode, she was also in panic mode. Brandt had her out in the street, marching across the muddy avenue as he spanked her soundly, not once but at least four times. She could hear men cheering and laughing, and it only served to fuel her agitation.

Finally, Brandt moved to set her on her feet. Realizing that he was releasing her, Ellowyn started smacking at him as he set her down, hitting him on his vulnerable ear and neck. But Brandt didn't react; he simply set her to her feet as she took a few more angry swings at him.

"You brute!" she hissed. "You... you uncivilized fiend! I will never forgive you for this, do you hear me? *Never!*"

Brandt drew in a long breath, still fighting off the grin that he had struggled with for the past few minutes. He crossed his massive arms calmly.

"Is it not exhausting being so aggressive all of the time?" he asked.

The comment only seemed to inflame her. "Beast! Monster! Son of a...!"

He cut her off, casually, losing the battle against the grin. "Are you finished?"

Ellowyn scowled. "Not by any stretch of the imagination," she jabbed a finger at him. "I have met my share of infuriating and callous men, but you are the worst of the lot. What possessed you to do what you just did?"

"Do what?"

She threw up her hands. "Throw me over your shoulder like a... a...."

"Common wench?"

Now her eyebrows flew up in outrage. "Common?" she was turning red in the face; he could see it even in the moonlight. "Now I am *common?*"

"Given the behavior I have seen from you since the onset of our association, you have given me little else to go on," he replied steadily. "Therefore, in response to your demands earlier today, I have delivered your father's men as ordered. You will find all of them over there to the left, by the livery stables, and none of them have been fed since earlier today. I hope you have made arrangements to feed and shelter them until the morrow, because they are very weary and will not be able to make the trek back to Erith Castle in their present condition. They need food and rest, which you will now provide. Good evening to you, Lady Ellowyn."

Ellowyn's outrage fled in favor of genuine surprise and, if she were to admit it, apprehension. She should have been wildly furious at his insult, but she could only seem to focus on the fact that he was literally dumping almost six hundred weary soldiers on her doorstep.

"Wait," she stopped him as he turned away from her. All of the agitation had disappeared from her tone. "I have no means with which to house and feed over five hundred men tonight. You were supposed to bring them to me tomorrow."

"You were not clear on what time of day to return them to you," he said. "I assumed you wanted them as soon as possible. Now you have them. Good eve to you."

Ellowyn's mouth popped open as she watched the enormous man turn on his heel and walk away from her. She was stunned but she wasn't going to give him the satisfaction of knowing it. He had made it clear he wanted nothing more to do with her so to seek assistance from him was out of the question.

She's already made a fool out of herself in front of the man, and he had duly insulted her. Perhaps rightly so. She'd always had a temper, and a bit of a mouth as well, so mayhap he was entirely correct.

Certainly, they had gotten off to a very bad start. He had ignored and then insulted her, and she had taken his head off for it. If she thought very hard about it, he'd tried to apologize but she wouldn't hear of it. She'd been too angry at the time. Damn her temper!

Exhausted, and now faced with a very large and unexpected problem that she had more or less brought down on herself, she couldn't help the tears of exhaustion and despair that sprang to her eyes.

Wearily, she planted her bottom on the edge of a stone watering trough, trying to figure out what she was going to do next. It was growing late and she had no idea how she was going to feed and shelter all of those men. She looked over to the inn, looking for a sign of her escort but noting instead that de Russe and another big knight were mounting their chargers. So he really *was* leaving her with all of those exhausted men. Maybe she deserved it.

As Ellowyn floundered in self-pity, Brandt mounted his snappish charger and turned the beast around to return to the docks near the Thames where he had left the bulk of his army. As he put his helm back on dark and sweaty head, he couldn't help but noticed that Ellowyn hadn't moved from where he'd dropped her. In fact, she was sitting on the edge of a water trough, looking at her hands.

Brandt's movements slowed as he gazed at her lowered head. Oddly, he was coming to feel some remorse. She wanted her men back, so he had obeyed her wishes, only he had done it in a fairly vindictive fashion. He knew very well that she wasn't equipped to handle all of them this night, but he had brought them to her anyway. That had been his spiteful-self talking and he could indeed be spiteful when the mood struck him. Maybe he had been too harsh about it.

He didn't like feelings of remorse. He wasn't a remorseful man by nature. His confusion trickled into brusque movements, which his charger sensed. The animal was feisty and exhausted, dancing nervously as they headed back the way they had come. Brandt tried not to look at the lady as he rode past her, but a creeping sense of guilt was eating at him.

More than that, he suspected his actions would meet with de Nerra's ears and the man would become incensed at him. He didn't need that kind of an enemy. Perhaps he should try to ease the situation before the daughter's version of the story roused all of Erith against him.

With a heavy sigh, he pulled his charger to a halt and turned back in the lady's direction, but his horse wasn't cooperating. The beast fought him and kicked up great clods of mud that flew right at Ellowyn, hitting her squarely in the chest and neck. She was so startled by the flying mud that she lost her balance and toppled back into the trough.

Brandt was off his mount, rushing to pull her from the water. She was sputtering by the time he reached her, grasping her by both arms and pulling her effortlessly from the cold, dirty water.

"I am sorry, my lady," he said. He meant it. "I fear my horse is to blame for your misery."

Ellowyn was cold, upset, and pushed beyond her endurance. She opened her mouth to yell at him but the words wouldn't come forth. The fight had gone out of her. Instead, she burst into tears.

"Just... go away," she sobbed softly, picking at the sopping garment. "Go away and leave me alone."

"But...."

"I asked you to leave me," she snapped, sounding more like her aggressive self. She struggled to gather up her very wet, and very heavy, skirt. "I do not require your assistance. You have done your duty by delivering my father's men and I would be grateful if you would simply go away and forget we ever met, for certainly, I will try and do the same."

Brandt watched with regret as she gingerly picked her way back across the muddy, rutted road and back towards the inn. She was absolutely soaked and trying to avoid dragging her dripping surcoat through the dirt. As he stood there and debated what to do, the door to the inn flew open and the knight that Ellowyn had stabbed in the hand came barreling through.

The man was all fire and curses, shoving men out of the way that didn't move fast enough. The bloodied hand flailed through the air like a monument to his injury, held high for all to see. But the moment he spied Ellowyn in the middle of the street, his manner changed. He went from simple rage to a deadly malevolence all in a split second. He may have even growled. Ellowyn had her head down and didn't see the man as he headed right for her.

"You are brave when your husband is about," he snarled. "Does your bravery hold true when you are alone, you little bitch?"

33

Ellowyn's head snapped up at the sound of the voice, her eyes widening with fright when she saw who had uttered it. Her escort picked that moment to round the corner of the inn, having no idea of the danger she was in. They were only focused on her and not the angry knight advancing on her. Ellowyn tried to back away from the knight but was hindered by her very heavy and very wet skirt. She ended up stepping on the hem and falling to her backside as the knight closed in on her.

She might have uttered a cry because her escort was suddenly moving very quickly in her direction, but before they could reach her, a massive form moved between her and the advancing knight. She couldn't see much other than big, armored legs, and then she heard a strangled grunt followed by the sounds of something snapping. A body hit the ground next to her, splattering mud, and she shrieked.

Startled, she looked over to see the knight with the bloodied hand lying in a heap next to her, and he was quite dead. His head was bent at an odd angle and, horrified, she looked up to see de Russe standing over her. Before she could say a word, he reached down and pulled her to her feet.

"Are you all right, my lady?" he asked. "Did you hurt yourself?"

Ellowyn was feeling disoriented, astonished and sickened. Everything she could possibly feel all rolled in to one. Her exhaustion, coupled by the events, all fell in to line and before she realized it, she was feeling rather woozy. She couldn't look at the man with the snapped neck on the ground next to her and she tried to turn away, but she couldn't quite catch her balance. She could see the trough in front of her and she thought she might make her way to it and sit down again, simply to collect herself, but her body had other ideas. She hadn't taken two steps when the world faded to black.

# CHAPTER FOUR

*It was that field again, the one with the men dying upon it, as plentiful as driftwood upon the sea.*

*She was slugging through the bloody mud, trying not to step on the dead and avoiding the desperate hands of the dying. She should have felt guilty for ducking those who needed care, but she couldn't manage it. All she could feel was a desperate yearning to seek out something, something that drew her to it like a moth to flame. She could think of nothing else and her heart was near bursting with fear and anxiety because of it. God, if she could only find it!*

*The bottom half of her surcoat, shift, and cloak were soaked with mud that smelled like the bowels of hell. The stench was everywhere. She thought perhaps she would smell that scent forever, like a fog that would never leave her. It was horrifying. As she pushed through it, her cloak snagged on something and as she reached down to yank it free, a hand grabbed at her from one of the countless bodies strewn about and took hold of her glove. He yanked it off as she drew her hand back in horror. Her naked hand, exposed to the dark and heavy hair, glinted oddly. Gazing at her exposed flesh, she could see a ring on it.*

*A wedding ring.*

\*\*\*

Something was popping and crackling, and there was a great deal of warmth on her face. Ellowyn gradually became aware of heat on her body and the smell of smoke, and her eyes rolled open to the sight of an enormous fire a few feet in front of her.

Somewhat startled, she pulled away from it, realizing that she laying on a floor in only her shift. It was dirty and cold. Her heavy brocade surcoat was hanging above her head on exposed rafters, drying in the heat of the blaze.

Confused, frightened, she looked around the small, dark room. She had no idea where she was, or what had happened, but as she rolled into a sitting position, bits of her memory began to return. She remembered the inn, the aggressive knight, and de Russe's appearance. Hand to her aching head, she remembered tripping on the road when the aggressive knight came after her but nothing after that. Looking around the small room again that smelled heavily of unwashed bodies, she had no idea what was going on.

Standing up unsteadily, she reached up for her surcoat and realized that it was wet. Parts of it that were nearer the fire seemed to warm and moderately dry, but other parts were almost sopping. Curious, she was in the process of fingering it when the door to the chamber jerked open.

Startled, Ellowyn jumped away from the door. Her first instinct was to protect herself and she grabbed the first thing she could find, which happened to be a well-used ash shovel propped up near the hearth. She raised it like a club just as an enormous figure emerged from the dark hallway and into the weak light of the room.

It was de Russe. He spied Ellowyn pressed against the far wall with a small, dented shovel in her hand. She was poised, ready to brain him if he came any closer. He paused in the open door, inspecting the woman who was half-illuminated by the firelight.

"Are you planning on using that?" he asked somewhat drolly.

He was nodding his head in the direction of the shovel. Ellowyn's attention flickered between Brandt's face and the spade in her hands, not wanting to admit that it looked rather ridiculous. It was like trying to fight off a bull with a twig. But she didn't lower the shovel.

"That depends," she said. "What am I doing here?"

He came in to the room, slowly, and shut the door. He didn't want to make any sudden movements because he could see that she was genuinely frightened.

"I brought you here," he said. "You fainted."

Ellowyn thought hard on her last memories of the angry knight and de Russe's involvement in... something. She couldn't quite remember. After a moment, she shook her head.

36

"I do not remember much," she admitted. "What happened?"

Brandt shrugged. "You were overwrought, I assume," he said. "You fainted in the street so I brought you back to the inn and secured a room. You were wet so I put you in front of the fire to dry off."

Her gaze flicked up to the hanging surcoat. "Did... did you remove the coat?"

He nodded. "I did, but one of the tavern wenches assisted. Never was I alone with you, I swear."

It was a rather chivalrous statement and something he wanted to be clear on. Ellowyn eyed him; she had known a lot of knights in her life, as her father and grandfather were great knights, and it was her grandfather who had taught her to be a good judge of character. He had instilled the caution and the protocols in her.

From the moment she'd met the Duke of Exeter, he'd come across as arrogant and rude, that was true, but never lascivious. He wanted her to be clear that he'd not molested her and her instincts told her to believe him. At that moment, she started to see something more in the man, not simply the haughty warrior.

More than that, he was starting to make some sense about the situation so she slowly lowered the shovel. As she eyed him, she also recalled the army he had dumped on her, leaving her to fend for the shelter and nourishment of nearly six hundred men. Her head was throbbing and she was feeling nauseous, made worse now that her memory was returning. She was remembering every sickening and frightening thing. With a heavy sigh, she tossed the shovel aside.

"I thank you for your concern for my safety," she replied, "but I have several hundred of my father's men I must attend to. If you will kindly vacate the chamber, I shall dress and be gone."

Brandt shook his head. "It is not necessary," he told her. "I have tended to the men."

She regarded him some doubt. "Why would you do that? They are no longer your concern. At least, that is what you told me."

He could feel the brittle peace between them and sensed she was not particularly the forgiving type. At least, not with him. Not that he blamed her. He'd had a momentary flash of guilt when she had fainted and had sought to make amends by taking charge of her welfare. Now he was starting to feel stupid for allowing himself to feel any compassion for her. The woman was still as hostile towards him as she had ever been.

"My concern is with the men," he said. "With you incapacitated, someone had to tend the weary troops so I took the initiative."

Truth be told, Ellowyn felt marginally better knowing she didn't have to worry over housing and feeding all of those men this night. However, along with her relief was a measurable amount of awkwardness. She wasn't particularly comfortable with de Russe, nor did she care for him much, so she was determined to vacate his presence as soon as possible.

"You have my thanks," she said. "Now, if you will kindly leave the room, I shall dress and find my own way."

He didn't move. "It is late, my lady," he said. "You may sleep here tonight. I have ordered food and your cloak is still being cleaned. It would not due for you to be out and about at this time of night."

Her brow furrowed as she looked at him. "You do not need to be concerned for me. I can take care of myself."

He lifted an eyebrow as if he did not doubt her. "Be that as it may, your father would never forgive me if something happened to you. Please be my guest this eve, enjoy the room and the meal, and that will be the end of it."

"The end of what?"

"Our association. I apologized that it has not been pleasant."

Ellowyn was caught off guard by the apology. She was smug in her acceptance of it, gratified he had been the one to acknowledge and make amends for their rough relationship, but it began to occur to her that he was not entirely to blame. If she thought hard on their first meeting, she realized that she had been the first one to throw a metaphorical punch. True, he had been rude, but she had taken it to an entirely different level with her reaction. Perhaps if he was apologizing, she should give it a try as well. But swallowing her pride was easier said than done.

"It...," she tried again, shrugging in resignation. "It is not solely your fault, my lord. I... well, I believe I was quite angry with you this afternoon when you ignored me and I should not have been so...furious."

"You were belligerent."

"Aye, that too."

He fought off a smile. "You, my lady, have a bit of a temper."

"I do. I admit it. But if you know my father, then you also know it is an inherited trait. He is a de Nerra, after all."

Brandt's grin broke through, a surprising gesture. "Your father and I have fought a few battles together," he said. "Fortunately, I was always on his side. There were times when I pitied the enemy."

Ellowyn couldn't help but smile in return; she really couldn't. It came so easily when he smiled first. She also couldn't help but notice de Russe was a truly handsome man with a dashing smile. He had straight white teeth and big dimples in both cheeks. Embroiled as she had been in her anger towards the man, it was the first time the thought of his handsome looks had occurred to her.

"He has considered taking me into battle with him, in fact," she said. "He is convinced I would make a fine commander."

Brandt's grin broadened, an unusual gesture for him and one he did not readily display. But Ellowyn, in spite of everything, seemed to easily provoke it. Perhaps it was because she was truly a beautiful woman, more beautiful when she smiled, and her smile erased her bad behavior from his mind. Something about that warm, angelic face just made him want to smile as if he had no control over such a thing.

"I would believe that implicitly," he said. "You have shown tremendous bravery in the short time I have known you, an admirable quality. And you showed no hesitation in showing me that side of you."

He meant earlier by the Thames. Ellowyn simply lifted her shoulders. "I was angry," she said, realizing she was feeling rather bad for her behavior now that the conversation was becoming civil. Warm, even. "I am sorry if I was insulting."

He waved her off. "You already apologized," he said. "Further apologies are not necessary. I am as much to blame as you are. I am willing to forget about it if you are."

She nodded fervently. "I am."

"Then you will accept my hospitality tonight?"

She had to admit, the bed looked inviting. "I will. Thank you. You are very kind to offer."

He continued to smile at her, his smoky dark eyes acquiring something of a glimmer. "And you are very kind to accept."

Ellowyn giggled, something she didn't normally do. She wasn't silly or flighty by nature, but the duke, in a complete swing of the situation, had taken her from suspicious to giggly. It was rather remarkable, Ellowyn thought, but she didn't give it much thought beyond that. She was a little too naive of her own emotions to realize the man had managed to garner her interest.

"Have... have you eaten yet, my lord?" she asked. "I would be honored if you would partake with me. As you are friends with my father, I would like to hear what you know of his valor. He has been ill most of my adult life, you see, so I do not know the man as a great knight. I only know from the stories I have heard. Perhaps you know more stories?"

Brandt's lips twitched with a smile. "I have never met a lady who was interested in tales of valor. That is a man's inclination."

She shrugged, almost embarrassed. "I come from a long line of great knights. I can remember tales of my grandfather's exploits as far back as I can remember. And my father... well, I love him dearly and it is sad that so great a knight has suffered such bad health. I am always eager to hear stories of his greatness."

Brandt's smile broke through at the tender sentiment, something that, even an hour ago, he would not believe her capable of. He could see in that statement that she had a very soft side. She was capable of deep emotion, like attachment. He liked that side of her much better than the aggressive side.

As he gazed at her, softly illuminated by the firelight, he found himself thinking of all of the duties he had awaiting him; the king was expecting his report as a result of the Black Prince's wars in France, plus he had a meeting with his subordinates that needed to take place before they could begin moving men and material again. So many things awaiting the Duke of Exeter's attention, but at the moment, all he could see was a lovely red-head before him who had invited him to sup. He wasn't a man normally given to accept such a thing; in fact, he made it a policy to avoid women in general. Too much trouble. But her gently-uttered invitation had him thinking of accepting.

"Very well," he agreed quietly. "It would be my pleasure to sup with you and tell you what I know of your father. We have had a few adventures together, Deston and I."

Her entire face lit up happily and a strange, giddy feeling fluttered in his chest. It was odd but not unpleasant. It was another of those feelings that made him smile before he could stop himself, a trigger release that was quick and before he realized it, he was smiling in return.

A soft knock at the door interrupted the repartee, returning Brandt to the grim and imposing knight as if he was afraid someone might see him with warmth in his expression. He didn't reply to the summons, choosing to open the door instead. A serving wench stood outside, a heavy tray of food in her hands, and he silently summoned the woman inside. When the food was set out on the very small table, which leaned a little so the food slid to the edge, Brandt kicked the woman out and shut the door.

When he turned back to the table, he saw that Ellowyn had dragged it over to the bed. She was also trying to keep the tray from sliding over the edge. When she looked up and saw that his attention was on her, she smiled weakly.

"There is only one chair," she said. "I can sit on the bed and you may have the chair."

Brandt dipped his head in thanks, in acknowledgement, as he accepted the only chair. He wasn't entirely sure it would hold his weight, being that it leaned about as much as the table did, so he tested it out before allowing his entire weight to rest on it. Meanwhile, Ellowyn had planted herself on the bed opposite him. By the time he glanced up from the chair, he noticed the butt-end of a knife in his face.

"Please serve yourself," Ellowyn said as she extended the utensil.

He took it without a word.  The meal, as it turned out, was a mostly silent affair, but he didn't mind in the least. It wasn't an uncomfortable silence but it was as if they had moved past the rough introduction, the words of apology, and were now simply settling in to what had now become a tolerable association. More than that, with all of the bad blood between them reconciled, there was definitive warmth settling.  Brandt couldn't put his finger on it, but he could definitely sense it. He didn't particularly want to admit it but the more he tried to ignore it, the more it would not be ignored.

As Brandt silently served both himself and Ellowyn, he realized at some point that he stopped viewing her as de Nerra's spoiled daughter. Now, he was starting to view her as a woman.

And a very beautiful one at that.

# CHAPTER FIVE

Ellowyn was fairly certain she had been miserable for quite some time, but by the time she fully awoke and became lucid, she was coughing her head off and dealing with generally uncomfortable symptoms. Her nose was running, her chest hurt, and her head was killing her. She could only surmise that the dousing of both cold water and mud had somehow weakened her and she was back to a thoroughly grumpy mood as a result. Misery claimed her with swift and unjust claws.

The fire in the small room had gone out some time ago. All that remained was ash. Coughing, she struggled up from the bed and called for warm water and firewood from a serving wench lingering in the corridor outside her room. By the time the woman returned with a big, burly man who smelled like a privy, Ellowyn was sitting on the bed, wrapped in the coverlet and shivering uncontrollably.

The smelly man in torn breeches had brought wood with him and started the fire, waiting until it sparked up before fleeing the room with the serving wench. When the door slammed, Ellowyn shuffled over to the leaning table, now with a big bowl of steaming water that was leaking over the side due to the angle of the table, and inhaled the steam deeply. Then she coughed some more, trying to clear her lungs.

At some point towards the end of her meal with the Duke of Exeter, her escort had brought her satchel. Ellowyn wondered where they had been the entire time she had been unconscious and subsequently alone with de Russe, but no one seemed to offer an explanation and, by that point, she didn't much care. De Russe had ceased to become a horrible beast and had somehow morphed into a man capable of amiable behavior. Sniffling, Ellowyn turned away from the steaming water and heaved her bag upon the mattress. Digging through her belongings, her thoughts drifted to de Russe.

He'd not spoken a great deal through their meal. In fact, he'd only really answered her questions. He'd never offered anything of his own volition. Ellowyn had asked him a dozen questions about her father, what de Russe knew of him, of the adventures they'd had together. De Russe had answered thoroughly, speaking of a man of great power and cunning before the ravages of swollen joints had forced him to retire.

Now, Deston could scarcely walk, a true tragedy for so great a knight from a long line of great knights. As de Russe had recalled a story involving saving several knights from captivity in a well-guarded castle, Ellowyn had been enthralled at the prowess and daring. She could picture her father, young and strong, and his much younger and much stronger companion, de Russe, as they charged out to save the world.

But the stories or answers to her questions had been dotted with stretches of silence. Although not uncomfortable, Ellowyn had found herself thinking on what more to say to him just so they wouldn't have to sit in silence and as she pondered her next question, she stole glances at the man sitting across from her.

De Russe was enormous, as she'd noted from the start, and he had the biggest hands she had ever seen. She'd noticed his male comeliness before but at close range she noticed his thick dark lashes and the surprisingly smooth skin of his face. And his eyes... she had thought they were the color of smoke but upon closer inspection, she could see they were a very dark hazel. They were quite attractive, as was the rest of him. When she stopped viewing de Russe as her mortal enemy and started seeing him as a man, she realized that he was an extraordinarily handsome one.

But that was where those thoughts ended. She knew nothing about the man other than what her father had told her and she suspected she didn't want to know any more. Men weren't something, as a group, that particularly interested her, although she'd had more than her share of suitors. She was far too pretty a lass not to, but she had no patience for pretty words or wretchedly sweet wooing. Men of bravery and skill on the battlefield interested her most, but those men were usually so wrapped up in their own glorious ego that she could not, and would not, compete with such a thing. After her conversation with de Russe the previous night, as great as the man was, she suspected he fell into that category.

Digging in to her satchel, she removed a clean shift and the only other surcoat she brought with her. She also brought forth a carefully wrapped bar of white soap that smelled of lavender. Whereas most people bathed infrequently, Ellowyn was not that sort. She washed, and washed often, mostly because it kept her skin clear because she was prone to ugly blemishes on her chin. She had found that washing daily kept her skin clean and unfettered, so it was something of a daily routine.

With the same linen cloth that the soap had been wrapped in, she quickly lathered up the soap in the steaming water and proceeded to wash herself down. Thoughts of de Russe would not go away as she washed her body before the snapping fire, rinsing off as best she could and drying herself with her worn shift. Dressing in the clean lamb's wool shift and heavy dark blue woolen surcoat, she put on the rest of her warm things before wrapping the soap back up and re-packing her satchel. Her last act of dressing was to run a bone comb through her long blond hair and braid it, draping the single braid elegantly over her right shoulder. And with that, her bags were secured and she was prepared to move out.

Her health had other ideas, however. Her nose was running terribly and the cough, having briefly died down, was now enjoying a triumphant resurgence. She hacked like an old woman dying of the damp. As she pulled out a linen kerchief from the depths of her satchel to wipe her nose, there was a soft knock at the door. Holding her kerchief to her nose, she went to the door and unlatched it only to find de Russe standing in the doorway dressed for battle.

It was the de Russe she remembered from the wharf, the massive warrior in mail and steel so wrapped up in his knighthood that it was difficult to ascertain where the armor ended and the man began. His helm wasn't on, but his broadsword was, strapped to his hips and right thigh with heavy leather binds to keep the scabbard stable. His smoky eyes were oddly soft as he looked at her.

"I could hear you coughing downstairs," he said. "Are you ill?"

She blew her nose into the rag in her hand. "I am," she said, her nose stuffy. "I fear that I have somehow caught a chill."

He wriggled his eyebrows in agreement. "An understatement, my lady," he said. "I came to see if you were ready to move out but I see that perhaps we must wait until you are feeling better."

She shook her head firmly before the words even left his mouth. "I will return today," she said. "I will feel poorly here or on the road so it does not matter... hold a moment, my lord; what did you say?"

She was cocking her head at him curiously. He had no idea what she meant. "What do you mean?" he asked. "What did I say?"

She blinked as if surprised. "We?" she said. "You said *we* would move out?"

"I am not staying here."

"Ah... I see," she seemed to understand. "Then you are going home as well."

"I am going to Erith."

She was back to being surprised. "To *Erith*?" she repeated. "Why?"

He cleared his throat as if suddenly uneasy. Why *was* he going to Erith? He'd spent all night wondering the same thing after he'd decided, at his conclusion of the meal with Ellowyn, that he would be accompanying her home. He wasn't sure why he had made the decision, much less possess the ability to explain it to her. But she was looking for an answer and he looked her in the eye whilst giving one, mostly because he didn't want her to sense anything but sheer, unadulterated decisiveness from him. He didn't want her to see his uncertainty.

"Because," he gestured with a big gloved hand towards the avenue outside. "You have nearly six hundred men to take back to Erith and not one knight to take charge. I am concerned that Deston sent you to retrieve troops without anyone to control them, so I will therefore escort you, and them, back to Erith Castle."

By this time, she was looking at him with greater surprise than ever. "They will take orders from me, although I thank you for your concern. Truly, it is not necessary."

*Refuted.* Brandt found himself in a very odd position as she rejected his offer of escort. He still wasn't sure why he felt compelled to escort her back to Erith, but as he gazed down at the woman with the red nose and exquisite face, he knew it had nothing to do with the six hundred men outside in the rain. It had everything to do with that damnable conversation last night when he had conversed with her as he'd never conversed with anyone in his life. She listened intently to him and made him feel as if he had something worth saying.

Certainly, in his position, everyone had respect for his word but it was because of his title. The Duke of Exeter was not a man to be ignored. But last night, he felt as if Ellowyn de Nerra listened to him not because of his title, but because of who he was as a warrior. As a man. He was feeling foolish and unbalanced by it but he also knew that it made him feel as he'd never felt in his life.

"Perhaps," he said after a lengthy, and contemplative, pause, "but it would seem I have business with your father as well, so we may as well travel together. Are you opposed to this?"

Ellowyn wiped at her dripping nose. "Nay, my lord," she shook her head. "But you never said anything about having business with my father. This is the first you have mentioned it."

He was starting to feel like an idiot. "I had forgotten," he muttered, then pointed towards the bed behind her in the hopes of changing the subject. "Perhaps you should retire for the day. Our trip can wait until you are feeling better."

Again, Ellowyn shook her head firmly. "I do not want to linger here," she said, moving back into the room to claim her satchel. "I am strong enough to travel home. Where is my escort? The men I brought with me?"

Brandt could see that she was determined. In fact, if there was one quality about Ellowyn de Nerra that stood out to him, it was her determination. She was fierce about it.

"They are down in the main room," he told her. "My lady, it is my sincere hope that you will reconsider traveling today. It is raining fairly heavily outside."

She acted like she hadn't heard him as she brushed past him, exiting the room. "I will ask the innkeeper if he has something hot to drink. Perhaps that will help my cough. I will be well enough – you'll see."

With a sigh of regret, Brandt followed. The great room of the inn was fairly quiet at this hour, bodies strewn about the room in sometimes noisy slumber. Ellowyn reached the bottom of the stairs with Brandt shortly behind her, making her way to the rear of the tavern in search of the innkeeper. Brandt watched as her escort, having been huddled near the smoking hearth, spied the woman and moved to greet her. As the lady went in search of something for her cough, Brandt headed outside into the howling elements.

It was pounding in buckets as he made his way across the avenue where all of the de Nerra men were huddled under the trees, seeking shelter from the rain. Late last night, after the conclusion of his meal with Ellowyn, he had sent Dylan de Lara back to the wharf to disband his army.

The bulk of four thousand, two hundred and thirteen men headed back to the duke's seat of Guildford Castle while a smaller portion of skilled foot-soldiers had broken off from the main body and marched to Gray's Inn along with five of Brandt's most skilled and trusted knights and a few lesser knights. As Brandt moved closer to a thick cluster of trees, he could make out the features of his senior knights lingering in a group near the road.

Dylan and his identical twin brother, Alex, were the first faces to greet him. The two were so alike that most people couldn't tell them apart, but Brandt could. Alex was slightly bigger and led with his left hand, whereas Dylan led with his right. As Alex acknowledged his liege with a silent salute, Brandt's gaze fell on the knight standing next to him.

Brennan St. Hèver was perhaps the very best knight to have ever swung a sword, eldest son of the Earl of Wrexham. A tall man with enormously wide shoulders, he had white-blond hair and eyes the color of the sea. He was extremely fast, witty, and intelligent. He was also extremely young and twenty years and two, but had a maturity well beyond his years.

Standing next to Brennan were the remaining two knights that rounded out de Russe's top generals, Magnus de Reyne and Stefan le Bec, le Bec being the grandson of the legendary Guildford le Bec. Both young knights were from very fine families, descended from the bloodlines of illustrious warriors, and were two of the best knights Brandt had ever seen. Their strength and cunning was beyond measure, and Brandt considered himself extremely lucky to command such a fine senior stable. He had one hell of an arsenal.

"Good men," Brandt greeted the group, the focused on Dylan. "Have my orders been carried through?"

Dylan nodded. "Aye, my lord," he replied. "Most of the men have been sent back to Whitestone, but we retained five hundred for your service. They have broken their camp and are awaiting orders."

Brandt moved so that the rain wasn't pelting him in the head from the branches above and ended up turning around, his back against the tree trunk as his gaze fell on the inn across the avenue. The rain was so heavy that it was misting as well, giving the land a foggy appearance. His eyes lingered on the inn.

"We will be going to Erith Castle," he said. "I have business with de Nerra and since his daughter will be taking his troops north anyway, we will be traveling with her party."

Dylan was the only one who reacted. His eyebrows lifted, slowly, as if he was genuinely shocked by what he was hearing. "The woman who threatened you, my lord?" he asked.

"The same."

"Will we need to guard your safety against her, then?"

Brandt tore his eyes off the inn and looked at Dylan, who was fighting off a grin. He could see the man was teasing him. He turned away quickly so Dylan would not see the beginnings of a smile; Dylan did not know that he had supped with Ellowyn the previous eve and settled all hostilities. The truth was that Brandt didn't want his men to know he'd paid attention to a female, even if it was in the line of duty. Well, mostly. What he did and who he did it with was his own business.

"Perhaps," he said vaguely. "In any case, she will be traveling with us. You will show her all due respect."

"The woman *threatened* you, my lord?" Alex repeated, as if the gist of the words suddenly sank in.

Brandt was thinking to the moment in time when he and Ellowyn first met, that fiery misunderstanding that had left him both angry and intrigued. "She did," he conceded. "But it might have been because I accused her of being a whore."

Over his shoulder, le Bec burst out snickering as St. Hèver and de Reyne looked rather surprised. "A whore, my lord?" de Reyne clarified. "De Nerra's daughter is a whore?"

Brandt shook his head, folding his enormous arms across his chest as they continued their wait for Lady Ellowyn to appear.

"She is not," he said flatly, "but she boldly addressed me down by the wharf yesterday and before she could introduce herself, I took her for a whore and tried to chase her away. She did not take kindly to it and became rightfully angry."

Dylan looked at the group, elaborating on the encounter he had witnessed. "He mistook her for a whore but when her identity became clear and he tried to apologize, she told him to bite his tongue and proceeded to berate him." He watched the various expressions of disapproval around him. "Somewhere in the scolding, she told him that if he did not deliver de Nerra's men to her as instructed, she would return home and tell de Nerra all of the terrible things our lord said to her. She was furious, sassy and disrespectful and if our lord had allowed me, I would have spanked her on the spot."

The knights were horrified at such behavior towards their liege. The Duke of Exeter was the most respected of men, a mentor and military equal to the Black Prince, and highly esteemed by the king himself. For a woman to publicly humiliate him was beyond their comprehension.

Brandt knew their thoughts. He glanced over his shoulder at the expressions of outrage around him and thought perhaps he should pacify his loyalists before they vilified the lady.

"It is true she was angry," he said. "But I offended her so I am sure I deserved everything she said to me. That being said, since I was the one who wronged her, in no way will you show this woman any less measure of respect. I was able to speak with her last evening after she had sufficiently calmed and she was kind, intelligent, and rational. We were able to solve our differences. However, I will say one more thing and then speak of the incident no more."

Dylan was deeply curious, about everything. "What is that, my lord?"

"She has one hell of a temper so if any of you set her off, be warned that I will not step in to defend you. You are on your own."

As Brandt returned his attention to the front door of the inn, the five knights behind him glanced at each other with various expressions of curiosity and dread. They even started muttering. Brandt, however, wasn't paying attention to them; he was more interested in what was unfolding at the inn. He could hear things breaking and furniture being smashed inside. It sounded as if someone was tearing the place down, never a good sign, and he had little doubt that Ellowyn was somehow in the middle of it.

Unsheathing his sword in a flash, he charged back across the avenue with his arsenal of knights behind him.

# CHAPTER SIX

The innkeeper had made Ellowyn a brew of hot wine with cloves, honey, and boiled apples. It was very sweet and very soothing to her sore throat, and felt wonderful going down as she took a few timid sips. Ellowyn explained that she would be traveling and wanted to take it with her, so he gave her a huge portion of it in a big earthenware mug with a cloth over the top to keep the brew protected from the rain.

He also gave her a sack with warm bread, cheese, and several apples. As she was sipping on the brew, his wife gave her a bowl half-filled with mush and honey, forcing her to sit down with all of her lovely booty and eat the porridge because she couldn't very well carry it with her. Quickly, she slurped it down, knowing that hundreds men were waiting for her outside in the rain. So was de Russe

Her coughing had eased but she was still very stuffy and, if she were to admit it, more than likely running a fever. Her eyes felt hot, a sure indication that her temperature was elevated. But she would not mention it to anyone for fear of being forced to remain in London until her health improved, for she very much wanted to return home.

As she was finishing the last of her delicious porridge, someone abruptly swiped the bowl away from her, causing the remains to spray out onto her and onto the floor. It had been an angry gesture, not one of happenstance or accident. The hand intentionally slapped her in the arm as it swept past her. Cloak littered with splotches of goo, Ellowyn turned with outrage towards the source.

A man dressed in rag-tag pieces of mail and armor stood next to her table, his weathered face dark with danger. He smelled of alcohol and sweat, and Ellowyn's outrage dissolved into that of tempered fear. Before she could move away, he grabbed her by the arm.

"You are the one who killed my brother," he snarled. "He was dead in the street yesterday and I was told that you did it. I hope you are prepared to pay for your actions, my fine lady."

Ellowyn's fear upped a notch at his statement, knowing the man had swept her food away with a purpose. "I have not killed anyone," she said, yanking her arm from his grip. "My husband is...."

He cut her off, advancing, as she backed away from him, just out of arm's reach. "Your husband killed him because of you," he muttered ominously. "I came yesterday to meet my brother and was told your husband killed him because he showed attention towards you. I have been waiting all night for you to appear so I could make you pay for what you did."

Ellowyn continued to back away. "Leave now and you leave with your life," she said, trying to sound as threatening. "Continue on this path and you will end up like your brother."

The knight snorted. "Your husband is outside waiting for you and can be of no use to you now."

"You are mad!"

"We shall see."

Ellowyn began to scamper back, away from him, as her escort rushed forward to protect her. But along with the ragged knight were two companions, who came rushing in from the back door of the inn to take care of Ellowyn's escort. Soon, a full scale brawl erupted and the entire room was in turmoil. In the cold, dirty depths of the tavern's main chamber, life and death was beginning to play out.

Ellowyn realized very quickly that her escort was occupied by the other men. Even though there were four of them, one man had already been disabled and, as she watched with horror, a second man was stabbed in the neck. Terrified, and knowing she would have to fight for her life until she could get free of the inn, Ellowyn spied a knife on the closest table and without missing a beat, she grabbed it and hurled it at the man pursuing her.

The knife bounced off his mail, flipped up, and clipped him in the mouth. The man roared as he brought a hand to his lips, coming away bloodied. Meanwhile, Ellowyn was running for the door.

"You foolish chit," he yelled. "I will pain you for this, do you hear me? You will pay with your sweet tender flesh and you'll not be so beautiful when I am finished with you!"

He was booming by the time he spit out the last few words and Ellowyn's fury dissolved into pure panic. She threw a stool at him, and finally a wooden plate, before she could get to the door. She was hoping to slow him down but her tactics didn't seem to be working. He was closing in on her as the entire room was shuddering with the impacts from the fight. As she finally reached the door, the portal that promised safety beyond its wooden borders, the panel suddenly burst open.

The force of the door opening shoved her back on her arse. Knights were flooding into the room. Ellowyn sat on her bum, astonished, as de Russe and five of the biggest men she had ever seen rushed into the room and began engaging those who had assaulted her. De Russe himself went after the man who had been pursuing her, the ragged knight who unsheathed his broadsword at the sight of so many armed men pouring into the room. Now the man and de Russe were engaged in a violent battle, but it was a short-lived one. As Ellowyn watched, de Russe was able to subdue the man in about six strokes, completely dispatching him in eight. The man collapsed in a groaning heap, felled by the Duke of Exeter's mighty broadsword.

Meanwhile, de Russe's knights had gone after the other two assailants and had made short work of them. A few sword thrusts and several punches later, both men were down, one of them bleeding out all over the dirty inn floor. The de Lara brothers picked up one man who was simply knocked unconscious and tossed him out the back door, flopping him into a vast swamp of mud that had once been the kitchen yard. Behind them, an enormous blond knight and another big warrior with dark hair and bright blue eyes tossed out the second man, leaving a trail of blood across the floor. As Ellowyn sat on the floor and observed all of this, overwhelmed, de Russe came up beside her.

"Are you injured?" he reached down and picked her up off the floor. "Did he hurt you?"

She let him pull her to her feet and dust her off. In truth, she was a little stunned by the whole thing and somewhat muddled.

"I am not hurt," she said, finally tearing her gaze off the chaos of the room and looking up at him. "He said you killed his brother yesterday. I believe he was going to kill me, too."

Brandt shook his head. "I sincerely doubt he could have completed the task," he said, eyeing her. "You put up too much of a fight."

He was gently teasing her and it took Ellowyn a moment to realize that. Understanding she was finally safe after the past few harrowing minutes, she exhaled heavily and slumped.

"Perhaps if I was feeling better, I might have made it more difficult for him," she returned the humor as much as she could at the moment. "But it would seem that you have once again saved my life, my lord. I am not entirely sure I can ever repay you for it, but please know that you have my undying gratitude."

Brandt's smoky eyes gazed steadily at her, a flicker of a smile on his lips. "Hmmm," he said thoughtfully. "Yesterday you hated the sight of me. Today I am your savior. I am not sure I am comfortable with your abject adoration."

Ellowyn knew enough to know that he was trying to ease her mood, her fears, after such a terrifying ordeal. She appreciated the attempt.

"Would you rather I throw things at you?" she said helpfully. "Would that make you more comfortable?"

He broke out in a smile, those straight white teeth gleaming in the weak morning light. "Perhaps not," he said, glancing over his shoulder at his knights who were now filtering from the room and back out into the rain. They hadn't even raised a sweat at the battle. "I would rather we remain comfortable acquaintances. Is that acceptable?"

"It is."

"Are you ready to leave, then?"

Ellowyn nodded as she turned around to see that two of her escorts were dead on the floor of the inn while the other two, being tended to by the innkeeper and his wife, were fairly thrashed. Her humor faded.

"Oh... no," she murmured.

Brandt watched her move across the room to the remains of her escort. After a moment, he followed, coming up behind her as she was growing increasingly upset over the death of two of her men. He watched her a moment, understanding something that he'd known from nearly the start of their association - she was a woman of deep compassion and deep feeling. Most people wouldn't have shown much concern for men who were simply paid to do their bidding, but Ellowyn did. It would seem that human life meant something to her which, in Brandt's eyes, gave her some depth of character. Increasingly, he was seeing her through different eyes.

"My lady," he caught her attention as she examined the injured soldier's arm. "May I make a suggestion?"

She nodded eagerly. "Of course."

He pointed to the dead man. "Perhaps we should pay the innkeeper to see that your man is buried," he said, "and pay him further to tend the injured. We cannot take the dead or wounded with us."

Ellowyn's first instinct was to contradict him, but she knew he was right. She just didn't like the idea of leaving any of her faithful men behind. But de Russe was correct; they couldn't drag along the dead and wounded. She sighed.

"Very well."

As Ellowyn made arrangements with the innkeeper to tend her men, Brandt quietly ordered his knights from the inn and instructed them to ready the troop to move out. As the five knights made their way out into the increasingly inclement weather, Brandt stood near the entry of the smelly old inn and waited patiently for Ellowyn to finish her affairs. When she finished paying the innkeeper a few coins from the purse she kept tied to her waist, she collected the food sack that the innkeeper had given her and bid farewell to the injured man.

Turning for the entry where de Russe was waiting, she was followed by her two remaining escorts who had collected her baggage from various places in the room. It had been kicked around in the brawl. Brandt waited patiently as she approached.

"If my lady is ready?" he asked.

She nodded, pulling the hood of her cloak up over her head. The cloak was heavy wool, very well made, and oiled so it would repel the rainwater. As her men gathered behind her, luggage in hand, she sneezed in succession, several times, violently.

Brandt took a pause as he opened the door, looking at her with some concern, but he refrained from commenting because she would only disagree with him. She looked red around the eyes and the nose but it wasn't any concern of his.

At least, that's what he told himself. He couldn't decide if it was because Deston would become truly angry with him if some evil sickness befell his daughter or if it was because he was, in fact, concerned for her.

## CHAPTER SEVEN

Rain was pouring outside. Brandt's knights were waiting for him astride their beastly war horses but one of Ellowyn's men had to run off to gather her horse. Without the two additional men in her escort, the two that were left were sorely strained so one remained with the lady while the other collected the horses. Ellowyn preferred her leggy mare against a carriage or wagon, so the man returned shortly leading three very wet horses.

Brandt didn't say a word as Ellowyn and her escorts tied off the baggage and mounted their steeds. In fact, he left her with her men and went to collect his charger. The horse had seen more action than most men and was a violent, bad-tempered beast that snapped at anything that moved. The horse was muzzled tightly as Brandt collected the reins from the wet soldier holding him, mounting the horse smoothly which was no easy feat considering the weight of his armor coupled by the weight of the water collecting on him. He turned to Dylan and Alex behind him.

"The lady will be protected by two knights at all times," he said. "Surround her and her escort with at least a dozen men."

Dylan nodded smartly. "Aye, my lord," he replied. "And our road?"

Brandt flicked a finger off to the west. "Harrow road," he replied. "That will take us to the road to Gloucester and points north."

Dylan nodded smartly, turning to the men behind him. "Five point formation," he snapped. "St. Hèver , you take point with le Bec. De Reyne and I will ride center with the lady and Alex will take the rear. Get the men on their feet and moving; *go*."

The knights slammed down faceplates, going in different directions to carry out Dylan's orders. Five point formation was one of de Russe's traveling formations – usually two knights to the front, two to the rear and one in the center, with de Russe fluid throughout the column. There were sixteen lesser knights in de Russe's corps, young men from good families who were not in the chain of command.

Brandt was very rigid about the men he trusted, and about men in general, and these knights were not in his inner corp. They served him but they mostly commanded the foot troops. With his five hundred troops and de Nerra's nearly six hundred, he had a very sizable army heading north and he had Dylan and Alex position the eight additional lesser knights accordingly.

It was into this monstrous collection of men and weapons that Ellowyn found herself absorbed. As the rain pounded and the thunder rolled, she ended up in the middle of the column with her two escorts, slogging through the muddy roads on their way out of London. Kerchief clutched in her hand, she sneezed and sniffled in to it, all the while eyeing the big knights riding near her. She knew they were there to keep watch over her and protect her. Maybe they were even there to report back to de Russe on her every movement.

The truth was that she found herself thinking about de Russe more and more. He was like a completely different man since last night when they'd supped together. His eyes didn't hold that hard edge any longer. Not that she cared. Well, perhaps she was coming to care in the slightest, and that thought scared her to death. She'd never shown interest for a man in her life and she wasn't about to start now.

The trek was slow because of the rain, unfortunate because the weather seemed to be worsening. Everything was gray; the sky, the air, and even the land to some extent. Because the road was so traveled, it was wide and very well used which meant the mud made from the loose earth and rainwater turned portions of it into swamps. The men on foot were covered in mud up to their hips and even the horses had some trouble maneuvering through it. Ellowyn made sure she was very careful when they came to such soupy patches; that last thing she wanted to do was end up in the mud again.

There wasn't anything spectacular about the travel as they made their way out of London. It was cold and wet, and although

Ellowyn had initially felt better after her warm brew and porridge, the cough was starting to make a return and her throat was becoming very sore from all of the hacking. More than that, she was very cold in spite of her layers of clothing, making for a truly miserable ride, so she kept her head lowered and the oiled cloak pulled very tightly around her as the minutes and then hours passed.

*Acton. Penvale. Gutteridge.* The line of unspectacular towns passed in succession. The party was so enormous that they would literally swamp the small villages with men and animals as they moved through. If the weather hadn't been so poor, people might have actually turned out to see them, but as the thunder rolled it was as if they were passing through ghost towns. Worse yet, Ellowyn's illness was making her extremely drowsy and after four hours in the saddle, she was struggling to stay awake. Twice, she had nearly fallen off her horse. She hoped no one had noticed.

She tried everything to stay awake, including eating the bread and cheese that the innkeeper had given her but, much to her chagrin, a full belly only made her sleepier. She was deeply thankful when the column finally came to a halt outside of a small village. Ellowyn could see the huddle of houses in the distance, with smoke from the fireplaces heavy upon the air. She heard someone say that the village was called Beaconsfield, and as she sat upon her horse, soaked to the skin and coughing, she very nearly gave up any hope of surviving the trip. She was feeling horrible and it surely would kill her. Perhaps she should have stayed in London as de Russe had suggested. Perhaps he had been right.

"My lady?"

A deep, quiet voice roused her from her thoughts and she looked over her right shoulder to see de Russe standing there. He was soaked too, his mail rusting in the bad weather and creating black streaks on his chin and cheek. His nose was pinched red from the cold but the glimmer in his eye was rather warm. Weary, but warm.

"I have secured a room for you in town," he told her. "It is not much, but at least it is warm and dry."

Ellowyn was deeply grateful. In fact, tears popped to hear eyes as she thought of actually being warm and dry. It was a great relief.

"Thank you," she sighed, appreciative. "I must be honest when I say that I was coming to think I would never be dry again."

His lips twitched with the flicker of a smile. Silently, he took the reins of her horse and pulled the beast along towards his charger. As lightning lit up the sky overhead, he managed to mount his steed still holding on to the reins of her horse, and proceeded to lead her into town.

There was a small town square, or at least the semblance of one, and an inn tucked deep amongst the poorly constructed buildings. Brandt dismounted his war horse and tethered the animal before moving to Ellowyn and helping her from her mount. The problem was that she was so stiff from having ridden all day, and ill to boot, that she could hardly dismount, so he pulled her from the horse and carried her into the inn.

Entering the establishment was like walking through the gates of hell. They were hit in the face by a blast of hot, smelly air, and the great room was filled to the rafters with people. It smelled like an ocean of unwashed bodies as Brandt set Ellowyn carefully to her feet.

As hardened as he was to people and places, even he was a bit put off by the sheer smell and volume of people. He glanced at Ellowyn, apologetically, before emitting a shrill whistled that almost immediately silenced the writhing throng. When the sound died down, he bellowed.

"Barkeep!"

Ellowyn jumped at the sound of his voice. It was like the voice of God, echoing off the walls, powerful in its timbre and baritone resonance. As she coughed into her hand, a skinny man with a crooked back appeared.

"M'lord?" he stammered nervously.

Brandt's intense gaze zeroed in on the man. "You have a room for the Duke of Exeter."

The man's eyes widened slightly and he bowed swiftly once or twice. "Aye, m'lord," he began to walk, motioning them to follow. "This way, if ye please."

Ellowyn stumbled after the man, following him to the rear of the building where there was a small corridor with three doors. The hunched man led her into the last door, shoving it open because it was stuck in the ill-crafted doorframe. Beyond lay a rather large room with two beds and a snapping fire. In fact, Ellowyn came to a halt just inside the doorway, shocked at the room. For all of the crowded dirtiness of the inn, she hadn't expected something as spacious or well-kempt as this. Her eyes widened.

"All of this?" she asked no one in particular. "For *me*?"

The barkeep slipped past her. "I will bring food, m'lady."

He vanished back into the busy inn, leaving Ellowyn and Brandt standing in silence until Ellowyn began hacking and Brandt stepped further into the room, shutting the door behind him to keep the warmth in.

"Perhaps you should remove your cloak," he said quietly. "In fact, perhaps you should undress completely so your clothes may be dried before we embark again on the morrow. And a hot bath probably would not hurt, either."

Ellowyn coughed again, realizing how very cold she was. Her brain was moving rather slowly, slandered with fatigue and illness. With freezing fingers, she fumbled with the ties at her neck.

"If one could be arranged, I would be very grateful," she said.

Brandt noticed she was having trouble with her cloak ties so he gently pushed her fingers away and politely undid the tie. Then he pulled the cloak off of her and went to hang it on a peg next to the hearth so the radiant heat would dry it.

Ellowyn watched him, aware that his presence was comforting. She wasn't sure why, but it was. She was also aware that she was glad to see him, having traveled essentially alone for the past ten hours with no conversation or company. She had been lonely, and he offered company. Unusually for the lady who liked to be alone.

But she was sure he did not feel the same. She watched him quit the room and close the door softly behind him, a bit disappointed at his departure. He didn't even say a word to her. With a heavy sigh, she went over to the fire and began the laborious process of undressing with cold and wet clothing. Her shoes were the first to come off, placed neatly by the fire before pulling off her hose, which ended up draped over a stool as close to the fire as she could get it without igniting it. Then came her surcoat, of which the entire bottom of the skirt was soaking and muddied. She was untying the stays at her waist when the door opened again.

Brandt was there, holding the door open as a heavy-set man with a mashed face and curly black hair entered lugging a big copper pot. There were a pair of women behind him struggling to carry buckets of hot water, which were dumped into the pot. As they left to get more water, Brandt turned to Ellowyn.

"I will have someone bring your belongings," he said. "Do you require anything else?"

Did she? Probably not. Just someone to talk to would have been nice, and she had very much enjoyed their conversation the previous night when the duke had spoken of Deston. But the entire conversation had been out of polite duty out of respect to de Nerra, she was sure. It hadn't been anything personal, because he wanted to speak to her personally. She understood that.

"You have been most kind and accommodating, my lord," she said, her voice hoarse and scratchy. "Please know that I appreciate your attentiveness greatly, but I do not want you to feel obligated. Surely you have more important duties than seeing to my comfort."

Brandt's dark gaze lingered on her. "None that I can think of," he replied. "Seeing to your comfort is an important duty as far as I am concerned.

She gave him a weak smile, ruining the effect when she burst into a series of harsh coughs. "You are very kind," she repeated. "You are coming to make me feel very guilty about our first meeting. Had I only known I was becoming irate with a saint."

He broke into a grin. "I thought we were going to forget about that."

She grinned in response, shrugging as she turned back for the fire. "We were," she said. "Eventually. I do not suppose there is anything I can do to make up for that encounter except... oh, wait a moment... perhaps there is."

He was more than curious. "There is nothing to make up for, but I would be willing to listen to suggestions."

She stood up on her cold, bare feet and pointed to the two beds in the room. "This," she said. "There is only one of me but there are two beds in the room. Perhaps we could string a curtain between the two, for propriety of course, and you could sleep in one and I could sleep in the other. It seems an awful waste for one of these beds to remain empty while you sleep outside in the foul weather. That way, you can enjoy a dry bed as well."

He looked at her, seeing that she sincerely meant what she said. She also meant it quite innocently, which disappointed him, although he couldn't figure out exactly why except that an inappropriate offer would have flattered him deeply. But she hadn't meant it that way, mostly because he was sure she didn't find anything about him remotely attractive. It was a kind offer, but inappropriate. After a moment, he shook his head.

"You are very generous to suggest such a thing," he said, "but I am afraid I cannot."

She cocked her head. "Why?"

He lifted his eyebrows at her. "My lady, if your father got wind of such a sleeping arrangement, he would cut off my... head. He would be furious to say the least."

Her brow furrowed. "But there is no reason why... oh...." She cooled. "Do you mean to imply that I suggested something inappropriate? That was not my intention, my lord. Not in the least."

He could see she was mildly offended. "My lady, I did not take it as an improper suggestion, but there are others who would wonder why I was sleeping in your room. It is an unfortunate fact that men talk and if word got back to your father, I would be in for a row."

Ellowyn simply nodded and turned away from him, resuming her stool next to the hearth. She was rather disappointed that he had refuted her offer, but she recognized what he was saying. He made sense.

"I understand," she said softly. "Please know I was not truly trying to suggest something inappropriate. I was rather hoping we could continue our conversation from last night. It has been a long time since I have enjoyed such conversation and… well, I do not have the opportunity to converse with many people so I suppose I was… forgive me, I am rambling. I am sure you must return to your men, so I will thank you again for your kindness and bid you a good eve."

Brandt's gaze lingered on her as she faced the fire, holding out a hand trying to rub some warmth back into it. As he stood there, the heavy set man and the two women came into the room again, dumping more buckets of hot water into the copper tub. When they left, Brandt followed. He quit the room without a word and shut the door.

Ellowyn turned when she heard the door softly shut, seeing that she was quite alone in the room. With a sigh, she rose from her stool and went over to the door, bolting it. Going over to the pot, she put a hand into it to feel that it was very hot. She wanted to get it badly but decided to wait for her things first; it would be of no use were she to get in now and then have to get out again when her satchel was brought about. Fresh clothes and toiletries were in the bag. So she went back over to the fire and sat, waiting for one of de Russe's men to bring her possessions as she tried to figure out why she felt such a sense of disappointment with de Russe's departure. .

She didn't have to wait long. Several minutes later, there was a knock on the door and she rose to open it. A wench with an enormous tray of food entered, moving to set the tray down on the small table next to the hearth. The wench fled, leaving Ellowyn to inspect the tray of mutton, carrots and turnips boiled together in gravy, plus a big slab of cheese and an entire loaf of bread. There was also a cup with something steaming in it, which turned out to be spiced wine. Ellowyn slurped it down as it soothed her irritated throat. It was so good that she had the wench bring her another one, but the wench brought two more. They were large tankards nearly filled full. Ellowyn was almost done with the third large cup of spiced wine when there was another knock on the door.

Feeling tipsy and warm, Ellowyn went to answer the door. Brandt was standing in the doorway, soaked to the skin, with her large traveling satchel in his hands. Before he could say a word, she grabbed her bag, then his hand, and yanked him into the room.

"Come in," she demanded. "'Tis cold and wet outside, and you should sit."

She punctuated the 'sit' by shoving him into the nearest chair. Brandt let her do it, mostly because he was baffled by her behavior and wasn't quite sure how to respond, but when he saw her taking a deep drink out of a fairly large tankard, he began to suspect what had happened.

"How many of those have you had?" he asked.

Ellowyn stopped sipping and looked at him with big eyes. "Of what?"

He pointed at the mug. "That."

She stared at his pointed finger, then looked around until her gaze came to rest on the cup in her hand. "This?"

"Aye."

It looked as if she was thinking very hard on the question. "I am not sure," she said. "I may have had two or three."

He was coming to understand the situation. "I told them to bring you something hot to drink," he said. "Wine, I would presume?"

She stared into the cup as if trying to figure out what was in it. "Aye," she said, then walked over to him and shoved it in his face. "See? There are bits of things in it."

He had to dodge his head quickly or risk getting hit in the nose when she tried to show him what was in the mug. He was mostly watching her face as he spoke.

"Things? You mean bits of spice?" he said.

She was staring down in to the cup, her brow furrowed. She was also very close to him, in fact; their heads were nearly touching. Brandt just watched her face, studying her long lashes and creamy skin, as she gazed into the cup.

"Things," she repeated as if unsure how else to describe it. "Floating dark things. Mayhap they are bits of bugs."

"I doubt they are bugs."

That was good enough for her. She proceeded to toss her head back and drink the last bit of spiced wine, at least three big gulps worth. She nearly toppled as she tried to set the cup down and would have fallen had Brandt not reached out a long arm to steady her. She smiled at him when she realized he was trying to help her. Brandt tried not to smile back but it was difficult when she was grinning so openly at him.

"Perhaps you should go to bed," he suggested. "It has been a long day and we will depart at dawn."

Ellowyn continued to stare up at him. Then, she reached out and grasped the hand that was steadying her, tearing her gaze away from his face to look down at his gloved hand. It was big, the glove well-used and very well made. She inspected it closely.

"You have the biggest hand I have ever seen," she said. Then she sneezed on the glove, wiped away the spittle with an apologetic glance, and then proceeded to pull off the glove. She began to run her hand over his palm, inspecting the worn flesh. "Your hands are so rough. They have callouses. Is that from holding your sword?"

In truth, Brandt was having a rather difficult time keeping his head. There was something decidedly erotic about her running her finger all over his hand, something that made his heart race and his stomach quiver. He was shocked at himself for his reaction to her, but not shocked enough to pull away. He rather liked the strange, alien feelings she was managing to provoke.

"Aye," he muttered.

She looked up at him, smiling sweetly. "I heard tale that you were called the Black Angel," she slurred. "Is there truth in this?"

He lifted an eyebrow. "I suppose it depends on what side of my sword one is on."

"The enemy would call you this?"

"As the right arm of Edward, the Black Prince, I suppose they had to come up with a name for me. Black Angel, Bringer of Death, has followed me around for some time."

She gazed up at him seriously. "But that is *not* true," she said flatly. "You are kind and you are considerate. Who has said these terrible things about you? Tell me now and I will seek them out

67

and berate them for their slander and misinformation."

A twinkle came to his eye. "You would champion me, then?"

Ellowyn nodded, so forcefully that she nearly toppled over again. He had to grab her again to keep her from falling.

"You have been very kind to me in spite of what happened when we met," she said, waving a careless hand at him. "Oh, I know we were not going to discuss it anymore, but you must understand that I have been conducting my father's business for at least three years, ever since my brother, Fenton, joined the cloister. Since my father is so ill most of the time, someone has to conduct his business for him so everyone in Cumbria knows me and treats me with the same respect they would treat my father. But *you* did not."

His lips twitched with a smile at the way she said 'you'. She dragged it out so it sounded as if it had four or five syllables.

"I did not know you," he said. "I will deeply regret the way I spoke to you, always."

She cocked her head, exaggerated with her drunken state. "You will?" she asked, awed. "But, truly, you should not. I am very sorry I became so angry, but you called me a whore and, well, I have never had anyone say such things to me."

"I should not have called you that."

She was staring up at him thoughtfully. "Do you think it would be a terrible thing to be a whore?"

He fought off laughter because she was truly silly and ridiculous with this line of conversation. "I would not know," he said, biting his lip. "I suppose it would depend on the circumstance."

Her brow furrowed. "What if you had an entire family to feed and that was the only way you could make money?"

"Then it would be the means by which to achieve an end."

"Do you think whores like being whores?"

He couldn't stop himself from chuckling now. "I have not given it much thought," he said, then tried to change the subject. "Perhaps you should go to bed now. It is growing late and...."

She cut him off, yanking him over to the table where the food was. Snatching away the cloth that was covering the now-cooling meal, she pushed him down onto the bed next to table. In spite of being more than twice her size and probably three times her weight, she was able to push him down simply by her manner. He was afraid of what would happen if he didn't do what she wanted.

"Eat," she commanded. "There is plenty of food."

He tried to stand up but she pushed him down again. "Lady, my mail is wet and it is getting the bed wet," he explained. "May I please stand?"

Her response was to grab an arm and pull him up. He pretended to let her.

"My father and mother call me Wynny," she informed him. "I will give you permission to call me Wynny, too. Addressing me formally seems peculiar under these circumstances."

He just smiled at her as he began to remove his helm. "Thank you," he said, pulling the helm free and setting it on the table. "I am honored."

Ellowyn watched, weaving and half-lidded, as he proceeded to peel his hauberk off and move to drape it near the fire. The tunic followed. He was standing with his back to her and her gaze began to wander from the top of his extremely broad shoulders down his back and to his buttocks and legs. He had enormous legs. She grinned, liking what she was seeing, more inebriated than she had ever been in her life because she never really drank wine. She didn't particularly like it, so three large tankards of very sweet wine had gone straight to her head. She just stood there staring at his broad backside.

"Are you married, my lord?" she asked.

Brandt began to peel off his mail coat. "I was," he said. "She died a few years ago."

"Oh," Ellowyn pondered the death of his spouse. "I am sorry for you."

He shook his head. "No need," he replied, pulling the rest of the mail coat off and shaking off the excess water on the hearth. "She hated me and everything about me. She took our two daughters and moved to France years ago. I have not seen my daughters very often since that time and was only recently contacted by them because they wish to marry and require a dowry. That is all I am to my daughters; a source of funds to elevate their marital prospects."

Ellowyn was listening to him seriously. "How old are they?"

"Margarethe is fifteen years and Rosalind is seventeen years."

She cocked her head. "Were you very young when they were born? You do not seem old enough to have grown daughters."

The corner of his lip twitched. "Their mother and I were married very young," he said. "In fact, I was twenty one years of age. She was fourteen. I had been an earl since my father passed away when I was nine years of age so I was already well established and she was from royalty."

"You were only an earl when you married her?"

He nodded. "I was not granted the Dukedom of Exeter until King Edward bestowed it upon me ten years ago after the Battle of Crècy. It was my reward for serving his son, and England, flawlessly."

"I see," she said, very interested. "Now, back to your marriage. You said you married very young."

He nodded, back on the original subject. "We did," he replied. "It was an excellent contract but for the fact that we discovered shortly after our marriage that we hated each other. Rosalind, born a short time after we were wed, was supposed to be a boy, or at least I prayed for one so that my duty as a husband would be done, but when she turned out to be female, my wife and I agreed to one more pregnancy in the hopes of having a male child but she failed at that, too. The girls were still infants when she took them back to one of my properties in France, and I have only seen them twice since. They cannot stomach the sight of me."

She was listening to him with a heavy heart. "I am sorry for you," she said sincerely. "I cannot understand daughters that would not love their father because I love my father a great deal. I also do not understand a wife who would not at least be fond of her husband because my mother and father are very fond of one another. I hope that when I marry I am madly in love with my husband."

He turned to look at her, grinning. "Love, is it?" he said. "You are optimistic."

She nodded firmly and nearly toppled again. "I will only marry for love."

"What does Deston have to say about that?"

"He does not know."

"You should probably tell him before he betroths you to someone you cannot stand."

She shrugged, averting her gaze and noticing the big copper pot a few feet away. She wandered over to it and stuck her hand into the still very-warm water.

"I am sure that will not happen any time soon," she said.

"Why?"

She went over to the bed where she had tossed her satchel and began to pull it open. "Because he knows I must approve of any betrothal and so far, I have not approved of a single fool who has come to our door."

"Not one?"

"Not one."

"Then you set a high standard."

She shrugged as she open the satchel wide and began to pull forth her toiletries; a bar of soap that was made with precious oils and smelled heavily of lavender, a frayed reed and tooth cleanser that was made with mint and cloves, and a big hair comb.

"I will not be saddled with someone I do not like or do not approve of," she said simply, then sneezed a few times in rapid succession. "It is not foolish to want to be happy."

Brandt turned to look at her. "Nay, it is not," he agreed quietly. "I wish you good fortune in your search."

Pensive, drunk and sniffling, Ellowyn made her way back over to the copper pot. She set the stuff down on the bed next to the pot and looked at Brandt seriously, as if her muddled mind was in the midst of concocting something. Then she pointed at him.

"You will remove your wet clothing and put it before the fire," she said, sounding as if she was once again commanding him. "Then you will sit in this chair with your back to me while I bathe. I will not look at you if you will not look at me and, being a knight and a duke, I will trust your word when you swear you will not watch me bathe. Are we clear?"

71

He was back to fighting off a grin. "My lady, I am...."

"Wynny!"

He corrected himself. "Wynny, I am not entirely certain that is wise," he tried to make it simply so her alcohol-soaked brain could understand. "Do you realize what you are saying? You are telling me to take my clothes off, and you will take your clothes off, and the only thing keeping propriety as our cloak and shield is a promise we will not look at each other. Does that sound fitting to you?"

She blinked, thinking hard on his words. "Aye," she said, looking up at him as if confused by his statement. "I will trust you if you tell me you will not look."

Brandt had never before seen such naked, complete and utter trust. It was in her eyes, her expression, everything about her, and he didn't find her drunken state so funny anymore. He'd had the faith of many people over his life, mostly out of fear and out of respect for his skills as a man and as a warrior, but never had he seen it so trusting and blatant as he did at this very moment in that lovely little face. She was trusting him as a man, not as a warrior or a duke. To refute her would be to insult her. He didn't want to do that. More than that, she was determined to take a bath and in her condition, he was coming to think it would not be wise to leave her alone. She could hit her head, pass out, or worse. He didn't want that to happen.

"I will not look," he said softly.

Satisfied, Ellowyn went about undressing in a very uncoordinated fashion. Brandt turned away, acutely aware of every sound she made, as he pulled off his heavy padded tunic, so wet and uncomfortable, and put it out by the fire to dry out. Off came the boots as well as they ended up in front of the flame. As he sat with his back to Ellowyn, he began to carve into the cooling mutton when he heard the water behind him slosh as she climbed in. He was hit in the back of the neck with warm water as she began to splash about.

"My lord?" she called.

"I must tell you something," he said, mouth full of mutton.

"What is that?"

"Since you have so graciously given me permission to call you Wynny," he said, "I must tell you to call me Brandt in private. Agreed?"

"Agreed," she said, splashing around some more. "Brandt?"

"Aye?"

"Do you have any friends?"

"A few."

She fell silent a moment, sneezing as she splashed. "I do not," she said, rather forlornly. "Not really. I have cousins, of course, but it seems as if I only really have my family. We are related to Simon de Montfort on my father's side, so when people find out, it seems no one wants to know us. After all these years, that part of the family is still frowned upon."

"Did you not make friends when you fostered?"

"I did not foster."

He was surprised. "You did *not* foster?" he repeated, turning around to look at her but remembering his promise not to watch her bathe, so he quickly turned back to face his meal. "That is unheard of. Who took charge of your education, then?"

"My grandfather," she said. "Braxton de Nerra. He was a very smart man. He taught me everything from when I was young. Did you know him?"

Brandt nodded as he tucked into the bread and gravy. "I knew him," he said. "He was a great knight."

In the tub, Ellowyn was busy soaping her feet. "He passed away six years ago," she said softly. "But he was healthy and vital right until the end. My grandmother misses him every day, you know. They loved each other very much. I suppose they are why I am determined to marry a man I love. I saw what they had together and I want that, too."

Brandt chewed on his bread, digesting their conversation, reflecting on the intelligent and loyal woman he was coming to know. She was talking quite a bit, that was true, but he knew it was because of the alcohol. He was coming to learn a lot about her, understanding her, and liking it. In fact, sitting in the little room with the blazing fire, he was more comfortable with her than he had been with almost anyone in his life. There was something pure about the woman, open to a fault, but also strong-willed to a fault. She reminded him a lot of her father. She was a woman who knew what she wanted in life and would get it. He admired that.

"Brandt?" Ellowyn cut into his train of thought.

"Aye?"

"Do you think you shall ever marry again?"

He swallowed the bread in his mouth and went for the wine. "I have not given it much thought," he said. "Perhaps."

"You should, you know," she said. "You should have sons to carry on the de Russe name. Who will inherit your dukedom if you do not?"

"As I said, I have not given it particular thought."

"Are you returning to war again?"

"Eventually."

"Then you should think about marrying again and having a son," she said, splashing around behind him. "You should do this before you leave again, just to be safe."

"I will take it under advisement."

"Perhaps I will help you find a wife," she said decisively. "I can do that, you know. I will search high and low for someone worthy of you."

He smiled into his cup. "Although I am honored you would think so highly of me, marriage is not a priority at this time. I have many other things that need my attention and wife is not among them."

She wasn't put off in the least. "When you are ready, you will let me know."

His expression turned distant, pensive, perhaps interested more than he cared to admit. "I will let you know."

He finished off the wine as she finished off her bath. She sneezed and coughed, but it was far less than she had been doing earlier. True to his promise, he didn't turn around to look at her as she slithered out of the tub, dried off with a corner of the bed linen, and dressed.

By the time she came into view, she was clad in a simple shift that was of one piece, like a dressing gown. It was some kind of heavier fabric, perhaps cotton or even lamb's wool that clung to her figure almost indecently. In fact, Brandt had to make an effort not to stare at her as she passed in front of him and sat down on the opposite side of the table. Her long blond hair was damp, and braided, and he caught distinct whiffs of lavender. It was a clean and delicious smell. He was starting to realize that he'd never in his life seen such a radiant and pure creature.

"You are breaking your promise, you know," he remarked as she began to pull the bread apart.

Curious, she looked at him. "What do you mean?"

He was looking at his wine. "You promised not to look at me in my half-dressed state."

She stared at him a moment before dropping the bread and slapping her hands over her face. "You are correct," she muttered through her hands. "I will not look if you wish to dress."

"Did you not even notice that I only have my breeches on?"

She nodded. "I did, but I did not give it much thought. Forgive me."

He fought off a grin. "My, but you are comfortable around half-naked men."

She shook her head, hands still over her eyes. "I suppose I was not paying attention," she said. "I was more focused on eating. My head is beginning to spin from too much drink."

He pursed his lips wryly. "So much for making an impression on you," he grumbled. "Take your hands off your eyes. I suppose if you do not even notice me, then it is of no worry. I might as well be a horse sitting here for all you would notice my state of dress."

She giggled as she uncovered her eyes. "I *have* noticed you," she insisted as she resumed her bread. "You are a very handsome man, Brandt. I am sure if you decide to marry, your wife will be a very fortunate woman and she will notice you all of the time."

His eyes glimmered at her. "Flattery will get you everywhere," he said in a low, and nearly flirtatious, voice, "but I am still not sure if I am comfortable with your abject kindness. It scares me."

Her hands came away from her face. "Why?"

A smile played on his lips. "I am not entire certain," he said, looking down at his food. "Perhaps I want to believe it."

Ellowyn gazed at him, still somewhat inebriated, but there was lucidity to her thoughts now as well. As Brandt cut off a hunk of

75

cheese, she did, in fact, take a look at the man's naked torso. Not being an expert on men's naked torsos, she really didn't have anything to compare it to, but she did know that he was exquisitely muscled with enormously wide shoulders and a narrow waist. He had the biggest arms she had ever seen and his fair share of scars, all illuminated softly by the orange firelight. She could see his veins through the skin. As she looked at him, she realized she was feeling quite warm and breathless at the sight and she knew, instinctively, that she liked it.

"You should believe it," she said, averting her gaze to find her bread. "It is the truth. I wish you much success with a future wife. She will be a fortunate woman."

He looked at her, noting she was focused on her food and not on him. Strangely enough, her comment didn't sound like a passing remark. It sounded sincere, something that peaked his interested more than he cared to admit. He also noticed, even in the weak light, that she was rather flushed. It didn't occur to him that it was, in fact, because of him. He thought it was her illness. Wiping his hands off on his breeches, he reached across the table and trapped her head in his big hands. Feeling her forehead, he hissed.

"You have a fever," he said somewhat grimly.

Head contained in his massive palms, Ellowyn looked surprised. "I do not believe so," she said as he felt her warm cheeks. "It is because the bath was warm."

He just shook his head. "This has nothing to do with the bath," he told her. Then, he stood up and went over to the bed closest to the fire and pulled back the linens. "Get into bed. I will go in search of a physic."

He said it in a manner that invited no resistance. Ellowyn stood up, bread still in hand, and looked at him with curiosity and bewilderment.

"I am fine, truly," she said, punctuated by first a sneeze and then a hiccup. "I do not have a fever."

"Get in bed. That was not a request."

He had the innate ability to give an order that sounded as if the devil himself had just given a command. Ellowyn tried not to be intimidated. "But I am hungry," she said, pointing at the food

76

behind her. "Can I please eat first?"

Brandt grunted, unhappy, but he relented. "Very well," he said, ripping the coverlet off the bed and wrapping it around her like a babe in swaddling. He guided her back to the chair next to the table and pushed her down on it. "Sit there and finish your meal. But the very moment you are finished, I want you to get into bed. Is that clear?"

She gazed up at him, indecisive, preparing to refuse, but the look on his face killed any sense of resistance. She nodded with resignation.

"If you insist."

"I do."

"I do not need a physic. I am sure I do not have a fever; it is only the warm bath."

"I would feel better if we had a physic make the diagnosis."

With that, he pulled on his nearly dry padded tunic, his boots, his armor, and his overtunic with the dark green and black dragon of the Duke of Exeter. Ellowyn picked her bread apart, dipping it in the cold gravy, as he dressed. She found herself watching him more than she was paying attention to her food. When he was finished dressing, he quit the room with a lingering glance. But not word came forth out of his mouth.

He didn't need to speak, however. Ellowyn understood the silent words radiating forth from his eyes more than if he had shouted at her.

# CHAPTER EIGHT

*The rain was back.*

*She was in the field of bodies again, avoiding the pleading hands of the dying, staring at her left hand and the gold and garnet ring upon it. She was married and somehow, somewhere in this mess, was her husband. That must be why she had come; to find him. She wasn't sure how she knew, only that she did. In this sea of death and destruction, littered with the dead like flotsam upon the sea, she had to find him. She would do it or die trying.*

*She was knee deep in unfathomable mud, now a dark brick red in color because of the blood mixed into it. Rivers of it coagulating, creating dark veins in the mud. She struggled to walk through it, panic in her throat.*

*She looked up at the sky, that great steel-colored mess, thankful for the lack of sun; it would dry up the mud and would trap the dead within it. She had to find her husband before that happened, heightening her sense of urgency. God, please help me, she prayed. Please help me find my love.*

*My love, she thought. Aye, he is my love, my life. As she moved towards a grove of stripped trees, the mud became shallower and less binding, and she struggled to get up onto firmer ground. But she slipped and fell to her knees, bracing herself with one arm to keep from falling completely while the other arm went around her belly. A big, swollen belly.*

*Shocked, she looked at her midsection to realize she was pregnant.*

\*\*\*

"I am with child!"

Ellowyn started herself awake with those words, disoriented for a moment until she realized she was on the back of her mare, riding in the midst of de Russe's column of battle hardened warriors. She glanced around, sheepishly, realizing she had fallen asleep and praying no one had seen her.

"My lady?"

She heard the soft, deep voice over her left shoulder and she closed her eyes briefly, tightly, for a moment. She just knew she'd been caught. Slowly, she turned.

"Aye?" she asked.

It was the very young and very blond knight. The lad was absolutely enormous, with a fair face, white eyelashes and brows, and intense blue-green eyes. They almost looked too bright within his pale face as he focused on her with polite concern.

"Did you say something, my lady?" he asked.

She shook her head and faced forward. "Nay," she said, demurred. "Nothing of import. Thank you for your concern."

"The Duke has ordered us to stop at the next town," he said. "We will make camp there for the night."

Ellowyn merely nodded. There wasn't much excitement in the fact that they were stopping for the night. It was the sixth day of their journey to Erith, which would take another ten days at the very least. De Russe was driving a fairly swift but steady pace, something that thoroughly exhausted Ellowyn but she wouldn't let on. She had gone to great length to convince the man that she was strong and hearty, even with her sniffles and coughing, but that really wasn't the case. She was putting on a big show when the truth was that she was sick, weary, and verging on tears nearly every second of the day. Traveling with all of these strange men unnerved her and she didn't feel well, a bad combination. De Russe, as kind as he had been, was her only solace.

Fortunately, it was no longer raining and hadn't been for two days as they had made their way north. Still, it was cold and the winds from the west had been brisk. From what she had heard that morning, if all went well enough, they would be at Coventry by evening's fall. As the army plodded north through a series of small hills, she gazed off towards the west, towards Wales, and could see flat and green lands below with a very small and dark ridge on the horizon. It was a very faint crest, but she could see it because of the angle of the sunset and the clearness of the air. She pointed.

"Knight," she said, addressing the young knight with the pale hair. "What is that over there?"

The knight turned his helmed head in the direction she was indicating. He flipped up his visor so he could see more clearly. "Wales, my lady," he replied. "The Welsh mountains that define the Marches."

She watched them a moment. "They look rather peaceful now."

The knight cocked an eyebrow. "They look dark and jagged to me, like teeth preparing to bite. They are a testament to the darkness in the soul of every Welshman and their desire to tear the English apart like wolves to the feast."

Ellowyn glanced back at the man, studying him a moment. "You are a poet."

He looked at her, fighting off a grin. "Alas, I am not," he replied. "Merely an observation."

"What is your name?"

"Sir Brennan St. Hèver, my lady."

"Do you know much about the Welsh?"

He nodded. "I grew up at Kirk Castle," he replied. "It is very close to the Welsh border. My father is the Earl of Wrexham and we have seen much of what the Welsh can do."

She cocked her head. "Yet you serve de Russe. His seat is in Exeter, far from the Marches."

Brennan nodded. "That was my father's decision," he replied. "He and the duke have known each other for years. It was his wish that I serve the duke for a time before returning to assume my station."

"How old are you?"

"I have seen twenty years, my lady."

Her eyebrows lifted. "And you are already a knight?"

"Fully sworn, my lady."

"Then you are exceptionally talented to be knighted so young."

He shrugged modestly, not having an answer for her. Sensing their conversation was at an end, Ellowyn's gaze moved back to the horizon, how illuminated with the fading sunset. There were clusters of small forests around them the closer they drew to Coventry and the hilly road leveled out. She could no longer see the sunset or the western horizon.

Bored, weary, she began picking at her cloak, thinking on what they would have for sup that night. She was hoping for beef or fowl as she was growing weary of mutton. It always tasted old, to her at least. But those were her last coherent thoughts before something nicked her chin, slammed into her right shoulder, and sent her hurling to the ground.

Horses were screaming around her as men began shouting. Everyone was in a panic. Conscious but stunned, Ellowyn's only thought was to pull herself out of the mud but there was so much pain in her right shoulder that she was having difficulty sitting up. An enormous armored body was suddenly beside her, scooping her up. With her clutched against him, he ran towards a tightly packed grove of trees. As they bounced along, she could see the forest looming as a dark and protective embrace.

There was more shouting going on around her followed by the distinct sounds of fighting. They entered the grove of trees and knight surrendered his burden to a few waiting soldiers, waiting to help, and Ellowyn was lowered to the ground by several pairs of hands. As they settled her on the ground, the knight knelt beside her and flipped up his visor. She could see it was St. Hèver .

His young face was flushed but he was in control. Their eyes met and he nodded his head at her, firmly, in a move that was both encouraging and business-like.

"So sorry, my lady," he said, and she could feel more hands holding her still. "I must remove this."

She had no idea what he was talking about until he yanked something from her right shoulder, an evil projectile that had embedded itself near the joint. Now the shoulder pain was starting to make sense. It had been painful going in but it was excruciating coming out and she screamed as he removed it and tossed it aside, accepting a wad of boiled linen from someone and pressing it hard against the wound to stop the bleeding. But Ellowyn wanted no part of his battlefield medicine; she cried and squirmed, eventually kicked and beat at his hands as they held that damnable wad over her wounded shoulder. She didn't want anything to do with it. She wanted out.

"Bren!" Someone shouted from the direction of the road. "Leave her! You are needed, man!"

He held pressure on the wound a moment longer before passing the duty to one of the soldiers. The man took the position occupied by St. Hèver , pressing firmly, as the knight ran off towards the fight.

At that point, Ellowyn was nearly hysterical. She was injured, bleeding, exhausted and ill, and truly wanted out. She began fighting the soldiers so badly that they eventually had to let her go or she would have probably hurt herself more. But they didn't move far enough away from her, fast enough, so she screamed and kicked at them until they did.

The majority of the fighting was out on the road but there were dozens of men in the shelter of the trees as they had moved the wagons off of the road. There were many men protecting what they were carrying while the bulk of the army did the fighting. Trembling, on her knees, her right shoulder and arm virtually useless, Ellowyn watched the madness go on.

"What... what has happened?" she demanded, her voice cracking.

"We were attacked," said one of the soldiers left to tend her. "M'lady, we need to wrap your shoulder. I promise...."

"Nay!" she snapped, struggling to her feet. Her right shoulder felt as if it weighed more than her entire body, dragging her down. "I am getting out of here. I am leaving."

The soldiers followed her for a few feet as she backed away from them, eventually stumbling and falling onto her bum. Then she turned around and, on her hands and knees, tried to crawl away but her right arm wouldn't support any weight so she ended up tumbling. A charger suddenly roared up and kicked dirt and rocks on her. As she tried to brush off the cloak that was covered with mud and blood, someone grasped her by the arms.

"My lady?" It was Brandt. St. Hèver  had shouted to him of the lady's wound and even though there was a fairly nasty fight going on around him, all he could seem to think of was her. He'd fought his way through a passel of determined Welshmen to get this far. Now all he could see was blood and her pale face. "Wynny, what happened? What are you doing?"

Ellowyn gazed up at him and, seeing his handsome and familiar face, burst into frightened tears. Deeply concerned, Brandt moved to pick her up but their safe haven of trees was suddenly overrun by the enemy, and Brandt stood up, fending off an onslaught of angry men with blades. There were at least three of them intent on harming him as he practically stood on top of Ellowyn in order to protect her, his heavy broadsword wreaking havoc against the enemy. But he knew, very quickly, that they were in a bad way.

He couldn't maneuver with her on the ground at his feet and he very badly needed to. He'd managed to kill one man but there were two more, and perhaps even more. He wasn't quite sure because it seemed as if they were everywhere. Slugging the nearest enemy soldier in the face and sending the man to the ground, he ducked low when someone slashed a sword over his head and tried to decapitate him. He turned to Ellowyn.

"Wynny!" he snapped. "Get up! I need you to get *up!*"

Ellowyn had been stepped on twice. She was overwhelmed by the chaos and fighting over her head but she heard Brandt's voice, like a beacon in the darkness luring her towards it, and she grabbed on to Brandt's leg with her good arm, using him to help her get to her feet. Once, he took a big step back and knocked her down, but she continued to struggle to her feet. Left hand pressed to the wound on her right shoulder, she tucked in behind Brandt and prayed they would survive.

She wasn't the only one praying. Brandt was, too. He was using every part of his body to fight off the onslaught but trying to protect a wounded woman had him in a bad position. Fists met with jaws and feet met with bellies and groins. He'd already killed two men with blades through their chests. When he managed to disable the last man involved against him, he whirled to Ellowyn and put a big arm around her, battling his way out of the fight. He couldn't pick her up because if he did, he wouldn't have a free hand to defend them both. She had to walk on her own.

Men were ripping at his supply wagons and beating down his soldiers but Brandt didn't care about that. All he cared about was removing Ellowyn from the chaos, an unprotected woman in a sea of razor-sharp blades. As he headed towards a break in the trees, a man rushed at him and he had to push Ellowyn away so he would be free to fight.

Ellowyn stumbled, watching Brandt engage a man in heavy armor but, strangely, without a helm. Still, he seemed to be a fairly accomplished warrior because he was able to withstand Brandt's powerful thrusts. The duke was impressive to watch, in both strength and skill, and like a god, his skills were innate and flawless, his instincts without question. Ellowyn began to see what all men saw in de Russe; she saw the black angel of legend. She saw Death.

When the battling pair came close and Ellowyn was forced to move away lest she become swept up in the maelstrom, she ended up tripping and falling to her knee. Her left hand, bracing against the fall, fell upon a heavy piece of wood. Ellowyn grasped it. As Brandt gored his opponent in the groin and the man fell on his back, Ellowyn picked up the wood and smashed it across his face several times, beating in his features until they were a bloody pulp. There was panic to her movements, and there was fear. But there was also unmitigated bravery.

Brandt was somewhat surprised to see her rather brutal move, but in hindsight, he should not have been. Ellowyn de Nerra had thus far proven herself a strong and fearless woman, and she never failed to impress him. He looked at her, and she looked at him, and for a moment, they just stared at each other. Something was in the air between them, something inviting and curious no less, very misplaced in the middle of a battle, but they could both feel it. At that moment something ignited, at least for Brandt. Sword in his left hand, he went to Ellowyn and very carefully tossed her up on his broad and armored shoulder. Without a word, he carried her off to safety.

# CHAPTER NINE

"Welsh," Dylan said grimly. "Our scouts said that they raided Kenilworth Castle to the south earlier today. Then they saw us and apparently saw something worth taking."

It was just after sunset as Brandt stood outside of his tent, a massive structure that bore the black and white of the Duke of Exeter. The shelter, like all of the others pitched up around the edge of a small and dense forest to the south of Coventry, had seen more than its share of bad weather and use during Brandt's campaign with the Black Prince in France. Everyone knew Exeter's colors, announcing the onslaught of Edward's war machine.

"They were furious and they were determined," Brandt finally mumbled, scratching at his forehead. "To attack Kenilworth is foolish enough, but to attack a fully functional army smacks of madness. What is our final casualty count?"

"Eighteen dead and twenty seven wounded," Dylan replied. "Most of the dead are de Nerra men. When the Welsh hit us, they slammed into their column first."

Brandt grunted softly. "And they almost took the lady down with them," he grumbled, shaking his head. "'Tis a miracle she was spared."

"How is she?"

Brandt glanced around his senior Corp, standing in a semi-circle before him. They were still in full armor, battle-hardened men that were perhaps more comfortable in a fight than most. Alex and Magnus were sporting various cuts about the face but, for the most part, everyone had come through unscathed. His gaze came to rest on Brennan.

"Thanks to St. Hèver, she survived," he said, his gaze fixed on the blond young knight. "His quick thinking is all that stood between her and certain death. Brennan, you are to be commended. Your father shall know of your valor."

Brennan, standing between Stefan and Magnus, bowed his head modestly but didn't reply. He was a humble young man. Brandt's gaze lingered on him a moment.

"She will recover," he said, addressing the group as a whole. "I sent to St. Mary's in Coventry for a physic and two nuns were dispatched. They are with her now and barring anything catastrophic, the lady assures me she will be well enough to travel in the morning."

The knights glanced at each other, around the semi-circle, unspoken questions presented in the guise of eye contact. The past six days with the lady had seen her remarkably quiet and accommodating, not at all like the banshee of description they had first been introduced to.

De Russe, in fact, had shown her an inordinate amount of courtesy during the trip north and she had responded in kind. They had all seen it. Now, her injury had them all feeling rather guilty, as if they had collectively let her down somehow. Only men were supposed to be injured in battle; not innocent women.

"Camp is established, my lord, and posts set for the night," Dylan spoke up. "Is there anything else we can do for the lady?"

"Nay," de Russe shook his head. "She is well tended. For now, I would suggest you all take some rest. You have earned it."

With that, the group disbanded, wandering off towards tents and campfires and food. The de Lara twins stayed together, usually including St. Hèver because they had all grown up together, while le Bec and de Reyne formed their own little group. They were insomniacs, requiring very little sleep, so they tended to wander the night while the others slept. Brandt watched his men disappear into the night before turning for his tent and pulling back the flap.

Ellowyn was in the center of it, near the flat copper disc that, raised of the floor dirt with stones, contained burning peat or wood. Tonight, it burned wood and the soldiers who pitched his tent had opened a roof flap for ventilation. It made the tent very warm but also very smoky. It was enough to sting Brandt's eyes as he entered.

"My lady?" he said from the entry. "May I come in?"

86

Ellowyn was on her back on a mound of furs. She waved her good arm at him. "Please," she said.

He entered, his eyes adjusting to the dim light. Besides the fire, there were also three or four fat tallow candles sending greasy smoke to the ceiling. The tent was fairly well lit as he came to within a few feet of where Ellowyn lay but he was prevented from moving closer by one of the nuns. The woman in heavy brown robes, course but clean, rose from her seat near Ellowyn and nearly threw a body block.in front of him.

"Psh!" she hissed, putting up her hands. "No closer, my lord. Thou wilt keep distance."

Brandt lifted his eyebrows at the little nun, with her bird-thin hands and heavy Germanic accent. He didn't have much patience for pushy women and struggled not to physically shove her aside. She was denying him his wants and he didn't like that one bit.

"I have come to speak with the lady, not ravage her," he said somewhat wryly. "How is she?"

The nun still stood in front of him with her hands up. "She will heal," the woman said. "The wound was not deep."

On the ground, Ellowyn put her good hand over her face and groaned. "Please," she muttered softly. "Save me."

Brandt looked at her, brow furrowed. "Save you from what?"

The hand flew away from her face. "Boredom!" she hissed. "They have been reciting the Book of Job since they arrived. I am so despondent with his trials that I am ready to throw myself in the fire!"

Brandt struggled not to laugh. "It is not a very big fire," he told her. "I doubt it would kill you."

She grunted, unhappy. "Probably not," she said, looking him in the eye. "But they feel it necessary to not only heal my wound but save my soul."

"Why?"

She made a face. "They think I am a camp whore."

He did burst out laughing, then. It was a short guffaw that he quickly stilled. "That is madness," he said, looking at the little nun in front of him. "She is *not* a whore."

The little nun lifted her eyebrows at him as if she didn't believe him. "Thou wilt leave, my lord."

He frowned, putting his big hands on his hips. "I will *not* leave," he said. "She is... well, she is not a whore and I will not leave."

On her back, Ellowyn sighed rather dramatically. "I told them I was your wife."

His head snapped to her. "Wife?"

"Wife."

He caught on quickly to the lie. "Aye, wife," he confirmed, although he didn't sound sincere. He sounded off-guard. "This woman is my wife. It is you who will leave now. We no longer require your services."

The little nun took a rather surprising stance. Rather than outright believe him, she questioned him. "If that is true, my lord, why does she not wear a band signifying her marriage?" she asked. "Married women wear it as a symbol of their union."

Brandt was finished being polite. His dark eyes narrowed. "Get out," he growled. "I will not tell you again."

Ellowyn, who had been fighting off a grin to this point, heard the death in his tone. She didn't want him snapping the woman's neck out of sheer exhaustion and frustration. She lifted her voice to capture their attention before things deteriorated into unholy mortal combat. One enormous knight against a determined little nun would not have a good outcome.

"I do not wear a band because... because it was stolen when I received this wound," she told the woman quickly, fearful of what Brandt might do. "We were married in Kendal five years ago come May and... and we have two sons. Big, healthy sons. They live... with my parents in Cumbria because I went with my husband to France. We are going home now. Although I sincerely thank you for your assistance, I believe it is no longer required. My husband has surgeons with his army who can tend to me further if needed. Is there anything more you wish to know?"

By this time, the little nun and Brandt were both looking at her with some interest. The nun, in fact, was starting to back down. She glanced at Brandt with some uncertainty before replying to Ellowyn.

"It is my duty to protect you, my lady," she said rather firmly. "Although I mean no disrespect, lies do not please our Lord."

"Are you accusing me of lying?"

"I am simply saying that our Lord is displeased with sin."

Ellowyn fixed the woman in the eye. "As He is displeased with stubbornness and the lack of humility," she said, growing irritated. "Who are you to question us? My husband is the Duke of Exeter. He is an extremely powerful and influential man. You are unworthy of questioning his integrity. Now, you and your companion will leave. I no longer require you."

It was clear the nun did not believe them but she bowed out without another word, taking her silent colleague with her. Brandt simply stood aside as they quickly gathered their things and fled the tent. He stuck his head from the open flap to make sure the nuns were escorted back to St. Mary's, but that was the extent of his attention toward them. His focus quickly returned to Ellowyn. He smiled at her.

"You will have to say many Hail Mary's for lying to a nun," he told her. "In fact, we both will."

Ellowyn giggled. "I thought you were going to come to blows with her."

He wriggled his dark brows. "I thought so, too. Fortunately, you took charge of the situation and saved me. I could not possibly pray enough rosary novenas to save my soul from hell if I were to go to battle against a nun."

She laughed softly as he made his way over to her. "I will give her credit for being a brave woman. Not many would stand up to you as she did."

"*You* did."

"I was a fool."

He grinned as he crouched next to her, joints in his knees popping. His gaze never left her face. "How is your shoulder?"

She moved it gingerly. "It is sore," she admitted. "Honestly, I do not need to lay here like an invalid. I am perfectly capable of sitting up."

He shrugged. "Why would you want to?" he asked. "It is late and we will be getting an early start in the morning. It would do you good to rest until then."

She knew he was right, so she managed a reluctant nod. They were gazing at each other quite openly and Ellowyn could feel something warm in the air between then. It was that same warm feeling she had experienced with him after the battle, that moment when they had finished off the Welsh soldier together. It had been an oddly bonding moment and most unexpected. At least, it had been a bonding moment for her. She realized at that moment she was coming to feel something towards him more than simply camaraderie. It was a both terrifying and thrilling realization.

"I want to apologize for my behavior earlier," she said, finally averting her gaze. "In the battle... I suppose I was more frightened and overwhelmed than I realized. All I could think of was escaping to safety. I did not mean to put you in such danger and I know I did."

His expression was rather gentle as he looked at her. "You did not put me in any more danger than I already was," he said. "I was simply terrified that you were going to be killed. I apologize that my efforts to remove you from the battle were not immediately successful. That you should be in such peril for so long is inexcusable."

She looked at him, puzzled. "You did your best," she insisted softly. "With you as my protector, I never had a doubt that I would come through safely. You are quite impressive to behold in battle."

He gave her a half-smiled. "Have you seen many battles, then?"

She shook her head. "None, in fact," she said, her eyes on him growing intense. "But I know an excellent warrior when I see him. No wonder the French call you *l'ange noir*."

He could feel the intensity from her beautiful eyes; it sucked him right in and rather than curb himself, as he had been doing all along, he allowed himself to feel it.

"Compliments?" he asked, a twinkle in his eye. "I told you I was not sure I am at all comfortable with them."

"Because you want to believe them."

He stared at her before nodding, faintly. "I do."

"You may believe them, because they are the truth," she murmured. Then, she smiled. "I would lie to a nun, but not to you."

He smiled because she was. He even chuckled. Whatever was brewing between them had gone from a small spark to a healthy blaze fairly quickly, at least as far as he was concerned. It was so alien to him, these feelings of warmth and attraction, that he found he was actually somewhat giddy. His heart was pounding against his ribs and his palms were beginning to sweat. It was odd but wonderful. But being a man unused to romantic games of any kind, he had no idea how to deal with them.

"I appreciate that," he said after a moment. "I would never lie to you, either."

"Thank you."

The conversation fell into warm if not slightly awkward silence. He didn't want the conversation to die and struggled to come up with something more to say to her. He didn't want to leave.

"You said you were going to find me a wife," he said the first thing that popped into his head. "Did you have anyone in mind?"

She laughed softly. "Did *you* have anyone in mind?" she countered. "I told you that I do not have many friends, at least friends that I would consider an appropriate match for you, so surely you must have someone in mind? Tell me and I shall write her forthwith with an introduction."

Brandt had no idea how to play these flirtatious games, at least with a woman he genuinely respected and was genuinely attracted to. But he gave a good stab at it; if nothing else, perhaps he could discover what she thought of him. It might end his little infatuation with her fairly quickly without leaving him feeling too much like a fool. But he knew it would disappoint him a great deal if she was she not receptive.

"I am not sure," he shrugged, lowering himself to his buttocks next to her pallet. "Women are not usually interested in me and if they are, it is only for my reputation and title."

Ellowyn grew serious. "Surely there is someone who would see you as a man and not as a war machine."

"I am one in the same."

She shook her head. "Untrue," she countered firmly, softly. "Who you are as a man is completely different than who you are as a warrior."

He sat back, one big arm propped up on a bended knee. "Explain."

She looked thoughtful. "Well," she said, "as a warrior, you are bent on death. I saw you in the battle today and you were focused, alert, and skilled. That is the man they call the Black Angel. But right now, as you sit here and converse with me, you are kind, interested, and thoughtful. You are concerned for my shoulder and concerned for me. To me, that speaks highly of who Brandt de Russe is as a man. You are more than the Bringer of Death; have a heart and a soul as well."

He just stared at her. "Do you think so?"

She nodded firmly. "Of course I do."

He gazed at her a moment longer before slowly shaking his head. "I have never heard anyone say that to me," he said quietly. "I am not quite sure how to respond."

She shifted so she was laying more on her side, facing him. "May I ask you a question?"

"Of course."

"Do you *want* people to see that side of you?"

He shook his head without hesitation. "I do not," he replied firmly, but then he looked at her, hesitantly, before continuing. "But I do not mind if you see that side of me."

Ellowyn grinned brightly. "Do you know what else I see?"

"What?"

"You are afraid of nuns."

He shook his head, smiling, as she burst out laughing. "The Brides of Christ are frightening," he replied. "I can remember many a nun taking a switch to me as a child. My mother employed them as governesses."

"Your mother did not tend you?"

"Nay," he replied. "My mother was only a mother in the literal sense. She married my father for the Exeter title but there was no affection between them. Once I was born, she considered her duty complete and went on to other pursuits."

Ellowyn wasn't smiling any more. "How sad," she murmured. "What of your father? Did he care for you?"

Brandt shrugged. "I was his son," he stated the obvious. "As long as I did not shame the family name, he was civil, but he died when I was young so to be honest, I do not remember much of him. I do remember that he was very big and very intimidating."

"Like you."

"Like me"

"Any siblings?"

"An older sister that died in infancy."

As Ellowyn gazed at him, she began to feel very sorry for him. His upbringing, his life, had been so unlike hers. The things she took for granted, the familial love and affection, was evidently unknown to him. He was alone.

"Then you have never had any one close to you?" she asked. "No mother or father to love you? What about grandparents?"

He sighed faintly, thinking back to his dark and dismal childhood. "Nay," he said. "There was no one."

Ellowyn was deeply distressed. "No home, no one to care for you," she said, "and then you apparently married a shrew who was also very cruel to you and took your children away. I am so very sorry for you, Brandt. You are a man given so much in this world yet you have so little by way of personal joy. I wish I...."

She suddenly stopped, causing him to look at her. "What do you wish?" he asked.

Ellowyn rolled on to her back, looking away from him. "I suppose I am very sorry for you, 'tis all."

"That is not what you were going to say," he said, his voice low and rumbling. "What do you wish?"

"I do not know."

"You swore you would never lie to me."

She looked at him sharply. "How do you know I am?"

He met her gaze, a knowing grin on his face. "Because I can tell," he said. Then, he reached over and tugged on the sleeve of her dressing gown. "Tell me what you wish. I promise I will not laugh."

She made a face at him and looked away. "I wish... I wish you would go away."

He laughed softly. "Is that so? Well, I will not. Not until you tell me what you wish."

She was still making that funny scrunch-nosed face when she looked at him again. "You are a nuisance."

"I know."

"You are making my shoulder hurt."

"Nay, I am not."

"You are causing me great ache with your harassment."

He chuckled at her dramatics. "Do you want me to bring the nuns back to assist you?"

She sat bolt upright on the pallet. "God, no!" she gasped. Her left hand instinctively went to her sore shoulder. "Very well, you pest. I shall tell you. I was going to say that I wish I could help you. Are you satisfied?"

His dark eyes glimmered at her, a smile playing on his lips. "I am," he muttered. "But you should know that you have already helped me, more than you can ever know. I have spent the past year in France fighting in conditions you could not possibly imagine, dealing daily with death and destruction. I returned home a few days ago only to be confronted with a spitfire of a woman who threatened me the moment we met. But something odd has happened since that time."

Ellowyn couldn't help the smile on her lips, simply because his manner was so light and warm. "What?"

His grin broadened. "That woman has turned out to be the very best part of coming home," he said softly. "She is kind, compassionate, wise, and uproariously humorous. I consider it an honor and a privilege to have met her and even if I never see her again after leaving Erith, I will consider myself a better man for having known her. You, my lady, have brought light into my life and do not even know it. It is a priceless gift you gave to a man who insulted you when he first met you."

Ellowyn's mouth popped open. She had never heard such complimentary words and she knew doubtlessly that they were spoken from the heart. She could read it in his face. Without thinking, she rolled off her pallet and, on her knees, crawled over to him. As Brandt watched, she threw her left arm around his big neck and squeezed tightly. The right arm, injured and folded, pressed against his chest.

"No one has ever said such wonderful things to me," she murmured, ignoring the jab of the armor and mail. "I am so sorry you have had such a terrible life, Brandt. I feel as if I should hug you to make it all better. Perhaps we can be friends even after you leave me at Erith. I would like that."

Brandt, startled as he was by her hug, nonetheless recovered swiftly and wrapped a big arm around her. It seemed the most natural of things to do. In fact, his other arm wrapped around her, too, and he held her tightly as she squeezed his neck. He'd never in his life felt something so warm and wonderful, and he sorely wished his wasn't wearing his armor. He would have liked to have felt her against him, body to body. The feeling of her was overwhelming him.

"How do you to this?" he hissed.

She pulled back to look at him, frowning. "Do what?"

His face was very close to hers; he could feel her hot breath on his face. "*This*," he said again. "Show your emotions so openly? Give comfort to someone you barely know without thought?"

She shrugged, realizing that he still had both arms around her. He was so enormous that it was like being swallowed whole, but she knew that it was a sensation she could grow to crave. To think of him leaving her off at Erith and never seeing him again brought waves of disappointment.

"I do not," she murmured. "Not always. But my family is very affectionate so I suppose I grew up that way. When someone is hurt, friend or family, we comfort them."

"I am hurt?"

She nodded faintly, studying his handsome face. "I think your heart is hurt and you do not even know it. You have never known anything else."

"Would you heal it?"

It was a hugely open question; she sensed it obviously. She unwound her arm from his neck and sat back on her heels, gazing into his eyes. Brandt released her somewhat, but not entirely; his hands were still on her as they faced one another. The question had been presented; her response would determine the course of their association and quite possible their future. He held his breath, watching her as she considered the question.

"I would like to know what you mean by that," she finally said, her tone soft.

He shrugged and averted his gaze. "I am not entirely sure," he said. "All I know is that... Ellowyn, we have known each other a matter of days but since yesterday, I feel as if... I have never felt like this in my life and I completely understand if it is unwelcome, but I have to say that I find you beautiful and brave and gracious and sweet, and I would like nothing better than to come to know you better and perhaps...."

Ellowyn could feel her heart swelling with joy. She broke out into the most amazing smile. "Perhaps... *what?*"

He couldn't quite bring himself to say it. "Perhaps... well, perhaps you could...."

"Perhaps I could help you find a wife?"

He shook his head, realizing she was teasing him when she started to laugh. It was charming. He was stumbling over his words and she was mocking him playfully.

Throwing caution to the wind, he cupped her sweet face in his two enormous hands, studying her closely and deeply for the very first time. He felt giddy and quivering, but also elated and emotional. For a man who had learned to suppress his emotions long ago, it was both liberating and frightening.

"Perhaps...," he murmured, "you will consider me as more than an acquaintance. I realize that you may not be interested in me as a marital prospect, but I hope that given time you will consider it. I would very much like to explore the possibility if you are amiable to it."

Her giggles faded and her eyes widened. "*Marriage?*"

"Perhaps... well, if you find the prospect an attractive one."

She was genuinely shocked; it was more than she could have ever dreamed. "You find *me* an attractive marital prospect?"

"I do."

"Why?"

He gave her a half-grin. "Because I had no idea how dark my days were until I met you. In that short amount of time, you have shown me the sun and it is blinding. I would be very happy to be blinded by you."

"Surely you jest."

"I do not jest."

Ellowyn could hardly believe her ears. She began to giggle, growing louder as she threw her good arm around his neck again. Brandt, overcome and out of his element, hugged her so tightly that she grunted when he squeezed the air out of her. He also cracked her back. But neither one of them let go; they simply held one another in the first real and true romantic embrace either one of them had ever experienced. It was magic.

But Brandt eventually loosened his grip. The feel of her, the scent of her, was overwhelming him and he found that he had to taste her. Her lips were soft and sensuous morsels, calling his name, and he answered the call with the fires born of passion.

Ellowyn was started at first when his mouth descended on hers but her surprise was only momentary; his touch was firm but not harsh, soft but not sloppy, and she couldn't help but respond. She'd never kissed a man in her life but instincts took over and she began to suckle his lips just as he was suckling hers. Her belly began to quiver and her heart began to race, and soon she was pressed against him, her hand in his dark hair as they suckled one another feverishly.

But Brandt wanted more; his tongue licked her lips, snaking between them and licking her teeth, and when Ellowyn opened her mouth, he took great liberties in tasting her deeply. He could feel her hesitation at something so new and intimate, but she began to relax quickly. She even began to mimic him, something that drove him mad with desire. He pulled her closer, his hands in her hair and his mouth devouring her, when a voice from outside the tent stopped their building passion.

"My lord?" It was Dylan's voice. "A word, my lord?"

Ellowyn, lips red and wet from his seeking mouth, loosened her grip on his neck but Brandt didn't loosen his at all. He continued to hold her tightly. He could not believe de Lara had chosen this moment to interrupt them.

"Can it wait?" he called out to the man.

"Nay, my lord."

With a grunt of frustration, Brandt looked at Ellowyn apologetically. "I am sorry," he whispered, letting her go with reluctance. "I will return."

Ellowyn watched him rise, an enormously tall man who had to duck as he moved to the tent entry. He turned before he quit the tent, however, giving her an awkward little smile and a wink before ducking out completely. Once outside, Ellowyn could hear him speaking with de Lara but she could not hear their words. All she was aware of was the soft, deep warmth of his tone.

With a sigh, she went back over to her pallet and lay down, trying to get comfortable with her bad shoulder. She still could not believe what he had said to her and that kiss... well, it had been everything a first kiss should have been; passionate, sweet, and overwhelmingly sexy. Just thinking about it made her feel weak. But perhaps she was asleep, dreaming everything that had happened. As she lay there and stared at the ceiling, she knew that she would be terribly disappointed if that was true.

Brandt de Russe, as she had noticed from the beginning of their association, was an enormous and handsome man, much more perfect than any man she had ever seen. To think that somehow, someway, she had endeared herself to him was astonishing. She had no idea how she had done it.

Whatever it was, she would have to keep doing it. Now that she had his attention, she most assuredly didn't want to lose it.

# CHAPTER TEN

Erith Castle was a massive two hundred year old bastion that had been built for Henry II. It sat at the base of a range of mountains and protected the gap that led into an area of Cumbria that was heavy with ports along the western coast. The castle had remained in royal hands for over one hundred years until it was given as a gift to Simon de Montfort when he married Eleanor, Henry's granddaughter. After that, it had passed to their son, Richard, and then to his daughter, the Lady Gray de Montfort Serroux who had eventually married Braxton de Nerra.

Upon their marriage, De Nerra had given the castle to his step-daughter, Lady Gray's daughter Brooke and her husband Sir Dallas Aston as a wedding gift, but Dallas returned the castle to Braxton when his eldest brother died and he inherited his father's barony in Devon. That was how the castle came into the hands of Sir Deston de Nerra, Braxton and Gray's eldest son, and it was this man who waited impatiently in the bailey as Brandt brought the man's army home.

Deston wasn't a particularly tall man, like his father, but he had a muscular and powerful build. He had his mother's amber-colored eyes, his father's graying blond hair, but his personality was all de Nerra. He was aggressive, loud, passionate, highly intelligent, and lived for a good fight. However, a disease of the joints had hit him at a very young age, like his grandfather and one of his uncles, and his hands were so gnarled that he hadn't been able to hold a sword in many years. Still, he had fists like hamhocks and could still ball one up to deliver a devastating punch. When he saw Brandt ride into his bailey, he began to crow with delight.

"The great duke himself!" he yelled happily. "I see you survived your years in France!"

Brandt flipped up his visor, smiling at the loud man. He was glad to see him. Wearily, he dismounted and handed his snapping

charger over to a soldier as Deston marched up and slapped him
on his armored arm.

"You look whole enough," Deston said with satisfaction.

Brandt pulled his helm off, peeling his hauberk off his wet black
hair.  The army was trickling in after him, weary men kicking up
the dust and dirt of the bailey, creating clouds of grit.

"I am, fortunately," he replied, eyeing the worn army. "But it
was not for their lack of trying. The French have been trying to kill
me for years."

Deston sized up the man he hadn't seen in at least three years.
He started to say something more but a woman on a palfrey
caught his eye and he turned to see his daughter entering the
gates.  Deston forgot all about Brandt and walked towards her,
very quickly.

"Wynny!" he held up his hand in greeting.  When the palfrey
came close, he reached up and grabbed his daughter right off of
the horse. "My sweet little Pickle Snuff. Praise God you have
arrived home safe and whole."

Ellowyn let her father hug and kiss her, with the annoyed
patience that children often show, before pulling away. "Dada, stop
it," she hissed at him. "I am fine. Do not paw over me like that. And
do not call me Pickle Snuff!"

"Will you make the expression for me, please? I have missed it
so."

"Nay!"

Deston just grinned, not put off in the least. "I am happy to see
you," he said. "Your mother will be thrilled. But you were sent to
bring my men home, not bring de Russe with you. He is a busy man
with much to do; he is well out of his way up here at Erith."

Ellowyn looked at Brandt. "He said he had business with you."

Deston's eyebrows flew up as he looked at Brandt, at least a
head taller than he was. "Is that so?" he said. "Then I am honored.
But first things first; how many men are you returning to me?"

"Five hundred and forty-eight," Brandt replied. "Until four days
ago, there were five hundred and sixty two but we ran into some
trouble near Coventry. We were attacked and lost some men."

Deston grew serious. "I see," he said, looking at his daughter. "I am sorry to know that. Where was Wynny when this happened? Was she safe?"

"I was in the middle of it," Ellowyn said before Brandt could reply. "I was hit with an arrow but Lord de Russe saved me. He was heroic, Dada, truly."

Deston turned pale and his eyes widened. "Hit with a…?" He put his hand over his heart, unable to finish the sentence. "God's Bones, Wynny, what happened? Where were you hit?"

Ellowyn put her hand on her father's arm, patting him soothingly. "I was hit in the shoulder," she said, pointing to the spot. "Truly, Dada, it was of no consequence. I am fine."

Deston wasn't over his fright. He looked straight at de Russe. "And you allowed her into mortal danger?" he boomed. "God's Bones, man, what were you thinking?"

Ellowyn started to explain but Brandt cut her off; she had upset her father already with her casual telling of a near-death experience and he hastened to clean it up so that her father wouldn't think him careless.

"Your daughter we well protected in the center of the column when we were attacked," he explained succinctly. "The Welsh plowed into our column in the middle in an attempt to divide us, I would assume, and your daughter was struck in the initial wave. One of my knights carried her off to safety where she was initially tended, but later she was cared for by two nuns from Coventry. I assure you that she has been very well tended the entire time."

Deston eyed him as if he didn't believe him. He still had his hand over his heart. "To think of my daughter, my precious child in danger, is horrifying to say the least," he said, looking at Ellowyn. But then, he sighed. "I only wish I could have gone myself to London, but unfortunately, I cannot travel these days. The pain… it is too much. I had no choice but to send her."

Brandt glanced at Ellowyn, his gaze warm. "She is as competent as she is fearless," he told Deston. "You were wise to send her. She sought me out immediately and we made arrangements to bring your men back to Erith."

101

Ellowyn shot him an expression when her father wasn't looking, wondering why had concealed the truth of their first meeting so eloquently. Brandt winked at her.

"I have much faith in my daughter," Deston said, hugging her again so that she grunted because he squeezed too hard. "We are very glad to have her returned. And you also, my lord. Please come inside and we will discuss your business."

Brandt nodded as he began to loosen his gauntlets. "In a moment," he said. "I wish to settle my men first."

Deston understood. He stood politely for a moment until one of his knights caught his attention and he excused himself. Ellowyn collected her satchels from her saddles before a servant led her palfrey away, casually moving next to Brandt as the man focused on his men as they were settled in Erith's enormous outer bailey. His knights were yelling, animals were braying, and Brandt watched it all like a hawk.

"What business do you have with my father?" she asked.

Brandt didn't look at her. "I have a question first."

"What?"

"What is Pickle Snuff?"

Ellowyn rolled her eyes. "It is a nickname, from childhood," she said. "If you call me that, I shall be furious with you, so you would do well to remember that."

"I will."

She eyed him. "Will you answer my question now?" she asked. "What business do you have with my father?"

"That is between Deston and me."

She wasn't offended; in fact, since they declared their interest in one another, the mood between them had been pleasant and, at times, sweet, which was made difficult due to the fact that they were traveling with a host of witnesses including Brandt's very astute knights. Brandt had kept a distance from her most of the time as she rode most with St. Hèver or Alex de Lara, but Ellowyn wasn't particularly distressed by it. When they had been afforded a moment alone, Brandt had explained the need for discretion, at least until he could speak with Deston. She understood completely and she was thrilled. She still felt as if she was living some kind of wonderful and unexpected dream, for never in her life could she have imagined finding interest and affection with the mighty Duke of Exeter.

As she shifted her satchels to one hand, she looked up at him. "You have hardly spoken to me since the incident in Coventry," she said quietly. "Will you please tell me what you are going to speak to my father about?"

"I told you why I have kept my distance."

She turned to him fully. "Aye, you have," she said, her big eyes swallowing him up. "But we are no longer traveling. There are no ears to hear us. Will you please speak with me now or have you changed your mind about me?"

He looked at her, puzzled. "Of course I have not changed my mind."

"Then you intend to speak to my father about courting me?"

"About marrying you."

A light of joy came to her eyes. She was trying very hard not to smile. "You are still so certain about it?"

"I am. Are you?"

She giggled. "I am, but only if you will swear you will not keep a distance from me in front of your men once we are married. I do not like not being able to speak with you whenever I please."

He sighed faintly, the dark eyes glittering. "You make it seem as if it was easy for me to stay away," he said softly. "It was not a simple thing, you know. I had to force myself every single minute to keep from rushing to your side."

She was flirting with him by this time. "How flattering," she murmured. "Tell me more."

He fought off a grin and looked away. "I cannot."

"Why?"

"Because I will turn into a giddy, silly fool right before your eyes and I do not wish for anyone to see that side of me in public."

"But I would like to see it."

"You shall, when we are alone. It is for your eyes only."

She understood, but she was still flirting with him simply because it was humorous to see a man so big and powerful squirm uncomfortably. It was a fresh, new, and fun game to play between them, and she relished in it. Still, she did not want to be cruel so she mercifully changed the subject.

"I should go into the keep and see my mother now," she said after a moment. "Will you miss me when I leave?"

"I miss you now."

Her flirting softened. "As I miss you," she said. "But we will see each other at sup. Do you intend to speak to my father before or after we eat?"

"As soon as I can."

He dared to look at her and she smiled, blowing him a discreet kiss. "Good luck," she whispered. "Until tonight, then."

Brandt watched her walk across the bailey. In fact, he couldn't look at anything else. Her shapely back and luscious hair had his full attention. She had a way of moving that was fluid and lovely, and he had never been so entranced with anyone in his life. The kiss they had shared a few days ago was still as fresh and heated in his mind as if it had only just happened. It made his heart light simply to watch her, in a way it had never been light before. Whatever magic Ellowyn had, he was fully under her spell.

"Until tonight, sweetheart," he whispered to himself as he watched her go.

He made a vow at that moment that he was never, ever going to force himself to stay away from her again. From this day forward, they were joined at the hip.

He sincerely hoped Deston saw things his way.

\*\*\*

Ellowyn's mother, the Lady Annalora de Gare de Nerra, was a tall and elegant woman with blond hair and her daughter's big green eyes. Personality-wise, she was much like her husband with loud laughter and a rather pushy manner, but she had a heart of gold and was much loved and respected. When she saw her daughter in the hall of Erith, speaking with her grandmother, Annalora rushed the woman and nearly knocked her over in her joy. She hugged Ellowyn within an inch of her life.

"Wynny," she sighed, squeezing. "You are home. Are you well, darling? Did the trip go well?"

Ellowyn didn't mind being hugged by her mother because she had a much softer touch than Deston. She hugged her mother in return and kissed the woman on the cheek.

"It went very well," she said. "In fact, it was wonderful."

Annalora kissed her daughter on the forehead, smoothing her hair as she sat down on the bench beside her. In fact, the woman couldn't keep her hands off her daughter, touching her shoulder, her arm, her back, as if to reassure herself that her child was well and whole.

"Wonderful?" Annalora repeated. "In what way?"

Ellowyn shrugged, though there was a faint grin on her face. She glanced at her grandmother, sitting across the table from her. The Lady Gray Serroux de Nerra gazed steadily at her granddaughter.

"I am not entirely sure why Wynny's trip was so wonderful," she said. "She was about to tell me but we cannot get past the smile."

Ellowyn lowered her head, grinning broadly. "It was a good trip," she repeated, rather softly. "I returned with most of Papa's men, and I also returned with the Duke of Exeter and his fine knights."

That brought a reaction from Gray and Annalora. "The Duke of Exeter?" Annalora repeated. "I had no idea he had arrived with you. We must make all due preparations for his arrival."

With that, she began snapping orders to the servants who had been milling about the great hall. Annalora sent them scurrying with her specific commands for food, drink, and fresh rushes. When half of the staff was in an uproar because of the arrival of the duke, Annalora returned her attention to her daughter.

"This is so exciting," she said. "Rarely do we have such distinguished visitors."

Gray, an elegant, sweet and wise woman in her seventieth year, watched her granddaughter's face. She could see there was something more there, something thrilling and giddy, although she wasn't sure what. Perhaps one of the knights in the duke's corps had attracted her attention. Coming from a young woman who generally had no use for the suitors that had passed over their doorstep, it was certainly an event.

"Annalora," Gray said in her sweet, soothing voice. "Perhaps you should seek Deston and find out how many men we can expect for the meal. We want to have enough for them to eat."

Annalora nodded quickly. "Indeed," she said as she stood up. "I shall find him right away."

Ellowyn watched her mother go. "He was out in the ward last I saw of him."

Annalora waved her off as she quit the great hall. When Ellowyn returned her attention to her grandmother, she could see that the woman was studying her intently.

"Now," Gray said softly. "Why are you so giddy, young woman? Tell me the truth."

Ellowyn couldn't help the smile on her face. She stood up and went to the other side of the table where her grandmother sat, and she planted herself next to the woman. Gray put her arms around her, hugging her.

"You will not believe me," Ellowyn said, her head on her grandmother's shoulder.

Gray smiled. "Tell me and I shall believe you, I promise. Who has put this smile on your face, Wynny?"

Ellowyn giggled. She never giggled. "The duke," she whispered.

Gray couldn't help it; her eyebrows lifted with surprise. "*The* duke?"

"Aye."

Gray released her granddaughter and looked the woman in the eye. "De Russe?"

Ellowyn nodded, somewhat hesitantly because her grandmother seemed off-guard and she wasn't sure why. "Aye," she said again. "I am not entirely sure how it happened, but we went from hating one another to being rather fond of each other. He is going to speak to my father about marrying me."

Gray just stared at her. Then, her amber eyes took on a marvelous glimmer. "He wants to marry you?" she gasped. "Wynny, that... that is wonderful, sweetheart, truly."

Ellowyn was beaming from ear to ear. "He is not like anyone I have ever met," she said. "He was rude when we first met, that was true, but as we came to know each other, he is chivalrous and thoughtful and kind. But life has not been good to him; he was raised by nuns, his mother did not care about him at all, and then he was forced to marry a woman he hated. Is that not terrible?"

Gray was listening with some surprise. She had never seen her mature and level-headed granddaughter so passionate. It was astonishing but thrilling nonetheless.

"Horrible," she agreed. "But it is not unusual. Families such as ours are rare."

Ellowyn nodded, averting her gaze and picking at her nails. "I realize that," she said. "I suppose it has made me very thankful for my family and the way we are. I have told you this before, Grandmother; I know how you and Grandfather were with each other and I have always hoped for that, too. Perhaps... perhaps I see the same qualities Grandfather had in the duke. I realize I have not known him very long, but I have such feelings when I look at him. He is a good man in spite of his reputation; I know it."

"Of course he is," Gray agreed, listening to Annalora's loud voice as the woman came through the keep entry. "But until the duke speaks with your father, perhaps you should keep this to yourself. The last thing you want is your mother running to the man and...."

Ellowyn knew exactly what she meant; she knew how aggressive, though well-meaning, her mother could be. The woman's voice was growing louder as she bossed the servants around.

"I understand," she said, wriggling her eyebrows. "She would give the man no peace."

Gray fought off a smile as Annalora drew closer, her fair face pinched pink with excitement.

"Your father is escorting the duke into the keep," she said excitedly. "God's Beard, but he is an enormous man. I have heard tale about him and how he is the Black Prince's henchman. I would believe him evil simply by looking at him."

"He is *not* evil!" Ellowyn said indignantly, bolting to her feet. When she saw the expression on her mother and grandmother's faces, she hastened to recover. "He... he was very kind and diligently protected me during the journey from London. I... I would like to change into fresh clothing. Please excuse me."

With that, she nearly stumbled from the table, making haste to the great flight of stairs that wound its way to the upper floors of Erith's four storied keep. But before she could reach it, her father and Brandt entered the keep and Ellowyn nearly ran into them. In fact, Brandt had to reach out and steady her to keep her from bumping into him.

"My lady," he said, making a conscious effort to drop his hand from her arm when he very much wanted to keep it there. "Are you well?"

Ellowyn gazed up into his handsome face, now without his helm. He was so incredibly handsome with his angled jaw and black hair. Her heart was fluttering wildly.

"I am well," she said, forcing a weak smile. "I am simply going up to my chamber."

"Bon voyage, then," Brandt said, humor in his voice. "Now you will finally have a solid room about you and not a tent."

Ellowyn's smile turned real. "I did not mind the tent."

There was a glimmer in her eye when she said it, something only Brandt could see. And then she was gone, scampering up the stairs and disappearing from view. Brandt gaze lingered on her until she vanished before tearing his focus away. He knew Deston had seen the exchange so he hastened to sounds as if he had shown concern purely for chivalrous reasons. He didn't want the man to suspect anything more; at least, not until he was ready to plead his case.

"Your daughter showed remarkable strength throughout the journey," he told the man as he began to pull off his gauntlets. "She never complained once."

Deston stood there with his hands on his hips, watching Brant remove his gloves and the ruff around his neck that soaked up sweat and protected his neck from his chaffing helm. It was a soiled and bloody mess.

"Ellowyn is a good girl," he agreed. "She is strong of mind and heart, but I would imagine you have already discovered that for yourself."

Brandt looked at the man, wondering if he meant beyond the usual acquaintance. Maybe it was his paranoia suggesting it as he gazed at the man whose daughter he was in love with, but he thought perhaps Deston was only making a statement and nothing more. Still, he was careful in his reply.

"She is a proud daughter of the House of de Nerra," he replied. "And how is your son?"

Deston's prideful expression faded. "Being holy, I suppose," he said, heading into the great hall with Brandt in tow. "We have not spoken in almost two years. He has taken a vow of silence, you know. It is an unnatural thing for a de Nerra to be silent."

Brandt could see that the man was genuinely unhappy, which he found rather humorous.  As they approached the table, the women who had been seated stood up, their polite attention on Brandt.  He bowed respectfully when he came to the table.

"Lady de Nerra," he said to Annalora, whom he had already greeted out in the ward.  His attention moved to the second woman. "Lady Gray, it is a pleasure to see you again. It has been a long time."

Gray came out from the table, extending her hand when she came close to Brandt.  He took her small hand in his enormous one, shaking it gently.

"Brandt de Russe," she said softly, her amber eyes twinkling up at him. "Except for the fact that you are bigger and older, you've not changed a bit since we last met."

Brandt grinned, displaying his big white teeth. "And you have grown more lovely," he replied. "I can see where your granddaughter gets her astonishing beauty."

Gray laughed softly. "Did they teach you such flatter on the battlefields of France? Somehow, I do not think so."

He took her hand and gently helped her to sit on the bench around the table. "I learned much on the battlefields of France, but flattery was not amount them," he said as he sat down next to her. "I missed your husband there, my lady. Braxton was one of my mentors, you know. I miss his wisdom as well as his sword."

Gray's eyes were still glimmering. "He did so enjoy fighting with you," she said softly. "He said there was no one like you. He swore you were the first and last of your kind, the greatest knight he had ever seen."

"He was a liar, too."

Gray giggled. "He was no such thing, my lord," she scolded lightly. "He always told the truth. That is, he did until he became ill. Then, by the time he told us the truth, it was too late. I do not believe I shall forgive him for that."

Brandt's gaze was soft as he took her hand and kissed it. "How many years has it been now? Six?"

"Six years, two months, three weeks and seventeen days," Gray replied softly. "He is buried at St. John's in Leven if you want to go and yell at him, by the way."

"I miss him."

"As do I."

Brandt gave her a faint smile. Not wanting the conversation to deteriorate into something heady on the subject of Braxton de Nerra's passing, he shifted the subject.

"Well," he said, turning to Deston and Annalora, now seated on the opposite side of the table. "I suppose you would like a full report of my use of your men, my lord."

Deston waved him off. "I wish to hear more of this battle with the Welsh that nearly killed my daughter."

Brandt thought back to the fight and the fact that Ellowyn had indeed been in a good deal of peril. But he didn't want to frighten the family over something that was over with, so he did his best to be truthful yet tactful.

"There is not much more to tell," he replied. "I told you that the Welsh rebels had attacked Kenilworth earlier that day and set their sights on us as well. They plowed through the middle of the column first, blindsiding us, and that was where Ellowyn was riding. She took an arrow to the shoulder but she was taken to safety immediately where she was tended first by my knights and then by the nuns from Coventry. She recovered quickly and is in fine shape, as you have seen."

As Deston nodded his head, Annalora and Gray were in various states of horror. They had not heard of Ellowyn's injury and both of them bolted up from the table.

"My sweetling!" Annalora was already rushing for the stairs. "I must see to her!"

Brandt felt rather bad that he had startled them, but Deston yelled after the pair. "She is well," he told his wife and mother. "You saw for yourself – she is fine!"

Annalora muttered something that sounded suspiciously like an insult to her husband's sense of compassion as she and Gray disappeared up the stairs. Brandt turned to Deston somewhat sheepishly.

"I did not mean to upset them," he said. "I was not aware that they did not know of our Welsh encounter."

Deston waved a careless hand. "They are always looking for something to work them into a froth," he said as servants brought forth pitchers of wine and trays of cheese and bread. "You know women; they like to be upset and them blame us for causing it."

For some reason, Brandt thought back to the moment he and Ellowyn had first met. She had been furious and had blamed him; although there was blame on both sides, he could see Deston's point.

"I will admit," he said as he reached for a cup of wine, "that I upset your daughter when we first met. She did not announce herself right away and... well, I was not kind in my reaction."

Deston collect his wine cup, a twinkle in his eye as he looked at Brandt. "Did you chase her away?"

"Something like that."

He snorted as he drank. "Did she return with a stick and try to beat you? She is fiery like that."

Brandt gave him a half grin. "Not quite," he said. "She is quite bold, however. She did not hesitate to let me know what she thought of me."

Deston laughed. "You do not know the half of it," he said, reaching for the cheese and bread. "She possesses bravery and a sense of vengeance that exceeds that of most men I know. Had she been born a man, she would have made a magnificent knight.

Sometimes I wish... well, it does not matter what I wish. I still have Ellowyn and for that, I am grateful."

Brandt watched the man intently. "What about your son?" he asked. "Surely whatever profession he has chosen does not make him any less your son."

Deston cocked an eyebrow at him. "That is what my father said," he replied, drinking his wine in thought. "Fenton... he could have been the greatest knight we have seen yet. Do you know him?"

Brandt nodded. "I am acquainted with him," he replied. "When your father and I served together in France for a time, he spoke of him. He was very proud of Fenton."

Deston regarded his wine, the pensive look of a disappointed father evident. "We all were until he joined that damnable cloister," he said. "He said he felt as if his true calling was to God and not the knighthood. He broke my heart on that day."

Brandt could see the sadness, the frustration, in the man. He could see that it was a sensitive subject.

"Well," he said quietly as he reached for his own bread and cheese, "the knighthood is not for every man. Sometimes I wish it was not for me, but alas, I am too entrenched in the very fabric of the profession to ever retire from it. I will die on the battlefield and not warm and safe in my bed as most men."

Deston watched him as he took a healthy bite of the tart, white cheese. "When do you return to France?"

Brandt chewed and swallowed the bite in his mouth. "We spent the last year raiding the Aquitaine," he said. "Edward may be young, and fairly hot–headed, but he is a brilliant leader. He knows what it takes to lead men to victory. We moved through the Aquitaine raiding and weakening strategic towns and those we did not raid, we set about building alliances. France is still quite divided with many houses laying claim to the throne. Edward intends to gain a foot-hold there."

Deston was listening carefully. "Edward? Or you?" When Brandt shook his head, Deston put up a hand to silence him. "Brandt, we all know it is you who is the military intelligence behind Edward. It is *you*. You have planned the systematic weakening of the

Aquitaine and you are the military leader planning the Black Prince's movements. Edward may be a great leader of men, but you are the man behind the leader. Make no mistake; England understands that and so do those in France. When all of this is over, you will be an extremely powerful man in both countries."

Brandt didn't have much to say to that. He returned to his bread and cheese, ripping off great hunks of bread and washing them down with the rich red wine. Deston could see the man was silent on the matter of his greatness, as most great men were. He was not humble, but he knew the truth. He saw no need to confirm it. Deston poured himself more wine.

"It is well known that you are a master of *chevauchèe*," he continued quietly. "Quite an effective tactic – burn, pillage, and loot, and then move on to the next town. I understand that Edward has used your tactics for the past year quite heavily. That is what has weakened the Aquitaine most of all and I am sure that is why the French call you *l'ange noir*. Even they know who is truly the master behind the prince – Exeter, the Angel of Death."

Brandt glanced at him. "Where did you hear things like that?"

Deston grinned. "Erith is well-traveled," he said. "We have many visitors. I hear many stories. Is any of this untrue?"

"Of course it is true."

"Then you must be a very wealthy man from all of the time spent looting the Aquitaine."

"I am well-rewarded for my service."

It was a mild way of putting it. Deston chuckled softly before draining the rest of his wine.

"When do you return to France?" he asked, shifting the subject slightly. "More importantly, how many of my men will you need when you return?"

Brandt sighed heavily; the wine was starting to relax him and his professional manner was easing.

"I will not be in England long," he said, suddenly looking very weary as he reflected on his future plans. His burdens were huge, dragging at him. "My directive from the Prince of Wales is to return for fresh troops and join him in the Aquitaine in three months' time. We are beginning the systematic weakening of the north of France. Without going into a huge amount of detail, it is our intention to take Chartres, Tours, and eventually Poitiers. The prince wishes to set up court in Poitier and rule from there."

Deston was looking at him seriously. "Is this true?" he breathed. "My God... you have a task ahead of you, man."

Brandt nodded faintly, slowing down his food and alcohol intake as a thought occurred to him; returning to France soon as he was, he would have to marry Ellowyn quickly if he was going to spend any amount of time with her before he left. Odd that now, instead of returning to France where Edward was waiting for him for fresh men and supplies, all he could think of was Ellowyn and how he did not want to leave, not while they were just becoming close.

"I will be soliciting men and material from the Duke of Carlisle, the Earl of Wrexham, and move across the middle of England soliciting what support I can," he said. "I will perhaps ride to Carlisle and Wrexham because their sons, St. Hèver and de Lara, serve me. I know the families well. To that end, what support can I expect from you?"

Deston took a deep breath, sighing heavily with thought. "Five hundred men at the most," he said, scratching his blond head. "The six hundred you brought back should expect to stay here. What kind of supplies do you need?"

"Arrows," Brandt said without hesitation. "The archers go through them at a maddening pace. They recover as many as they can, but supplies are short. We can also use any kind of combat weapons you can provide – axes, poleaxes, swords. Anything. Horses would also be well-met."

"I will see what I can do," Deston said. "How long will you be staying?"

"No more than a day; two at the most."

"Then let us spend tonight feasting and enjoying life. We will speak of the serious things tomorrow.

"Agreed."

They lifted a cup to each other before drinking deeply. Brandt was thinking heavily on re-introducing Ellowyn into the conversation for the purpose of asking permission to court her when his knights entered from the bailey.

They were exhausted, dirty, and hungry just as Brandt had been, so Brandt kept his mouth shut as Deston greeted them and the men settled down to wine and food. All the while, he kept thinking of how he was going to broach the subject of Ellowyn with her father, because it had become increasingly apparently during the course of the conversation that Ellowyn was Deston's pride and joy. He wasn't quite sure how the man was going to view someone who would take her away from him.

Downing his wine, he tried to think of a way to break it easy to the man.

# CHAPTER ELEVEN

Ellowyn was dressed very carefully in a ruby-red silk surcoat with a matching shift. The surcoat was stitched with silver thread and a flower made from red-colored glass decorated portions of her belly and trailed down her right leg. It was a magnificent dress that her father had purchased for her in York a few years ago. It had been one of the rare times he had traveled out of Erith because the weather had been warm and his health good, and she very much treasured the spectacular dress. She only wore it for special occasions.

Her first evening back at Erith was a special occasion. Her mother's maid had arranged her hair in a beautiful style with silver ribbons woven into a braid that draped over her right shoulder. The maid had scrubbed her face along with her body, so her complexion was particularly rosy, and she smelled strongly of lavender.

Furthermore, with a good deal of coaxing, the maid had borrowed some of Annalora's cosmetics and Ellowyn found herself with luscious red lips, faintly rouged cheeks, and a dark cosmetic on her lashes that was made of crushed coal, beeswax, and linseed oil. Her mother had bought it on a trip to Manchester, a major port, and was told by the merchant that it was a mysterious Egyptian cosmetic that was all the rage in Paris. On Ellowyn with her bright blue eyes, the dark lashes made her look like a goddess.

Standing to the rear of Erith's massive keep where the ponds and small flower garden was, Ellowyn stood by the still waters of the fish pond, watching the water creatures move amongst the lilies. The sun had set behind the hill that backed up to Erith, and the moon was full and bright. As she stood there, gazing into the water, she could hear foot falls come up beside her.

Brandt was walking fairly quickly. He came to within a foot of Ellowyn, gazing down at her with a good deal of pleasure. Ellowyn smiled brightly.

"You received my message, I see," she said.

He nodded. "Your maid delivered it," he replied. Then, he took a moment to look her up and down. "I have never in my life seen such beauty. I did not think it possible for you to grow lovelier since last I saw you, but I was wrong. You are an angel."

Her smile broadened. "My thanks," she said softly. "It has taken all afternoon for me to look like this."

"It was well worth the time spent."

She nodded her thanks, her blue eyes seeking his dark ones curiously. "Did you speak with my father?"

Brandt shook his head, the look of pleasure on his face turning to one of frustration. "I did not," he said. "There has been no opportunity as of yet, but I find that I am going to have to create the opportunity. I am planning on leaving in the next day or two and I would like to take you with me when I go. Time is of the essence."

Her expression grew serious. "Leaving?" she repeated. "Where are you going?"

"Back to France," he said, somewhat softly. "I am expected."

Her features fell. "Expected by whom? Why must you go back? You have only just returned."

There was a stone bench near the pond. Brandt reached out and took her hand, guiding her over to the bench which sat partially obscured by the moonlit shadows. When they sat, it was very close together. Brandt lifted her hand to his lips, kissing it sweetly, before continuing.

"You know that I have been with the Prince of Wales in France for the past two years," he said softly. "Whether or not I have told you directly, surely you were aware?"

Ellowyn was pouting now. "Of course I was aware," she said, frowning. "But I did not pay much attention to the details, to be truthful. All I knew was that my father loaned you six hundred men and that you were returning them to London at the end of January, but I heard nothing about you going back to France. Why must you return?"

He kissed her hand again. "Because Edward is expecting me to return with fresh men and supplies," he said. "That is the only reason I returned to England, Wynny. I brought your father's men home because they had been fighting for a solid year and needed rest. My orders are to collect fresh men and supplies, and return to Edward within three months of my departure. I have already been gone a month, so I must leave as soon as I can and go about my mission on seeking fresh men and supplies from other allies. Then, I must go back."

She was looking at him with big, bottomless eyes. "To fight."

"Aye."

She cocked her head. "What about me?" she asked. "Do you plan to marry me in haste and simply leave me here?"

He sighed faintly. "I plan to marry you, enjoy what time we have together, and then return to France," he said, trying to be gentle. "You may stay here at Erith with your family, or you may stay at my seat of Guildford Castle. As my wife, you would command much power and respect. I would be proud to have you at Guildford, administering my lands."

"I do not care about power and respect," she said, somewhat petulantly. "I only care about you. I do not want you to go."

He smiled faintly, cupping her face with one big hand and stroking her soft cheek with his thumb.

"I must," he said simply. "But know that it will give me no pleasure in leaving you. That has never happened before."

"What do you mean?"

"Leaving someone behind that I would miss. In fact, I do not ever believe I have missed anyone."

The smile was returning to her face, reluctantly. "Not ever?"

"Not ever."

She gazed at him, rather dreamily. "Why can't I come with you?" she asked softly. "I would not be any trouble. You said yourself that I travel very well. Won't you take me with you?"

He shook his head. "Absolutely not," he said firmly, but he kissed her hand as he said it. "You must understand that I am in harm's way every moment of every day. Men go out of their way to try and kill me because the death of *l'ange noir* would bring any man much prestige. Furthermore, I...."

He came to an abrupt halt because he could see her eyes welling up with frightened tears. He inwardly winced at his lack of tact and sought to make amends.

"The rainy season is upon us," he said quickly, covering his tracks. "There is mud such as you have never seen. Mud up to my waist. And the rain; it is torrential. We travel day and night in the stuff. I would hate to see you covered in mud day and night. It would kill my morale."

Ellowyn wasn't fooled. "I realize that you are a warlord and men are going out of their way to try and kill you," she said, unhappy. "Must you be so blunt about it? Must you give me such angst for your safety?"

He sighed faintly, kissing her hand again. "I am sorry," he said softly, his deep voice a gentle rumble. "I was not thinking. You must understand that I have no need to be tactful with those around me and I am unused to speaking with women on a personal level. This is all very new to me so I apologize if, at times, I am tactless."

His apology eased her somewhat and she even managed a weak smile. "Do you have property in France?"

He nodded. "I do," he replied. "In Brittany I hold Chateau Melesse, which became mine when my father died, and Chateau Gael, which is where my daughters live. Near Limoges I hold Chateaus Ruffec and Civray, which I confiscated last year whilst fighting."

"Why can I not stay in one of your castles? I would be safe there and you could come and see me every day."

He smiled at her, her naïve nature. "Would that I could," he murmured, his gaze drifting over her face. "But I would not put you in such danger. Besides, I would probably kill myself racing home to you every night after a day of fighting."

"It would be worth it."

He chuckled, pulling her into a snug embrace. "Aye, it would," he said. "Even on my deathbed, every moment with you would be well worth it."

Ellowyn held him tightly, relishing the feel of him in her arms. Her heart was racing madly, her limbs tingling with excitement.

As she opened her eyes to say something to him, she caught a shadow moving towards them quickly. She also caught a glint of steel heading in their direction. With a gasp, she managed to release Brandt and give him a shove sideways at the same time.

"Get down!" she cried as she fell backwards over the bench. "Behind you!"

Brandt didn't stop to question her; he rolled off the bench and onto his knees, turning to face whatever had Ellowyn's panicked attention. He was without his broadsword but he carried two daggers; reaching into the holster lodged into his big boot, he removed a dirk that was nearly a foot long and, taking swift aim, hurled it at the rapidly approaching figure.

The wicked-looking knife caught the man in the neck and he collapsed forward onto the bench. The broadsword in his hand clattered to the ground and Brandt swiftly retrieved it, turning it against the man in a split-second and driving it into the back of the man's neck. He still immediately as the blood gushed.

Ellowyn was on her bum just a few feet away, eyes wide and hands against her mouth. Before she realized it, Brandt was sweeping her into his arms and carrying her back to the keep.

"Come along, my lady," he said calmly. "That is enough excitement for one night."

"That... that man," she gasped. "He... he would kill us."

Brandt was quite composed. "Not us," he said. "*Me.* I told you that men were out to kill me. I did not exaggerate."

She lifted her head from his broad shoulder, looking at him with big eyes. "Men under *your* command?"

He wasn't looking at her; his gaze was focused on the keep. "An assassin," he said quietly. "It happens all of the time."

She struggled to overcome her shock. Pushing herself from his arms, they ended up facing each other just outside of the kitchen entrance. Warmth and noise radiated from the open door as they stood in the dark and quiet yard. Ellowyn was working herself up into one of those lathers he'd seen when he had first met her; he could see it in her eyes.

"Stop this instant," she said, holding up her hands to him in a halting gesture. "Do you mean to tell me that your own men are so disloyal that they try to kill you for... for *money?*"

He sighed heavily, hands on his hips as he shook his head. "I have French in my command," he said as if it was all quite normal. "Or I have men in my command who have French brothers or cousins. Our two countries are so intertwined that such things are not unusual. Men fight for those who pay the most. A few coins to a soldier under my command, a promise of finer rewards, and he becomes an assassin for my enemies. Loyalties to a liege are bought and sold, my lady. This is the world I live in."

Ellowyn gazed up at him, digesting his words. "What about loyalty to a man simply because you respect him?"

"There is far less of that than you think."

"So fealty is goes to the highest bidder?"

"Poverty, hatred, and greed do desperate things to a man's character."

Ellowyn stared at him. Then, she shook her head. "Your world scares me," she said softly. "Look around you; this is my world. It is a world of peace and contentment. Your world is frightening."

"Then it is best you learn what you will be marrying into before the deed is done. Shall I still speak with your father or have you changed your mind?"

Ellowyn felt sick to her stomach. She held his gaze a moment longer before looking away. "I fear I am already attached to you," she murmured. "I do not want anything to happen to you, Brandt."

"That is not an answer. Shall I speak with your father or not?"

She looked at him, sharply. "Are you so cold to all of this?" she snapped. "Do you not care what I am feeling?"

"Of course I care what you are feeling, but as I explained, it is the way of things. Marriage to you will not change it."

He was so cold in his delivery, so matter of fact. Ellowyn's injured expression regarded him carefully.

"Is marriage just another business transaction to you?" she asked softly. "Because if it is, then we can stop it right now, shake hands, and be along our separate ways. I do not consider marriage a business transaction. I told you once before that when I marry it shall be for love, not because I can broker a better deal or find a richer man. It is because I *feel* something for him. I wonder if you

121

can feel anything at all for me of if you look at me as another acquisition."

He was gazing seriously in the moonlight. "Do you love me?"

"I am very fond of you. I am sure it will turn into love at some point."

He continued to look at her, pondering her reply. These emotions were so foreign to him, so confusing because he had never experienced them before. Once, he believed that love was a fool's emotion. As he gazed at Ellowyn, he wasn't so sure of that any longer. "I do not know what to say to that," he said softly.

Exasperated, hurt, Ellowyn sighed with frustration and turned away from him, gathering her luscious red skirts as she started to march away. But Brandt caught up to her, grasping her by the arm to stop her.

"I am sorry," he said, his deep voice soft and sincere. "I did not mean... Wynny, you must understand that love, or to be loved, has no place in my life. At least, until now. I do not understand the emotion because I have never felt it before. I am not very good with words so you must forgive me if I am blunt or abrupt. I do not mean to be, especially with you."

Ellowyn wasn't entirely soothed, though he had softened her considerably. "May I ask you something?"

"Of course."

"If an assassin were to pounce on me at this moment and kill me, how would you feel about it? Think carefully before answering."

He did. "Rage," he finally muttered. "Deep and unbridled rage."

She lifted her eyebrows. "Would you feel sadness?"

He nodded thoughtfully. "Aye."

"Why?"

"Because... because you would be dead."

"*Why* would you feel sadness, Brandt? What emotion deep inside you would cause you to feel sadness for my death?"

He blinked, not quite sure what she was driving out, but reaching out with his thought processes to try and figure out what it was. He could tell she was very serious about it. And then, the answer struck him.

122

"Fondness," he murmured. "I am fond of you also. I would miss you a great deal. Your death would fill me with anguish because of my fondness for you."

She smiled faintly. "Fondness can turn to love quite easily," she said softly. "Perhaps one day you will indeed introduce the emotion of love into your life, Brandt. You have the capability. I can see it."

"You give me the capability, Wynny. You and only you. When I love, it will only be you."

Her smile broadened. "Then you may speak with my father tonight about marriage," she whispered. "And I will try to accept the terror of your world, but know it gives me no pleasure to fear every moment of every day for your safety."

Brandt didn't say anymore. He just went to her and swept her up into his arms, his lips seeking her warm mouth. The kiss was tender at first but quickly roared to life with fevered intensity as the scent of Ellowyn filled his nostrils. He'd never known anything like it. Soft and sweet, blond and buttery, she was all things delicious. His blood was beginning to boil.

Aloft in Brandt's arms as his mouth ravaged her, Ellowyn could do nothing more but hold on to his neck, embracing him, feeling his life and warmth against her. Every taste, every suckle, was better than the last. Just as she pulled him tighter, they were interrupted.

"Wynny!"

A hiss came from the direction of the kitchen door. Ellowyn and Brandt turned to see Gray standing in the kitchen yard a few feet away, waving her hands at them. Brandt quickly set Ellowyn to her feet.

"What it is, *ma mère?*" Ellowyn asked, concerned as she moved towards her grandmother.

Gray took her granddaughter in-hand, glancing at Brandt as she spoke. "Your mother is heading in this direction," she said softly, quickly. "The duke will go to the feasting hall and I shall bring you in shortly."

Brandt bowed swiftly and headed for the opposite side of the keep. But both Ellowyn and Gray caught the warmth in his eyes as he moved away. Ellowyn's gaze lingered on the man until he disappeared from view, thinking warm and wicked thoughts about him. When she finally turned to her grandmother, she caught the mirth in Gray's eyes.

"What is it?" Ellowyn asked. "Why do you look at me so?"

Gray smiled as she began to lead her back into the keep round about through the kitchen yard.

"Because I remember what it is like to be young and lusty," she said softly. "Your grandfather and I met when your Aunt Brooke was about fourteen, so I was still relatively young. Poppa was quite taken with me and I with him. I remember the first time he kissed me; he had brought your aunt and me a great many gifts. I was still leery of him, you understand, so I did not want to accept the gifts but your aunt was mad for such things. Poppa took my hand and kissed it so tenderly that I nearly fell over and that, my dearest, was the start of it all. Poppa pushed his way right into my heart and he has stayed there ever since."

They entered the warm, dim kitchens and Ellowyn looked at her grandmother. "I miss him," she said softly.

Gray smiled faintly, a distant look in her eye. "I miss his presence," she replied, "but he is still with me. We speak daily. He does not answer me, but we most definitely speak. I can feel him all around me."

Ellowyn sighed sadly, thinking of her grandfather gone these six years. "I wonder what he would think of Brandt. Will you ask him then next time you speak with him?"

Gray laughed softly. "I believe he liked the duke," she said. "He served with him in France years ago when the duke was a very young man. Even then, he thought a good deal of the man, so I believe he would have approved of such a match."

Ellowyn smiled. "I hope so."

As they entered the narrow, barrel-roofed corridor that led from the kitchens into an alcove that then connected with the great hall, they ran into Annalora. The woman was in a rush, like she usually was, her eyes widening with surprise when she saw her daughter.

"Wynny," she gasped, grasping her arm. "I have been looking everywhere for you. Some of the duke's knights are already in the hall and they have asked for you. Where have you been?"

"With me," Gray said before Ellowyn could speak. "We have been walking."

Annalora only half-paid attention to the explanation as she whisked her daughter towards the great hall. In fact, she hardly gave it a second thought.

"Go, now," she told her daughter. "Entertain the duke's men. They seem quite taken with you."

Ellowyn gave her grandmother a rather desperate expression, causing the older woman to follow her granddaughter right into the hall.

The great hall of Erith was a two-storied monstrosity with a gallery that ran along the western wall. There was a massive fireplace that, twenty years before, had been a big open pit with a hole high above for the smoke to escape. Ellowyn's grandfather, Braxton, had the fire pit enclosed with masonry so the unusual enclosure and chimney ran all the way to the ceiling now. It was surrounded by a sort of cage built from wood to hold it steady. The result was a two-sided hearth in the center of the enormous hall that warmed it quite adequately. The massive feasting table for the family and visiting guests sat on the east side of the hearth.

St. Hèver, both de Laras, and le Bec stood up when they saw Ellowyn and her grandmother approach. Le Bec had cups of wine in both hands, double-fisting his drink, but quickly set them down when Alex elbowed him. Ellowyn smiled at the men as she came upon the table, especially at Brennan with whom she had grown friendly with. The young, blond knight smiled back.

"Good eve, my lords," she greeted the group, listening to their polite replies. "This is my grandmother, the Lady Gray de Nerra. Her husband was Braxton de Nerra."

The name Braxton de Nerra carried a great deal of weight. The knights shifted their attention to Lady Gray.

"Lady de Nerra," Dylan greeted. "'Tis a great honor to meet the wife of Braxton de Nerra."

Gray smiled politely and indicated for the men to sit, which they did. Ellowyn sat down next to St. Hèver as Gray took the chair at the corner of the table.

"It is an honor for us to have the House of de Russe as our guests," Gray said, waving on the servants to bring forth more food and drink. "I understand that you have all seen an arduous year this long past."

Dylan reclaimed his cup. "No more arduous than most, I suppose," he replied. "Edward of Wales has a claim to France and the French people do not wish to honor it. We must convince them."

As the knights snorted, Gray grinned at the warring man's humor. "I am sure you see it that way."

Dylan looked surprised but it was all for show. "What other way is there to see it?"

Gray shook her head reproachfully, delicately sipping at her wine. "No other way, young man," she assured him. "You sound as if you have generations of warring spirit behind you."

Dylan nodded. "My father is Tate de Lara, the Duke of Carlisle," he replied. "My grandfather was Edward Longshanks. My brother and I are bloodthirsty from way back."

Gray's eyebrows lifted, impressed. "De Lara," she murmured. "Of course I have heard of him. My husband said many times he is the man who should have been king."

Dylan shrugged. "I believe he is often glad that he was not," he replied. "Although he was Longshank's firstborn, my grandfather and grandmother were not married. My father was in indiscretion of the king's youth, but he was treated as a royal son. My uncle, Edward the Second, granted my father the title of Earl of Carlisle but his son, Edward the third, granted my father the dukedom of Carlisle. My father is quite content, I assure you."

"He is still alive?"

Dylan took another gulp of wine. "Indeed he is," he replied. "Alive and stronger than I am."

Gray smiled. As she and Dylan engaged in further conversation, Brandt entered the hall with de Reyne trailing after him. Brandt and Magnus had gone back to the kitchen yard when Ellowyn and

Gray had vacated it to quickly remove the assassin's body. Clad in leather breeches and a rough linen tunic, with boots to his knees, Brandt looked utterly masculine and divine. At least, that was Ellowyn's first thought when she saw him. Another thought occurred to her also; he wasn't wearing his armor. She'd never really seen the man without all of his armor. Even outside in the kitchen yard, he'd had pieces of it on. He must have changed out of it rather quickly. Ellowyn's heart fluttered madly.

Brandt's gaze lingered on her as headed for St. Hèver , who was seated immediately to her left.

"You are in my seat," he told the knight.

Brennan, ever obedient, jumped up without question and went to sit further down the table. Brandt resumed his seat next to Ellowyn, accepted a cup of wine handed to him by a hovering servant.

"Lady Ellowyn," he greeted evenly, as if they had not just seen each other moments before. "You are looking lovely this eve."

Ellowyn flushed. "Thank you, my lord," she said, rather innocently. "It seems strange not seeing you ever moment of every day, as I did when we were traveling. Have you been busy today?"

Brandt began helping himself to the bread and cheese artfully displayed on the table. "Verily," he told her. "The de Lara brothers can attest to that."

Alex heard his name. Since his brother was still engaged in conversation with Lady de Nerra, he answered.

"I am not entirely sure we have had time to rest and relax in over three years," he said. "This afternoon, your father allowed us to inspect some green chargers he had recently purchased. Your father has a good eye for horseflesh."

Ellowyn nodded sincerely. "Indeed he does," she replied. "We both do. I purchased those young chargers, in fact."

"*You* did?" Brandt repeated, somewhat incredulous. "My lady, they are some of the finest horses I have ever seen. Your father said he would negotiate a good price for them."

Ellowyn looked at him with a cocked eyebrow. "*I* will negotiate a good price for them," she clarified. "I purchased them, after all. I will be the one to barter their sale."

Brandt bit off a grin. "You will be easy on me, will you not?" he wanted to know. "You frighten me."

Ellowyn giggled. "I will try."

"Pray do."

As Brandt and Ellowyn lost themselves in grins and warm glances, Deston and Annalora entered the hall. The noise level soared with the two of them, their loud laughter and conversation, and the servants began to bring out the main course of the meal. As Deston and his wife sat at the table next to Brandt, the table was set with an entire roasted pig, boiled apples, cherries soaked in wine and spices, pickled cucumbers and turnips, more bread with cheese baked into it, and great bowls of boiled carrots. Ravenous, the diners plowed in to the offered fare.

Ellowyn didn't say much as Brandt and his knights tucked into the food. She was more interested in watching Brandt. After he served her first of the succulent pork, he helped himself to a great heaping pile and plowed into it. She was staring at him but he was trying not to stare at her. In fact, Ellowyn was watching him so closely that she hardly remembered to eat until her grandmother, seated on her right, gently nudged her.

Picking up her knife, she tore her gaze away from Brandt long enough to spear a piece of meat. But her attention was diverted when she saw a thin young man entered the hall carrying a rather large box.

Curious, she watched as the young man took up a stool near the blazing hearth and pulled a large mandolin-type instrument from the box. He strummed and tuned his cat-gut strings.

"Papa?" Ellowyn caught her father's attention, pointing to the young man. "Who is that?"

Brandt had been in conversation with de Reyne. He glanced over his shoulder at the man tuning the strings.

"He arrived a short time ago," he replied, turning back to his food. "He is a musician separated from his troop. They are all in Milnthorpe but he did not want to travel at night and asked for shelter. I told him I would feed him if he would play for us."

Ellowyn was thrilled. "How wonderful," she said, excited. "It has been a long time since we have had any music in the hall. Papa, perhaps you should think about employing musicians so they can play at every meal."

Deston wriggled his eyebrows, making a face. "Too much extravagance," he said. "You spend my money far too easily."

"I spend your money on what it needs to be spent on."

He guffawed. "Child, you are my greatest joy and my greatest expense," he said as the musician began to play. "Someday, you will find a husband who will say exactly the same thing."

Ellowyn knew he was teasing her but she wondered what Brandt was thinking about her father's statement. She hastened to soften it.

"You complain too much," she told her father. "If I spend a pence to buy wine, you cry rivers over lost money. Truly, Papa, one would think I have spent us right into the poor house."

Deston was grinning. "I look forward to the day when I can laugh at your husband because you do the same thing to him," he said, glancing at the knights around the table. "Any takers? My daughter would be most happy to spend your money for the price of a marriage contract."

"I accept," Brandt said without hesitation. "She can spend my money and will have my blessing to do so."

Ellowyn looked at him, eyes wide with shock. Deston, still grinning, had no idea the man was serious. "Are you certain?" he asked. "The woman has fine tastes. You will be a duke living in a mud hut with rocks for your bed. But at least your wife will be well-dressed with all of the frivolous things she will buy for herself."

"As long as she is happy, that is my only concern," Brandt replied steadily. He could tell that Deston wasn't taking him seriously but he could feel the curious stares from his knights. "Well? Is it settled?"

Deston snorted, tossing aside a bone and moving in for another hunk of meat. "Is what settled?"

"That Ellowyn will be my wife."

That brought the table to a grinding halt. By this time, everyone was looking at Brandt, including Deston and Annalora. Deston's smile vanished.

"Your *wife?*" he repeated. "My lord, are you... are you *serious*? I was only jesting."

"And I was not," Brandt replied, his gaze upon Deston intense. "Ellowyn will be my wife. You offered her to the table and I was the first to accept. Now, will you draw up the contract or will I?"

Deston's jaw dropped. "You cannot mean it."

"Why not?"

"Because... because she is... and *you* are... you cannot be serious!"

"Again, I say that I am very serious," Brandt replied. "Why do you find it so hard to believe? I want your daughter for my wife. I was going to ask permission in a more private setting, but since you made the offer public, you have given me little choice but to take my desire public as well."

Deston just stared at him. His gaze moved between Brandt and Ellowyn, who looked rather hopeful. Then, reality hit him; this was not a random discussion or something Brandt had accepted without consideration. This was something that evidently Ellowyn and Brandt already had on their minds; he could see it simply by their expressions. That thought did not set well with him. He set down the meat in his hands and wiped his fingers on his breeches.

"We will discuss this in my solar," Deston's voice was low. He stood up from the table. "Come with me, my lord."

Brandt didn't hesitate. He stood up and followed the man towards the keep entry and the small solar off of the foyer. When they faded from view, the table sat there in stunned silence. Ellowyn got up and ran off before anyone could stop her.

She headed straight for the solar.

# CHAPTER TWELVE

"Would you mind telling me why this notion of marrying my daughter has possessed you?" Deston was surprisingly hostile. "What *else* happened on the trip from London that I have not been informed of, eh? You two did not become closer that propriety allows, did you?"

Brandt kept calm. "Nothing more happened than what I told you," he replied, "except that Wynny and I have grown quite fond of each other. I want her for my wife."

Deston's round face flushed with outrage. "But you are the Black Angel, for God's sake!" he said. "I *know* what you have done in France with Edward. I know your reputation for ruthlessness and horror. What about all of those women and children you murdered? Well?"

Brandt stood his ground. "Such things happen in war."

Deston wasn't satisfied with the answer. He began pointing fingers at Brandt. "You have used the *chevauchèe* strategy," he hissed. "Burning, pillaging, and looting farms and town. That is all anyone can speak of. Burning everything to the ground and then stealing the spoils. Does that mean women, also? How many women have you stolen, de Russe, to fill your lusty veins?"

Brandt's jaw ticked. "I do not steal women and I do not lust," he said. "What I do is in the quest for Edward's victory and I will be judged only by God. Wars are made in such ways, and victory is achieved because of it. But none of this has anything to do with my offer for Ellowyn."

Deston threw up his hands; he was a passionate man as it was, now more passionate on the subject of his beloved daughter. He was off-guard by the subject matter and defensive. Although he respected Brandt's military ability and valued the alliance, he did not want such a man for his daughter. Too much about him was dark and frightening.

"It has everything to do with Ellowyn!" he said. "You are asking me for my life and my heart – you, a man who kills women and

131

children and calls it warfare. Women and children do not fight you, de Russe. What you do is dishonorable!"

It was the magic word as far as Brandt was concerned. He would not be called dishonorable by anyone, not when he worked hard to uphold his knightly honor in a world that knew little. His manner cooled dramatically.

"As the son of a great knight, I should expect better treatment from you," he growled. "You are basing your entire argument on rumors and gossip, something that only women do. You never once asked me to explain the truth of the matter but instead insult me based on slanderous half-truths. I still hold the greatest respect for your father but for you, I now hold none. Anyone who would call me dishonorable without fact is a fool and you, my lord, are a blatant one. How on earth Braxton de Nerra could father someone such as you is beyond my comprehension."

With that, he turned on his heel and threw open the solar door. He heard a yelp, realizing as he stepped out into the entry that Ellowyn had been standing by the door. He opened his mouth to apologize to her but her focus was purely on Deston. She cut Brandt off before he could speak.

"How *dare* you say such horrible things to him!" she hissed to her father. "You always considered yourself a fair and equitable man but I heard nothing fair or equitable when accusing Brandt of dishonor. How could you do such a despicable thing?"

Deston stood in the doorway, flushed and emotional. "Wynny, this is none of your affair," he scolded. "Go away now. This is not your business."

"Not my *business*?" she repeated, outraged. "It is indeed my business because Brandt is the man I wish to marry. He is kind and compassionate and wonderful, Father, and I will not have you say such terrible things about him. You were not in France; you do not know what went on. Furthermore, Grandfather was there years ago and who is to say he did not do his share of terrible things? Did you not tell me once that war is full of terrible actions by honorable men? It is evident your words are empty and I am ashamed of you!"

Deston swallowed hard, refusing to look at de Russe at all. In fact, he turned back for his solar. "I will not discuss this," he muttered. "De Russe, the men you asked for await in the bailey. You will leave before dawn."

The door slammed, leaving Brandt and Ellowyn in sudden and terrible silence. Brandt looked at Ellowyn; he wasn't sure what to say to her. She met his gaze steadily in spite of the fact that she was still quite angry. Taking a deep breath, she forced herself to calm.

"He has denied us," she said quietly.

"I know."

"What will you do now?"

He sighed, shaking his head as he raked his fingers through his hair in thought. "I am not sure," he muttered. "Leave before dawn as I have been instructed, I suppose. Your father needs time to cool his anger. Then I will try again."

Ellowyn took a few steps towards him. Then, she reached out and took his hand; their touch was filled with sorrow. Brandt brought her hand to his lips and kissed it tenderly.

"I am sorry," he murmured. "I wish this had turned out for the better."

Ellowyn was deeply grieved. His touch made it worse. She clasped his big hand in her two soft, warm ones.

"I do not want you to leave without me," she said, her throat tight. "I am afraid I will never see you again."

He kissed her hand again. "Of course you will," he murmured. "This is only a small setback. It is not the end."

She was starting to tear up, wiping at her eyes. "My father is very stubborn," she whispered. "I am afraid he will never give in. The more you press him, the more he will dig in."

"Then what do you suggest?"

She gazed up at him, eyes brimming. "I will go with you when you leave on the morrow," she said. "We will be married at the first church we come across and that will be the end of it."

He wasn't surprised by the suggestion. Truth be told, he had been thinking the same thing but wasn't sure she would agree. "You would defy your father?"

"I would. For you, I would do anything. I cannot stomach the thought of being separated from you, not even for a moment. Please, Brandt; let us leave here and never look back."

He gripped her hands tightly, kissing them gently. He gazed into her eyes as he caressed her fingers.

"Sweetheart, you must understand that defiance of that magnitude would render you separated from your family, perhaps for eternity," he said softly. "I cannot stomach the thought of being separated from you, either, but I am not sure defying your father's wishes is a good idea."

"He would forgive me, eventually," she said with a shrug. "My father only has one child that he recognizes. He has disowned my brother but he will not disown me. If he does, then he is the fool you have accused him of being. Perhaps... perhaps all of these years I have been viewing him through the eyes of an adoring child. Now, I view him through the eyes of a grown woman and I do not like what I see. I cannot believe he would say such things to you without basis."

Brandt sighed, still caressing her hands. "They are not entirely without basis," he muttered. "Your father was correct in some aspects; I use ruthless tactics to gain my wants and the wants of Edward. I have looted, burned, and pillaged. I have killed innocents. It does not give me pleasure to say that, but it is true. They call me the Bringer of Death for a reason, Wynny. You must not be fooled by romantic notions. I have killed my share."

She gazed up at him, her expression even. "I realize that," she said. "I do not have silly romantic notions. But what you did, you did in the course of war. War does not always protect the innocents. I am sure you did not go out of your way to kill them, did you?"

"And if I did?"

She averted her gaze thoughtfully as Brandt watched her anxiously. "I cannot change the past, I suppose," she finally said, looking up at him. "But perhaps... perhaps for the future, you would reconsider killing those who are helpless, even if it is in the name of the prince. Would you at least consider it? I would like to think that you are a man of mercy, Brandt."

He regarded her a moment. "Perhaps," he said softly. "But the idealistic concepts of chivalry on the battlefield are unrealistic. Chivalry can get a man killed. We must do as we must in order to survive and achieve victory."

Ellowyn cocked her head. "That is logical thinking. "

"It is indeed pragmatic."

They gazed at each other for a few moments as Brandt continued to caress her hands, buried deep within his massive mitts.

"I will go with you," she whispered. "To the devil with my father."

He sighed. "I am not entirely sure that is wise."

"If you do not take me with you, I will simply follow you. It is your choice; in your caravan or behind it."

He cocked an eyebrow. "You would, wouldn't you?

"Aye."

He sighed, long and slow. He might have even rolled his eyes at her. But beyond that, he didn't put up much of a fight. He wanted her with him, too, in the very worst way. The feel of her, the visual sense of her, filled him up like nothing he had ever known before. Already, she was becoming what was most precious to him.

"Very well, then," he murmured. "Be ready before dawn."

She grinned. "And we will be married at the first church we come across?"

"Do you know any nearby?"

She nodded firmly. "In Levens," she said. "It is a mile or so to the east."

"Then that will be our first destination on the morrow."

She giggled happily, throwing her arms around his neck. Brandt responded by wrapping his big arms around her, hugging her so that her feet dangled more than a foot off the ground. Then he kissed her, warm lips against warm lips, tasting her sweetness as if he had been starving for it all his life. If he didn't know better, he might have suspected the love he had never known was already upon him.

"Come, now," he breathed against her mouth. "Let us return to the hall and finish our meal."

Ellowyn nodded, rather breathlessly, as he set her on her feet. "Not a word to my mother," she told him as he took her hand and tucked it into his elbow. "She might try to stop us."

"And your grandmother?"

"She will fight my father to let me go with you."

Brandt grinned at her as they headed into the warm, fragrant hall beyond. They had a plan, just the two of him, and he felt excited and nervous about it like a giddy young squire. But it was the best feeling in the world. He could hardly wait for the morrow.

As they moved back to where the feasting was taking place, the solar door creaked open and Deston stood there. He had heard every word through the door, as he had been listening with his ear up against it. He knew the scheme, and he knew he must stop it. For Ellowyn's sake, he had to. His beautiful young daughter was not meant for a killer such as de Russe.

Shortly before dawn, Ellowyn was locked in her room by her own father, who told it was for her own good. When Brandt found out, he unleashed his men and laid siege from his prime position of inside Erith's massive inner bailey. He wasn't leaving the fortress without Ellowyn.

It was a very bitter and exhausting day.

\*\*\*

If Brandt de Russe was one thing and one thing only, it was a military master mind. He knew how to get his wants, and he knew how to make things happen. His systematic and rather strange siege of Erith would be something they would speak of for years to come in military circles.

When Deston had told him, from behind the bolted keep door, that he had no intention of allowing Ellowyn to sneak disgracefully off with the duke, Brandt had not been particularly surprised. He stood on the steps leading into Erith's big keep, hearing Deston's refusal and looking at the de Lara brothers, standing next to him, for their reaction.

Their response, of course, was immediately; they spread the word to St. Hèver , de Reyne and le Bec, and the five knights spread out and sequestered their four hundred and ninety-two men from the de Nerra troops. Once they were all separated, Dylan returned to Brandt for instructions.

Brandt was still standing on the top step of Erith's keep. He was looking at his men, now separated from de Nerra soldiers, and he was assessing the situation, the strengths and weaknesses, and their probable loss ratio. By the time Dylan appeared, Brandt was prepared.

"Does the man really think I am simply going to pack up and leave?" he asked, somewhat rhetorically.

Dylan, in full battle armor, shrugged as his gaze moved up the side of Erith's towering keep. "Perhaps he is hoping," he said, focusing on Brandt. "Your orders, my lord?"

Brandt, too, was in full battle regalia. He was well prepared for any sort of military undertaking. He sighed faintly as he latched the chin strap of his helmet.

"De Nerra?" he called in his booming baritone. "I will ask you one last time; will you turn Ellowyn over to me peacefully?"

From behind the enormous oak and iron door, he could hear the muted response. "Nay!"

Brandt looked at Dylan. "Is the vault in the gatehouse?"

Dylan nodded. "Aye, my lord."

"How many people would you say it will hold?"

Dylan cocked his head thoughtfully. "There are four cells plus a sublevel. It would hold fifty men at most. "

Brandt came off the steps. "Then jam as many of de Nerra's soldiers as you can into it and lock it up," he said decisively. "Then I want you to strip the rest, of their weapons and clothing and everything else, and pin them in the outer bailey with fifty of my best archers trained on them. If anyone moves, kill them. The rest of us will lay siege to this big beast of a keep and breach it."

The corner of Dylan's mouth twitched. "*Strip* de Nerra's men, my lord?"

Brandt nodded shortly. "A man cannot fight and protect his privates at the same time," he said. "I guarantee you that if given the choice between having his head or his manhood cut off, a man will choose his head every time. Being stripped of everything should give de Nerra's men cause to think twice before trying to resist us. They will be too busy protecting what is most precious to them."

Dylan's smile broke through as he turned away from Brandt, barking orders, which the other senior knights took up in chorus. Two hours after sunrise, a full-scale siege was taking place in the inner bailey of Erith.

Brandt knew he would have to be very careful in opening the keep, mostly because he didn't want to use his usual tactics. Those normally resulted in fatalities and since Ellowyn was inside, he wanted to make sure she stayed safe and whole. Therefore, he was cautious with his plans.

Erith had two openings at ground level; the entry door and the kitchen door. Since it made sense to breach the keep at its most vulnerable point, he set dozens of men to ramming down the keep entry and dozens more to chopping down the kitchen door, which was smaller and thicker. Those who weren't involved in breaching the doors, since only so many men could work on it at a time, were sent to watch over the naked de Nerra soldiers who were quite upset that they had been stripped of their dignity. But, as Brandt had predicted, nakedness prevented them from rioting. One could not riot and protect his privates at the same time.

Brandt didn't do much other than watch his men work the doors. It was methodical and calculated. He knew they would eventually open the keep and he was under no illusion that de Nerra wasn't going to fight him once he entered, so they had a master plan – they would wait until both doors were open and create a bigger, louder diversion at the keep entry while Brandt entered through the kitchens and went in search of Ellowyn. He would be armed, of course, but he would try not to kill anyone. All he wanted was Ellowyn. So far, they'd managed to not to lose a single life and he wanted to keep it that way.

It was a simple notion, or so he thought. The entry was breached before the kitchen door was, and that proved a mess to bring down. Ultimately, they brought out a couple of axes and Brandt lent his considerably strength to chopping down the rest of the kitchen door.

When the gap was big enough for a man to slip through, he handed the axe off to le Bec as Dylan went to the door to see what was waited for them on the other side.  Unfortunately for him, he got too close to the breach and the panicked cook hit him on the head with an iron pot in a blow that sent him to his knees.

With Dylan dazed, Brandt tried to charge through but found himself fended off by several kitchen women using spits and pokers to keep him at bay.  When one came too close to his eye, he furiously reached out and tossed the spit outside into the yard.  That prompted the other women to start whacking him with their pitiful weapons.  Brandt grabbed at them, yanked them free, and tossed.

Soon the kitchen yard was full of iron kitchen implements because Brandt was genuinely trying not to hurt anyone.  He simply didn't want to be hurt in the process, either.  Those pokers were coming awfully close to his eyes and face to the point where he had to lower his visor. Then he looked terrifying and the servants were panicked even more.

Eventually, he had enough of the foolery.  He pushed his way into the kitchen, batting away the crude weapons the servants were using against him. St. Hèver  pushed in after him and actually pushed a woman onto her backside, which brought a chorus of screams.  Brandt glanced back at him to see what he done, to which the young knight only shrugged.  It was the oddest battled they had ever fought – weaponless and against women.  But all of Brandt's knights understood what he was trying to accomplish; they wanted Ellowyn and didn't want to have to kill everyone to get to her.

Brandt pushed his way through the close quarters of the kitchen, heading to the alcove that eventually led into the great hall, when he ran head-long into another woman. It was a rather violent collision in the dark. He reached out to prevent her from falling over only to realize it was Lady Gray.  And trailing after Lady Gray, holding on to the woman's skirts, was Ellowyn.

"Brandt!" she shrieked.

Gray shushed her granddaughter harshly, thrusting at Brandt when she realized who it was.

"Take her," she hissed. "Deston is at the entry. Take her now or you will have real blood on your hands."

Brandt didn't need to be told twice; flipping up his visor and with a loud kiss to Lady Gray's cheek, he whisked Ellowyn back towards the kitchens with St. Hèver covering their retreat. In the dim, smokiness of the close-quarters kitchen, Brandt and his men backed their way out of the keep and out into the sunlight. When Dylan de Lara saw them emerge, he began bellowing the retreat orders, eventually taken up by de Reyne, le Bec, and his brother who were at the keep entry creating all sorts of havoc.

The duke's men deteriorated into organized chaos as they scrambled for their mounts. The provisions wagons, having been positioned in the outer bailey by the gates, rallied and fled out into the countryside, followed by the retreat of the wagons. The senior knights managed to mount with Brandt and Ellowyn leaping aboard his muscular charger. Ellowyn nearly fell off as Brandt spurred the beast out of the front gates of Erith, leaving de Nerra's naked army behind, wondering why the duke's army had cleared out so quickly.

# CHAPTER THIRTEEN

*It was that dream again.*

*As Ellowyn moved towards a grove of stripped trees, the mud became shallower and less binding, and she struggled to get up onto firmer ground. But she slipped and fell to her knees, bracing herself with one arm to keep from falling completely while the other arm went around her belly. A big, swollen belly.*

*She put a hand to her gut, feeling the life kicking within. It brought a rush of joy and euphoria, feeling the tender life she carried. But it did not take away from her sense of urgency as she scratched and clawed her way up on to firmer ground, out of the mud that was sucking her down. Finally free of the cold, gray mud, she stood for a moment, gaining her bearings.*

*The dream was oddly fluid. Everything rippled, like movement upon a lake. She turned to look at the castle again, seeing the fingers of smoke spiraling upwards even in the rain, and as she gaze steadily at the broken walls and gray-stoned keep, she could see that every window in the keep was glowing red. They looked like eyes, pulsating a red and liquid reflection of the evil that surrounded it. As she watched, the red turned to blood and began dripping down the side of the keep. All of those windows, now dripping blood.*

*Horrified, frightened, Ellowyn tore her gaze away from the hellish castle, arms around her swollen belly as she began to walk. Tears filled her eyes, spilling over onto her cheeks, as she began to call for her love, her life, the man she was looking for. In dreams past, she had only come this far before the dream ended. So many times it had ended and so many times she had awoken upset and frustrated. But this time, the dream didn't end; she was able to keep going, searching with panic that swelled her heart so that she thought it might burst. Bodies were at her feet but she didn't recognize any of them. She kept going, feeling the cold rain against her face, feeling the cold howling winds that grabbed at her.*

*And then she saw someone she knew; her grandfather was standing by the edge of a grove of trees. His armor was clean, untouched, and dry. Rain was pouring down upon her, but her grandfather was completely dry. He looked at her with some sorrow. Ellowyn ran to him.*

*"Papa!" she cried. "Help me! I cannot find him!"*

*Braxton simply stood there, looking at her. When she tried to touch him, her hands went right through him. Then, he pointed.*

*Ellowyn's gaze moved in the direction he was indicating. She had no idea what he meant or what he was pointing at; all she could see was a sea of corpses that were beginning to turn into liquid, being absorbed into the ground. But as they drained away, into the mud and earth, she saw a figure propped up against a tree in the distance.*

*As she focused on the distant figure, Deston began to howl in her ear. It was a mournful and terrifying sound, enough to make her scream as everything else faded to black.*

141

\*\*\*

"They have not followed us yet but our scouts report that de Nerra is amassing his army," Dylan told Brandt. "He knows we have her and it is evident he intends to pursue."

Brandt gazed up at the man, his expression without emotion. It was towards midnight as he sat at a heavy, damaged table before a smoking fire in a public house in the village of Garstang. Twenty six miles south of Erith, it had been the logical place to stop for the night so Ellowyn could gain a few hours of sleep.

Garstange was a larger berg, with several public houses, that were well traveled and littered with all kinds of people. Brandt had his army park themselves south of the town in an open field that had a clear field of vision in all directions, while he took his senior knights to the inn on the edge of town called the Punchbowl. It was unusual comfort for the usually hard-core men, but in Brandt's opinion, they deserved it. Besides, it was his wedding night and he was feeling particularly generous.

"Of course he knows I have her," Brandt grunted as he rubbed his weary eyes. "Deston can pursue me to the ends of the earth but it does not change the fact that I married his daughter earlier today and that she is now my wife. He cannot destroy the bonds of matrimony. Whether or not he likes it, Ellowyn belongs to me."

Dylan shrugged as he claimed a seat next to St. Hèver. "I am sure he will be happy to discuss that with you when he catches up to us, my lord," he said, rather sarcastically and wearily. "Our scouts did not seem to think his army would be departing this night which leads me to believe he will be departing at dawn and, just as we have scouts, I am sure he has his own who are reporting back to us that we are holed up in Garstang."

Brandt took a long drink of his wine, watching Dylan rip into a warm and succulent piece of beef. In fact, all of his senior knights were seated around the table in various stages of a food-and-drink stupor. Le Bec and de Reyne, overstuffed and bordering on drunk, were arm wrestling at the end of the table while St. Hèver, the ever-proper and pious young knight, was trying not to look at a young and rather pretty serving wench who was trying very hard to catch his eye. Alex de Lara was aware of this and kept calling the girl over to the table to refill their cups while Dylan, newly returned from settling the men and debriefing the scouts, ignored everything else and tucked into his food.

Brandt watched it all with some amusement and, surprisingly, a great deal of relaxation. He was more at ease than he had been in quite a while knowing that Ellowyn was safely asleep over his head. He really didn't care about de Nerra in the least. Alcohol and a rush of emotions had seen to that. At the moment, he simply wanted to enjoy the situation and his new marriage. He'd never felt such contentment.

"We will not be here long enough for them to catch up to us," he finally said. "We leave this berg before dawn. If all goes well and the weather holds, we should be home in less than two weeks. If de Nerra wants to attack Guildford after a battle march across the whole of England, then I invite him to try."

Dylan wriggled his eyebrows, his mouth full. He was starving and had spent a good deal of time securing the men while the other knights ate their supper. He didn't want to talk anymore but he couldn't help stating the obvious.

"We are traveling with weary men and a woman, my lord," he pointed out. "If we make it back to Guildford in two weeks, we will be fortunate. Much can happen in two weeks, now with an angry father on our tail."

Brandt cocked an eyebrow at him. "Much can happen indeed," he agreed, not particularly pleased with Dylan's attitude. "In fact, I would suggest we send your brother to solicit support from your father and St. Hèver to the Marches to solicit support from his father. I have enough to deal with now with de Nerra nipping at my heels and preparations to return to France. I will not be able to attend the Duke of Carlisle and the Earl of Wrexham personally."

Dylan simply nodded his head, his mouth too full and his mind too weary to think on any more than evening. As a tense silence settled, le Bec entered the conversation.

"My lord?" he said. "Is your lady wife well? She seemed rather fatigued when we arrived earlier. I am sorry she was not able to join us for sup."

Brandt set his cup down, exhaling wearily. "She is well; simply exhausted," he replied, his thoughts turning to his wife. "She went upstairs, fell on the bed, and went straight to sleep. I should go and check on her.  Perhaps she is awake and will join us now."

He stood up, feeling every inch of his exhaustion, as Dylan muttered.  "Or perhaps you should simply stay in the room with her," he said, mouth full. "You are a bride groom, after all. Why would you wish to share your wife with us on this night?"

As the knights snickered, Brandt actually grinned.  He slapped Dylan on the shoulder as he walked past him and lumbered up the uneven stairs.

The corridor was dim, the only light from the common room down below seeping up through the floorboards.  Brandt headed for the room at the far end of the hall, the one farthest from the inn's main chamber.  He had tried to find a quiet spot for Ellowyn, something rather difficult in a packed inn, but as he inserted the crude key into the equally crude iron lock, he opened the door to a darkened and quiet chamber.  It seemed worlds away from the quagmire downstairs.

It was a long and skinny chamber that stretched all down the side of the structure with a big window that overlooked the stable yard below. He could smell the animals wafting through the oilcloth. The bed, barely big enough for two, was shoved against the far wall with the foot of it close to the small fireplace, now laying low and glowing with a mixture of peat and wood.

As he made his way quietly over to the bed, he realized there was noise coming from the darkened corner.  He could hear sniffles and sobbing. It took him a moment to realize that Ellowyn was weeping.

Brandt sank down on to the mattress, full of concern. "Wynny?" he asked softly. "Why do you weep, sweetheart?"

Ellowyn wiped furiously at her face. "It... it is of no worry" she whispered. "I suppose... it has been a long day. I am simply fatigued."

Brandt's brow furrowed as he stroked her dark hair. "But you were fine when I left you earlier," he insisted quietly. "You were dead asleep. Why are you crying now?"

The fact that he was pressing her on her the reasons behind her tears made her weep more. "I... I will not see my father or mother again," she sobbed. "I miss them already."

He sighed heavily; he wasn't about to remind her that he had warned her of such a thing. Now was not the time. He stroked her head again and kissed her forehead.

"Aye, you will," he assured her. "They will not stay angry with us for long, especially when their grandchildren come along. That will make them forget everything."

Ellowyn wasn't entirely convinced but she nodded anyway, wiping at her nose. "Mayhap," she said. "But I miss them just the same. And... and I had a dream."

He bent over her so that he was nearly laying on her, stroking her silken hair and kissing her cheek.

"What dream, sweet?"

She gazed up at him, shadows on her face as her tears glistened in the weak firelight. "I do not exactly know," she murmured, her tears lessening. "I have had the same dream for a while now. Sometimes I have dreams that come true and this one scares me."

He smiled faintly. "Are you a prophetess, then?"

She nodded seriously even though he had meant it in jest. "Since I was young, I have had dreams that sometimes come true," she said. "I dreamt that my brother would no longer be a knight but no one believed me, and then he left for the cloister. I also dreamt my grandfather was ill well before he told anyone. I have dreamt of other things, as well, that have come to pass."

He cocked an eyebrow. "You did not tell me you were an oracle. Perhaps I can use you to my advantage."

She grinned weakly because he was, wiping away the last of her tears. "I cannot divine your warring future," she told him. "But... but this dream. It *is* about war. There is a castle with a big keep and it is raining heavily. The castle is on fire and there are bodies strewn everywhere. I am walking through the mud and rain searching for my love but I do not know who he is nor can I find him. I am so terribly frightened and it is then I realize I am with child. I walk through this mud and blood, my hands on my swollen belly, looking for... someone. It is a horrible dream."

Brandt took absolutely no stock in prophetic dreams. He was a logical man and knew there was an explanation for everything. Moreover, the mind could do strange things when weary or frightened. He had experienced it for himself. He stroked her head again and kissed her cheek.

"Now I am here and I will chase these evil dreams from your mind," he said softly. "I will bring you comfort where you have had none before. Once you feel safe and cherished, this dream will stop. Do you feel like eating something now? Perhaps some food will help chase your nightmares away."

Ellowyn sighed wearily. "I am not hungry," she told him. "I simply want to sleep."

He didn't push her. "As you wish," he kissed her cheek again. "As your husband, may I join you?"

She smiled, a genuine gesture. "I was hoping you would."

Brandt didn't need any further prompting or conversation. He stood up from the bed and began pulling off pieces of armor and his mail. When he had it all gathered up, he sent a servant for his squires, who came on the run. There were two of them, big strapping lads, and they carried away the duke's expensive protection to clean it and have it ready for him in the morning.

When the young men fled, Brandt pulled of his tunic and sat down on the bed to remove his boots. He found that he was very eager to get into bed with his new wife, reminding himself that he had to take it slowly with her. She was sweet, sensuous and delicious, but she was also very virginal. He didn't want to frighten or hurt her, although he knew the latter was inevitable as an untouched bride. He found that he was actually shaking with anticipation as he slipped his leather breeches off and, in the darkness of the room, climbed into the narrow bed next to her. But the moment he went to pull her into his arms, she snored and sighed. It was so dark in the room that he had to get right up to her face to see that she had fallen back asleep.

He sighed faintly, feeling a good deal of disappointment. Then, he chuckled at the irony of the situation. He lay down quietly next to her, folding a big arm under his head and just watching her. The firelight was very faint but he could still see her features in the glow. She was such an exquisite creature. He was still having difficulty believing that she belonged to him now because the events of the past day, not to mention the past week, had been overwhelmingly swift. He felt like he was still trying to catch up with all that had happened.

Reaching out with his free hand, he gently touched her hair, her forehead. Then he touched her neck and shoulder and wound back up to her head again. She had such lovely hair. She stirred a bit but didn't waken.

Lifting a rather devious eyebrow, Brandt shook the bed a bit. She didn't stir. He wriggled harder, enough to move her fairly significantly, and she stirred again but she didn't awaken. Then, he bounced around like a fool two or three times, enough to jolt her out of a deep sleep. As big a man as he was, he nearly flipped her right out of bed. He lay there innocently as she sat up and rubbed her eyes.

"Did I wake you?" he asked, feigning concern. "I am sorry, sweetheart. Go back to sleep."

Ellowyn yawned, still rubbing her eyes before looking at him. "You did not wake me," she muttered, lying down because he was pulling her down next to him. "I was already awake."

She yawned again as he tucked her in next to his heated, naked body. "You should be asleep," he said, kissing the top of her head, "even if it *is* our wedding night."

Ellowyn didn't say anything. She simply snuggled against him, trying to find her comfort zone. But then, her eyes opened and she realized she was staring at his chest. His *naked* chest. More than that, she was in his arms, lying with him for the very first time. The contentment was unimaginable. His words began to sink in and her first instinct was to pull away from him, uncertain and a little frightened. But with those same emotions came feelings of excitement and joy such as she had never known.

Peering down under the covers without really moving her head, she could see he was completely nude; she could see his bare thighs and belly, but the shadows and darkness prevented her from seeing anything more. She knew what he meant by it being their wedding night. He meant doing what all married couples do.

He had come prepared. She had not.

Lifting her head, she looked into his handsome face. "I will stay awake," she said. "I am your wife, after all. It seems so strange to say that, does it not?"

She was giggling and he smiled. "I have never heard a more beautiful thing in my life," he said softly, stroking her cheek. "I never thought I would have a wife again and particularly not one I was fond of, so this is quite a miraculous event."

Ellowyn reached up, stroking his cheeks that were rough with stubble. "I have married the Duke of Exeter," she whispered. "It is only a title to me. I married Brandt de Russe, someone who has come to mean so very much to me. I would have married you had you been the lowliest pauper."

He kissed her fingers as they came near his lips. "Fortunately, I am not," he murmured. "I am the Duke of Exeter, Lord of the Western Gates, Baron Guildford and Waverley. You are now the Duchess of Exeter and Lady Guildford. If we have a son, then the hereditary title of Earl of Weston will pass to him. There are a dozen other titles that go with my dukedom so our children will be well titled and propertied. Most of Devon and parts of Surrey belongs to me, my lady. We shall build quite a legacy."

Ellowyn smiled faintly. "I only care that I belong to you."

He smiled in return, pulling her close against his warm, nude chest. She felt unbelievably delicious in his arms. His mind was screaming at him to take it slowly with her but his body wasn't particularly listening. He wanted her now, and he wanted all of her. He was a man who always got what he wanted.

"You belong to me," he whispered, kissing her forehead, her eyelids. "You, and everything about you, belong to me."

"I am so glad."

"As am I."

His seeking lips found her warm mouth, kissing her gently at first, but with increasing passion. Ellowyn was quickly becoming adept at returning his kisses but little more beyond that; she had no idea what 'more' there really was. Yet she was responsive and mimicked him when he snaked his tongue into her mouth to taste her deeply; however, when he rolled on top of her, trapping her,

she felt a little overwhelmed. All of this was so new and
wonderful, but it was also frightening. He was such a big and
powerful man. Brandt was taking charge and she had little choice
but to let him.

Ellowyn was still wearing the surcoat she had fled Erith in, a
durable broadcloth of deep blue. It was also complicated and she
was fastened and tied into it, and Brandt didn't have a lot of
patience for it. He snapped a strap on her waist but Ellowyn
stopped him before he could rip it to shreds.

"This is all I have," she whispered, pulling away from his
seeking mouth and putting a hand over his to top it. "If you ruin it,
I shall have nothing to wear."

He backed off as a chivalrous man would and lay back on the
pillow, watching her as she climbed out of bed and began
unfastening the dress. Even though it was dim in the room, when
it came time for her to finally begin removing the pieces, he turned
his head and stared up at the ceiling to allow her some privacy. He
wanted nothing more than to watch her strip to the skin, but he
thought perhaps it might embarrass her too much. He was trying
very hard to think of her comfort and not of his lust.

He could hear the fabric falling to the floor and then she was in
bed again, swiftly pulling the covers up to her neck. By the time he
turned to look at her, the covers were up so high that even her
ears were covered. All he could see was the top of her head and
her face. She looked as if she was swaddled and he struggled not
to smile.

Propping himself up on an elbow, he loomed over her in the
dim light. Ellowyn gazed back at him with a mixture of curiosity,
excitement, and apprehension. He let his smile break through as
he began to very gently peel back the coverlet, kissing every inch
of flesh he uncovered. She seemed fine with his attention, relaxing
even, until he began to peel it away from her breasts. Then she
tensed up but Brandt wouldn't have it; he tugged firmly, steadily,
as she tried to hold the coverlet, all the while kissing the bits of
skin that were being revealed. Eventually, he managed to uncover
her left breast completely and when she moved to yank the
coverlet up to recover it, he tugged hard enough to pull the entire

coverlet completely off of her body.

Ellowyn shrieked softly with surprise, and perhaps some fear, as Brandt covered her up with his big body and latched hungrily to a nipple. He was heated and virile and overwhelming, and Ellowyn was rather stunned by his onslaught. She'd truly had no idea what to expect on their wedding night, virginal and lacking any knowledge whatsoever, so she couldn't do much more than lay there and experience what he was doing to her. Truth be told, she was embarrassed that she was naked and he was touching very personal parts of her body. But she was also very interested. As he fondled and nursed at her breasts, bolts of excitement coursed through her.

Brandt remained with her breasts for a good long time, acquainting her with his touch. He was also very much acquainting himself with the feel and taste of her, and it was more than he could have imagined. He'd never known anything so sweet. The problem was that he was not a man of supremely great control; if he wanted it, he got it, and if he gave a command, it was fulfilled. He'd never had to practice great restraint. Therefore, as Ellowyn squirmed beneath him with awakening desire, Brandt's senses were overwhelmed. He had something in his grasp that he very much wanted to take. Therefore, he did.

Using his knees, he wedged Ellowyn's legs apart and settled in between them. As he continued to suckle her breasts, a hand drifted down her torso, feeling her flinch, before settling at the thatch of dark curls between her legs. Ellowyn stiffened with uncertainty as he stroked her, coaxing forth her juices, before inserting a finger in to her body.

Ellowyn gasped at the sensual invasion, instinctively bringing her knees up, and it was more than Brandt could take. Removing the finger, his manhood pushed into her, sliding half of his full, hard length on the first try. Beneath him, Ellowyn gasped and squirmed with the discomfort, the newness of the sensation, and Brandt withdrew only to come back firmer and harder the second time, driving himself to the hilt in one swift stroke.

Ellowyn cried out softly at the surprise and pain of it, her nails digging into his arms as he began his measured thrusts, his hips undulating against her pelvis, commencing with the sensual rhythm of mating. Legs wide apart as the massive form of Brandt de Russe settled between them, Ellowyn bit her hand to keep from crying out as he thrust into her again and again. The first several thrusts were filled with stinging pain, but the more the man moved and ground his hips against hers, the more another sensation began to take hold.

It was like a spark that struggled to grow into a blaze, but when it finally did, Ellowyn stopped biting her hand and began to ride the sensations. Brandt was a master at building a fire in her lions, something she had never before experienced. He would thrust into her but then he would also remove his manhood and rub it against her sensitive core, creating sparks and magic before he would thrust into her again.

He did it again and again until eventually she began to feel the build of something that sent her entire body into a spasm as it radiated out from her loins like lightning bolts of pleasure. When Brandt felt Ellowyn's climax begin, he thrust into her, again and again, until he achieved his own release. It was an explosion of passion, one of such power that he bit his tongue as he peaked. Underneath him, he could hear Ellowyn gasping as her tremors died down.

Full of warmth and passion and contentment, Brandt gently suckled her neck, toying with a tender nipple as he continued to softly thrust into her over-worked body. It was enough to send Ellowyn over the edge again as she experienced her second release, bringing her to delirious and confused tears. Her body was reacting in ways she never imagined possible and she had no idea how to process it. The only thing that came to mind was tears. She wept as Brandt continued to kiss her tenderly.

"What is wrong, sweetheart?" he murmured against her flesh. "Did I hurt you? Should I stop?"

Ellowyn sniffled, shaking her head. "No," she whispered. "You did not hurt me."

"Then why do you weep?"

She shrugged, the only answer she could give him, and closed her eyes. Brandt watched her face for a moment, concerned with her emotional state. He thought perhaps she was lying and that perhaps he had done something wrong. He didn't know why she would cry otherwise.

Carefully, he lifted himself off of her and lay down beside her, his big arm across her belly as he continued to watch her face, now in profile. He didn't want to upset her; he only wanted to make her happy. He'd never wanted something so much in his life. Eventually, her tears calmed and she fell asleep, a soft and deep slumber, but Brandt remained awake, watching her, pondering their new relationship and the course of their future.

Truth be told, their association had started it out on a rather violent note, but he wasn't sorry. He had Ellowyn and that was all he cared about. But he was a man who believed in controlling his destiny, his future, and the same thing applied to Ellowyn. He was determined to control her happiness as well.

He was gone before she awoke before sunrise.

## CHAPTER FOURTEEN

It was morning.

Ellowyn knew this because she could hear animals stirring in the yard below her chamber window. It was still dark as she sat up in the empty bed, momentarily disoriented until memories from the previous night came rushing back on her.

Clutching the coverlet to her naked chest, she recalled Brandt and his scorching touch, his lips and body that seemed to do miraculous things to her. She was very embarrassed about how she had reacted to him, unable to understand her body's responses. Mentally, she was still very virginal and naïve even if bodily she was not. To think of her reaction made her cheeks flame, even in the cool room.

Inching over, she pulled back a corner of the oiled cloth to see a heavy fog blanketing the land and a stable yard below. Smells of animals and urine wafted up, assaulting her nose until she closed the oiled cloth. Men were shouting out in the yard, bellowing for mounts, and Ellowyn snuggled back under the warm coverlet, eyes wide open and staring at the wall. Her thoughts began to move to the previous day.

So much had happened. Her sleepy mind was singling out thoughts and fixating on them. She thought of her mother, of her father, and how they had tried so hard to protect and shelter her. Tears sprang to her eyes as she thought of her parents, undoubtedly distraught over her disappearance. Of course they knew she had gone with Brandt; there was no other alternative. She knew her mother would be weeping and sorrowful, and her father would be both grief-stricken and irate. Discord had invaded their happy little world and had taken their daughter away from them.

Ellowyn wiped at the tears on her temples as she thought of Brandt, the man now her husband. She thought perhaps she had been terribly foolish to run off and marry him, but she did not

153

regret it. She only wished the circumstances could have been different. Yesterday, all she had considered was her own wants. She wanted to marry Brandt and would stop at nothing to achieve those wants. Today, she was regretting her haste at least to the extent it had hurt her family. But she knew that, given the choice again, she would have made the same decision.

The door to the chamber quietly opened and she sat bolt-upright, startled. Brandt stood in the doorway, his expression somewhat startled as well.

"Did I wake you?" he asked. "Forgive me. I was only bringing food and firewood."

With that, he sharply motioned to the servants behind him, who scurried into the room bearing steaming trays and cups, and wood for the fire. Ellowyn pulled the coverlet up to her neck, watching the chaos going on, before pulling the coverlet over her entire head and falling back onto the bed.

She remained there, a lump on the bed, as the servants stoked the fire and set out a rather plentiful morning meal. All the while, Brandt stood in the doorway, monitoring the situation. When the servants were finished, he snapped his fingers at them and they fled. But then he waved his big arm at another servant who was hovering in the hall with a pile of fabric in her arms. The woman dumped the massive pile into his arms and ran off.

Brandt entered the chamber and shut the door, bolting it. He eyed Ellowyn's lump on the bed as he deposited the bundle of fabric in his arms on the bottom of the mattress. The lump stirred. He poked it and it stirred again. It was difficult to keep the grin off his face.

"I wonder if my wife will come out of her hiding places if she knows that a bath has been ordered for her," he pondered somewhat obviously. "In fact, I have brought many wonderful gifts for her to inspect."

The covers came off in a flash and Ellowyn's messy blond head greeted him. His grin broadened.

"I see I have lured you out of your cave," he said. Then, he pointed at the pile on the bed. "I raided a merchant's shop early this morning and brought you these. You said you had nothing more to wear. I have remedied that."

Ellowyn peered at the heap on the bed with interest. "You *raided* the shop?" she clarified.

He shrugged, watching her as she crawled across the bed, keeping the coverlet around her nude body to protect her modesty. She began to rifle through the items with one hand while keeping the coverlet up with the other.

"A figure of speech," he said. "The man was preparing to open his shop for the day and I purchased these items for you. There are four surcoats, two shifts, various belts and scarves and hose, and a sack that contains a variety of soaps and oils and combs. You said you had nothing and I wanted to ensure that you had something until you could purchase items more suited to your taste."

Ellowyn looked at him, surprised and pleased. "You did this for me?"

He looked at her as if puzzled by the response. "Of course," he said. "You are my wife. It is my duty to provide for you."

Her gaze lingered on him, hearing his words, *you are my wife.* She felt such giddy joy at the reminder, chasing off the damp thoughts from just moments before. Aye, she'd run off to marry him, leaving her family to start a new life with a man she had quickly come to adore. She missed her family very much. But she realized it could not dampen the joy she felt at becoming Brandt's wife. Gazing up at him, she was very glad to be with him, no matter what the circumstances.

"I would thank you for your thoughtfulness, then," she said. "You are very generous, my lord."

He gave her a half-grin. "Not under usual circumstances, but you seem to bring it out in me," he said, his gaze moving over her appreciatively as his manner softened. "Did you sleep well?"

She nodded, a smile coming over her face. "Very well, thank you," she said. "Did you?"

He nodded, his dark eyes twinkling. "Surprising well considering my new wife thrashes about in bed. Twice I was smacked in the face by flailing arms."

Ellowyn's mouth popped open in outrage. "I do *not* thrash!"

He laughed, bending over to kiss her on the forehead. "Aye, you do, but I find it quite charming," he said. "In fact, I find everything about you quite charming. You are a true and rare treasure, my lady. I feel like the most fortunate man alive."

He insulted her and soothed her at the same time, leaving Ellowyn with a furrowed brow and a smile on her face. "Compliments and slander well played, Lord Husband," she said. When he snorted and shifted on his big legs, she noted that he was dressed in a full complement of armor. "I would assume that I have little time to dress?"

He nodded. "That is a fair statement."

"Then I will need something to pack these garments in."

"My men are searching out such a trunk as we speak," he said, "and I would appreciate it if we could be on the road within the hour. We have much traveling to do before we reach Guildford."

She was aware of that. As she looked at him, something else occurred to her. "Is my father chasing us?"

His humor faded. "My scouts indicate he has amassed his army," he replied. "He will not be far behind us so the sooner we depart, the better."

Ellowyn thought seriously on that. "Perhaps we should send him a missive and tell him we have married," she said. "Even if he did catch us and, for some reason, wrest me from you, the fact remains that I am your wife. My father cannot dissolve our marriage. Perhaps if we tell him that, he will give up trying to reclaim me. There is no point if we are married."

Brandt lifted his eyebrows. "If your father has any brains, then he knows I have married you already and he will come after us regardless. We are speaking of honor, Wynny – I defied your father and slandered his honor by taking you. He wants you back. He will try to kill me to achieve this."

She frowned. "I will not allow it," she said firmly. "Moreover, he cannot kill you. Frenchmen have been trying to do it for years and have not succeeded. What makes you think a crippled Englishman can?"

Brandt chuckled, shaking his head. "An angry crippled father is worth a thousand whole-bodied Frenchmen," he said. "Do not underestimate him."

He was half-joking but Ellowyn was still serious. "So what do we do? Retreat to Guildford and hope he gives up at some point? Perhaps he will come to Guildford and lay siege."

Brandt nodded. "It is a distinct possibility," he replied. "But my castle is well fortified. He will not succeed if he tries to bring me down."

"Do we just sit and wait him out?"

"Nay," Brandt said, rather firmly. "I will go about my business seeking fresh men and supplies for the Prince of Wales, and eventually return to France."

Her spirit dampened. "And leave me behind at Guildford with my father trying to beat down the walls?"

He sobered. Then he put his hand beneath her chin, tipping her head up to receive a sweet kiss to the mouth.

"We are not going to play out that scenario at this moment," he said softly but firmly. "You will get dressed and I will return for you within the hour. Agreed?"

She made a face but nodded. "Agreed."

He smiled, kissing her again. "I will station a soldier outside in case you need something."

She watched him head to the door. "Where are you going?"

He put his hand on the latch, his eyes studying her. "I have many tasks that require my attention," he replied. "But I will not go far, I swear it."

He winked at her before quitting the room and quietly shutting the door. Ellowyn sat there a moment, pondering his massive and handsome presence, before being interrupted by a soft knock on the door. Two serving women admitted themselves, carrying a big copper tub between them.

Lined with linen, the tub was dented and very used, but serviceable. Ellowyn remained on the bed, covered up to her ears, as men entered bearing buckets of hot water and proceeded to fill up the tub. She could also see a pair of Brandt's soldiers in the hall, watching everyone who entered and left the room. Already, they were protecting the duchess, Brandt de Russe's lady wife. The thought made her grin.

A serving woman remained behind to help her bathe. Once the water was filled about half way in the tub, the serving woman shut the door and locked it. Ellowyn climbed out of bed and rummaged around in the booty Brandt had brought her until she came across a sack made from dried grass soaked in oil to both strengthen and soften the strands. It was woven tightly and tied with another piece of long grass.

Untying the top, she dumped the bag onto the coverlet and was delighted to find two white, lumpy bars of soap that smelled like orange blossoms, a small bladder that was well-sealed and when opened revealed scented sesame oil for the skin, a wooden brush made with horse-hair bristles, and a decorative hair comb carved from tortoise shell. There was even a little pot of something that looked waxy, was unscented, and that she and the serving woman figured out must have been to keep her lips from cracking. Ellowyn recognized the consistency; she had something similar back at Erith.

Thrilled with the items, she climbed into the bath as the fire in the hearth gained steam and started smoking into the room. After the servant woman doused Ellowyn's hair with the warm water, she went to the window to lift the oil cloth so some of the smoke could escape. Meanwhile, Ellowyn was scrubbing herself furiously with the white soap that had pieces of orange blossom petals in it. The maid took charge of her hair and soaped it up into a slimy lather that took a great deal of water to rinse out. From the top of her head to the bottom of her feet, Ellowyn was soaped and rinsed, feeling warm and wonderful.

But the bath didn't last too long considering Brandt was anxious to get on the road. Once out of the tub, the servant dried Ellowyn with such vigor that her skin turned red and then sparingly rubbed the oil all over her. The result was silky skin that had a delightful smell to it, like flowers on a warm summer day. After that, the servant picked out one of the two new shifts off the bed and put it over Ellowyn's head, sitting her on a stool by the fire as she went to work drying the long blond hair.

The woman worked quickly but not quickly enough; with some of her hair still damp, the servant braided Ellowyn's hair tightly and helped her dress in one of the new garments Brandt had brought her; the shift was pale, soft wool while the surcoat was a finely woven linen dyed a dark blue. It had laced-up ties in the back that, when cinched up, gave Ellowyn an exquisite figure. Working swiftly and silently, the woman cinched it up too tight at first until Ellowyn begged for it to be loosened.

The servant then helped her with her hose and leather boots, and then took one of the two heavy woolen scarves that Brandt had purchased, and draped it over Ellowyn's shoulders, tying it to the rear so it elegantly covered most of her torso. The bright red color was striking; with her luscious figure in the shapely surcoat, red scarf, and braid draping elegantly over one shoulder, she looked every inch the Duchess of Exeter. It was, in fact, a vision not lost on St. Hèver and Alex de Lara when they showed up with a wicker trunk they had purchased from a nearby vegetable merchant.

Two male servants were hauling the half-filled and used bathtub away and the door to the chamber was wide open when the knights appeared. Ellowyn was standing over by the bed, carefully folding her new garments, when a soft knock on the open door distracted her. She looked up to see two armored men smiling at her.

"Come in," she said, waving them in. Then she noticed the trunk they were carrying. "For me? Lovely! I have all of these wonderful things to pack."

The knights set the tightly-woven reed trunk down, tipping it over and shaking out some of the leaves and roots left over from the vegetables that had been stored in it.

"It is all we could find at such short notice, my lady," Brennan said. "It will be serviceable for now, but the duke wishes to purchase you finer trunks when we reach a larger town. We should find more merchants with more of a variety of wares."

Ellowyn was already carefully putting things into the wicker trunk. "This will be fine," she told them. "Where is de Russe?"

"Your husband is outside tending to some business," Alex replied. "He has asked us to escort you outside when you are ready."

She grinned as she rolled up the blue shift and surcoat she had worn the day before. "I meant to ask where my husband is," she said as she turned for the trunk and tucked the garments in. "I have not yet gotten used to calling him that."

"And we have not gotten used to calling you his wife," Alex countered, returning her smile.

"It all seems so new and strange, doesn't it?" Ellowyn asked.

Both Alex and Brennan nodded, inevitably thinking back to the first day they met her. A marriage between their liege and the spitfire of a woman at that time seemed the most unlikely of things. Just like Brandt and Ellowyn, the knights of the duke's command were still getting used to the idea, too.

"It does, indeed," Alex replied quietly.

The sack of dried grass was the last thing to be packed in the wicker basket and Brennan secured the lid. Slinging the trunk over one big shoulder, he took it out of the room as Alex and Ellowyn followed.

The corridor outside was dim as Alex escorted Ellowyn to the stairs. The soldiers that had been guarding the hall were leading the way down the steps into the main room, which was dark and cold at this hour. The innkeeper and his employees were moving around, preparing for the coming day, and smells were wafting from the kitchen that was tucked back into one corner of the inn. Ellowyn most definitely smelled bread and she turned a hungry eye in the direction of the kitchen.

Alex must have sensed her famished state, or at least had already anticipated it, because he was already snapping commands at the kitchen staff. One of the women who had helped with Ellowyn's bath came forth with a basket containing what Ellowyn thought were small loaves of bread. She found out she was very wrong.

"You can take this with you, my lady," the woman handed her the basket, pointing at the contents. "These are little loaves of puffed cakes. I have put butter and honey on them for you. Eat them while they are warm."

Ellowyn was very interested. So was Alex. The quieter, more introspective version of Dylan evidently had a strong interest in food. She picked up a piece of one of the puffed little cakes, which were actually hollow inside, and popped it in her mouth. It was delicious. She offered one to Alex, who gladly took a piece. He, too, thought they were quite delicious.

"What are these puffed cakes made from?" Ellowyn wanted to know, stuffing another one into her mouth.

"Flour, eggs, a little milk and salt," the servant told her. "We bake them in fat and they puff up into little hollow cakes. Sometimes we douse them with gravy, which is also very delicious."

Ellowyn had already put another cake in her mouth by the time the woman had finished explaining how they were made. Alex took the last one. The serving woman ran off with the basket and returned with several more, all hot and delicious with white butter and golden honey soaking into them. She also included several cuts of well-cooked meat, which smelled divinely. It was crispy, salty and greasy, and Alex took a piece before Ellowyn could get to it. He crunched into it the brittle meat, pieces flying out of his mouth. Ellowyn selected her own piece and bit into it.

"What is this wonderful meat?" she asked, mouth full.

The servant woman grinned, displaying the only three discolored teeth she had. "*Bacoun* my lady," she replied. "It is cured, salted, and fried pork."

Ellowyn was sold. "Give me all you have. I suspect it will be stolen from me when the knights smell it."

The old servant was on the move. "I shall return, my lady."

Ellowyn devoured her fill of the puffed-up cakes while waiting for the *bacoun*, leaving a few for Brandt on the assumption he had not yet eaten. When the servant returned with a slab of *bacoun* wrapped in burlap that was quickly soaking with the grease, Alex carried it outside for her but Ellowyn kept shooting him threatening expressions to ensure the temptation of the pungent smell would not lure him into eating it. She wanted it for Brandt, protective and concerned for her new husband. He had displayed as much consideration for her; she would return the favor.

It was still quite misty outside in the breaking dawn. Water coated the buildings, landscape, and people, and there was an icy chill to the air. The army was packed up and ready to depart and Ellowyn could see the knights through the mist, making sure everything was set before they departed for the very long journey to Guildford Castle. As she stood on the stoop of the inn, watching the activity, a carriage pulled up in front of her.

The wheels kicked up some mud so Ellowyn stepped back, out of the way, as the carriage came to a halt. It was a sturdy vehicle with a driver perched at the front of it and an enclosed cab, drawn by two matching gray horses that blended in with the mist and fog. It was in decent condition and she kept waiting for someone to get out of it, but instead, Brandt roared up behind it astride his big black charger. Ellowyn had to move quickly yet again to avoid the splashing mud.

"My lady," Brandt greeted her as he climbed off his steed. His helm was on, his visor up, and his dark eyes were warm on her. "You look astonishingly lovely in your new garments."

Ellowyn felt warm and giddy at the sight of him. "That is because you have remarkable taste, my lord," she flirted gently. "Thank you again for these lovely things."

He looked like a man who was struggling to fight off a grin as he went to her and reached out, taking the hand that wasn't holding the food. He kissed her fingers sweetly, his gaze lingering on her as she grinned coyly at him. It was a sweet little moment. Then, he tilted his head in the direction of the carriage.

"What do you think of your new coach?" he asked.

Ellowyn's eyes widened as she looked at it. "This is for me?"

"Indeed," he replied, putting the warm palm of her hand against his rough cheek. "The livery had it, evidently acquired from a traveling merchant who could not pay them for its storage. The stable master was more than happy to sell it to me."

Ellowyn patted his cheek and removed her hand, stepping closer to the carriage and running a careful eye over it.

"The wheels look to be in good condition," she commented, peering into the cab. It was double-sided, holding passengers on a rear-facing bench and a forward-facing bench. "The leather on the seats seems adequate. How much did you pay for it?"

Brandt wasn't used to being questioned about his monetary transactions but he also knew that Ellowyn was a very astute businesswoman. He could see, in that moment, that his financial freedom and control was about to change; Ellowyn was used to controlling the purse strings for her family and he realized that was going to be the case within their marriage as well. It was the natural order of things. He felt very much as if he was answering to her as he replied.

"Five gold marks," he told her. "When we reach Guildford, I have a particularly talented smithy that will restore it like new."

Her eyebrows lifted at him. "Five gold marks?" she repeated, looking back at the carriage. "That seems a bit much. Perhaps I should speak with him and renegotiate the price."

Brandt fought off a grin. "Not today," he told her, opening up the door to the cab. "If we had the time, I would let you barter to your heart's content, but we must depart immediately unless you are keen to having your father catch up to us."

She sighed, perhaps in agreement, and he took it as a sign to assist her into the cab before she could argue further with him. Scooping her into his arms, he swept her up into the cab, depositing her neatly onto the seat. Alex, standing next to the carriage, handed her the wrapped *bacoun* through the window. Before she could thank him, Brandt sent the man back inside the inn on an errand to collect a heavy coverlet for his wife. Alex was off but the smell of the *bacoun* was heavy in the air as Ellowyn held the greasy parcel in her hand.

"Have you broken your fast yet?" she asked Brandt. "I have some wonderful food for you."

Brandt shook his head. "No time," he said. "We must depart."

He started to move away but she stopped him, unwrapping the *bacoun* and extending a piece to him.

"Here," she said in a tone that left no opportunity for declination. "Eat this. You must keep up your strength and we have a long ride ahead of us."

Brandt reached for the meat because she told him to. Also, he didn't want to upset her. It was easier to do as she asked rather than argue or refuse her. So he shoved it into his mouth and started to walk away when he realized that it was very good. He turned to say something to her about it but she shoved thrust more at him, plus the basket of still-warm puffy cakes. She told him to take one, so he did, putting everything in his mouth and chewing it all down.

She was directing him to eat so he did, like a child being directed by his mother, and in little time he had scarfed down everything. He had crumbs and grease on his expensive gloves but he didn't give it any notice; it was odd behavior from a man who did not take orders from anyone, now being bossed around by a slip of a woman. But he didn't give it any thought and neither did Ellowyn; again, it seemed to be the natural order of things and Brandt submitted quite willingly, loving it and not even realizing he was loving it. He was simply doing as he was told. It was the beginning of contentment he had never before experienced, a relationship with a woman he had never known to exist. It was symbiotic in every sense.

Shaking the crumbs off his fingers, he leaned into the door of the cab and kissed Ellowyn, mute thanks for being thoughtful enough to feed him. As he pulled his head out of the cab, he happened to glance at his knights standing several feet away; Dylan, Magnus, Stefan and Brennan were all watching him with rather curious expressions on their faces. They had never seen anyone order Brandt around, either, and they were somewhat stunned by the fact that Ellowyn was tending to the man like a mother to her child. The mighty Duke of Exeter had a wife who brought out a softer side of the man they'd never seen before and their astonishment was understandable.

When they realized that Brandt was looking at them, they suddenly began moving about as if they had something better to do. Magnus and Stefan actually bumped into each other in their haste to scatter.  Alex came out of the inn at that moment, bearing a coverlet and a pillow he had confiscated from the bed Ellowyn and Brandt had slept on the night before.   He handed both items to Brandt, who turned away from his confused knights long enough to put the pillow behind Ellowyn's back and cover her with the heavy blanket.

"There you are," he said, tucking the coverlet around her legs. "You will be much more comfortable traveling like this."

Ellowyn's brow furrowed. "But the carriage will slow us down considerably," she pointed out. "With my father pursuing us, I could just as easily ride a horse."

He shook his head. "You will let me worry about that," he said. "This carriage will travel much faster than you think providing the roads are in good repair."

"And if they are not?"

"Then we shall have to remedy the situation at that time. Until then, enjoy the ride."

With that, he took her hand and kissed it before securing the cab door closed.  Ellowyn could hear him speaking with Dylan and the subsequent shouts of the knights as the men began to move out.  The carriage lurched forward and she yelped, surprised, before settling in as the vehicle pulled out onto the road. Fortunately, the road was indeed in good repair so the ride was relatively smooth.

Chargers raced past the carriage, heading to the front of the column, and she caught sight of a big black beast as it whirled by the small carriage window.  In new clothing and bundled up against the chill weather, Ellowyn had truthfully never traveled in such luxury and she wasn't hard pressed to admit she liked it.

For a short while, she watched the mist-shrouded landscape pass through the small window, her mind wandering back to Erith and her family, wondering if her father was indeed planning to pursue.  She wondered if her grandmother had confessed her part in the escape, and if Lady Gray had talked her father out of his vengeance.  She wondered if her father would even listen.

Not an hour into her journey south, Ellowyn fell asleep against the gently rocking carriage.

# CHAPTER FIFTEEN

*Guildford Castle*

Thirteen days after the hasty departure from Erith Castle, the soaring keep of Guildford came into view.

Seated in her carriage playing a card game from a deck of lovely painted cards that Brandt had purchased for her in the larger berg of Warrington about a week prior, Ellowyn heard the shouts of the men as their home was finally within sight. Sticking her head out of the window, she caught sight of the big white keep on the horizon, a pale-looking mountain against the deep blue sky.

Cards still in hand, she looked around the nearest knight. There was always a knight riding near her coach, usually her husband, but today he was at the head of the column. She spied Magnus and waved him over.

"Is that Guildford?" she asked, pointing to the sight in the distance.

De Reyne nodded his helmed head. "Indeed, Lady de Russe," he said. "We will be there within the hour."

She shielded her eyes from the sun. "It seems so far away," she murmured. Then she removed her hand and looked at Magnus. "Do you think that Brennan and Alex have reached their homes yet?"

St. Hèver and Alex de Lara had been sent to their respective father's holdings almost two weeks before to seek men and material for Brandt's return to France. Their absences had been felt, mostly by Ellowyn who had become friendly with Brennan. He would talk to her as they rode along keeping her company when Brandt could not. The other knights just seemed to keep a polite distance with her. With the big blond knight missing, she had been rather lonely.

"I am sure they arrived at their destinations several days ago," Magnus replied. "In fact, I would not be surprised if they were already on their way to Guildford."

"How many men do you suppose they will be bringing?"

Magnus shrugged. "That is difficult to say," he replied. "The Duke of Carlisle has an enormous compliment of men, but he is close to the Scots border and does not like to diminish his strength. The same can be said for the Earl of Wrexham on the Welsh Marches."

She was thoughtful. "Then perhaps my husband will need to solicit men elsewhere."

"That is a distinct possibility, my lady."

Ellowyn though on the fact that Brandt might need to spend more time in England before heading back to France and the thought did not displease her. As she pondered that possibility, she began looking around, taking an interest in the landscape for the first time in days.

"It seems as if I have been caged in this coach for years," she said, shielding her eyes from the sun again. "I have not paid much attention to the lands we have passed through. It seems rather flat around here, does it not?"

Magnus looked around, too. "You come from land that has many mountains and valleys," he said. "Compared to that, it is indeed rather flat around here. You have never been this far south?"

She shook her head. "I have been to London, of course, but never this far south. The castle rather looks like a mountain amongst all of this flat land."

Magnus wriggled his eyebrows. "Do not let this land deceive you. It is very rich soil. The farmers make a small fortune off of their crops, which in turn makes the duke a very wealthy man."

Ellowyn simply nodded, watching closely as the village surrounding Guildford came into view. She could see a church, built from pale stone in a squat and powerful design, and the cloister surrounding it. There were people out tending the fields, beasts of burden pulling plows as the serfs toiled in the dirt. The weather was very moderate; in fact, it was rather warm and there were few clouds in the vibrant sky. The ground didn't seem to be saturated with too much rain as the land she came from tended to be, but the fields and hedges were very green and overgrown.

On the edge of the town, the gutters were full of muck as they drew closer to the areas of human habitation. With the warmth of the day, the smell of urine and feces wafted in the air now and again. Children ran about with their friends, playing games, while other children hauled buckets or accomplished tasks for their masters.

There were a great many people milling about and Ellowyn put her cards away to watch the comings and goings. She was so involved, in fact, that she hardly noticed when the column came to a halt. She only noticed when de Reyne slammed his face plate shut and bolted in the direction of the castle. Suddenly, men were shouting in chorus and the carriage was turned around, nearly tipping it at the speed in which it was moving, and making haste away from the castle.

The cards scattered, and Ellowyn held on for dear life.

***

Hours later, the town was vacant and people were in hiding as the sun began to set on a bright and glorious day. A half mile from Guildford Castle, Brandt had set up a small encampment but it wasn't meant for rest; it was in preparation for a battle.

Ellowyn sat in Brandt's tent with her cards, her possessions, and her husband's material comforts. The flat copper disc was once again called into service and it sat in the middle of the tent, raised on stones, and burning a small pile of wood for warmth. Smoke escaped through the hatch in the room. It was the same tent she had stayed in nearly every night, with rare exception, for almost three weeks. She and the tent were friends now. A boring friend, but a comfort nonetheless. She was thinking on giving it a name.

Seated on a heavy rug atop the ground, she lay her cards out absently, playing a solitary game, before losing track of what she was doing and collecting the cards, only to shuffle them out again. She knew something was going on but no one had come to tell her what it was. She knew it had something to do with the castle but beyond that, she had no idea. Boredom was settling heavy on her and she was thinking of putting her cards away altogether when she heard voices close by.

One of the voices was Brandt; he was giving a directive to someone, more than likely Dylan. The two men were practically inseparable. Ellowyn watched the tent flap with anticipation, cards still in her hands, waiting for Brandt to make an appearance. She didn't have to wait long.

He blew into the shelter, slapping back the tent flap so violently that he nearly pulled half the tent down. Ellowyn put her arms over her head as the tent lurched dangerously but Brandt managed to steady it. When Ellowyn finally lowered her arms and looked at him, he smiled sheepishly.

"Greetings," he said softly, perhaps wearily. He let go of the supporting pole and made his way towards her. "Have you eaten?"

She shook her head. "Not yet."

He pulled off his helmet with a heavy sigh, tossing it on to the pile of his possessions. "Good," he muttered, scratching his scalp as he faced her. "Then we may at least share a meal together. Considering I have not seen you all day, I am grateful for whatever time I can spend with you."

Ellowyn watched the man, his exhausted movements, his pale and shadowed face. He stood there, pulling off his gauntlets as she watched him closely. His expression was hard, his eyes distant.

"What is the matter?" she asked softly. "Why are we here and not within the walls of Guildford Castle?"

Brandt tossed the gloves down and rubbed at his eyes. "Because it would seem that Arundel is occupying my castle," he said, looking at her. "He says that the king asked him to garrison my property while I was in France but I know that to be a lie. I have given him until the sun sets to be off the grounds."

"Or what?"

He sighed again. "Or I will lay siege and kill every one of Arundel's men," he said. Then, he grunted ironically. "Fitzalan and I have fought together, many times. I know the man. He thought perhaps that I would not return from France and set about staking his claim early for my holdings."

Ellowyn was confused by the entire situation. "Is he your enemy, then?"

Brandt shook his head. "He is a greedy bastard. His father and my father had a tenuous relationship and the son carries on the tradition. He occupies my castle while I am away, takes my revenue, rapes my lands...." He righted a stool that had been lying near his bedroll and planted it next to where Ellowyn was sitting. He plopped on it heavily. "When I docked in London, I had over two thousand men with me. When we departed for Erith, I sent three-quarters of my men here with sixteen of my lesser knights. Arundel's commander tells me that when the army tried to return to Guildford, he sent them to one of my lesser castles at Farnborough. De Reyne and several soldiers ride there now to collect them and bring them back here. I have sent le Bec to Canterbury for reinforcements."

Ellowyn cocked her head. "You are allied with Canterbury?"

He nodded. "The House of de Russe and the House of de Lohr have long been allied," he replied, rubbing at his eyes again before refocusing on her. "James de Lohr, the Earl of Canterbury, is a friend. Le Bec can make it to Canterbury in a few days, but we cannot expect reinforcements from de Lohr for a couple of weeks at the earliest. I am therefore hoping that Arundel's commander obeys my directive and vacates my castle by the dictated time."

Ellowyn gazed up at him as he rubbed his eyes again. The man was so very weary, burdened by days and months and years of strife. She began to think back to moments when she had seen her father weary or in particular pain, and how her mother had rubbed away the worries and the ache. It always seemed to work for her father. Perhaps it would work with Brandt. She felt strongly that she needed to do something for the man; he appeared edgy and brittle.

Silently, she stood up and moved in behind him as he sat on the stool. Brandt tried to turn around to look at her but she put her hands on either side of his head, forcing him to face forward. With her hands still on his head, she got in behind him so that she was right up against his back. His head was level with her breasts.

"Relax your head," she murmured, gently pulling it back so it was resting against her chest. "Just... relax."

Brandt did as he was told, leaning his head back slightly until it came to rest against her. He didn't even ask her why; he simply did as she asked. He was rewarded for his obedience when Ellowyn's fingers began to gently massage his sweaty scalp, his temples. It was heavenly. Brandt groaned with delight and closed his eyes as Ellowyn proceeded to rub his head, her fingers applying slight pressure, ironing out the worries and stress he was overloaded with. Her gentle fingers moved all over his scalp and forehead, and partially down his neck but his hauberk prevented her from doing much with his neck and shoulders.

So she focused on his head, rubbing his temples and tenderly stroking his forehead. It was a gentle touch, a loving touch, something Brandt had never experienced before. He had so much on his mind; the weight of a young prince's dreams and the expectations of the royal father. If he failed, Edward failed, and the monarchy's quest in France failed. Everything rested on one man's shoulders. Days like today, he felt the burden more heavily than others.

Ellowyn seemed to sense that. By magic or intuition, she seemed to sense what was troubling him and was prepared to do what she could to help him in a way he'd never been helped before. It was on a deeper level, an emotional level, and he'd never known such comfort. He was quickly becoming languid, dozing, enjoying every rub, every stroke. He felt her kiss the top of his dirty head.

"You have had a very trying day," she whispered. "Right now, at this moment, I want you to think of nothing else but peace and relaxation. Can you do this?"

His eyes were closed as he leaned back against her. "I can try," he mumbled.

She smiled at his sleepy reply. "I want you to think of a peaceful lake on a warm summer's day, and of cool grass beneath your feet," she murmured. "I want you to think of me sitting next to you on the shores of this lake. I want you to...."

She was cut off by a rattling snore. She laughed softly, continuing to rub his head, pleased that he had fallen asleep against her. At least for a few moments, she had given him that peace she had hoped for. The poor man was exhausted.

As she stood there and rubbed his head, she realized it was the first time she had seen the man with his guard down. Even in times of intimacy between them, and there had been several since they had been married, he hadn't fully let his guard down. There was always some manner of control to his behavior. But at this moment, he was at his most vulnerable. Underneath all of the pomp and circumstance, he was just a man with all of the needs of a man. Ellowyn intended to provide for those needs. She intended to take care of him.

Brandt's snoring was deep and even. He was dead asleep against her, sitting up, as she massaged his scalp. It went on for several minutes until the tent flap slapped back again and Dylan appeared. Before he could say anything, Ellowyn barred her teeth at him threateningly and he came to a wide-eyed halt, seeing that Brandt was sleeping the sleep of the dead as his wife drilled her fingers into his head.

"Wake him and you shall feel my wrath," she hissed softly. "Let him rest, for Pity's sake."

Dylan's gaze moved from her face to Brandt's and back again. He was apologetic. "Forgive me, my lady," he said quietly but politely. "He must know that Arundel is on the move. They are vacating the castle."

Brandt's head popped up and he was on his feet before Ellowyn realized it. "Well and good," he growled, moving for his helmet and slapping it back on his head. "Is the portcullis lifted yet?"

"Aye, my lord."

"Then move my troops in and make sure anything that is Arundel is cleaned out," he said. "I do not want that man's stench in my castle."

Ellowyn ran after him. "Wait!" she called. "Where are you going?"

He paused before quitting the tent and she bumped into the back of him. He took her hand and brought it to his lips for a sweet kiss.

"I will return," he assured her, looking remarkably awake for a man who had been passed out moments earlier. "You will remain here until I do. I will have someone bring you something to eat."

She peered at him closely. "Are you well?" she asked, concerned. "You were so exhausted and...."

He kissed her hand again, her palm, and her lips swiftly in that order, cutting her off. "I can move mountains," he assured her quietly. "You, Lady de Russe, have that effect on me."

She smiled as he winked at her and quit the tent. She could hear his voice outside, relaying orders and receiving information. Listening to his strong, confident voice kept the smile on her face for some time to come. Returning to her cards, she settled in to wait for Guildford to be cleared.

## CHAPTER SIXTEEN

It was a spectacular castle.

Near sunset, Ellowyn's carriage was escorted into the extensive grounds of Guildford Castle and gazing from the coach window, she could immediately see the majesty and wealth of the Duke of Exeter. The castle was truly something to behold.

The entire complex was surrounded by a massive ditch that was partially filled with water. It was a moat of sorts, with steep sides that made it treacherous and uninviting. An enormous gatehouse built into the colossal outerwall protected a vast bailey that contained a number of wood and stone outbuildings and stables, the roofs heavily thatched. It looked like an entire little village in the bailey.

The most obvious feature of Guildford was the gargantuan motte, or hill, on the northern edge of the complex upon which a tall, block-shaped keep had been built. There was another moat around the motte and there were any number of defense structures surrounding the motte, most notably the dozens of spiked logs jutting out from the sides of the hill. It gave the motte a rather terrifying and unenticing appearance.

As the carriage pulled through the bailey, Ellowyn could see Brandt and Dylan standing at the base of the stairs that led up the side of the motte to the keep on the top. They were speaking with three knights, all of them dressed for battle, and as the carriage drew close, Ellowyn saw Dylan advance menacingly towards the three unknown knights. Brandt put out an arm to stop the man, eventually putting himself between Dylan and the knights. His demeanor seemed to be very threatening. As Ellowyn watched, Brandt lashed out a massive fist and caught one of the knights squarely in the face. He sailed backwards, into his companions, and the entire trio went down.

The carriage turned away from the view and she could no longer see what was happening as it eventually came to a halt.

Before anyone could assist her from the coach, Ellowyn opened the door herself and climbed out. The first thing she did is rush straight to Brandt and the knights now picking themselves off the ground.

"Are these the men who tried to steal your castle?" she asked.

Brandt hadn't seen her coming; she had run up behind him and caught him off guard. He turned to say something to her but she was already fixed on the knights who were now standing, one of them with his hand to his face. Ellowyn advanced on the group, fingers pointing.

"Are you Arundel's men?" she demanded.

The man with the hand over his bloodied nose scowled at her. "Who in the hell are you?"

Ellowyn felt Brandt come up behind her, preparing to deliver another crushing blow for the harsh question, but she put out a hand to stop him. She was used to taking charge because Deston had let her; it seemed that her behavior and sense of control would not be contained in a different environment. Wherever she was, she was in control. She was well prepared to punish and scold, protecting what was hers. She was not afraid.

"I am Lady de Russe," she said, her tone hazardous, "and you have usurped the castle belonging to my husband, the Duke of Exeter. How on earth your liege thought a challenge like this would go unnoticed and unanswered is beyond me, for it was a foolish and ridiculous attempt, and you may tell him I said so. You may also tell him that we fully expect reparation for the year's worth of revenue he stole from my husband, an accounting of which I will send to him with in the week. If we do not receive immediate compensation for Arundel's thievery, I will send a thousand men to claim what is rightfully ours from every farm, village, church, and individual within a twenty mile radius of Arundel until the debt is paid. Is this is any way unclear so far?"

She had delivered the demands so succinctly, so smoothly, that the three knights were staring at her with some shock and a hint of intimidation. Brandt and Dylan, standing behind her, were equally astonished. The knight with the bloodied nose nodded after a moment.

"Aye, Lady de Russe," he replied.

Ellowyn wasn't finished. "You will further tell your lord that I am personally offended by his attempts to confiscate my husband's property and he has earned my great displeasure for the angst and strife he has put my husband through. An offense against my husband is an offense against me. He had better think of some way to ease my displeasure and pray that I am in forgiving mood when he presents his case. I will expect his full and unrestrained apology when he delivers the compensation for what my husband is owed. Do you understand?"

"I do, my lady."

"Get out of my sight."

The knight and his comrades turned away from her, swiftly, and made haste towards the stables. Ellowyn watched them go before turning to Brandt and Dylan, still standing behind her.

"There," she said decisively, as if she had just finished some manner of simple business that she conducted every day. "Now, will you show me this magnificent keep?"

Brandt was staring at her. He was still rather stunned with her aggressive behavior but strangely, it did not displease him. He was rather amused. He was also rather proud. It was the same manner she had used when they had first met, only he had been on the receiving end just as Arundel's knights had been. The more he saw of Ellowyn, the more he liked.

"Lady, your negotiation skills are a force to be reckoned with," he said, a twinkle in his dark eyes. "Those men never stood a chance."

She cocked an eyebrow and took his elbow. "Which do you think they would choose to face? My ultimatum or your fist?"

He grinned, patting the hand on his elbow as he turned in the direction of the keep. "My fist, without question."

Ellowyn's expression softened and a grin surfaced. "Unfortunately, today they received both. They will think twice before they attempt to take your castle again."

He simply lifted his eyebrows. "Of that I have no doubt."

The keep of Guildford was strictly for the duke's residence, as Ellowyn quickly discovered. After mounting a long flight of steep and at times treacherous stairs, the keep itself was three storied, with a big armory on the lower floor, accessible by an exterior door. A wooden flight of stairs led to the first floor of the keep, which only contained one big room with a massive fireplace, and a latrine. Brandt used the room as his solar, his war room when he was in residence. There was a big oak table, scattered rubbish, and a pair of dogs near the hearth, but for the most part, the room looked stripped.

A very narrow spiral staircase built into the wall of the keep led to another big room on the second floor. This was Brandt's bed chamber, but Ellowyn could see from the expression on his face that it was not how he left it. It had been looted and items scattered, just like the solar below. There was a wardrobe and an enormous bed that was a big, jumbled mess. Surveying the chaos, Brandt shook his head.

"I apologize for the state of the room," he said. "Whoever was staying here was most careless."

Ellowyn ventured into the room, surveying the chamber as she went. When she came to the bed, she peered at the linens and coverlet without touching them. She made a face when she saw the state of the linen.

"No matter," she said, eyeing the bed distastefully before turning to him. "I shall clean it up. Are there any women servants to assist me?"

Brandt shook his head. "I did not keep female servants," he replied. "They are far too much trouble. My father never had female servants, either."

Ellowyn eyed the dirty bed again. "Then if you can simply provide me with two or three soldiers, I can make due. It is apparent that this keep has not seen a woman's hand in some time. It shows."

"I will not dispute that point."

Ellowyn began to remove her wrap and gloves. "Not to worry," she said. "I shall make this place livable in no time."

A smile creased his lips. "Of that I have no doubt," he said softly. "If it will make your life easier, then I will find a few female servants to assist you."

She pulled the gloves off, looking at him. "I would appreciate it," she said. Then she started rattling off her priorities. "But until they arrive, I will need lye and vinegar and... oh, never mind. I can find it myself. I am sure you have more important duties to attend to."

She was taking charge again. "Nothing is more important than you," he said softly.

Ellowyn paused in her bustle, eyeing him with a somewhat flirtatious smile. "That is a very sweet statement," she said. "You are becoming quite adept at being sweet to me."

He wriggled his eyebrows. "It is becoming easier with practice."

"You may practice all you wish."

They grinned at each other for a moment until he made his way over to her and wrapped her up in his big arms. She was sweet and soft and supple, smelling of that lovely sesame oil that made her skin so soft. He nuzzled her neck, inhaling her fragrance, losing himself in her deliciousness.

"This place has been in my family for many years," he murmured. "It is where I was born, in this very room in fact. But it has only been a possession. It has never been a home. Perhaps it is the closest thing I have to a home, however. Now, with you in its walls, perhaps... perhaps it will start to feel more like a home for my heart than a house for my body. Perhaps it will become something that means something to me rather than just a possession where I lay my head. Does that make any sense?"

Ellowyn pulled away to look him in the eye. "You lied to me."

He looked shocked. "When did I do such a disgraceful thing?"

She smiled, touching his rough cheek. "You told me you were not good with word, but you lied," she murmured. "You are very good with words. You say the most wonderful things."

His soft expression returned. "You have made it easy," he whispered. "You have made a great many things easy for me, Wynny. It has endeared you to me more than you can possibly know."

Gazing into his magnificent face, Ellowyn was struck with how much she loved the man. She didn't know exactly when it had happened, but as she looked at him, she couldn't remember when she hadn't loved him. Powerful, commanding, handsome, kind, and sometimes socially awkward, Brandt had quickly come to mean everything to her. And then he was going to go back to France and leave her all alone. The knowledge of that tore her to shreds and tears filled her eyes. She threw her arms around his neck, squeezing him tightly.

Brandt had seen the tears no matter how quickly she had moved to hide them. He held her snuggly, his face in the side of her head.

"Why do you weep?" he murmured. "What is the matter?"

She shook her head. Then, she sobbed. "I do not want you to leave me," she whispered tightly. "Brandt, the thought of you returning to France, the thought of us being separated, claws at me like a great fanged beast. Being apart from you will surely kill me."

He didn't say anything. He simply continued to hold her, but the truth was that he was thinking very heavily on what she had said. Although he didn't want to admit it, he was becoming increasingly distraught at the thought of leaving her behind as well. He knew he had to, but that didn't change the emotions he was feeling. He loosened his grip on her, taking her face between his two great hands.

"If I said that the mere thought does not eat away at me as well, I would be lying," he muttered, his dark eyes boring into her. "But I know, as a warrior, that I cannot bring you with me. My thoughts would be on you constantly, worrying over you or dreaming of you, and that would be the death of me. If my mind is not on what I am doing, then it makes it easier for someone to kill me. Do you understand?"

She sniffled, nodding her head as she wiped her eyes. "I do," she said, unhappy. "I hate that I do, but I understand."

He rubbed her cheeks with his thumbs, kissing her forehead. "I find myself in a very peculiar position right now," he said. "My focus, my career, has always been on Edward. Until I met you, I was anxious to return to him. Now I am not anxious at all. I am dreading it."

"As am I."

He sighed sadly and kissed her forehead again. "Then let us make the most of this time together. Let us build happy memories to cling to for the times we are separated. I promise I will not bring up my departure to France in your presence until such time my departure is imminent. I will not constantly remind you of something we are trying to ignore. Is that acceptable?"

She frowned. "When are you departing?"

He was serious. "Four weeks at the most."

Ellowyn closed her eyes, already miserable although she was struggling not to be. Finally, she nodded. "Very well," she whispered. "We will pretend you are not leaving and that you shall always be with me."

He put a finger under her chin, tipping her head up. He kissed her softly on the mouth. "I will always be with you no matter where I am," he kissed her again. "My heart is with you, Wynny. Surely you know that."

She gazed into his dark eyes, unable to control herself. "I do love you, Brandt," she murmured. "Always remember that. You have all of me."

His features when through the range of emotions - shock, realization, and finally awe. He wrapped her up in a fierce embrace, squeezing the breath from her.

"Wynny, my love," he murmured. "I do not know what to say except...."

Ellowyn buried her face in his neck, trying to avoid the chain mail. "Except what?"

"Except... I am sorry I called you a whore when we first met."

Ellowyn froze, her eyes flying open. Then, she pulled her face from the crook of his neck, looking at him with such surprise that her mouth popped open. Brandt looked back at her with equal surprise until she broke down into screaming laughter. Soon, the two of them were howling with laughter, so much so that Ellowyn was nearly weak with it. She struggled to catch her breath.

"It was probably the best thing you ever did," she chortled. "As sweet and slick as a marriage proposal."

He shook with mirth. "I was at my most charming that day."

She shook her head, wiping the happy tears from her eyes. "You are a devil, Brandt de Russe."

He grabbed her face and kissed her soundly. "Aye, but I am *your* devil, Wynny. I am your devoted, humble, and loving devil."

She sobered as he kissed her, the moment so warm and fluid between them. "Do you love me, Brandt?"

He slowed his aggressive kisses, running his hands over her soft cheeks. "I have never loved anyone before but I suspect that I do. What I am feeling for you could only be love."

She grinned, returning his sweet kisses, until they turned amorous. The fire that ignited so easily between them roared to life. Brandt picked her up and headed to the bed, but she balked.

"Nay," she breathed. "Not on that mess. It is filthy and full of bugs."

Brandt hardly slowed down. He began pulling off his gloves, unfastening the ties of her girdle with a free hand. Ellowyn felt his sense of urgency, feeding off of it, and in little time she had her surcoat off, helping Brandt with his mail. It was more cumbersome to undress him but they managed it, everything from the waist up. His broad, muscular chest drew her lust and she kissed his chest, toying with his nipples just as he toyed with hers.

Brandt yanked the shift over her head, leaving her clad in her hose and boots. She had a fabulous figure, soft and round in the right places, and already he was suckling her breasts and fondling her buttocks, pulling her up against him. She had such soft skin and he lapped it up, starving for her. Nothing on earth fueled him like she did.

Ellowyn, meanwhile, managed to unfasten his breeches but he had to lower them; he could do it faster, anyway. With his breeches down around his knees, he turned her around, braced her arms against the bed post, and lifted her buttocks up against his pelvis. His manhood, hard and demanding, thrust into her from behind.

Since he was so much taller than she was, he had to literally hold her up off the ground as he thrust into her. It was nothing for his considerable strength. Ellowyn gripped the bed post, wrapping her legs around him as he drove into her soft and yielding body. He had a firm grip of her pelvis, holding it tightly against him, his gaze on her slender back and supple buttocks, driving him insane with desire.

Bending over, he wrapped a big arm around her torso, holding her against him as his free hand roamed her breasts, delighting in the silken texture. Then his fingers moved to the curls between her legs, fingering her, listening to her gasp and groan as he stroked her. He felt her release and he answered shortly, spilling his seed deep into her womb.

Still embedded in her, he held her close, kissing her back, stroking her breasts gently, digesting everything about the woman that he was so closely joined with. Every tremor, every breath, every sigh was engrained in his brain. She was becoming a part of his very makeup, the fibers of his being. As he stood there and held her, his body still joined to hers, his mouth was against her back.

"Aye, I love you," he whispered into her flesh. "I will never love another."

Eyes closed, trying to catch her breath, Ellowyn could only smile.

# CHAPTER SEVENTEEN

*The dream was back, picking up where it had left off.*

*She had no idea what her grandfather was pointing at. Through the rain and mist, all she could see was mud and dead bodies. Even this far away from that horrid, smoking castle, the bodies were thick. So many dead.*

*Her heart was pounding in her throat, her hand on her belly as the child kicked. The kicking was becoming painful, in fact, and she rubbed at her belly as she tried to see what her grandfather was pointing at.*

*There, Wynny, he said. Do you not see him there?*

*She was frantic as she tried to determine what he was talking about. There was something in the distance to catch her attention, something deep and dark and ugly. She could feel it. She wanted to know what he was pointing at but then again, she didn't want to know.*

*Who is it, Papa? she cried.*

*Her grandfather simply pointed, his handsome face edged with sadness.*

*Go to him, Wynny. You must save him.*

*Frustrated, terrified, she began to cry. The baby kicked, painfully, and she cried harder. But she could see something through the rain and mist beneath the trees in the distance. It was a man in armor, lying beneath the canopy. There was blood all around him, the color of a ruby In an otherwise black and white and gray landscape, it was the only spot of gruesome color.*

*She tried to move towards him but the mud had become a great sucking cauldron, refusing to let her move. She clawed at it, scratching her way towards the man lying beneath the trees. The hands of the dead began to sprout up through the mud, grabbing at her, clutching at her.*

*She screamed.*

\*\*\*

During those first few days of the duke's return to Guildford, the servants, soldiers, and knights would be hard-pressed for an answer when asked who the sterner task-master was - the duke or his wife. Popular opinion was leaning towards the formidable and lovely Lady de Russe as she took over the castle like a conquering hero.

The evening they took possession of the castle and keep, Brandt had sent four soldiers to assist his wife in making the keep habitable to her standards, which wasn't a simple or quick task. Ellowyn had very high standards. The first thing she did was set a giant iron pot to boiling in the kitchen yard and ask the soldiers to find some lye. A search of the entire castle didn't turn up a trace of it, so Ellowyn set forth making some. She'd seen the women at Erith make it dozens of times so she understood the simple process. In order to effectively clean, she had to have lye.

One of the soldiers found her an old wine barrel, which she had propped up on some stones so that it was off the ground. Then, she had the soldiers put rocks all over the bottom of the barrel and covered the rocks with a thin layer of hay before making a hole near the base and plugging it up with another rock.

With all of that done, she had them make a fire of oak. The hard wood burned long and low, so it wasn't until the next morning that they had the desired ash from the burning. While waiting for the oak to burn down, Brandt had tried to talk her into sleeping on the dirty bed but she wouldn't touch it, so he fashioned a pallet for them on the floor of the chamber and they slept on that. His first night back at his castle had him sleeping on the cold, hard floor, but he didn't mind. As long as he had Ellowyn in his arms, he was a content man. However, she didn't sleep very well at all. She had cried and muttered all night in her sleep.

At dawn the next day, Ellowyn made no mention of her restless night. She was more concerned with her chores. The oak wood had burned away overnight and she had her pile of ashes, so she had the men scoop up the white flakes and pour it into the barrel along with gallons of rainwater. The white mix blended, settled, and sat for three days while Brandt and the other men went about their business, watching Lady de Russe's mysterious experiment carefully. Ellowyn, too, went about her business of doing what she could to clean up the keep but everything was really dependent upon the lye she was making. It would be the key ingredient to a clean keep of her standards.

At the end of the third day, Ellowyn took an egg from the chicken coop and, opening the barrel, cracked the egg into the murky water. Brandt, Dylan, Stefan, and her four helpers watched curiously as the egg floated on the top and Ellowyn declared her satisfaction. The lye was sufficiently leeched. Unplugging the hole and the bottom of the barrel, she had her assistants fill buckets with the white stuff, now ready to be used.

The giant iron pot was filled with water again and put to a boil along with a bucketful of the white lye concoction. The bed linens were all thrown into the pot and the massive bed was broken down, brought outside, and scrubbed with lye.

Meanwhile, Ellowyn and one of the soldiers went inside and began scrubbing the floors and walls down with the lye. When Brandt caught sight of his lovely wife on her knees, scrubbing like a washer woman, he sent Stefan into the village to acquire servant women to do the dirty work. He had promised her, after all, and the truth was that it had slipped his mind until he saw her on the floor with a horse bristle brush in her hands. Then, he was fired into action.

Stefan returned with four women by the evening, a widow and her three daughters, and Ellowyn was thrilled. She had already managed to scrub most of the bed chamber but was happy to turn it over to someone else. While two of the daughters got to work finishing the master's bower, Ellowyn spoke to the old widow, Miss Maude, and discovered that she was mostly deaf but seemingly very willing to work and very knowledgeable. Ellowyn put the old woman to work with the now-boiled bed linens while the third daughter, a surprisingly attractive red-head, started to work on scrubbing down the solar.

The keep was lit up with torches that the soldiers had ignited when the sun began to set. The narrow windows of the keep made it a fairly dark place, even in broad daylight, so there were a variety of wall sconces for the torches and black soot on the walls above them. Satisfied that her new worker women were proceeding nicely with their tasks, Ellowyn went in search of her husband.

Descending the long and edgy stairs that led down the motte and into the bailey, she headed for the great hall. It was nearing supper time and she could smell the roasting meat.

A few soldiers and male servants were already in the hall, milling about. It was a long and slender room with a greatly angled thatched roof and a massive fireplace built of stone against the southern wall. The chimney wasn't in good repair so smoke seeped into the room, clouding up near the ceiling. Two long, well-used tables filled the room, each one of them seating at least thirty men.

Ellowyn hadn't really made it into the feasting hall since her arrival because she and Brandt had taken their meals in the keep, and she hadn't much been out of the big stone structure. But now, she looked about with interest as an old male servant put fresh bread upon the feasting table. It was brown bread, course, but there was plenty of it. Ellowyn got the man's attention.

"Have you seen the duke?" she asked.

The old man was very old and very tiny. He shook his head. "Nay, my lady," he replied. "He has not been here."

Ellowyn's face twisted thoughtfully. She looked around the room, her thoughts moving from one to the other.

"What is your name?" she asked the servant.

"Gilbert, my lady," he replied.

"Who does the cooking here?"

Gilbert pointed to his right, towards a darkened alcove. She could see an open door at the end of the alcove.

"Servants, my lady," he replied. "Men servants. They served the duke's father."

Ellowyn's eyebrows lifted. "They must be very old."

Gilbert simply nodded, both fearfully and eagerly, and skittered after Ellowyn as she proceeded through the alcove and out of the feasting hall.

The kitchen yard was vast, backing up all the way to the outer wall. There were various small structures; chicken coop, pig pen, goats roaming free, sheep penned near the outerwall, a buttery that was made of uneven gray stone and resembled a bee hive. There was also an enormous stone oven that was blazing in the early evening and a fire pit near the oven contained a carcass of a sheep, roasting on the open flame.

Everything was fairly open, unlike the kitchen at Erith that was actually enclosed on the lower level of the keep. There were two big, burly men carting around sides of meat and other things, obviously preparing for the coming meal. Gilbert, a nervous little man, made haste to run them both down and bring them to Ellowyn.

As the men drew near, Ellowyn could see that they were indeed quite old. If they served Brandt's father, then they had to be nearly ancient. One man was big and bald, perhaps once muscular that had now gone to fat, and the other man had long gray hair, huge hands, and was missing an eye. Ellowyn was a bit taken aback at the 'cooks' of Guildford. She had only known women cooks, not two old men who looked more like thieves or murderers.

"I am Lady de Russe," she said, introducing herself. "I wanted to see who it was that prepares the meals for the duke."

The two big men bowed to her while Gilbert fluttered at her side nervously. "This is John, my lady," Gilbert said, pointing to the man with the long gray hair. "His companion is Lune. Lune cannot speak, my lady, but he will understand you."

Ellowyn nodded in understanding. "I am told you both served the duke's father."

Eyeless John nodded. "My father served the duke's father, my lady," he replied. "I have served Exeter all of my life. We travel with his army."

She cocked her head. "Truly?" she said. "I never saw you."

"We did not go with the duke to Erith, my lady," John replied. "We came straight from the docks."

"Ah," she understood. "Then you were with the group that Arundel sent away."

"Aye, my lady."

Ellowyn understood now. She thanked the men and headed back to the hall, still on a quest to find her husband, but she felt as if she was coming to know Guildford a little better. It was to be her home, after all. It was important she understand the workings so she could better oversee the operations.

The hall was staring to fill in with some of Brandt's lesser knights, whom he had not yet introduced her to. In fact, Ellowyn realized that he had mostly kept her to himself bottled up in the keep for the past three days. Furthermore, whenever she had moved from the keep, he or another knight had been by her side. She had never been alone. Just as she pondered that particular realization, she ran straight into Brandt, who was just entering the hall.

It was a collision of sorts as he reached out to keep her from falling over. Startled, she gasped until she saw who it was. Then, a smile lit up her face even though she saw that he wasn't smiling in return. In fact, he looked rather perturbed.

"What are you doing here?" he demanded quietly.

She picked up on his tone but wasn't sure why he was irritated. "I came to look for you," she said. "The women are working on the keep right now but I need straw for the mattress. There was no one to ask so I came to find you."

He sighed sharply, looking around at the men milling in the great hall, and took her by the arm. Leading her out into the deepening night, he spoke as he escorted her towards the motte.

"You must never go anywhere without an escort," he told her. "Too much can happen and I do not want you in danger."

She looked at him curiously. "What do you mean?"

He looked down his nose at her. "Do you remember when we were in the garden of Erith?" he asked, watching recognition register on her features. "I told you there are assassins in my ranks. You have seen the evidence with your own eyes. You should have thought about that before you went wandering around without an armed escort."

She was contrite and defiant at the same time. "So I am to have no freedom at all?"

"You can have all the freedom you want provided you have a proper escort."

She didn't like that answer. "What about after you leave for France?" she demanding, coming to a halt just as they reached the stairs leading up the motte. "Am I to be kept caged in that stone prison of a keep until you return?"

He let go of her and faced her. "I thought we were not going to speak of my leaving for France."

She threw up her hands. "Evidently we must speak of it because I must know if I am to be held a prisoner until you return." She put her hands on her hips. "It is not fair to expect me to stay caged until you come back, Brandt."

"Stop saying that you will be caged," he said irritably. "That is not the case. I realize you are used to having free reign at Erith, but this is not Erith. You must adapt, Wynny. You must understand your environment now. Dangers lurk everywhere. It would destroy me if anything happened to you and you know it."

She just shook her head in frustration; she wasn't happy about it but she didn't want to argue with him.

"As you say," she said, holding up a hand to signal surrender, although they both knew it was not the end. "Now, back to my original question; may I have some hay so that I may have the mattress stuffed? As much as I like sleeping on a hard floor, I do believe I would prefer a real bed tonight."

He was glad she wasn't going to argue the point further; in fact, he had been fairly terrified when one of the soldier's assisting her up at the keep had told him she had gone wandering down in the outerbailey. It had been a panicked flight to find her and he was grateful she was whole and safe. Still, he let the subject go for the moment, and gratefully so. He didn't want to fight with her about it.

"As would I," he said, glad to change the subject. "I will take you over to the stable and we shall see about getting some hay."

The stable master was able to provide them with a great deal of soft, dry hay, which made for a wonderful night's sleep in their newly boiled bed linens. In fact, it was so wonderful that Ellowyn slept well into the morning even when Brandt rose at dawn to go about his duties. He let his wife sleep, watching her as he silently dressed, and thinking he'd never in his life been so happy or content. It was a remarkable feeling.

Ellowyn probably would have slept until noon had the sentries not awoken her mid-morning and Brandt went to make sure she was awake. It would seem that the Duchess of Exeter was required to make an appearance.

Visitors had arrived at Guildford.

\*\*\*

Lady Sabine de Ferrers, Baroness Albury, and her daughter, Daphne, had been sitting in the cold and rather darkened great hall for a half-hour before Brandt made an appearance. Wife and daughter of Lord Albury, a vassal of Brandt's, they were dressed in their finest for their visit to the duke's. Lady Sabine had a pure white wimple on that was surely cutting off the circulation to her head while her daughter, dowdy and round, dressed in scads of flowing robes, jewels, and a corset that was so tight that her bosom was nearly pushed into her chin. Couple that effect with her plain dough-like face and the results were truly hideous.

Brandt didn't have time for visitors so his patience was strained. The only reason he agreed to greet them was because Lady Sabine's husband was very wealthy and commanded nearly eight hundred men. Propriety dictated that Brandt be polite to his vassal, so after he made sure his wife was up and getting dressed, he begrudgingly made his way to greet the visitors.

He met the pair in the great hall where he had purposely made sure they were not offered anything more than a small cup of wine. He didn't even want them up at the keep, and he certainly didn't want to socialize with them beyond necessity. He simply wanted to know their business so he could get on with his day. When Lady Sabine saw him enter the cold hall, she bolted to her feet.

"My lord de Russe," she said happily. "It is so good to see you alive and well after your campaign in France."

Brandt barely cracked a polite smile. Lady Sabine extended her hands to him in greeting and he forced himself to respond. Her icy fingers clutched at him.

"Ladies," he greeted the pair, trying not to look at the blob-like daughter. "I am honored by your visit. How may I be of service?"

Lady Sabine wouldn't let him go even when he tried to force her to sit. "We heard that you had returned to Guildford," she said. "Imagine our horror when we heard Arundel had possession of your castle. What gall! Were you forced to throw him out to regain your seat?"

Brandt finally peeled her fingers off of him and indicated for her to sit. He sat opposite the pair at the table, a safe distance away.

"Not in the least," he replied. "When Arundel realized I had returned, they were happy to leave."

"Why did they confiscate it in the first place?"

"I was told that they possessed it in the event I did not return from Edward's wars. Evidently, Fitzalan wanted first claim." He shifted the subject, mostly because Lady Sabine was a terrible gossip and he didn't want to fuel her imagination. "Now, I would be happy if you would tell me the reason for your visit. I am afraid I have much to do and little time to spare."

Lady Sabine's face fell somewhat that he wasn't prepared to engage her in a nice, long visit, but she recovered. She wasn't going down without a fight.

"My husband sends his regards," she said. "When he heard you had returned, he wanted to make sure you were welcomed properly."

"Where is your husband?"

"Ill with gout, my lord. He cannot travel."

"I see," Brandt replied, his patience evaporating. He was done with pleasantries and stood up from the bench. "I thank you for your welcome, my lady, but you must excuse me. I have many tasks requiring my attention."

Lady Sabine couldn't hide her disappointment any longer. She stood up as well, dragging her plump daughter to her feet also.

"Are you planning on remaining in England, my lord?" she asked quickly. "Surely you have been away long enough."

Brandt shook his head. He was already moving around the table in preparation for escorting them out of the hall.

"I do not plan to remain long," he said. "I am returning to France within the month."

"Oh," Lady Sabine appeared crestfallen. "I am sorry to hear that. We were hoping you would stay for a time."

Brandt had the woman by the elbow. He looked at her curiously. "Why?"

Lady Sabine blinked. "Because... well, because we simply were, my lord. My husband is fond of you and I believe he feels secure when you are in residence at Guildford. We never had a son, you see, and I believe he has often times looked upon you as a son in a manner of speaking."

Brandt resisted the urge to roll his eyes at her statement. Baron Albury was a selfish man with bad health and a penchant for heavy drink. He didn't care for anyone unless they carried a bottle of wine with them. More than that, he and Brandt barely knew one another beyond their acquaintance. But Brandt remained polite.

"Then I am flattered," he said. "Please give him my regards."

He was effectively shutting the conversation down as he forcibly escorted Lady Sabine to the door. Her daughter trailed along behind. But Lady Sabine would not be cut off so easily.

"I will, of course," she said. Then, she grabbed at her daughter, pulling her forward. "Daphne is home from fostering at Portchester Castle. I do not believe you have seen my daughter for many years."

Brandt paused as the neared the hall entry, facing the round and pale young woman. She was even uglier at close range. "Lady Daphne," he greeted with forced politeness. Then he looked at Lady Sabine. "Considering I have only seen you four or five times in my adult life, I will admit that I have only met your daughter once. She was very young, as I recall."

Lady Sabine looked at her daughter with a beseeching expression that she was trying very hard to mask. *Say something, you silly girl!* Fortunately, Daphne received her mother's silent plea and cleared her throat nervously.

"I was ten or eleven years of age, my lord," Daphne said, her voice thin and weak. "Did you enjoy your time in France?"

Brandt could see through the paper-thin attempt to keep the conversation going and it was a genuine struggle not to rudely chase them away.

"I was at war, my lady," he said frankly. "I do not consider that an enjoyable time. Now, if you will...."

Daphne cut him off. "How long have you been in France this time?" she asked. "You have been there before on campaigns, have you not?"

Brandt sighed impatiently; he couldn't help it. "I have been there almost three years," he said with increasing annoyance. "Before that, I was in France on two separate campaigns, each one lasting nearly four years. During that time, I have spent no more than a year in England intermittently. All of my focus is on Edward and his desire to claim what is rightfully his. Now, if you ladies will excuse...."

"Perhaps you will come and visit us at Albury before you depart for France," Daphne said, clumsily interrupting him again. "My father would like to see you and we would have a great feast in your honor."

"Although I appreciate the offer, you will understand if I decline," Brandt said, moving them through the front door and out into the mid-morning sun. "I have a great many thing to accomplish and do not have time for social events."

Daphne's hopeful expression dampened. "I am sorry to know that," she said sincerely. "I was hoping... well, perhaps you will allow me to return to Guildford and play for you. I am most accomplished on the harp and I would consider it an honor to play for you."

Brandt eyed the woman; now he was coming to understand the purpose of their visit and it had nothing to do with welcoming him back to England. He didn't know why it hadn't occurred to him before now; Lady de Ferrers was on a husband hunt for her daughter and evidently thought the duke would be easy prey now that he was newly returned from the wars in France. He quickly sought to make his position very clear.

Kathryn Le Veque/LORD OF WAR: BLACK ANGEL

"Although your offer is gracious, I will have to ask my wife if she would be agreeable to such entertainment," he said. "I will send for you if she has an inclination to listen."

Both Lady Sabine and Lady Daphne appeared shocked. "Your *wife*?" Lady Sabine repeated, incredulous. "You... you are *married*?"

Brandt nodded. "Indeed I am," he said, rather pleased at their expressions. "Now, you will excuse me, ladies. I will bid you a good day."

With that, he turned away and headed back to the keep. But he was detained by Dylan, who pulled him into a private conversation somewhere near the smithy shack. Unfortunately, he was blocked from Ellowyn's view as she descended the stairs from the keep; although she was keeping her eye out for him, she missed him entirely but clearly saw the women standing near the great hall. They were just standing there, looking rather lost, so Ellowyn made her way towards them.

"Greetings, ladies," she said pleasantly as she approached. "I am Lady de Russe. I am not sure where my husband is, but I should be happy to entertain you until he can join us."

Lady Sabine and Lady Daphne looked at Ellowyn with shock, outrage, and curiosity. It was an odd combination. Lady Sabine seemed the most incensed, shamed by Brandt's treatment of her and now faced with his glorious wife. The bitter, petty woman had little control but in the midst of her tantrum, she was also very sly. If she could create problems, she would.

"He has already joined us," she snapped. "He was quite rude and... and inappropriate. We are leaving now."

Although Ellowyn wasn't surprised that Brandt had been rude, considering his behavior at their first introduction, she didn't like the way the woman spoke of him. Already, her dander was up.

"What do you mean?" she asked, her pleasant attitude fading. "What did he do?"

"*Do*?" Lady Sabine repeated, flustered and exaggerated. "My lady, do you know what manner of man your husband is?"

Ellowyn was finished being polite. Already, the conversation had taken a terrible turn and she crossed her arms impatiently.

194

"I believe that I do," she said. "If you think to slander him, I would not do it if I were you. You will not like my response."

Lady Sabine began pointing fingers. "How long have you been married to the man?"

"That is none of your affair."

Lady Sabine's eyes widened with indignation. "He is a man of immoral and lascivious character," she declared, then dramatically lowered her voice, speaking as if scolding. "He made inappropriate suggestions to my daughter that would clearly compromise her moral standards. I heard it myself; he asked her to play her harp for him. *Alone*. What kind of man would do this? If I were you, my lady, I would make all due haste back to your family and away from that... that *monster*. Being exposed to French whores and immoral women has taken away his sense of propriety."

By the time she was finished, Ellowyn was looking at the woman in complete shock. Her mouth fell open.

"Are we speaking of the same man?" she asked incredulously.

"We are!"

Ellowyn wasn't over her shock, but she was fully aware of the fury overtaking her. No one could speak that way of Brandt and get away with it.

"I do not know who you are and I do not care," she said, her gaze riveted to Lady Sabine. "Do you seriously think to come to my husband's home, slander him and call him a monster, and expect me not to defend him? You are a low-bred, foolish woman to say such things to a man's wife and I have no doubt you are lying about his proposition to your ugly daughter; my husband has far better taste than that fat little toad. Now, you will remove yourself from my sight immediately before I find a switch and beat you both within an inch of your lives. Now, *go!*"

She was roaring by the time she was finished. Lady Daphne shrieked, grabbing her mother by the hand and yanking her towards their fine carriage.

"Oh!" Lady Sabine gasped as he daughter dragged her along. "How dare you say such things to me! You ill-mannered...!"

She didn't get the words out fast enough before Ellowyn was hitting her in the mouth with a clod of earth she had scooped up at her feet.

"Get out!" Ellowyn bellowed as she picked up another handful of dank, dirty earth and threw it again, hitting the woman on her pristine-white wimple. "Get out of here, you stupid cow, and take your revolting child with you!"

Lady Sabine and Lady Daphne were running, with Ellowyn following and intermittently stopping to pick up more dirt to toss it. She was a good aim; she hit them five out of the six times she had thrown. But they were attracting attention, including Brandt's, and he turned away from Dylan when he heard the yelling. He wasn't particularly astonished to see his wife chasing after Lady Sabine and Lady Daphne, but he was surprised when he saw her snatch a rock from the ground and throw it at Lady Sabine with all her might. Lady Sabine shrieked when it the rock hit her on the arse.

Both Brandt and Dylan ran towards the women. Brandt intercepted his wife just as she collected another handful of dirt. He grasped her wrist to keep her from pitching it.

"No more," he said softly, firmly. "What on earth are you doing?"

Ellowyn was mad enough to spit. "That... that image of a woman's vagina called you a lascivious monster," she said angrily. "She said you made an indecent proposal to her daughter."

Brandt had to slap a hand over his mouth to keep from laughing at her rather vulgar insult; it was funny as hell. But he refrained, instead, rolled his eyes in disbelief, turning in time to see Dylan quickly usher the ladies into their carriage. As Dylan waved the driver on, Brandt forced Ellowyn to open her hand and he scraped the dirt from it. Then he brushed off the remaining dirt from her hand with the hem of his tunic.

"She is upset because she did not know I was married and had brought her daughter here with the hopes of perhaps making her an attractive marital prospect to me," he said firmly but gently. "I am sorry that she upset you so."

Ellowyn was cooling but still unhappy. She frowned at her husband. "Who is she?"

He sighed faintly, putting his arm around her shoulders and turning her for the keep. "Lady Sabine de Ferrers," he said. "Her husband is one of my vassals."

Ellowyn shook her head. "I do not care who she is," she declared. "I will kill her if I see her again for saying such terrible things about you."

He smiled, giving her a squeeze as they walked. "Your defense of me is flattering."

"You are my husband and a fine example of man. I will kill anyone who says otherwise."

He was genuinely touched. "There are many who do."

She looked up at him, her anger gaining speed again. "Who are they?" she demanded. "Tell me right now."

He laughed softly. "Well," he pretended to be thoughtful, "there is the King of France, the Lords of Navarre, the entire population of the Aquitaine, and...."

She cut him off, understanding that he was jesting with her. He was trying to calm her down and she appreciated his gentle, humorous manner. As Sabine and Daphne's carriage tore off for the gatehouse, Ellowyn realized just how irate she had been. She eyed Brandt, trying not to look too ashamed.

"I understand," she said, fighting off a contrite grin. "Everyone in France hates you. Well, you must start a list, then, so I know who it is I must defend you against. According to you and to my father, it might take a very long time for me to work my way through the ranks of haters."

He smiled, his dark eyes twinkling. "It would take you more than one lifetime, for certain," he said, pleased she was calming. "You are very gracious to want to defend me. I have never had anyone defend me before."

She gave up the fight altogether and collapsed against him, her arms around his waist. "I would kill for you," she said. "And if that foolish sow ever comes back here again, she will be very sorry."

He laughed low in his throat, hugging her. "Aye, she will," he replied, kissing the top of her head. "Return to the keep now and I shall join you in a short while for the nooning meal."

She nodded and let him go. "It would seem that I slept overlong this morning. I do not normally do that."

He eyed her. "You do not seem to sleep very well."

She shrugged, averting her gaze. "Sometimes I do not."

"More dreams?"

Her head shot up, looking at him. "How would you know that?"

"Because you mutter in your sleep."

She averted her gaze again, thinking on the murky, terrible dream she had been having for some time now. It wasn't every night but it did come to her every few days, pieces of this same dream like chapters of a book. The dream exhausted her; she always woke up feeling heartsick and weary. She didn't want to talk about it.

"Sometimes I dream," she said evasively, changing the subject. "Brandt, do you suppose we could go into town today? There are a few things I would like to buy."

He gave a reluctant nod. "I suppose," he said, well aware she was shifting the focus away from her poor sleeping habits. "What do you need to buy?"

"Thread, if I can find it," she said. "I have put a hole in one of my new stockings and must repair it."

"I can have the smithy make you a spinning wheel and we could provide you with all of the wool you need for thread," he said.

She shook her head. "I was never any good at spinning," she told him. "My mother and I would buy our thread from a merchant in Milnthorpe. In fact, I could use a great many sewing items."

Again, he nodded. "If that is your wish."

"Can we go today?"

He shrugged. "That depends," he replied. "Dylan told me that St. Hèver is approaching. The man sent scouts ahead to announce his arrival with six hundred of his father's men. I should like to be here when they arrive."

Ellowyn smiled. "Brennan is arriving?" she repeated. "I am glad to hear he has made a safe journey. He is a nice man."

Brandt was surprised by the stab of jealousy he felt at her innocent statement. He knew it was innocent; from what he knew of his wife, she didn't think covertly and she had never shown anything other than polite regard for his knights. She had spoken to St. Hèver more than most, more than likely because she felt a connection with him after he had saved her life. It never bothered Brandt until this moment. Her positive assessment of Brennan had him fighting off an unexpected surge of jealousy.

"Then you will understand when I say I want to be here when he arrives," he said, trying to keep his manner even. "However, if you can promise me that our trip to town will not take more than an hour, I believe I can take you now."

Ellowyn nodded eagerly. "Let me gather my things and I shall be ready to go."

On tip-toes, she pecked him on the cheek and ran off towards the mighty motte with the keep perched on top. Brandt watched her go, still feeling the kiss to his cheek and the warm adoration that brought about. But he was also still fighting off the last pricks of jealously and forced himself to shift focus, ordering the nearest sergeant to bring forth chargers and a palfrey for his wife. Whatever hateful envy he was feeling, it was unexpected and unnecessary. He had no reason to feel so. But as a man untried in the realm of romance, his control when it came to his feelings wasn't as practiced as it should have been.

Unfortunately, his jealously was going to make an ugly return.

# CHAPTER EIGHTEEN

The trip into the village of Guildford has produced a great deal of goods for Ellowyn.

It started with what she had originally sought – thread in many different colors.  But the purchase of thread triggered the purchase of fabric, and she selected five different types in all colors and weights.

Brandt, lured into the shopping mood by his gleeful wife, selected ribbons he thought were nice and she purchased those, too.  He also purchased a lovely gold and garnet wedding band, which Ellowyn wore with great pride.  It was a lovely ring, signifying a marriage that was quite palatable for them both.  They were content, in love, and deliriously happy.

Brandt went a bit overboard in purchasing luxurious items for his wife, simply because he liked them, she liked them, and he thought that she should have them. He'd never purchased items for a woman, ever, so it was a new and exciting experience.  There was a tailor in town that had several ready-made, loosely-basted garments hanging in his shop, including three or four beautiful cloaks lined with animal fur.  Brandt purchased a gray cloak lined with white rabbit and a golden-rod yellow woolen cloak that was lined with fox.  They were a big large for Ellowyn's petite frame, but terribly beautiful and soft.  While she loved up her new cloaks, Brandt walked around the shop and bought four more dresses simply because he liked the colors.

The booty haul was huge from the tailor's shop, loading up the escorts horses with goods.  More goods were to come, however, when Brandt took Ellowyn into the stall of a merchant who had all manner of perfumes, soaps, candles, dyes, gloves, and jewelry.  It was a veritable feast for the eyes and Ellowyn moved excitedly around the stall, selecting soaps, perfumes, and a pair of doe skin gloves.  Brandt told her she could buy whatever she wished, and she did.

Ellowyn was a paradox as far as he was concerned; she would roam the shop giddily, selecting pretty things, and then turn on the merchant like cunning bird of prey when it came time for payment. Brandt watched her swoop in for the kill, something she seemed to enjoy. She had purchased the thread for nearly what it cost the man to make, bartered the tailor down to the point where the man was barely making a profit, and then she started in again on the man with the perfumes.

Brandt stood in the doorway with Dylan, watching his wife verbally beat down the perfume merchant to the point where the man was so twisted up he had no idea what he had really said.

Eventually, Ellowyn was triumphant when she was able to purchase her soaps and perfumes for a very good price, leaving the old perfume merchant sweating and weary, and Brandt trying not to grin at his aggressive wife. He was coming to see that was standard behavior with her when dealing with the sale of goods. He had once jested with her about her fearsome bartering skills when the fact was that it was true; Lady de Russe was indeed formidable. And Brandt could not have been prouder.

All the way back to the fortress, Ellowyn verbally accounted for every cent spent, storing it in her memory while Brandt just listened to her rattle on. She had a head for mathematics and he was impressed. As they passed through the gatehouse of Guildford, they could see that there were hundreds of unfamiliar men in the bailey and that put an end to Ellowyn's aimless chatter. She quieted as Brandt reined his charger close to her, keeping her in arm's length, as he entered his bailey with gangs of unknown soldiers in it.

"St. Hèver must have arrived," Dylan said to Brandt. "Look; these men are bearing Wrexham tunics."

Brandt could see the red and white of Wrexham. His attention began to move through the hordes, searching for the big knight with the white-blond hair. Brennan wasn't difficult to spot, near the great hall speaking with le Bec and de Reyne. Assisting his wife from the palfrey while servants rushed to gather her goods and take them to the keep, Brandt escorted Ellowyn in Brennan's direction.

The young knight spied his lord on the approach through the crowd of men and animals and immediately went to him. He looked weary and dirty from days in the saddle, but he was sharp and alert.

"My lord," he greeted Brandt smartly, acknowledging Ellowyn with a nod. "My father sends his greetings and his support. I have brought six hundred and six men from Wrexham to support Edward's efforts in France."

Brandt passed a practiced eye over the group. "Good men," he commented. "Seasoned. I can tell by their clothing and weapons."

Brennan nodded. "He kept most of the green troops with him and sent his more seasoned soldiers to you," he said. "My father said you would need them more than he does."

Brandt smirked. "Your father is a wise and gracious man," he replied. "I am sorry I did not get a chance to visit with him. Is he well?"

Brennan nodded. "Well enough," he said. "My sister has just given birth to her third child, another boy, and he is understandably thrilled. It was all he could speak of."

"And you mother and brother?"

Brennan grinned. "My mother is doing very well," he said. "She sends her regards and is verily pleased to hear that you married. She says to tell you that it is about time."

Brandt laughed softly. "Your mother was never one to mince words."

Brennan shook his head. "Nay, she is not," he said. "My brother, Evan, is doing well and is in his last year fostering at Culpepper Castle. My father says he is bigger and smarter than I am."

"If he is anywhere close to the caliber of knight you are, then I will demand he swear fealty to me."

"My father says he is already in demand."

Brandt cocked an eyebrow. "I will fight for him if I have to."

"No one will fight you, my lord. You are too frightening."

Brandt was back to smirking, glancing at Ellowyn as she grinned at Brennan. *Is she looking adoringly at him?* He suddenly thought, startled by his uncontrolled notion. *Oh, God, I am surely going mad to give regard to such things!*

"My lady wife and I will expect to hear all about your travels," he said, trying to stay neutral and normal. "Get the men settled and we shall see you at supper."

Brennan nodded, having no idea what thoughts were crossing Brandt's mind. He turned to Ellowyn as Brandt grasped her elbow.

"My mother has sent you a wedding gift," he said. "Shall I bring it to you now?"

Ellowyn was thrilled and touched. "Did she truly?" she said. "Oh, please bring it to me now."

"You have enough finery and gifts from your shopping this afternoon," Brandt said in a nearly scolding tone. "Allow Brennan to finish his duties. He shall bring you your gift at supper."

Ellowyn's mood wasn't dampened in the least. She shrugged, waved at Brennan, and allowed Brandt to lead her off. As they approached the steps leading up the motte, she turned to him.

"What do you suppose Lady St. Hèver has sent me?" she asked. "She does not even know me. 'Tis a terribly kind gesture."

Brandt nodded, pushing down remnants of his jealousy. He didn't like feeling that way, especially when there was no good reason. Was it a territorial thing? Ellowyn belonged to him and he was extremely protective over her. Was it the fact that she was showing friendliness towards another man, even someone as good and moral as Brennan? Brandt didn't know but he didn't like it. Ellowyn made him feel so many things, among them insecurity. She was such a glorious creature and he actually felt insecure with her, as if he wasn't great enough to hold her attention. He'd never known jealousy or uncertainty in his life and it was a struggle to push it all aside.

"She is a kind woman," he said. "In fact, she reminds me a great deal of you."

"Why?"

"Because she is feisty and speaks her mind," he said. "The woman rules her house and hold with an iron fist. No one goes against Lady St. Hèver and lives to tell the tale."

Ellowyn wound her hands around his forearm, gazing sweetly up at him. "Am I feisty?"

"You are indeed."

"Most men do not like that quality in a woman."

"I am not most men."

She laughed softly as they began to take the terrible steps. In fact, she held on to Brandt tightly as they mounted them. She was careful to watch her feet as she climbed.

"Brandt," she said, picking up her skirts so she wouldn't trip. "Do you think we can put some kind of a rope or rail along these stairs? I am always afraid I am going to break my neck on them."

He looked at the steps, at the slope. "If it would make you comfortable."

"It would."

"Then it shall be done."

Happy, she continued to hold on to him tightly as they proceeded up the steps. They were nearly to the top when a shout from below caught their attention. They turned to see Dylan waving a hand at them, taking the steps very quickly.

"What is it?" Brandt asked as the man drew close.

Dylan was focused intently on him. "Reports, my lord," he said. "Our patrols are telling us that they have sighted an army about three leagues out. It is a big army, my lord, and unlikely that it is my brother."

"Colors?"

"He could not see, but he thought green and yellow."

Brandt knew who it was without another word. "De Nerra," he muttered, somewhat agitated. "St. Hèver just brought six hundred men into the fold not two hours ago. Why did he not see this army on his tail?"

"Because Brennan came in from the westerly road," Dylan said. "This army is coming in from the north, well shielded in the vales."

Brandt's jaw ticked, irritated, but he accepted the explanation. Brennan was an excellent knight and very astute; he would not have missed something like this. *Am I trying to find fault with the man now?* Brandt shrugged off the thought.

"Then mobilize the men," he commanded. "De Nerra has finally caught up to us. Lock down the castle. All men to their posts. Put St. Hèver's men on the walls as well; get everyone out of the bailey. And roll out the mangonels."

Dylan was already on the move, calmly and efficiently. Ellowyn watched him go, apprehension in her heart as she turned to her husband.

"So he has come," she said softly. "We have been so peaceful and happy the last few days... I had forgotten. I was hoping he would not come at all."

Brandt patted her hand. "I did not forget and I knew he would come," he said quietly. "It was simply a matter of when. If a man took my daughter, I would chase him down as well."

She looked up at him, his handsome face in the sunlight. "If it is my father," she said, "please let me speak with him. I will tell him we are married and that he will have to accept it."

Brandt began to lead her up the last few steps to the top of the motte. His manner was very composed. "You are going to stay safely bottled up in the keep."

She held on to him as he took her to the top before releasing him. "Please, Brandt," she begged quietly. "My father will listen to me."

Brandt cupped her sweet face and kissed her on the mouth. "For now, I want you in the keep," he reiterated. "If your father starts a battle right away, I do not want to chance you getting injured. If I need you, or if there is the opportunity for you to speak with your father, I will come for you. Do you understand?"

She was unhappy but she nodded her head. "But I am sure that I can...."

He cut her off with another kiss and took her hand, nearly dragging her to the keep. "What did I tell you earlier when we discussed your father and his need to regain you, Wynny? What did I say?"

She pouted as he pulled her along. "I do not know."

"Aye, you do. I told you it was a matter of honor. This is no longer about you; it is about your father and his damaged pride."

She didn't like being dragged and dug her feet in. "But you do not know how to deal with him," she insisted. "I do. You must let me speak with him."

He dragged her all the way to the keep entry. She yanked her hands free, facing him somewhat angrily.

"Do you hear me?" she demanded. "You must let me speak with him,"

He put his hands on his hips. "I hear you," he said steadily. "But you will hear me or you will feel the sting of my hand to your backside. You will go into the keep and bolt the door. Do not open it for anyone but me or my knights. When I see how the winds of war are blowing with your father, I will return to you, but for now, I want you safe where I do not have to worry over you. Is that clear?"

She sighed angrily, suspecting he wasn't going to give in to her demands this time, and she had no doubt he would do as he said. She had no desire to be spanked by him. So she stomped past him, up the steps into the keep, and slammed the door. Brandt grinned as he heard her throw the bolt.

With a chuckle, he proceeded down to the bailey of Guildford where his army was in the throes of mobilizing.

It was going to be a very long night.

# CHAPTER NINETEEN

Deston de Nerra hadn't gone on a battle march with his troops in almost twelve years. His failing health and diseased joints had seen to that, crippling him to the point of inactivity. But this march was different; Ellowyn had been abducted as far as he was concerned and he would regain her no matter what the cost. She was the only child he had left that was worth anything, so he would stop at nothing to regain her. Not even his mother could stop him.

Aye, she had confessed her role in Ellowyn's abduction. Lady Gray was not one to lie or shy from her responsibilities, and she had confessed everything the day after de Russe's army fled with Ellowyn as their prize. Gray had spent the entire day discussing the situation with her son and trying to convince him that Ellowyn and Brandt were better off together, but Deston would not listen. He wanted his daughter home, with him, and not as the concubine of the Black Angel. It seemed that de Russe's reputation was all he was fixated on. Brandt de Russe ceased to be an alliance that Deston was proud of and became instead an obsession for his shame. The obsession grew worse by the hour.

So he scrambled his army in spite of his mother's protests and departed four days after Ellowyn's abduction. He had also sent word ahead to an allied lord for troop reinforcements; Gareth le Mon of Clun Castle had been allied with Deston's father, so the man provided an additional four hundred men to Deston. They were waiting for him on the road as he traveled south, and with the blended de Nerra and le Mon armies there were almost fifteen hundred men. It was a sizable force.

Deston and le Mon's son, Dallan le Mon, drove the big army south. Dallan had seen his twenty-seventh year and was married with one child and another child on the way, and wasn't particularly happy to be on a vengeance mission. He was a big, handsome man with a quick wit about him, and Deston took to him fairly quickly. He was always attaching himself to men that were his son's age as if they were surrogate replacements.

Dallan knew the basic reason behind their march to Guildford Castle but he had shown extreme reluctance to lay siege to the Duke of Exeter. Everyone knew the man was the Black Angel and Dallan had argued with his father endlessly over attacking a man who was part of a larger war machine.

Ultimately, Gareth had committed resources to Deston's cause so Dallan went along to make sure Deston, the emotional father, wasn't too reckless with his actions. Dallan didn't want to lose more men than was absolutely necessary.

Guildford Castle was a massively formidable bastion. Deston had never seen it, and neither had Dallan, so laying eyes upon the soaring walls and massive motte of the fortress set them both back a bit. There were moats within moats, walls within walls, and everything about it reeked of power.

From a distance, Deston and Dallan had observed the soaring gray-stoned walls of the keep and the curtain wall that had to be at least four times a man's height. Nearing sunset, the golden rays of the sun warmed the stone, creating an almost glowing effect. The gates were closed and men were upon the walls, watching them suspiciously. The scent of battle was in the air, making them all edgy. Dallan finally turned to Deston.

"What will you do, my lord?" he asked, rather ironically. "Shall we burn it down now or wait until the morning?"

It was a sarcastic question, one that had Deston casting the man a withering glare. He hadn't expected Guildford Castle to present such a difficult target. In pain, exhausted, he shook his head irritably.

"Settle the men," he barked. "I will speak with de Russe before this night is out. Perhaps he will understand the folly of what he has done and we can come to an agreement."

Dallan was coming to think this truly was a fool's venture, served by the pride of an embittered old man. He reined his horse around, shouting orders to the men as he thundered back into the column and leaving Deston alone, staring at the soaring walls of Guildford and wondering if he would ever see his daughter again.

\*\*\*

"He wishes to speak with you, my lord."

Brandt heard the quiet statement. Seated in his solar on the first level of Guildford's keep, he glanced up at Dylan, standing in the doorway. Torchlight flickered and the glow from the burning hearth cast shadows all around the room. Sitting up from where he had been hunched over a well-worn map of England exquisitely etched on vellum, he stretched out his big legs.

"Who does?"

"De Nerra, my lord."

Brandt paused before replying. "De Nerra has brought a sizable army with him."

"He is reinforced with troops from the Lords of Clun. His messenger was more than happy to inform us of that."

Brandt thought on that a moment, folding his big arms across his chest. As he pondered the offer, the situation in general, the fire snapped softly and one of the dogs left behind by Arundel wandered over for a pet. Brandt, being rather fond of dogs, obliged the lanky, hairy beast. He stroked the dog pensively.

"Greetings, Dylan," Ellowyn said, interrupting the silence. She came off the narrow spiral stairs with a cloak or blanket of some sort in her arms and headed for one of the chairs near Brandt. "Any vital news to report from the war front?"

It was a rather quippy question, one that had Dylan giving her a half-grin. "Nothing of note, my lady," he said, eyeing Brandt. "I have simply come to relay a message to your husband."

She sat in the chair and spread out the blanket, which he noticed was something she was knitting. She had a big ball of woolen yarn, colored a dark blue, and she had a single very large needle with which she was looping the material with. She seemed very calm for a woman who had a hostile army at her front door, but Dylan suspected it was because Brandt was here to keep her company. He also suspected Brandt was here to keep her from running off to talk with her father. The man had left the walls of Guildford hours ago and had not returned since, unusual for the normally hands-on commander.

"A message?" she repeated curiously as she straightened out her yarn. "From whom?"

Brandt looked over at her. "Your father," he said. "It seems he wishes to speak with me."

She stopped fumbling and looked at him with wide eyes. "*I* will speak with him," she told him. "Brandt, the only conversation he wishes to have with you is one full of threats. He will not do that to me. Please allow me to speak with him and inform him of the situation."

Brandt sighed heavily. He knew she would question him again about speaking with her father and he'd been thinking for the better part of the evening on how to dissuade her. The problem was that he really couldn't think of a solid reason why she shouldn't and he realized he was seriously considering her request. Still, his pride stood in the way. He ultimately shook his head.

"That would be the coward's way," he told her quietly. "What man would send his wife to do his talking for him? Nay, sweetheart, I will speak with your father face to face and explain the way of things."

She grunted in frustration. "Would you not wish for a peaceful end to all of this?"

"Of course I would."

"Then you must let me speak with him. You will only upset him."

Brandt gave her a disbelieving glance before returning his attention to Dylan. "Tell Deston I will speak with him," he replied. "But I will set the terms - we will meet at the gatehouse in one hour."

Dylan bowed and silently quit the keep. Brandt watched the man go, thinking on the conversation he would have with Deston, when he caught sight of his wife from the corner of his eye.

Ellowyn was staring at him, her big needle in hand. Her expression was one of disapproval.

"It is not cowardly to want a peaceful end to this," she said quietly. "I do not want to see you hurt and I do not want to see my father hurt. There are many men out there with sharp weapons and if I can end this without a drop of blood being shed, I will happily do so. Why do you resist me?"

He shook his head. "Why must we discuss this again?" he asked. "Do you think me so weak that I must have my wife do my talking for me?"

She appeared rather taken aback. "Of course not," she said softly. "But if I can help...."

"If I want your help, I will ask," he said, rather sternly. "But if I do not, you will kindly cease badgering me."

A frown appeared on her delicate features. "I do not badger."

"Aye, you do."

The frown deepened. "If I do, it is because you are hard-headed and stubborn."

He rolled his eyes and stood up. "I will not have this discussion with you," he said, moving for the plate armor he had removed a few hours before, perched as they were on a frame near the door. "You will stay to this keep until I come for you. If you do not, I will catch you and lock you in a room. Mayhap I will even throw away the key. I do not like to be constantly questioned as if you do not trust me and I will like it even less if you disobey me. Do you comprehend?"

Still frowning, now feeling scolded, Ellowyn dropped her face and focused on the knitting in her lap. She kept her mouth shut as Brandt silently donned his plate armor and strapped on his weapons. When he was finished, he came over to her as she sat by the fire with the great half-knitted cover on her lap.

"Give me a kiss," he said, bending over. "I will return as soon as I can."

She turned her face petulantly and he ended up kissing her cheek. Fighting off a grin, he could see that she was pouting.

"You will be sorry you did that," he told her as he moved for the door. "What if I am struck down by lightning in the bailey? What if the earth opens up to swallow me as I move down the motte? You will be very, very sorry that you did not kiss me farewell. You will regret being so terrible to me."

By now, Ellowyn was trying not to grin at his dramatic account of the dangers awaiting him outside, none of which had anything to do with an impending battle.

"Nay, I will not," she said callously, focused on her yarn. "If you are struck down or swallowed up, it will be God's way of punishing you for being so mean to me."

He stopped at the door, his eyebrows lifted. "*I* am mean?" he repeated, feigning outrage. "Madam, you have a twisted sense of perception. Are you going to kiss me or not?"

She lifted her gaze, fixing him in the eye. "Why should I?"

"Because you love me. You said so yourself."

She bit her lip to keep from smiling. "I can love you and still be annoyed with you."

"Nay, you cannot. Come here, you silly wench. Kiss me."

She indicated the heavy blanket on her lap. "I cannot," she said. "You must come back over here if you want a kiss."

He stomped back over to her, so loudly that the dogs began to bark. Then he growled as he swooped down on her, listening to her squeal as he nibbled her ear, her neck. She giggled uncontrollably as his nibbles turned to kisses, and his mouth eventually slanted hungrily over hers. Ellowyn responded eagerly to him and the knitting needle fell to the floor.

"The next time you do not kiss me on demand, I shall not return for a second attempt," he murmured rather lustily. "You will obey me the first time, do you hear?"

She grinned at him slyly, causing him to kiss her hard enough to snap her head back. She gasped, and giggled, as he nibbled her lips, her cheeks, and her face. It was a sweetly tender moment yet wholly passionate moment.

"I hear you," she whispered.

"Hear me and obey."

"I will."

"For how long?"

She giggled again. "At least until you leave the keep."

With a grin, he kissed her again and made his way to the keep entry, turning to glance at her before he left. She was illuminated by the firelight and the torch in the room, giving her an ethereal quality. Brandt had never seen anything so beautiful in his life, reiterating the fact that she was indeed worth fighting for.

He hoped it wouldn't come to that, but he had his suspicions.

\*\*\*

"You *married* her?"

Brandt couldn't understand why Deston was genuinely shocked. It was a struggle not to sound sarcastic in response.

"I told you I wanted to marry her," he said steadily. "Did you truly think I would not?"

Standing in Guildford's great gatehouse, separated by the lowered portcullis, Deston and Brandt faced each other. Knights stood around both men, in the shadows as silent and deadly support, while torches burned hot and dense, sending black oily smoke against the low ceiling. Brandt held a torch simply so he could see in the darkness, but Deston was somewhat obscured by the blackness. It was difficult to see the man very well; even so, he could still see the outrage on his face. *This is not going well already*, Brandt thought.

That was an understatement. As he watched, Deston's face turned shades of red, even in the darkness.

"I told you that I did not want you for my daughter," he snarled. "You had no right to take her."

Brandt remained cool. "It is strange how I was your ally and comrade when I returned your men to Erith," he said, "but the minute I spoke to you of marriage to Ellowyn, I became your enemy. I am as good if not better than any man in England for your daughter, and your weak argument of war tactics and brutal rumors are without merit. You insulted me without basis."

Deston was furious. "Basis or not, she is my daughter to give," he said. "I denied you yet you still took her. It is thievery!"

"It is marriage."

"I shall take this to Edward!"

Brandt couldn't help it; he smirked. "Do as you must," he said. "I am sure Edward will tell you to shut your mouth and go home, but you are welcome to bother the King of England with something as petty as a man marrying your daughter without permission. Don't you think the king has greater things to worry about?"

Deston started to snap back at him but held his tongue; he knew, as everyone else did, that Brandt was much favored by Edward. It wouldn't do him any good to go to the king and try to charge de Russe with thievery. In fact, it might upset the king and work against him. So he cooled, eyeing the man through the iron grate, and thought of his next move. He was exhausted, in pain, and furious beyond reason. Because of it, his thought processes weren't as clear as they should have been.

"You had no right to take her," he said, sounding despondent now. The anger was fading. "Why did you do it? Why did you show me such disrespect? You call yourself an ally but an ally would not have shown such disregard for my position."

Brandt wouldn't admit that the man had a point. "Deston, you had no basis for denying us," he said, with some emotion. "Would you hear me tell you that I love your daughter and she loves me? Would you hear me tell you that she means everything to me? I would have told you all of this but you did not allow me to. We are not speaking of possession in this case; we are speaking of passion and adoration. Your daughter is the most important thing in the world to me and I could not leave Erith without her. I *would* not. If you must condemn me for being a man in love, then so be it. But I would hope the fact that I care for your daughter outweighs any shame you might feel."

Deston stared at him without saying a word. The blue-green eyes just stared at Brandt to the point where it made him uncomfortable. When he finally spoke, it was low and deliberate.

"If a man came to you to ask permission to marry your daughter and you denied him, what would you do if he married her against your wishes?" he asked.

Brandt knew the question might come and he was prepared. At least, he thought he was until visions of a beautiful blond daughter with Ellowyn's features flashed before his eyes. He already knew he would love her more than anything on earth. If a man absconded with her, he knew exactly what he would do – he would kill him. After a moment, he cleared his throat softly and averted his gaze.

"I would do what you are doing," he said quietly. "I would want her back."

"Would you want to kill him?"

"Of course."

"Why?"

"Because she would be my daughter. I would kill any man who laid a hand on her."

Deston sighed faintly; he suddenly looked very old, and extraordinarily weary. The anger had eased but the fight was still there.

"I want her back," he finally said.

"You cannot have her. She is my wife."

"Then I demand satisfaction."

"Name it."

"You and I will battle to the death at dawn. Just you and me, de Russe; the armies will stand down. This is between you and me, and no other."

Brandt looked at the man as if he was mad. "Deston, I cannot fight you."

"Why not?"

"Because I will win. I cannot kill you."

"Then I will kill *you*."

Brandt shut his mouth, eyeing the man a moment. "Are you truly serious about this?"

"I am."

"Ellowyn will not be happy about this. She will be the one ultimately affected by your death."

"It could be your death."

"Would you hurt her so?"

"She is worth fighting for and, if necessary, dying for. She is my daughter. I demand satisfaction for what you have taken from me. If I win, she will come back to Erith and if you win, well... all I ask is that you return me home. I would be buried next to my father."

Brandt understood him completely, mostly because if Ellowyn had been his daughter, he would do the same thing. He began to feel sick in the pit of his stomach, knowing how Ellowyn would react to all of this. This was going to tear her apart, a battle between the two men she loved best in the world. He couldn't even think of himself at the moment; all he could think of was her.

"Are you sure you want to do this?" he asked hoarsely.

Deston's jaw was set, his mouth a firm line. But his lips were trembling. "Aye."

Brandt's jaw ticked. There was nothing more he could say; the man had a right to his own sense of satisfaction. He was already devastated for Ellowyn at what would surely be the outcome.

"Very well," he murmured. "If that is your wish. I will meet you at dawn."

Without another word, Deston turned and faded off into the darkness, his soldiers closing in around him as they headed off towards their encampment in the distance. Brandt just stood there, watching them go, until they faded from sight. Then, he turned to the men surrounding him.

Dylan, Brennan, Magnus and Stefan were all looking at him with varied degrees of seriousness. They had heard the challenge. Already, they knew the outcome. Dylan locked eyes with Brandt.

"If you kill him, she will hate you," Dylan muttered what they were all thinking. "If he kills you, she returns to Erith. Either way, you lose your wife. This is a battle you cannot win."

Brandt's jaw ticked as he pondered the scenario. "I do not have a choice," he said. "The man has a right to seek justice."

"So you agree to a duel against him? If you die, he wins and if he dies, he wins. How is this justice?"

Brandt didn't have an answer. All he knew was that he had to see Ellowyn. Pushing past his knights, he made his way across the darkened bailey, heading for the keep at the top of the motte. He gazed up at the structure, seeing weak light emitting from the windows. It was like looking into his heart and seeing the light there; Ellowyn was in the keep, and she was also in his heart. Wherever she was, there was light. He raced up the steps to be with her, to tell her what had happened.

Ellowyn wept when Brandt told her of Deston's challenge.

# CHAPTER TWENTY

*The dream had come again, like shadows and mist, and she struggled to see through the fog until that scene of death and mud came clear again.*

*She was moving for the trees where the armored figure sat, slogging through mud that was as thick as honey on a frozen winter morning. It made moving almost impossible, but she couldn't stop. Her heart was pounding in her ears, louder and louder. Her breathing was coming in short gasps. She had to get to the man beneath the trees, the man she loved with all her heart.*

*She glanced behind her to see if her grandfather was still there; he was gone, evaporated like a puff of smoke. The castle in the distance was still burning deep, although somehow it had changed. The walls were no longer black with soot but now red, like blood. The entire structure looked as if it was melting, a blobbish mass that was slowly collapsing. Blood gushed from the lancet windows, now twisted in macabre fashion.*

*The sight panicked her. She had to get away from the collapsing castle, terrified that she was going to be caught up in the collapse although she was a good distance away from it. The castle was sinking into the mud, just like everything else, and she was frightened. She clawed and struggled, trying to get away from it and towards the man in armor lying beneath the trees.*

*Somehow, she found her footing. She was on firm ground again, straining with exertion as she made her way onto solid ground once more. She could move more quickly now and she began to run as fast as her swollen body would allow. Closer and closer she loomed, finally catching a glimpse of the man beneath the tree. The first thing her gaze fell on was the man's chest; there was an arrow embedded in it.*

*She slowed. The man didn't move. She inched towards him, terrified, feeling overwhelmed with sorrow. The man's breastplate had an insignia on it and she peered closer; there was a massive bird*

*of prey on the metal. It looked a good deal like the de Nerra falcon.*
*Ellowyn awoke with a scream.*

\*\*\*

It was an hour or so before dawn. Brandt knew this because the moon had gone down; he could see the black sky from the chamber window. The birds were starting to come alive, soaring across the still-dark sky in search of their morning meal.

He didn't think he had slept at all. He had spent the night with Ellowyn wrapped up in his arms, listening to her mutter in her sleep. He was just drifting off when she suddenly screamed and pitched herself up into a seated position. He sat up alongside her, wrapping his arms around her to comfort her.

"Everything is all right," he told her softly. "You are safe. All is well."

Ellowyn began weeping hysterically. "My father," she sobbed. "He is dead!"

Brandt had his mouth against the side of her head. "He is not dead," he assured her softly. "It was a dream, Wynny."

She was still half-asleep, burying her face in his chest. "He will be dead at dawn," she wept.

Brandt sighed heavily, snuggling her into his warm embrace and laying back down on the bed. "Go back to sleep," he murmured.

Ellowyn was becoming more lucid, struggling to shake off the effects of the bad dream. "I cannot," she sniffed. "Brandt, I cannot sleep knowing that my father will be dead in a few hours. Please let me go and speak with him; let me end this madness."

Brandt caressed her as he stared off into the darkness. "It will not do any good," he told her. "His honor is damaged. He must reclaim it at any cost."

Ellowyn closed her eyes, hot tears finding their way down her temple and on to Brandt's chest. "What do I do?" she whispered. "I do not want to see my father die."

He pulled her closer. "Are you so sure he will? I could die, you know. He could just as easily kill me."

She pulled her head off his chest and looked up at him. "If you were to die, I would not want to live," she told him seriously. "Although I love my father, I will survive his death. But I could not survive yours, Brandt. There would be nothing left to live for."

He gazed down at her, only the weak light from the glowing embers in the hearth illuminating her face. He stroked her cheek, kissing the end of her nose.

"You have married a lord of war," he murmured. "There is always the possibility that I will perish in battle. You *know* this, Wynny. If I die, it would make me very happy if you would live your life with the dignity and grace befitting the Duchess of Exeter. You could do me no greater honor and every man would envy me my strong and virtuous wife. But to take your own life... that is shameful. Would you shame me so?"

She shook her head, reaching up to run a gentle finger over his lips. "Nay," she whispered. "But living without you would be a hollow, dreadful thing."

"I understand completely," he muttered, "because living without you would be the same." He paused, thinking of Dylan's prophetic word before continuing. "I must say something, Wynny."

"What is it?"

He hesitated again, a moment rife with uncertainty. "This challenge between me and your father," he ventured, forming his thoughts as he went. "I do not want you to hate me for killing your father. Just as I could not live with your death, I could not live with your hatred, either. I feel as if I am in a situation where I cannot win, and that grieves me deeply."

Ellowyn gazed up at him, thinking seriously on what he was saying. It was evident that he meant what he said; she could read the emotion in his face. She was careful, and thoughtful, with her reply.

"I told you when we were at Erith that I had ceased to view my father through the eyes of an adoring young girl because of the way he treated you when you asked for my hand," she said softly. "That man was rash and rude and cruel. He would not even listen to me when I attempted to speak with him about it; he turned me away completely. Then, that same man rouses an army to come to

Guildford to challenge you. I have never known my father to be so reckless. Of course I do not wish his death, but he is the one who started all of this. He challenged you and I support your right to answer the challenge and defend yourself."

"You say that now, but when it comes time to cut your father down, I will wonder if you will ever look at me the same way again."

She sighed heavily and laid her head on his chest again, hearing his heartbeat strong and steady in her left ear. Her thoughts lingered on her father, his rash behavior and uncharacteristic anger. A thought suddenly occurred to her.

"I saw him turn on my brother the same way he turned on you," she murmured, thinking back to that dark and turbulent time. "He was very angry and abusive to my brother, eventually disowning him. My brother was devastated; all he wanted to do was serve God in his own way, but my father acted as if he had betrayed him."

"As you have betrayed him by going against his wishes and marrying me," Brandt said softly.

"He will disown me as well."

"If he was intent to disown you, he would not be here. He wants you back."

"I am not going back."

"Then I must fight him for the privilege of keeping you."

Ellowyn fell silent, listening to his beating heart, feeling it reassure her like nothing else ever had. He was her husband, a part of her in more ways than she could express. In the short time they had been together, she had never known such happiness or fulfillment. Brandt had become her entire world and everything about him caused her to live and breathe. She could not lose that. As much as she loved her family, her father, Brandt had become what was most precious to her. Still, the thought of losing her father, however rash and foolish he was, tore at her.

"When the time comes with my father," she whispered. "I will not ask you not to kill him because he has challenged you for your life and, as I said, you have every right to defend yourself. However... if you do not have to kill him, I would be grateful. But if you do... then I trust your judgment. I am sorry it had to come to this."

"As am I."

"Whatever happens, you must stay alive. Do you understand me?"

"Aye, madam."

"Promise me?"

"With all that I am, I do."

She lifted her mouth to his and they lost themselves in a powerful, passionate kiss. In little time, Brandt's hands were roving her body, a form he was now so intimately familiar with, and when he finally thrust into her, it was with the sweetest of movements. Ellowyn clung to him, his scent filling her nostrils, his body filling hers, feeling pain and fear and longing such as she had never experienced.

All she wanted was her husband and the ability to live a normal life with him, without the constant threat of her father hanging over their heads. If Brandt had to subdue the man to give them such peace... aye, even kill him... as much as it pained her to think such thoughts, so be it. If she had to choose between her father and her husband, she was not ashamed to choose her husband. The love she felt for him, the bond, ran too deep for words.

When the pink light of early morning began to fill the eastern sky and she found herself on the wall watching the mortal battle between her father and Brandt unfold below, the first glimpse of her father in weeks had her weeping at the sight.

\*\*\*

The presence of Brandt's army was heavy on the wall facing southwest where the gatehouse was located because outside of the gatehouse a great event was taking place. The foot soldiers were crowded on the parapet and an entire squadron of archers was poised with weapons cocked to keep de Nerra's army from charging. Even though terms of the challenge had been laid out, Brandt wasn't taking any chances. He wanted insurance that de Nerra wouldn't try to trick him once the portcullis was lifted. A fleet of obvious archers would keep anyone from getting too cocky.

Aware of the archers lining Guildford's walls, de Nerra's army was held back from the gatehouse by a line of sergeants, far enough so that they were out of the archers' range but close enough so that they could see what was happening. They had been told the previous night that there may not be a battle after all, as their liege had called out the Duke of Exeter to settle the matter between them. A challenge was not an unusual spectacle, but in this case, it was sure to be very one-sided.

The Duke of Exeter appeared at dawn in the gatehouse, behind the great fanged portcullis. He was dressed from head to toe for combat, the type of combat he had seen in France where men would fight brutally and with every part of their body to attain victory. Loaded down with mail, plate army, and a variety of weapons, the duke was deadly. He was also far stronger, more skilled and more experienced than Deston de Nerra, who had not seen a battlefield in over twelve years.

The portcullis lifted, spilling de Russe and his five frightening-looking knights forth across the drawbridge and into the clearing that fanned out from gatehouse. As the heavily armed knights stood back by the portcullis, Brandt came forth into the clearing and faced de Nerra's enormous army. He just stood there, waiting, while the tension mounted. They all knew what he was waiting for.

De Nerra wasn't long in showing himself. A big man who had been muscular back in his prime, most of that muscle had gone to fat with age and inactivity. It caused his armor not to fit very well and he struggled with it even as he made his way towards Brandt. He kept pulling at the mail. Not a man watching the spectacle didn't feel a sense of what was about to happen; the once-great knight was about to face a man who inarguably was the most formidable warrior on any battlefield, ever. It was like watching a lamb to slaughter. The drums of doom beat silently, growing louder with each footstep Deston took as he approached his executioner.

Brandt felt it, too. As Deston advanced, he knew the moment he drew is sword it would only be a matter of time before he was the victor, and probably a short time at that. Deston was not in any sort of battle condition. He was out of practice and weak. What he was doing was pride and honor driven alone, which made him foolish and careless.

"You may as well throw yourself on your own sword, de Nerra," Brandt said as the man drew close. "What you are doing is suicide."

Deston slowed as he came near. "Mayhap," he said. "But is something I must do."

"Is there no other way?"

"Unless you want to hand my daughter over, there is no other way."

"I will not hand her over. She is my wife. Why is it so hard to accept that?"

Deston didn't say anything. After a moment, he unsheathed the broadsword that had once belonged to his father. It was a wicked-looking thing, exquisitely crafted, and with the blood of thousands of men on it. It was an instrument meant to kill, and far out-weighed the capabilities of its master.

"Lift your sword, de Russe," he said after a moment. "Let us get on with it."

Brandt looked at him. *Really* looked at him. He knew that Ellowyn was on the wall, watching. He still had fear that she would grow to hate him for killing her father no matter what reassurance he had from her. Emotions had a way of changing people's minds, so he deduced at that moment he had two options – he could either draw out the fight and make it look like Deston had a chance before goring him, or he could refuse to fight at all and see how Deston reacted. He couldn't imagine the man would kill him in cold blood. Perhaps if he refused to fight, Deston might consider it a stroke of good fortune and back off. It would be a way for the man to save his pride in a sense if the great Brandt de Russe refused to fight him. For Ellowyn's sake, he was willing to take the chance.

"I am not going to fight you," he finally said.

Deston's helmed head cocked. "What do you mean?"

"Just what I said; I am not going to fight you. Deston, this is foolish. You know I am going to kill you. I cannot and *will* not fight my wife's father because of what it will do to her. Did you know she woke up weeping last night because she'd had a dream that you were dead?"

Deston faltered somewhat. "She has many dreams. That is not unusual with her."

"So you would have me kill you in front of her and give her nightmares the rest of her life? She is watching right now, you know."

Deston's head turned upward, towards the wall behind Brandt. "Where is she?"

Brandt turned around, scanning the wall until he caught a glimpse of a blond head with a scarf on it. She was near the seam where the curtain wall met the gatehouse. He pointed a massive finger in that direction.

"There," he said. Then, he lifted his voice. "Ellowyn? Show yourself to your father."

The men on the wall shifted and Ellowyn's pale face came into view. She was wrapped in a deep blue surcoat and scarf, all wrapped up against the chill morning air. Brandt's gaze lingered on her, drawing strength from the sight, before returning his focus to Deston.

"Please do not make me kill you in front of her," he muttered. "Go home, de Nerra. Go home and forget this foolishness."

Deston flipped up his visor, his gaze fixed on his child. His expression was wrought with longing.

"Wynny?" he called. "Come down from there. I have come to take you home."

Ellowyn boosted herself up so she could see him better. "I am *not* going home," she called down to him. "I demand you stop this foolishness right now. You are making a spectacle of yourself and I am ashamed."

The wistful expression on Deston's face changed to one of irritation. "You shame me by running off with a man not worthy of you," he bellowed, pointing his sword at her. "It was stupid!"

Ellowyn's face disappeared. Brandt kept searching for her on the battlements but she was nowhere to be seen until she suddenly appeared in the gatehouse, skirts gathered as she ran beneath the portcullis. Dylan tried to grab her but she slapped him as she pulled free.

"I will not embarrass myself further with a shouting match for all to hear," she barked at her father, pointing a finger at him. "How dare you come here with an army to bring me home. If I'd wanted to stay home, I would have never gone with Brandt."

She appeared as if she was headed for her father to punch him, so Brandt grabbed her before she could get near him. He held on to her, fearful of what would happen if he let her go.

"How could you do this to me, Wynny?" Deston said, his control slipping now that he was faced with his daughter. "I cannot believe you would disobey me so."

"And I cannot believe you would deny me the man I love!" Ellowyn shot back. "Think about what you are doing; even if you kill Brandt today and bring me home, I am still his wife. I am still the Duchess of Exeter, and this entire empire would be mine. You cannot take me back to the days when I was only your daughter. Those days are gone forever. I am Brandt's wife now and I love him, and it would make the situation so much better if you were simply to accept that and give us your blessing. I do not understand your reservation."

Deston's face was dark but his sword was still lifted, still in-hand. "He has done terrible things, Wynny. How could you love such a man?"

"I love you and you have done terrible things," she countered swiftly. "You were a young man when Roger Mortimer and Isabella stole the throne from young King Edward. Mama said you served Isabella and Mortimer, and when young Edward attacked Nottingham Castle and took Mortimer a prisoner, you turned on Mortimer and killed several of his personal guards so the king could be victorious. That makes you a traitor, Da. That makes *you* terrible."

Deston tried not to look too contrite. "Times were different then, lass," he said, lowering his sword. "It was a much harsher time."

Ellowyn shook her head. "It was *not*," she said. "It was war and you did what you had to in order to survive. That is what Brandt did, too. He does what he has to in order to survive."

Deston shook his head. "He is *not* defending a king," he pointed out. "He is simply furthering the claim of a greedy man."

"If that is the case, then you are supplying him men for the cause. That makes you just as guilty as he is."

Deston's jaw ticked furiously. He averted his gaze, wondering how this entire situation had veered so out of control. He couldn't surrender now, not when he had come so far.

"Do you not understand that I want something better for you?" he finally hissed, his hesitant gaze lifting to Ellowyn's beseeching face. "You are meant for far better things in this world than a man who lives and breathes battle for a selfish young man. I know that vocation all too well, for I was involved in something like it years ago. You may be de Russe's wife, but war will always be his mistress. You will have to share him. Even now, he prepares to leave you for France. You are not the most important thing to him, Wynny; Edward is. You will always be second. I wanted something better for you than that."

It was an extraordinarily valid point. Brandt heard it like hammer blows to his heart; he didn't dare look at Ellowyn, mostly because they both knew it was true. He had never heard his life put into those terms before, but Deston was entirely correct. It was a sickening realization.

"I understand your words," Ellowyn replied, more subdued than she had been during the entire conversation, "but this is a choice I made. You must let me make my own decision and, if necessary, live with the consequences of my choice. I am a woman grown, Da; you must accept that."

Deston drew in a long, deep breath. "I want you to come home with me, Wynny. De Russe is going to France as it is and you will more than likely never see him again. I want you to come home with me now."

Ellowyn frowned. "He is going to France and I am going with him," she told him frankly. "Edward may hold his fealty but I hold his heart and he holds mine. The only way that will change is if he is dead."

"He *will* die," Deston was growing heated again. "It is only a matter of time before he is dead and when that happens, I will take you home."

Because he was growing angry again, so was Ellowyn. "I will *not* go home," she said hotly. "Guildford is my home now. If Brandt is dead, I will administer his dukedom in a manner that will honor him. I will not run home to my father who only seeks to shame and demean me."

Deston's mouth fell open. "I do nothing of the sort," he fired back. "You are a stubborn, willful wench, Ellowyn de Nerra. You disrespected and shamed your family when you ran off with de Russe. You are fortunate that I forgive you for that."

They were back on the same old subject and Ellowyn would not be sucked into it. She pulled free of Brandt's grasp and took a few steps towards her father, shaking a finger at him.

"I do not care if you forgive me or not," she told him sternly. "Go home. I do not want to see you here ever again. You are hateful and nasty, Da. Go home and never return."

Deston was starting to turn shades of red. "You cannot order me about, you little fool."

Ellowyn put her hands on her hips. "I just did," she snapped. "Go home. I do not want to see you anymore. Everything I ever believed in, my father whom I loved so dearly, has all been a lie. The father I knew and loved would have never hurt me this way. If you do not go home this second, I swear that any love I ever felt for you will be forever turned to hatred."

Deston was struck with the devastating impact of her words. He sensed the conversation was at an end and he was furious, shattered, and all things in between. He had never heard Ellowyn speak to him like that, not ever. It was de Russe's doing, he was sure. The man had turned his loving, sweet daughter against him. He could hardly believe it. Rational thought gave way to irrational thought. He had to eliminate what stood between him and

Ellowyn; only then would things be right between them again. De Russe had caused all of this and the man would pay.

With a growl, he brought his sword up again. He was aiming for Brandt but Ellowyn heard the noise, saw what he was intending, and all she could think of was preventing it. She was deeply protective of Brandt, in any situation, and this was no different. With a scream, she threw up her hands and charged at her father, putting herself between Deston and Brandt.

Unfortunately, there was a sword between her and Deston, and it was the beloved and powerful sword of Braxton de Nerra that accidentally carved a searing path into the right side of Ellowyn's torso.

It all happened so fast. Brandt saw Ellowyn rushing towards her armed father but he was unable to get to her in time. When he saw the blade pierce her torso, he shouted something; he wasn't even sure what it was. All he knew was that it was a cry of pure anguish. As he shouted his agony, a nervous St. Hèver archer thought it was a command to fire and let loose an arrow that hit Deston in the throat. As Ellowyn went down with a sword wound, Deston slammed onto his back with a spiny arrow in his throat.

Chaos ensued.

## CHAPTER TWENTY ONE

Brandt stood at the lancet window in the master's bower, his gaze moving out over the bailey of Guildford. It was dawn and the eastern sky was turning shades of pink and purple as gray ribbons of clouds lingered on the horizon. He thought he could smell rain but he wasn't sure.

Behind him on the big bed, Ellowyn was sleeping heavily. She had been sleeping for nearly two days. The physic from Guildford, a thin wiry man by the name of Seever, had given her a poppy potion for the pain on the day of her injury that had knocked her out cold. He continued to give it to her every time she woke up, sending her back down into the black abyss of slumber where she would heal and forget the turmoil of her last lucid memories. Brandt was grateful for the merciful unconsciousness.

So much had happened since that fateful accident. Deston's lingering and gurgling death as his daughter lay in the dirt several feet away and witnessed the horror, the painful hysteria of transporting his wife from the gatehouse to their second floor chamber, Ellowyn's grief at her father's passing, his own stunned grief at her injury... God, it had all passed in a blur.

As Ellowyn had lain wounded and sleeping, Brandt had tried not to drink too much simply to help him cope but that plan had seen multiple failures. He wasn't a weak man by nature, nor did he drink much, but seeing his wife gored with a broadsword had taken something out of him.

Seever had been summoned from the village because Brandt didn't want his surgeon, a burly bear of a man, touching his wife. The old surgeon had a penchant for molesting young women and Brandt didn't want to have to worry that the man was lusting over his wife. So he had sent Stefan into town to retrieve the best physic he could find and the knight had returned with the lanky physic recommended by the priests and the man's wife. The pair had sat with Ellowyn, tending her carefully under the duke's watchful eye.

As Brandt's focus was on his wife, a knight by the name of le Mon had bundled up Deston's corpse and made haste for Erith. Brandt probably should have paid more attention to the care of Deston, but he couldn't manage it. Not with Ellowyn so badly injured. Therefore, he consigned Deston's fate to God and trusted le Mon to take him home... and that was the end of it as far as he was concerned. He couldn't invest any more time and emotion in it than that.

Now, at dawn of the third day, Brandt was emotionally and physically exhausted. He never left Ellowyn, not for a minute – not even when Alex de Lara returned the day after the incident with twenty five hundred men from the Duke of Carlisle and another eight hundred from his father's ally, the Earl of Richmond. Now, here were almost five thousand men swelling the bailey of Guildford and even at sunrise Brandt could smell the stench of too many men. He knew his time was drawing short before he had to return to France because he had what he'd come for – men and support. But he also had a wife he didn't want to leave.

"Brandt?"

He heard the softly uttered question, turning with a start to see that Ellowyn was awake. She was watching him from her stew of pillows and blankets, and he quickly left his post by the window and went to her.

"Why are you awake?" he asked, concerned, as he sat on the bed and put a hand on her forehead to see if she was with fever. "You should be sleeping."

She gazed up at him, groggy. "If the physic sees that I am awake, he will give me some of that damnable potion again and put me back to sleep," she muttered. "Where is he?"

Brandt was relieved to see that she was without fever and he took her hand in his big one, kissing it. "He and his wife are sleeping," he said softly. "They have not left you in two days. I told them to sleep and I would watch over you."

Her groggy gaze turned warm. "I suspect you have not left me, either."

He shook his head, whispering. "Nay."

"Have you slept?"

"Not much."

Ellowyn continued to gaze up at him, perhaps seeing the mighty Duke of Exeter through new eyes. She knew he loved her. She knew he would do anything or her. But the measure of devotion she was coming to see from him was something she could have never imagined. Reaching up a weak hand, she gently touched his face.

"I will be well again very soon," she promised. "Already, I can feel the wound healing. It does not pain me terribly."

He kissed the fingers that lingered on his lips. "I am pleased to hear it."

"I do believe I could sit up and take some nourishment."

"Are you sure?"

"I am famished. Will you help me to sit up?"

He nodded, kissing her fingers again. "Of course I will," he said as he stood up. He began hunting around for pillows to prop her up with. "What do you feel like eating?"

Ellowyn shrugged. "Something warm," she said. "Perhaps broth or gruel. And bread with butter."

He nodded as he reached out to take her hands. "Ready?"

"Ready."

Very gently, he pulled her up from the mattress, watching her make faces as her wound pained her. Groans accompanied the effort. Eventually, she was sitting up enough so that he could wedge several pillows behind her back to support her. Ellowyn, however, was struggling not to become ill. She was pale and gray as she tried to get her balance.

"Oh, heavens," she gasped. "I do not suppose I feel as well as I thought."

He looked concerned. "Do you want to lie down again?"

She feebly shook her head. "Nay," she said firmly. "I would sit here a moment. I shall be fine."

He watched her with concern as she struggled to acclimate herself. "Is your injury paining you?"

Again, she shook her head. "It hurts, but the pain does not consume me," she said. "I can stand it."

He adjusted her pillows carefully, trying to help her. "The physic said it did not cut anything vital and that it was not particularly deep," he said. "We can be thankful for that."

"Thankful indeed," she grunted. He was so busy fussing with her pillows that he didn't notice she was tearing up. "My father... where is he?"

He heard the weepy tone and stopped adjusting the pillows, looking her in the face. He was immediately stricken with her sadness, wiping at the tears on her cheeks.

"I sent him home," he told her softly, kissing her forehead even as he helped her wipe her tears. "I am so sorry you had to witness all of that, sweetheart, but I promise that we took care of him. Your father is on his way home, as he requested."

She sobbed softly. "What happened?" she begged. "Why was he fired upon?"

He sighed heavily, thinking back to that moment in time when Deston lay on the ground drying and Ellowyn lay several feet away, screaming as her father bled to death in front of her. Brandt's only concern had been Ellowyn at the moment and not the mechanics of what had happened. He didn't care why, only that it had. But he had certainly found out after the fact what had happened. Now, it was time for Ellowyn to know.

"It was an accident," he said quietly. "When your father advanced, the archers thought I gave a battle command. It was a nervous mistake and nothing more."

She looked up at him with her big watery eyes. "So they killed my father?" she whispered. "I tried to stop him... he was going to kill you, Brandt. I could not let him do it."

His jaw ticked with sorrow as he cupped her head in his big hand, pulling her cheek to his lips to comfort her. She had every right to be distraught. But, then again, he was fairly distraught himself. He'd spent two days living that moment over and over again, astonished that Ellowyn would put herself in danger to save him. He was having difficulty accepting that someone other than a loyal knight should be so devoted to him. His knights were loyal out of respect to him and respect to their oath; she was devoted purely out of love.

"I am the most fortunate man on earth," he said after a moment. "That you should try to protect me with your life, Ellowyn... I do not know what to say except how fortunate I feel to have such devotion. But he could have killed you."

Ellowyn didn't reply; she was still weeping softly, wiping at her cheeks, and he left her long enough to find a kerchief among the goods strewn about the room and bring it back to her. She wiped her face off

"If given the chance, I would do the same thing again," she said softly. "I could not let him kill you. I will not let anyone kill you."

"You are very brave."

She shook her head, fixing him in the eye. "I am not brave," she said. "I am in love with my husband and there is nothing I would not do for him, even if it cost me my life."

He stroked her head with a big hand. "As I said," he whispered, "I am the most fortunate man on earth."

Ellowyn smiled weakly, blowing her nose and wiping off the remainder of her tears. It was evident that she was attempting to regain her composure. But the tears weren't finished yet.

"Dear God," she sighed, gazing up to the ceiling, the window, as if seeing things beyond. "What is my mother going to say? She will be crushed. And my grandmother... I cannot even fathom what she will be feeling."

He watched her a moment. "Do you want to return home?"

Her head snapped to him, eyes wide with surprise. "Home?" she repeated. "Why would you ask that?"

He shrugged. "To tend to your mother and grandmother in the wake of your father's death," he said softly. "If you wish to return to Erith, I will send you with an escort."

She cocked her head. "You will not go with me?"

He sighed heavily, again, and moved towards the lancet window that overlooked the bailey. The day was cool and breezy at dawn as the men below were already awake and going about their affairs.

"Alex returned yesterday with over three thousand men," he said. "I have what I returned to England for; I have men to support Edward's war in France. There is no longer any reason for me to remain here. I would be happy to send you back to Erith to stay with your mother and grandmother, but I must return to France."

Ellowyn stared at him. "Just like that?" she asked. "With everything that has happened and everything we have said to each other, you would leave me behind without a second thought?"

He turned to look at her. "It is not how you make it seem," he said, rather perplexed that she should seem so emotional when they'd had the same conversation a dozen times. "Of course I do not want to leave you, but I certainly cannot take you with me. I...."

"Why not?"

He shook his head firmly, leaning up against the windowsill. "We have been over this subject, Wynny," he said. "You know why I cannot take you."

"But I do not want to go to Erith. I want to go with you."

"You cannot."

Emotional, exhausted, and wounded, she burst into angry tears, falling over on the bed and sobbing into the pillows that surrounded her. Then she screeched somewhat when her wound pained her from the sudden movement. Brandt came away from the window and went to the bed, trying to soothe her. She was lying awkwardly and he carefully gathered her up and tried to move her, but she cried out in pain when he tried so he simply left her. His big hand stroked her hair.

"Please do not do this," he begged softly. "Please do not upset yourself so. You know I must go and you cannot go with me. Why do you torment yourself so?"

She wept pitifully. "My father is dead," she sobbed. "Now you would leave me. I will be all alone."

"You will not be alone if you return to Erith," he reminded her gently. "You will be with your mother and grandmother."

"Please do not leave me," she cried, acting as if she had not heard him. "I am afraid that this heaven that we have known, this bliss that has become everything to me, will cease to exist once you are gone and will never be the same. When you return again, we will be as strangers and perhaps things will be different, and if you do not return at all, I do not want my news of your death to be delivered by cold and unfeeling men who have no regard for the love you and I share. Please, Brandt... I beg you... take me with you."

He sighed sadly; unfortunately, he was feeling himself relent. He had been now for some time. It was true that he had many properties in France and it was true that she could live there and he could see her far more often than if she remained behind in England. Aye, he wanted her with him. He wanted her more than he would admit. He struggled to make one last stand against the pleading that was breaking down his walls like a battering ram.

"Wynny, I cannot," he whispered. "All of France is in turmoil. It is no place for you."

She covered her face with her hands. "Then it is true," she wept. "What my father said is true. War is your mistress and Edward is more important than I am."

"That is *not* true."

"Aye, it is," she nearly screamed at him. "If it were not true, you would ensure that we were never apart. But your prince, and your wars, are by far more important than I am. What a fool I was to think a declaration of love would change all of that. You are a warrior, Brandt, and a husband second. That pains me more than you will ever know and if I mean no more to you than that, I may as well return to Erith."

He looked like a beaten dog. "You told your father that you would stay here and administer my lands," he reminded her softly.

The hand flew away from her face, the pale eyes blazing. "I will *not* stay here and be reminded of my loneliness at every turn," she snapped. "I will go home to my mother and grandmother, and try not to think of my husband who thinks less of me than his horse. At least his horse gets to go to France."

It would have been a comical and petulant statement had he allowed himself to think so, but he couldn't because Ellowyn was off on a crying tangent. Brandt gazed down at her, feeling incredible sadness and guilt. He just stood there, looking at her, listening to her sobs and feeling more turmoil than he had ever felt in his life. He was a man of strong decisions and a firm mind, never one to be swayed by another and certainly never one to be swayed by a woman. But this wasn't just a woman; this was his wife whom he loved with all his heart. He didn't want to leave her, either.

As Ellowyn eventually cried herself to sleep, Brandt stood over the bed, lost in thought. He was coming to think that somehow, someway, his battles with Edward were no longer the most important thing to him. It was more that the prince's warfare was all he knew; it was his life, his vocation.

King Edward had personally asked Brandt to control and manage young Edward's wars in France because he knew that Brandt de Russe was a lord of war from a long line of warlords. The de Russe family was well known for breeding the biggest and the meanest and the best. The Prince of Wales was young and rash at times, and de Russe was the perfect balance with his wisdom and strength. It had been a perfect partnership until the moment Brandt knocked Ellowyn into the water trough outside of Gray's Inn.

After that, everything changed.

\*\*\*

"My lady, I must state quite clearly that the duke will be furious if he discovers you have left the castle," Brennan said. "More than that, he will be furious with me for enabling such a thing. I beg you to reconsider."

Five days after her encounter with a sword, Ellowyn was on her feet. She was moving very stiffly, but at least she was moving. Dressed in a mustard-colored silk surcoat with an eggshell-colored shift beneath, she looked radiant except for the smudge of dark circles beneath her eyes. It was the only outward appearance that she had suffered a brush with violence.

As Brennan spoke the words, she eyed the stiff young knight. "He is off doing things that are more important to him," she said briskly. "I had the servants help me pack this morning. I am going to Erith today and I want you to take me."

Brennan was in over his head; he knew that already. "Lady de Russe, I have many pressing duties to attend to today," he told her. "Although it would be a great privilege, I cannot escort you to Erith."

Ellowyn looked at him as if he had just grievously insulted her; her emotions, aggravated by her injury, had been raging over the past couple of days since Brandt had told her he planned to return to France right away and refused to take her with him. She had convinced herself that he had lied to her when he told her that he loved her. A man couldn't love his wife and then leave her behind as far as she was concerned.

Her father had been correct; she would always be second to Brandt's ambition and devotion to the Prince of Wales. She felt demeaned, humiliated, and terribly hurt. She just wanted to go home with the people who truly loved her. She needed to tell her father, who would surely be in his grave by then, how sorry she was for everything.

Perhaps that was the crux of the entire situation; had she not run away with Brandt, Deston would more than likely still be alive so, in a sense, she killed her father. Her guilt was great, perhaps great enough to taint her views on Brandt. He had expressed fear once that she would change her mind about him if he had killed her father and she assured him that nothing would change. Perhaps she had been wrong, about a lot of things.

"Very well," she snapped. "If you cannot do it, then I will ask you to find someone who can. If you cannot find anyone by the nooning meal, I will leave on my own. Do you understand?"

Brennan was quite aware that he was being bullied. "Aye, my lady, but I must tell your husband what you have asked of me."

She shook finger at him "If you tell him, I shall never forgive you or trust you again, Brennan St. Hèver . You will promise me that you will not say anything to him at all."

He shook his head but took a step towards the door as he did so. "I regret that I cannot make that promise, my lady."

"Do you mean to tell me that you would violate my trust in you?"

"I mean to tell you that I am sworn to your husband, my lady, and it is Lord de Russe that I answer to. If he found out that I aided you on a flight from Guildford, he would have my head."

Furious, Ellowyn pointed imperiously at the door. "Out!" she commanded. "I will find someone else I can trust!"

Brennan moved swiftly for the door, a rather comical sight because it looked as if the man was truly afraid of the very angry lady. Once outside the door, he breathed a sigh of relief but made haste to locate Brandt.

A perusal of the entire castle had not turned him up. Dylan was missing, too. Le Bec, who had the watch upon the wall, could only tell him that de Russe and de Lara had ridden off towards the town but he didn't know any more than that. He suspected that the duke had ridden south to Godalming to a smaller castle inhabited by the wealthy and refined Lady Catteshall, because the woman was wildly wealthy. Part of his mission for the prince was to seek monetary support, and the knights suspected he was doing just that.

Surprisingly, Lady Catteshall had a damn good army of three hundred men and owned a great deal of land, and she ruled the province perhaps more than Brandt did. She was very respected and very generous. Nervous about Lady de Russe, Brennan remained upon the wall, watching anxiously for Brandt's return.

Unfortunately for Brennan, Lady de Russe sent for her carriage just before noon. He knew this because he saw the thing brought around from the stables, pulled by the two fine gray horses. Just as he was preparing to descend the wall to prevent Lady de Russe from leaving by any means necessary, including throwing himself down in front of the carriage, Stefan sighted incoming riders. There was a small group approaching from the south and one of the sentries, with particularly good eye sight, was convinced it was Brandt. The shout went out and the race against time was on.

Brennan came down from the wall and went to intercept the carriage. As he drew close, he could see movement at the top of the motte as Lady de Russe made an appearance. She had three out of the four female servants with her, carrying satchels and sacks with them as they carefully made their way down the motte steps.

Brennan was watching, feeling the distinct onset of panic. Once Lady de Russe loaded the carriage, there would be nothing to truly stop her from leaving unless Brennan made himself a human sacrifice before the whip-driven horses. His mind moved quickly, trying to think of a way to delay her until her husband arrived.

One of the gray horses shifted and kicked, and his attention was drawn to the hitching mechanism that connected the harnesses to the coach. A thought occurred to him; keeping his eyes on Lady de Russe as she descended the stairs, he edged his way over to the harness and, casually, reached down and plucked out the pin that held it all together. Using the iron pin, he poked one of the horses in the butt hard enough to cause the animal to bolt, and the entire rig pulled apart.

The coach staggered sideways as the team stumbled off. Soldiers and grooms went running after them, corralling them, as Ellowyn, now at the base of the motte, looked on in concern. Brennan pretended to be concerned as well, trying not to look at Lady de Russe as she wondered what had happened to her coach and team. In fact, he ignored her even as she began to load her own baggage into the cab.

When she wasn't looking, he slipped around to the oppose side, popped open the door, and unloaded her baggage from the other side. Then he would slip it under the cab where she had set all of her bags to be loaded. Ellowyn ended up loading the same bags at least three times before she thought something was amiss, and by that time, the gates of Guildford were opening for the returning duke.

Brandt thundered into the bailey alongside Dylan and with two other horses following close behind. The first thing he saw as he rode into the bailey was his wife's carriage near the motte, which both surprised and concerned him. The doors were open and as he drew closer through the crowds of men, he could see two of the female servants near the coach and baggage on the ground. Then, he saw his wife.

Clad in a rich wool surcoat of mustard yellow and wearing a deep blue cloak, she looked magnificent. He allowed himself a moment simply to gaze upon her because she really hadn't spoken to him since that day she accused him of loving warfare more than he loved her. He's wrestled with her statement for a full day until that morning when he decided to do something about it.

He'd gone to see Lady Catteshall because he knew she could help him. He'd been rather excited to return to Guildford and let Ellowyn in on his decision, but the longer he gazed at her, the more he began to realize that something was amiss. The baggage near the carriage was hers and she had absolutely no interest in making eye contact with him. Spurring his charger through the crowds, he roared up to the coach.

Ellowyn was hit by flying pebbles when Brandt's steed came to a clumsy halt. Grunting with annoyance, she brushed a few flecks of dirty off her cloak as she turned towards the offender. Realizing it was her husband, she stiffened when their eyes met before swiftly turning away.

"What is all of this?" Brandt demanded as he dismounted his sweaty steed. When his wife kept her back turned to him, he grew irritated. "Ellowyn, I am addressing you. What is all of this?"

She turned to him, a look of defiance and stubbornness on her face. "I am returning to Erith as I said I would," she told him coldly. "I will find my own escort so you do not have to trouble yourself."

He just stared at her. Nearly two days of her surly, somber attitude and bouts with the silent treatment had his emotions surging. He was frustrated and he was angry. More than that, he was hurt. He'd never been hurt before. Reaching out, he snatched her by the hand.

"You are coming with me," he growled.

Ellowyn immediately started to fight him. "Let me go," she demanded, trying to pull away. "I am not going anywhere with you."

Brandt didn't want to hurt her; her injury was still paining her and he didn't want to cause her any more agony, but he was genuinely furious. He swooped down on her and picked her up.

"This will end now," he rumbled.

He carried Ellowyn, kicking and struggling, all the way up to the keep. She beat her hands against his plate armor, demanding he put her down, but he wouldn't listen to her. By the time he got her into the keep, she had torn her surcoat in her struggles and her carefully braided hair was unraveling. He set her on her feet when they reached his solar.

Ellowyn twisted her way from his grip as he tried to put her down and ended up straining her injured torso. She hissed in pain, pressing a hand against the wound as she staggered away from him.

"What is the matter with you?" she demanded. "How dare you handle me like a common wench!"

He stood by the entry to make sure she couldn't escape. "How dare you behave like one," he fired back quietly. "You are the Duchess of Exeter. Your recent behavior does not suit that position."

Ellowyn scowled. "I do not know what you mean," she said. "You told me I could return home. I am doing that."

He faced her, hands on hips, jaw ticking. "Wynny, I am not entirely sure how the mood between us has deteriorated so, but it will end now," he said, struggling to calm. "I do not like it when you ignore me. I realize the past few days have been disruptive to say the least, but you are taking all of your frustration out on me. Is that fair?"

Ellowyn's features relaxed somewhat as she considered the question. After a moment, she appeared to deflate. Her gaze lowered. Then, she turned away from him, hand resting gingerly on her injured torso.

"You are going to France," she said with a shrug. "You said yourself that I should go back to Erith."

"I *asked* you if you wanted to return to be with your mother and grandmother," he said. "I never told you to return to Erith. Furthermore, while you have been stomping around like a petulant child and ignoring me at every turn, I have been busy making arrangements for my return to France, the plans of which now include you."

It took her a moment for his words to sink in. When they did, she whirled to face him, eyes wide with astonishment.

"*Me?*" she gasped. "I am going with you?"

He put his hands on his hips. "I should just as well leave you here for all of the tantrums you have exhibited over the past few days."

She could see that his irritation was real. His mood tempered her joy with uncertainty. "Then why did you decide to bring me?"

He lost some of his irritation. "Because... oh, hell, I suppose it is because your words the other day meant something to me," he said. "You must understand that until recently, all I knew was war. It is in my blood. But somehow, someway, you are in my blood now, too. You have shown me a life I never knew existed, Wynny. You are my wife and you are the most important thing in the world to me. When I return to France, it is because I said I would. It is not because my heart is in it. That particular part of me seems to belong to you."

All of Ellowyn's hurt and anger evaporated and she smiled at his sweet confession. "I am sorry if it seemed as if I was being difficult," she said softly. Then she shrugged awkwardly. "You said you were leaving and all I could think was that I would never see you again. Everything we have now, between us, would be gone forever. I started to think on my father's words, of how I would always be second in your life behind Prince Edward, and I was deeply hurt by it. Mayhap... mayhap ignoring you was a way of saving my heart. It is so fragile where you are concerned."

He sighed heavily, his eyes raking over her lovely face. "Being ignored by you for two days has hurt my heart deeply," he said softly. "I wonder what you will do to make it up to me?"

It was an invitation and a peace offering. Ellowyn didn't hesitate; she moved to him, putting her arms around his neck as he swallowed her into his enormous embrace. Feeling him in her arms, alive and vibrant, brought relief and joy. She shoved her face into the crook of his neck, smelling him and feeling the texture of his skin against hers. It was heavenly.

"I will do whatever you wish," she whispered, squeezing him. "Thank you for taking me with you, Brandt. I swear I will be no trouble at all."

He kissed her, hard, because he hadn't kissed her in two days and he found he was fairly starving to taste her. His big hands stroked her face, her hair.

"I have travelled with you before and know what to expect from you," he said. "But I went on an errand this morning to a neighbor, a Lady Catteshall. She is old and matronly but, as I remember from my younger days, she is a woman of tremendous grace and wisdom. I went to ask her what I should do in order to make your travels more comfortable and she was kind enough to provide me with two of her ladies."

Ellowyn cocked her head. "Ladies?"

He nodded and released her from their embrace. "Lady Catteshall is well-known for schooling young women who have gone on to be fine ladies for countesses and duchesses and even royalty. Even when I was there, she had at least twelve or fifteen ladies with her. She provided me with two she feels would make good companions for you so you will not be entirely lonely."

Ellowyn looked dubious. "Women I do not know?" she said, pursing her lips. "I do not believe that I need companions, Brandt. You will be my companion."

He nodded. "I realize that, but there will be times when I will not be with you," he said. "I will be away, fighting, and I want to make sure you have suitable companionship while I am away. Most titled women have ladies in waiting, and you shall be no different."

She still looked doubtful. "Can I at least meet them?" she asked. "What if I do not like them? Can I send them away?"

He took her hand and led her towards the entry. "If you do not like them, I shall take you to Lady Catteshall and you can choose your own companions."

It was enough to pacify her reluctance, at least until she could look the women over. He took her from the keep, holding her hand as they moved down the treacherous motte stairs which had recently had a rope hand-rail installed. The coach was still there, now with the gray team reattached and the baggage loaded inside. It was ready and waiting for the determined Lady de Russe.

Brennan was standing with the driver, watching Brandt and Ellowyn descend the stairs. He could tell by their body language that things were well between them once again. He met the pair at the bottom of the steps.

"Shall I arrange for an escort to Erith, my lord?" he asked Brandt.

Brandt cocked an eyebrow. "She is *not* going to Erith," he said frankly. "Did you arrange for this carriage, St. Hèver ?"

Brennan opened his mouth to reply but Ellowyn cut him off. "I ordered the carriage," she said. "Brennan did everything possible to discourage me from going and even refused to help me find an escort. In fact, he did everything he could to prevent me from leaving, the sly devil. He should be commended for being so loyal to you."

Brandt eyed her. "I can only imagine how you verbally pummeled the man because he would not do your bidding."

She turned her nose up at him, although she was smiling. "I did nothing of the sort," she said. "Even if I did, he is too chivalrous to say otherwise."

Brandt was still inclined to feel some jealousy over Brennan but it had been fading as of late. The more secure he felt in his relationship with Ellowyn, the more his jealousies seemed to fade. Still, he wasn't entirely free of it. He nodded curtly to Ellowyn's statement.

"Indeed," he said, eyeing Brennan. "Get this damnable coach out of here."

Fighting off a grin, Brennan did as he was told. As he whistled loudly between his teeth and ordered the carriage away, Brandt took Ellowyn by the hand and led her over towards the great hall.

It was very warm inside the hall, almost too warm on the temperate day. A fire sputtered in the enormous hearth and the two dogs that had been up in the keep had somehow made their way down to the hall, sleeping near the fire. Ellowyn immediately spied Dylan at one of the tables with two young women, seated and with cups before them. Gilbert, the old servant, was filling the cups with rich red wine. Brandt led Ellowyn to the table that was strewn with a collection of dried fruits, cheese, and bread.

"This is my wife, the Lady Ellowyn de Nerra de Russe, Duchess of Exeter," Brandt introduced Ellowyn to the women. "Wynny, this is the Lady Annabeth du Gare and the Lady Bridget St. John."

He indicated the lush brunette first and the pale redhead second. Both women jumped to their feet at the introduction and very gracefully curtsied.

"My lady," the greeted Ellowyn in unison.

Ellowyn was polite as she acknowledged them. "My husband just told me I am to have ladies accompany me to France," she said. "That being the case, mayhap we should become acquainted."

Lady Annabeth was petite, pretty, and big-breasted. She was also very young. She smiled at Ellowyn as she moved down the bench.

"Will you sit, Lady de Russe?" she said, indicating the open spot next to her.

Ellowyn took the offered seat. When Brandt moved to sit as well, she stopped him. "Nay, husband," she told him rather pointedly. "I will sit with the ladies alone for now. I am sure you have other duties to attend to and women talk would not interest you."

Brandt wriggled his eyebrows and grabbed Dylan by the arm, pulling the man with him. "As you wish, my lady," he said. "I will station a soldier outside the entry should you require anything."

"Thank you," Ellowyn said, smiling sweetly.

Brandt's lips twitched with a smile as he pulled Dylan with him from the hall, basically being thrown out by his wife. But he understood; she wanted to speak with the women alone and make her own determination as to whether or not she thought they were suitable companions. As he reached the hall entry, Brennan, Stefan and Alex were standing right outside the door. Brandt nearly plowed into them.

"What are you doing crowded around?" he wanted to know.

Brennan looked innocent, Stefan shrugged, and Alex was the only one to answer truthfully.

"I saw the redhead, my lord," he said. "I wanted to get a better look at her."

Brandt just shook his head. "I brought these women for my wife, not for you," he said, thumping Alex on the chest and turning the man around. "Get on with your tasks, all of you. You will not hound those women like dogs on the prowl."

"A pity," Dylan muttered. "The brunette is something to behold."

Before Brandt could scold him, he scattered with the rest of them. Brandt should have gone along with them but he just couldn't seem to do it. He stood outside of the hall entry, listening. For several minutes it was very quiet, but soon enough, female voices could be heard lifted in humor and every once in a while someone would laugh. Eventually, he heard his wife laughing. It was good to hear. After what she had gone through, he was pleased to hear that she hadn't lost her ability to laugh.

With a smile, he went about his business.

# FRANCE

# CHAPTER TWENTY TWO

*August 1356 A.D.*
*Chateau Melesse*
*Brittany*

Ellowyn and Annabeth were giggling so hard that they were nearly crying. They could hear Bridget screaming at the French chatelaine of Melesse Castle, a severe woman who had to be at least seventy years old. She was precise, nasty-tempered, knowledgeable, and a bully. Ever since Brandt and Ellowyn had arrived nearly seven months prior, the woman went out of her way to make the duke and duchess comfortable but she was horrid with their retainers.

It had proven something of a challenge for Annabeth and Bridget. Both young women had turned out to be wonderful companions and Ellowyn was very fond of them both, and they both seemed to have a somewhat wicked streak when it came to the haughty French servants of Melesse. The chatelaine, Mme. de Simpelace, was the queen of the roost and Ellowyn's two ladies had taken to calling her Mme. de Pimpleface. The chatelaine was not amused when she caught wind of the nickname and the battle for supremacy was on.

Ellowyn had brought up the subject of dismissing the woman but Brandt wasn't keen on hiring anyone new; they were, for all intent and purposes, in an enemy land, and he didn't want a new chatelaine, perhaps with a great hatred for the English, so close to his beloved wife.

Meanwhile, old Mme. Pimpleface would go out of her way to make things difficult and this moment was a perfect example. On this warm and lazy afternoon in the last week of August, Ellowyn had asked for warmed cider and the woman had produced a scorching product that was anything but cider. Very protective of their young duchess, Bridget had gone after the woman and even now was demanding that the squeeze the apples herself and boil the juice. Mme. de Simpelace was not inclined to do so, and the catfight was on.

So Ellowyn and Annabeth giggled like fools as they sat in a richly appointed solar that Brandt had assigned to Ellowyn for her personal use. She sat in a very comfortable chair, perhaps the most comfortable in the entire castle, and held her swollen belly as she snorted.

"Mayhap I do not need any cider after all," she finally said, sobering. "It seems to be too much trouble for Madam."

Annabeth made a face. "It is not too much trouble for her," she sniffed. "She simply likes to make things difficult, and I am positive she likes to argue with us. I think she feels she is doing her duty to France to protest the English in her own small way."

Ellowyn, still grinning, picked her knitting up off her lap and looked to resume where she left off. "I suppose," she said. "Brandt trusts her because she has been with the family for so long so I suppose there is not much we can do about her."

As Ellowyn resumed knitting a large and lovely blanket that was to be part of the baby's trousseau, Annabeth picked up the needlepoint she had been working on. She watched Ellowyn out of the corner of her eye, her slow and steady stitches with the soft white wool. Having spent every single day with the woman since the moment she met her, not only had they become good friends but she was also very attuned to Ellowyn's moods. She could tell by her mannerisms, her behavior, and her movements what she was feeling. And she knew that today she was feeling particularly blue.

"Mayhap the duke will return today," she said as she stabbed at the material in front of her. "He has been gone for quite some time now. He never leaves you for long."

Ellowyn was carefully stitching her blanket. "Forty-seven days," she said softly. "It is the longest he has been away yet. Sometimes I think I forget the color of his eyes or the feel of his skin. It seems like such a long time."

Annabeth sighed faintly; they had the same conversation almost every day since the duke left. Since the moment they arrived in France back in February, the duke would go off with the Prince of

Wales for days or weeks at a time, but he would always return. Strangely, the prince had never come to Melesse and Annabeth had heard the knights whispering that it was because he was jealous of the woman who had stolen the Black Angel's heart. For whatever the reason, they had never met the man.

"But the duke will return," she insisted softly. "When he left this last time, he said he would be in the Aquitaine, did he not? That is some distance away. It will take time to return home again."

"And Dylan with him?" Ellowyn glanced up, grinning at Annabeth when the woman blushed.

"I would hope so," Annabeth said softly. "And Bridget is most anxious for Brennan to return."

"I know she is," Ellowyn looked down at her knitting again. "Has he even kissed her yet?"

Annabeth shook her head. "Not yet," she said. "But Bridget is determined that he will very soon. She wants to be married to him before the end of the year."

The door to the solar opened, interrupting their conversation. Bridget entered the room, the pale and lovely redhead, with a cup in her hand wielded high like a trophy.

"I have it!" she said. "Cider, my lady. I had to kill several Frenchmen to get it, but here it is."

Ellowyn and Annabeth were back to giggling. "Really, Bridget," Ellowyn admonished softly. "Warmed cider is not worth murder."

Bridget grinned as she carefully handed Ellowyn the cup. "I beg to differ, my lady," she said. "The infant demands apples and apples he shall have. Whatever goes into your mouth goes directly to him to make him big and strong like his father. We are quite anxious to meet him, you know."

Ellowyn rubbed her belly. "Not too soon," she said. "He is not due until October. We do not want to meet him too soon."

Small talk bounced between them as Bridget went to one of the three long and slender lancet windows in the room to secure the oilcloth that had come loose from its binding. There was a nice breeze, cooling the warm air as she gazed out over the enormous bailey of Melesse.

It was a massive bastion that had been in Exeter's family for nearly two hundred years, part of a dowry from a grandmother several generations back. Situated on the top of a wooded hill with vast views of the surrounding countryside in all directions, it was a truly magnificent structure of golden stone and soaring towers. It was at least twice the size of Guildford and four times the size of Erith, with rooms and passages, kitchens, two halls, and innumerable miscellaneous chambers. For the first several months of their residency, they'd had great fun exploring it all until Brandt put a stop to it, fearful his pregnant wife would hurt herself going up and down narrow stairs or squeezing through tight passages.

It wasn't particularly strange that a man so devoted to his wife should become even more devoted with the event of her pregnancy. Ellowyn had felt fine since the beginning and ate like a horse as Brandt watched every move she made with a nervous edge. He was thrilled and deeply thankful for the pregnancy, which made it extraordinarily difficult for him to leave from time to time to go on campaigns with Edward.

In fact, the situation was heating up with Edward's wars as he drove north from Aquitaine on a campaign to grow his base and strengthen his troops, and Brandt was simply going through the motions. His heart wasn't in it; he wanted to be home with his wife and he certainly wanted to be present for the birth of the baby. Rumor had it, according to the knights, that Edward and Brandt were growing increasingly hostile towards each other because of it.

Why was why Bridget knew Brandt wouldn't be away for too much longer. They had been counting the days. In fact, as she stood in the window watching the bailey below, a group of soldiers flooded in from the gatehouse. Because of the angle of the road and the trees surrounding it, it was often difficult to spot visitors to Melesse until they were upon them. Curious, Bridget peered closer to the worn-out group, suddenly realizing a knight from Brandt's Corp was with them. She recognized the charger.

"Magnus has returned," she said, bolting away from the window. "He is in the bailey!"

Ellowyn was so startled that she jumped up, her knitting falling to the floor. "Is Brandt with him?"

She was rushing to the window with Annabeth on her heels. Bridget closed in on them and the three of them crowded around the window, straining to see the dusty bailey below. Ellowyn couldn't see much now that the party had fully entered the bailey and, frustrated, she turned away.

"I am going to see Magnus," she declared as she moved for the door. Then, she froze, eyes wide. "You do not suppose... Sweet Jesus, you do not suppose he is here to give me bad news?"

Annabeth and Bridget tried not to look fearful. Before they could reply, Ellowyn was bolting from the room and making haste towards the massive spiral staircase at the end of the hall that led to the first floor beyond. She was in a panic now, terrified that Magnus had come bearing news of Brandt's injury or worse. By the time she reached the lower floor and fled to the keep entry, she was in tears.

Cooler heads prevailed with Annabeth and Bridget as they followed. They caught up to Ellowyn as she reached the entry and grasped her gently by the arms, stopping her panicked flight. By this time, most of the keep had been made aware of a knight's return and even old Mme. Simpelace appeared. When she saw Ellowyn's hysteria, she was naturally concerned.

"What is it?" she demanded. "Why is my lady so upset?"

Annabeth cast the woman a long look and shook her head, *do not ask more.* The old woman, silly and vindictive as she might be, took the hint. She may have been at odds with the ladies but she was not at odds with Ellowyn. She was genuinely concerned.

"I will bring her something soothing," she said as she scooted off.

Annabeth and Bridget exchanged relieved glances that the old biddie had left them alone. Ellowyn, however, was insistent that they go down to the bailey where Magnus was, so they calmly escorted her down the big wooden stairs to the dusty, rocky bailey below.

It was windy upon the mountain top, gusts whipping around hair and hemlines. Magnus was with several other soldiers near the stable block to the south.  Melesse had a wide-open and sloping bailey because of the shape of the mountain top they sat upon, and the stables were lodged on perhaps the flattest part. Ellowyn pulled free of her escorts and gathered her skirts, racing across the dust until she came to the smelly stables.  She didn't want to wait any longer for whatever news Magnus brought.

"Magnus!" she called as she approached. "*Magnus!*"

Magnus was just removing his helm as he heard Lady de Russe's voice.  Startled, he whirled around to see that she was racing towards him. With her big belly evident, he did what her ladies often did – he made haste towards her and tried to stop her momentum.

"Lady de Russe," he said, grasping her by the arms. "Why are you running? You should not be exerting yourself so."

Ellowyn would have none of his mothering.  "Stop telling me what I should and should not be doing," she snapped. "Everyone tells me that and I hate it, do you hear? Tell me where my husband is this instant."

He wasn't surprised by the tone of the demand. Lady de Russe was well known for her snappish manner at times, made worse by the babe she carried.  In fact, all of the knights had lived in fear of it, including her husband, making going to war somewhat of the less fearful option.

"He is a few days behind me, my lady," he replied steadily. "He has sent me back to Melesse to wait for him."

Ellowyn cocked her head, calming now that her husband was the subject of the conversation. "Wait for him?" she repeated. "What do you mean?"

Magnus sighed faintly and it was then that Ellowyn noticed he looked particularly pale. So pale, in fact, that the circles beneath his eyes were almost green in tint.  She peered closely at him.

"Magnus, are you well?" she asked. "What is the matter?"

He took her elbow and turned her for the keep.  As they walked, Ellowyn and her ladies noticed that he was moving particularly slow.

"I was wounded nearly two weeks ago," he replied. "I have been unable to keep up with Lord de Russe although I have tried.  I was nearly killed yesterday because my reflexes are slow, so the duke asked me to return to Melesse and rest until he returns."

Ellowyn was very concerned for him. "Where were you wounded?"

Magnus gingerly touched his right hip area. "Here," he replied. "We were in a skirmish near the town of Niort and I took a bad blow. At least the poison seems to be diminishing now, but I am fairly useless in battle at the moment."

Ellowyn watched his face carefully. "Is there a lot of battle now?"

They had reached the steps leading up into the keep. Magnus' gaze fell on the heavy woods stairs, the rocky ground, and the massive keep. Anything but her face. When he finally spoke, it was quietly.

"Aye," he replied. "There is a lot of it now."

"More than usual?"

Magnus looked at her, then. "Edward has begun his push for supremacy," he said. "We have been pushing north from the Aquitaine for weeks now, burning and looting and raiding the likes of which I have never seen before. We will push all the way to Paris and finally conquer this country. It has begun."

Ellowyn didn't like the sound of that. "What has begun?"

"The beginning of the end for the monarchy of France."

Apprehensive, she put a hand over her mouth in mounting horror at the very thought of what he was suggesting.

"Where is my husband?" she hissed. "What is he doing?"

"He is in the middle of it," Magnus said quietly. "The Angel of Death has been unleashed. Edward has driven the man to a frenzy and the *l'ange noir* is doing what he was bred to do. He is killing and he is conquering, making a path for Edward to follow. I have never seen anything like it in my life."

Ellowyn could feel the tears in her eyes. "What has happened that Edward would drive him so?" she asked. "Is my husband well?"

Magnus nodded. "He is well," he replied. "But he is like a man possessed; the prince has denied him repeated requests to return home for a short time, so he is quite angry, as you can imagine. He fights with the Earl of Warwick and various other lords, all of whom have tried to maintain calm counsel with him, but he is not a happy man these days. He wants to return home to you. He told me to tell you that he will see you very soon and he hopes you are of good health."

She lost some of her apprehension and sadness as Magnus mentioned Brandt's thoughts for her. The man was destroying a country for a greedy young prince and still, his thoughts were of her.

"I am quite well," she said. "When do you suppose he will return?"

They reached the base of the steps leading up into the keep and Magnus came to a halt.

"Soon, Lady de Russe," he said. "I cannot tell you exactly when, but soon."

That seemed to satisfy Ellowyn for the most part. She allowed Annabeth and Bridget to guide her up the stairs as Magnus slowly followed. When she got to the top, she asked Bridget to assist Magnus because the man obviously wasn't well. Magnus was grateful for the assistance but kept a safe distance from the redhead because he knew St. Hèver would murder him in his sleep if he was forward with the woman.

As Ellowyn went to rest with Annabeth in attendance, Bridget and Mme. Simpelace tended to Magnus and put the man to bed. They discovered he was far worse off than he let on and the old chatelaine sent for the castle surgeon, a tiny rot of a man who had seen better days. He wasn't a particularly good physic but he was all they had. A midwife tended Lady de Russe and she wouldn't let the old man near the young mother.

While Magnus suffered through a wound cleaning, Ellowyn slept away the afternoon, her dreams filled with visions of Brandt.

\*\*\*

The battle outside of Le Haye against Jean de Clermont, the Marshal of France, had been particularly bad. Brandt and his army had held the front line of a very nasty skirmish in a rather sticky summer downpour, creating the epic mud he had warned Ellowyn about. Brandt, however, had used it to his advantage.

De Clermont was arrogant and rash. Knowing this, Brandt had planted a line of knights and men in the distance for him to see while keeping the bulk of his forces, including his archers, hidden in the thick forests surrounding the fields just outside of Le Haye. When de Clermont charged at the decoy army, Brandt brought his archers out of the woods and fired heavy volleys of arrows into the flanks of the charging horses. The armor on the horses tended to be much weaker than the armor on the men, and the English arrows pierced the armor easily, bringing down hundreds or horses in a very short amount of time. More than that, with the mud, they couldn't maneuver very well or escape. They were like sitting ducks.

The results were devastating for the French. Brandt unleashed his entire army on de Clermont's foundering men and it was a slaughter from the onset. Brandt himself was in the thick of the battle, using his massive broadsword to bring down heavily armed knights. The Black Angel was in his element in the midst of a battle, slugging through the mud and rain, weakening de Clermont's army to the point where the man eventually called a retreat. He vacated with heavy losses.

Brandt canvassed the battlefield with the rest of his men, looking for their own dead and wounded before moving to the French dead and wounded. Those who were badly wounded were put to the blade and those who could walk or at least function were corralled as prisoners of war. Brandt also had his men round up the chargers who hadn't been mortally wounded in the arrow onslaught, and he ended up with some very fine horses that could be healed. Those who were too badly injured were more mercifully put down than their human counterparts.

With their booty of horses and a victory for the prince, Brandt and his eight hundred men retreated to Edward's encampment near Chavigney, east of Poitiers. Brandt had secured a massive moated castle for Edward's use and an enormous English and Gascon base camp had been erected around it. As they approached from the north at sunset, the entire area around the castle was glowing with campfires and the air smelled like cooking meat.

Crossing the rebuilt drawbridge, the one that replaced the original bridge that Brandt had burned in the siege, Brandt couldn't remember feeling so weary or so disillusioned. He hadn't seen Ellowyn in nearly two months and he felt his need for her in every pour of his body. He was so desperate to see her that he couldn't even think straight, so after the success with de Clermont, he had made the decision to return to Melesse with or without Edward's approval. He was tired of fighting. He just wanted to see his wife.

Chateau des Eveques was one of the biggest castles Brandt had ever seen. Inhabited by the Bishops of Chavigney, it hadn't been a difficult thing to invade it. It was beautifully protected and built to withstand sieges, but the bishops and their somewhat aged ecclesiastical army was no match for the Black Angel. He burned the gates and breached the gatehouse in under four hours.

Now, as he rode into the massive innerbailey that looked more like a neat and tidy cloister, his thoughts were of finding Edward. He had to make a report, which he planned to do, but at the end of that report, he would tell Edward that he would be returning to Melesse for a few weeks. He found himself growing increasingly edgy as he dismounted his charger and headed wearily for the hall, hoping that Edward was in a giving mood when he told him of the success with de Clermont. If that man wasn't, and if he was unfortunate enough to deny Brandt's wishes to go home, then he honestly couldn't vouch for his reaction.

The great hall was built into the massive curtain wall of the chateau. Entering the cavernous chamber, Brandt was hit in the face by the heat and smell of it. It was cloying and uncomfortable. Removing his helm, he peeled back his hauberk because he was starting to sweat in the heat of the hall. There were quite a few people in the room, eating and milling about, and dogs were underfoot. He had to shove one out of his way as he made his way deeper into the hall.

"Brandt!"

He turned in the direction of the shout, seeing Edward standing at the table nearest the hearth. Brandt acknowledged the prince and made his way over to the table.

Edward was thrilled to see Brandt. Relatively tall like his great-grandfather, the young prince was slender but strong, with a head of dark gold curls. At twenty and six years, he was young but extraordinarily experienced. Much of his training as a soldier had come from Brandt, and men like him, so the Prince of Wales had learned from the very best. As Brandt drew near, the prince reached out to grab his hand and shake it.

"I was told of your victory over de Clermont," he said, excited. "My Angel of Death strikes again. Brilliant, my friend, truly. We are pleased."

Brandt smiled weakly as he sat at the table and the prince began shouting for food. In little time, Brandt had an enormous trencher in front of him piled with well cooked beef and boiled carrots. He dug in without another word.

"You did what you set out to do," Edward sat down beside him, watching him eat. "I never had a doubt that you would weaken de Clermont. We needed that, Brandt. You know this."

Brandt nodded. "Our intelligence on de Clermont's movements was correct," he said, mouth full. "It was simply a matter of waiting for him. He played right into our hands."

Edward was vastly pleased. "How many men would you say he lost?"

Brandt swallowed the bite in his mouth. "He must have had fifteen hundred men with him, but we felled several hundred. I would estimate when he retreated, he was down by half."

"Excellent," Edward said. He digested the victory, savored it, and collected his cup of wine. "You have been away for several days. Much has happened in that time, and your victory is a major contribution for our cause."

Brandt looked up from his meat. "What has happened?"

Edward sipped his wine. "My dear friend, King Jean, has rallied his troops at Chartres," he said, somewhat quietly. "As we speak, Suffolk, Salisbury, and Oxford are moving to reinforce my armies. Warwick is already here, as you know. I have received word from Jean that he wishes to discuss the situation to avoid what is sure to be a massive battle right here on this very spot. I want to move to

Paris. He does not want me to move at all. It should be interesting here at Poitier to say the least."

Brandt considered the information. "How many men has the king rallied?"

"Our scouts tell us ten to twelve thousand."

Brandt looked at him a moment before returning to his food. "They outnumber us."

"Not by much."

"Did you tell the king you would negotiate?"

"I told him we could speak but I do not negotiate."

"When is this conference to occur?"

"By the end of the month. I have given no specific date."

It was already the third week of the month. Brandt knew that if he was going to see his wife, he had to do it now. There was no time to waste. Too much was happening, building to what would surely be an explosion of epic proportions. He swallowed the bite in his mouth, took a long gulp of wine, and stood up.

"Then I am going to Melesse before these negotiations take place," he told Edward, weaving wearily on his feet. "If King Jean truly has as many men as you say he does, and we sit here with seven thousand men at best, this conflict near Poitiers will come fast and furious. It could be devastating for us. If that is the case, I wish to see my wife before this battle to end all battles comes."

He was already moving and Edward jumped up beside him, his hand on the man's arm. "Wait," he said urgently. "Brandt, you cannot go, not now. Did you not hear me? Jean is on our doorstep and...."

Brandt pulled his arm from the prince's grip, cutting him off. "I heard you," he said, his voice low and bordering on threatening. "I told you I am returning to Melesse. Make this conference with John at the end of the month and I will be back in time."

Edward put both hands on him this time, the friendliness out of his expression. "You cannot go," he said, his voice low. "I forbid it. I need you here."

Brandt knew this moment would come. He had been expecting it, and he was prepared. Very calmly, he looked the prince in the eye.

"Edward," he said, his voice so low that it was a growl. "I am going home and you cannot stop me. If you try, I will leave here, take my three thousand men with me, and fight for King Jean. You heard me correctly; I will take everything I have and side with the French. I have spent eleven years of my life doing everything you have ever asked of me and I do not like it when you deny me the small things I ask of you. At this moment, all I want to do is return to Chateau Melesse and see my wife. If you deny me, you will lose everything. Is this perfectly clear?"

Edward had a temper but he held it admirably. His jaw ticked, his face turned red, and his body tensed as if preparing for a fight. He wasn't used to having his wants denied and he certainly wasn't used to sharing someone he wholly depended on. He was possessive. But he also knew that what Brandt said was true; the man didn't bluff.

"I will have you arrested if you try to leave now," he muttered.

"Try it and there will be blood spilled everywhere. Is this truly what you wish?"

Edward's expression turned incredulous. "You would do that?"

"My wife is more important than you are," Brandt's dark eyes drilled into the man. "You have denied me long enough the privilege of returning home and I will be denied no longer. I am going home but I will return in time for your negotiations with Jean. If you do not like these terms, then find someone else to plan your foolish wars. I will return to England and forget I ever knew you."

Edward just stared at him. For several long moments, it was a tense stand-off to see which way the pendulum would swing. Brandt would not bend; Edward knew that. Although unused to bending himself, he knew he would have to if he wanted to retain his Black Angel. He was unused to the new terms of their relationship but he knew he had no choice. Finally, he broke out in a smile. Then, he started to laugh. He laughed heartily and slapped Brandt on the shoulder, hoping to ease the tension.

"Go home, you big lout," he snorted. "I will tell Jean we will meet to discuss on the last day of the month, so you have eleven days to spend with your wife before returning to me. Is that acceptable?"

Brandt wasn't in a humorous or forgiving mood. "It is a start."

Without another word or a hint of a smile in return, Brandt quit the hall. He was riding hard for Melesse less than ten minutes later.

## CHAPTER TWENTY THREE

*Oh, God... the armor... I recognize it!*

*She was in that awful mess of a dream again, gazing down at the injured knight beneath the tree. What she thought was a de Nerra coat of arms on the breast plate wasn't de Nerra at all. It was a bird of prey with great talons ready to spear its enemies. It sat upon a broad, broad chest, much bigger than her father ever was. In fact, the man was enormous.*

*All she could feel was sheer terror as she gazed down at the man beneath the tree. He was leaning up against the trunk, his helmed head facing away from her, and she crouched down on shaking legs next to him.*

*Angst and terror and panic gripped her. It was raining again and the tree provided minimal shelter. She felt wet all over. A nervous glance over her shoulder showed the castle in the distance to be half-melted now, bleeding out into the fields around it. It was horribly unsettling. The mud fields were churning now, churning the bodies in the ground , making them appear as if they were rolling over and over in their graves.*

*Frightened, she turned back to the knight against the tree. With a shaking hand, she reached out and lifted the visor so she could see his face. Then, all she could see was his eyes.*

*She knew those eyes.*

\*\*\*

Ellowyn was entrenched in the awful dream when she felt the bed give slightly. It wasn't a big shift, but big enough to rouse her somewhat. She was so exhausted, however, that very soon she was drifting back to sleep, snoring softly. The dream was gone but the anxiety was still there. Someone gently kissed the hand by her face and Ellowyn slowly opened her eyes.

Brandt was lying next to her, smiling into her sleeping face. Mind foggy from the terrible dream, it took Ellowyn a moment to realize she was looking at him and when realization dawned, it was as if the sun had emerged from behind the clouds. All was bright and well in her world again, and her apprehension had vanished. She smiled sleepily.

"Are you real?" she whispered.

"I am real."

"I am not dreaming?"

"Nay, sweetheart, you are not dreaming."

"Tell me you love me."

"With everything I am, I love you more with each breath I take."

That was enough for her. She reached out and wrapped her arms around his neck, overwhelmed with joy and ecstasy as he pulled her into his muscular embrace. She pressed tight against him, and he against her, but when he realized how big her belly was, he backed off.

"I am sorry," he whispered, one hand on her stomach as the other held her. "Did I hurt you?"

Ellowyn didn't like being held at arm's length. She resumed pressing herself against him. "Of course not," she murmured, her lips on his face. "You have finally returned to me. It seemed as if you were gone forever."

"It seemed that way to me as well," he said, his hand still on her hard belly, feeling the growing life within with awe and gratitude. "My son has grown quite large."

She grinned. "He will become bigger still," she said. "He is not due to be born for another few weeks yet. His is very restless, however; I believe he wants to be born now."

Brandt was grinning because she was. "What is he doing?"

She rolled onto her back so he could get both hands on her belly; it seemed that he was most interested in that at the moment. She put her hands on his as he felt up her stomach.

"He kicks constantly," she said. "Sometimes I cannot sleep because he is kicking me."

Brandt's grin broadened. "He will be a strong knight."

263

"The strongest," she insisted. "You have given him a great standard to live up to. He will not fail you."

Brandt took his eyes off her belly and looked at her face. She was round and rosy, but she looked very tired. He stroked her head with his big hand.

"And his mother?" he whispered. "How is she feeling?"

Ellowyn's smile was back. "So you noticed the mother, did you?" she said, laughing when he did. "I am feeling quite well. Hungry and tired most of the time, but quite well."

He leaned down and kissed her reverently, a sweet gesture that quickly turned hungry. Ellowyn wrapped her arms around his neck, feeling the familiar passion warm her vein, the heat of contact that flashed so brightly between them, but when he refused to do more than kiss her lustily, she backed away.

"Why do you not touch me?" she whispered hungrily. "I have not had my husband in weeks, yet you do not touch my body?"

He gazed back at her rather fearfully. "I do not want to injure you or my son," he told her. "I cannot make love to you although I would dearly love to."

She frowned. "That is ridiculous," she said. "You will not injure me."

As he lay there indecisively, she struggled to sit up in bed. He helped her, wondering where she was going, when she pulled off her shift and displayed her naked, pregnant body for him. She was beautifully proportioned with her swollen belly and full breasts, and he had to admit he was wildly aroused. Her pert breasts were perfect, large, and very perky, and her belly was so beautifully round. She was perfect.

He folded. Silently, he pulled her down to him and turned her around so she lay facing away from him. Pulling off his breeches, he pulled her back into his embrace and suckled on her shoulders and back as his hands roamed her breasts and belly. Ellowyn closed her eyes, savoring every touch as he wordlessly told her how very much he loved her. She could hear every syllable as if he had shouted the words.

She was hot for him, aroused as she had never been aroused in her life when he finally entered her from behind. He was careful

264

about it, not wanting to hurt her or the babe, and the slow pace was both erotic and maddening. Her senses were so highly aroused that in little time she was climaxing, feeling the release more strongly than she ever had. The pregnancy seemed to magnify the sensations.

When he found his own release, she wouldn't let him withdraw. She kept him trapped deep inside her until he grew hard once more and they made love again. It went on four times that morning until Brandt fell into an exhausted sleep and Ellowyn, feeling energized and relaxed, rose from bed to get on with her day.

The Black Angel was evidently weaker than a pregnant woman.

\*\*\*

By early afternoon, they had unexpected visitors.

Ellowyn was in her solar working on her knitting alone because Annabeth was with Dylan and Bridget was with Brennan. She had given her ladies permission to spend time with their respective interests and in truth she was enjoying the quiet time. As much as she loved her ladies, and she very much did, she was coming to crave being alone.

One of her three big windows faced the bailey, so she could hear the sentries when they began to sound off the alert that visitors had arrived. It wasn't unusual for the sentries to announce various visitors, and there always seemed to be people coming in and out of Melesse, but this announcement seemed different. It seemed to go on and she could hear soldiers in the bailey shouting back to the sentries on the wall. Curious, Ellowyn set her knitting aside and struggled to her feet. Making her way over to the window, she peered outside.

The day was dry and sunny, and a fairly strong breeze kicked up from the west. Brandt was flying the dark green and black standards of the Duke of Exeter upon the walls, and when Ellowyn didn't spy the visitors right away, she glanced up at the snapping standards because there were two of them in her line of sight. She'd seen them hundreds of times but never particularly paid much attention to the details of the standard. However, they were snapping loudly on this blustery day and she happened to look up at them. They were moving so swiftly in the breeze that all she could see was part of the talons from the Exeter dragon.

The sight of the talons gripped her. She began to feel a creeping sense of foreboding. She had seen those talons before, of course, but she was experiencing an odd sense of déjà vu as she looked at them. They looked just like the talons in her dream, those emblazoned on the breastplate of the faceless knight who lay dying beneath the tree. *Dear God....*

"My lady?"

Jolted from her thoughts, she whirled to see Bridget and Brennan standing in the entry to the solar. Bridget smiled when Ellowyn's gaze fell on her.

"My lady, there are visitors in the bailey," she said. "They have introduced themselves as heirs to the Dukedom of Exeter and say they have come to see the duke."

Shaking off the odd feelings that the talons had provoked, Ellowyn looked at Bridget curiously.

"Heirs to the dukedom?" she repeated, confused. "Did they give their names?"

Bridget shook her head but Brennan, standing behind her, spoke. "They are two young women, my lady," he said. "Knowing the duke has two daughters leads me to believe they are his children."

Startled, Ellowyn pushed out of the room with Bridget and Brennan on her tail. "Good Heavens," she exclaimed softly. "Do you really think so?"

"It is very probable, Lady de Russe."

Ellowyn was still quite baffled by the whole thing. "But how did they know he was here?"

"Most of France knows he is in residence at Melesse," Brennan replied. "News travels. Mayhap it has traveled to his daughters."

It made some sense. Knowing Brandt was still sleeping, Ellowyn didn't want to wake him until she solved the mystery of the visitor's identity. He'd only spoken of his daughters once and that hadn't been in the best of terms, so she would see for herself who these young women were before allowing them access to her exhausted and overworked husband.

In fact, the as she made her way down the wooden steps into the bailey, she found that she was fairly worked up about it. Brandt had stated that his daughters only looked upon him as a bankroll for their dowries; was that the reason they had come to Melesse? Only for his money? She felt some anger at that.

There was a small party off to her right near the smithy shacks. The horses were rather fine and there was a very fine carriage with two simple bench seats, white washed and decorated with elaborate painted patterns. Two young women, dressed in fashionable clothing, sat atop one of the bench seats. Ellowyn, now with the entourage of Dylan and Annabeth as well as Brennan and Bridget, headed straight for the wagon.

"I am Lady de Russe, Duchess of Exeter," she announced to the group on and around the wagon. "I understand you have come to see my husband."

The women on the bench looked over at her and she could immediately see Brandt's features reflected in their faces. They were quite lovely, dark-haired and dark-eyed, as they gazed at Ellowyn with surprise as well as suspicion.

"Lady... Lady de Russe?" one of the girl's repeated.

Ellowyn focused on her. "How may I be of assistance?"

The girl looked at her and her obviously pregnant belly before turning to the girl next to her. They both seemed at a loss for words. Then they started to appear nervous.

"I am the Lady Rosalind de Russe," the young woman finally said; she had darker hair than the woman seated next to her and finer features. "This is my sister, the Lady Margarethe. The Duke of Exeter is our father."

Ellowyn smiled politely. "He has mentioned you," she said. "Welcome to Chateau Melesse. May I ask what your business is?"

The young women seemed genuinely overwhelmed. It was an odd reaction, truly, and seemingly a bit extreme, but given the unfriendliness Brandt had described with his daughters, she shouldn't have been surprised. As the women struggled to find their tongues, she took charge of the situation.

"The duke is a very busy man," she said, clipped because she was frustrated with their seeming reluctance to tell her the nature of their business. "You will tell me what your business is with him."

Still, neither woman seemed willing to answer. They kept looking at Ellowyn and then whispering between them.

"Ladies, I am addressing you. What is it that you want?"

Rosalind finally looked at her. "Our business is with our father," she said with strained politeness. "Is he in residence?"

"You will tell me what your business is with him or I will have you escorted out."

Margarethe, silent until this point, looked at her with fury. "You cannot have us escorted out," she said. "We are his daughters, his flesh and blood."

"And I am his wife."

"Our mother is his wife!"

"Your mother is dead."

"Nay, she is *not*!"

Rosalind slapped a hand over her sister's mouth and the two of them struggled on the bench seat as Margarethe tried to yank her sister's hand off her mouth. Ellowyn, alarmed by the younger girl's angry reply, rushed to the wagon and grabbed Margarethe by the arm as she fought with her sister. She yanked so hard that Margarethe nearly came off the bench seat.

"What do you mean by that?" she demanded.

Margarethe was fearful and angry. She tried to peel Ellowyn's fingers off of her wrist and finally took to smacking her hand. Meanwhile, Brennan and Dylan had rushed forward to break up the tussle, pulling Ellowyn away as gently as they could while trying to keep Brandt's daughters calm.

"You will tell me what you mean by that!" Ellowyn would not be eased. "What do you mean your mother is not dead?"

"Ellowyn!"

The boom came from the direction of the keep. Everyone turned to see Brandt heading towards them, his features tight. He had been awakened by the cries from the sentries announcing visitors and by the time he dressed and exited the keep, he had been confronted by his wife in some kind of altercation with two women on a wagon.

Furious, he hadn't realized who the women were until he came off of the steps leading from the keep and by that time, he was in full blown rage. He wasn't sure how the altercation got started but anyone who touched his wife was sure to pay, even his daughters whom he had not seen in several years. They weren't hard to recognize; they looked just like their mother, and he was unmoved by their appearance. Perhaps a bit surprised, but unmoved.

"Take my wife inside," he instructed Brennan as he came upon the group.

"I am *not* going inside," Ellowyn told him, slapping at Brennan when the man tried to politely grasp her. She pointed at the women on the wagon. "Those young women say they are your daughters. Furthermore, that one said that her mother was not dead and I want to know what she meant."

Brandt hadn't heard any of the conversation; all he had seen was the struggle. As Ellowyn told him what had been said, the reasons behind the scuffle, his head snapped in the direction of his daughters.

They were sitting upon the wagon bench looking at him apprehensively. They had grown quite a bit in the past several years, that was true, but they still looked just like their mother. There was beauty there, but there was also coldness. He honestly felt no reaction as he looked at them. Just as they had been conditioned to hate him, he had been conditioned not to care. It was safer for him that way. They were strangers to him and he wanted to keep it that way. He turned to Ellowyn.

"I am sure she only said it to upset you," he said quietly. "Please return inside. I will be in shortly."

Ellowyn geared up for an argument but she could see by the look in his eye that he would not have tolerated it. The appearance of his daughters had him edgy and she didn't want to add to his burden. With a sigh, she forced herself to calm.

"Very well," she said. "Please come inside as soon as you can."

"I will."

"I want to know why they are here."

"So do I."

With a lingering glare at the young women in the wagon, Ellowyn retreated back to the keep with Annabeth, Bridget, and Brennan. Dylan remained behind with Brandt, who was watching his wife retreat into the keep. When she was out of view, he returned his attention to the wagon.

"Now," he said, his voice low and dangerous. "You will tell me why you are here immediately."

They did.

# CHAPTER TWENTY FOUR

"You will forgive me if I do not believe you. And I do not appreciate having my wife upset so."

Brandt, Rosalind, and Margarethe were in one of the smaller solars of Melesse, one that was tucked back near the kitchens and used by the staff for storage. Brandt wouldn't take them into a finer chamber to discuss their business because he truly didn't want them there, so he showed them the same consideration they had always shown him; none.

As he had escorted them into the keep, Rosalind had smiled tremulously at him and he remembered that the last time he saw her, she had stuck her tongue out at him. It was difficult for him to move past that last impression. Margarethe wouldn't even look him in the eye.

"But... it is the truth," Rosalind insisted to his statement. She looked at her sister for support. "Margarethe, tell him."

Margarethe was much like her mother with a quick temper and rash mouth. But at the moment, she was quite apprehensive of her massive father as he stood by the door of the small and crowded chamber.

"Several years ago, Mother met a man by the name of Louis of Ghistelles," she said, her voice quivering. "She fell in love with him. She wanted to be with him but because she was married to you, it was impossible to marry him. So she told him her husband was dead and that she was a widow. He married her but before she left with him, she told us to tell you that she had died. She wanted you to believe that she was dead and gone, which is why we told you she had perished of a fever. It is God's honest truth, my lord."

Brandt hadn't truly believed their story until that moment. Now, he felt the fingers of doubt clutching at him and he didn't like it. The girls seemed sincere.

"I remember when you sent me the missive informing me of her death," he said, jaw ticking. "I came to Gael to see you, if you recall. You were young."

"I was ten and Rosalind was eleven."

"I asked you if you wanted to live with me and you told me that you did not. In fact, I seem to remember you were rather adamant about it."

Margarethe nodded, glancing at her sister. "We had three governesses already," she said. "We did not need parents. I suppose we hoped that Mother would return some day, but she never did."

He was coming to feel just the slightest bit sorry for them but he fought it. He reverted back to his historical feelings for them, his children who had been taught to hate them. He didn't trust them in the least and even though the story sounded genuine, he chose not to believe them. He couldn't. It would turn his world upside down if what they said was true, and that would destroy him. He couldn't let that happen.

"You told me she was dead and that is what I still choose to believe," he finally said. "It makes no difference that you have come to me with this ridiculous story now. I have remarried and my wife and I are expecting a child. If you repeat that story again about your mother running off with another man and possibly still living, I will purge you from Chateau Gael and you will live in the streets. I will take no notice of you and officially disown you. Is that clear?"

The girls looked terrified. Rosalind nodded emphatically. "It is, Father."

"Do not call me that," Brandt said coldly. "You will address me as 'my lord' or 'Lord de Russe'. Now, why did you come here?"

Both young women looked beaten and scared. Brandt refused to feel pity as Rosalind, a very well-spoken young lady, struggled to explain.

"We do not remember you from childhood, my lord," she said quietly, fumbling through her words. "Mother took us from England when we were quite young. All we knew was what she told us or what we had heard from others. We had heard that you were a lord of war and advisor to the king. Mother said you were a brutal man."

"That still does not tell me why you have come."

Rosalind looked at Margarethe for support. The younger sister, looking at the floor, spoke.

"Bearing the name de Russe has been a curse," she said unhappily. "Everyone in France hates us. Our lives are hell because everyone is suspicious of us, made worse now that you and the Prince of Wales are waging such terrible warfare on the land. We are spat upon at church, hissed at in the street... we have come to you because we cannot live here any longer. We have come to ask you to send us back to England where we will at least have a chance of living normal lives and mayhap securing a decent marriage prospect, because no one in France other than dishonorable men will consider us."

Brandt saw a good deal of himself in his younger daughter. She was unafraid and strong, but very sad. For the first time, he was starting to feel like their father. He had never felt that way before and he struggled to shake it off. He didn't want to feel anything for the pair but it was becoming increasingly difficult.

"It was not I who brought you to France," he said. "It was your mother. If you must blame someone, blame her. I have dutifully provided you with a roof over your head and a comfortable living arrangement but beyond that, I will not do anything more. I am sorry you wasted your time coming to see me."

Margarethe looked at him, stricken. "How can you be so cold?" she blurted "We had no choice when Mother took us away; we were children! She only told us what she wanted us to know about you. We never got to know you personally to make our own judgments about you, but from what I see right now, everything Mother told us about you is true. You are a mean and cruel man!"

Rosalind hissed at her sister, quieting her, as she tried to salvage the conversation. "It is true that our mother hated you," she said. "She wanted us to hate you, too. She told us you never wanted us and that you hated us. Now we see that it is true and if we have wasted your time, then we apologize."

Brandt looked at her, his harsh stance wavering. He knew he shouldn't engage them in this level of emotional conversation but he couldn't help it. His relationship with Ellowyn had allowed him to realize and understand his feelings, so he was perhaps more emotional than he should have been. He still wasn't very good at controlling his emotions once his guard was down. Rosalind and Margarethe were trying very hard to pull it down.

"I never hated you," he told them. "No matter what your mother told you, I never hated you. You are my offspring and to hate something I have created is not within me. I realize that you were children and she fed you lies about me, so hear me now: I never hated you. I never sent you away to France; that was her decision. She did her best to keep you from me and turn you against me, and I know that she has succeeded. You have come here asking me to send you to England because my reputation in France has made you outcasts. Mayhap that is true and in that respect, I will reconsider your request to send you back to England. Given your historical relationship, you will understand that consideration is the best I can do right now."

The girls nodded demurely before glancing at each other, passing expressions of uncertainty and hope. Rosalind sighed with some relief.

"Thank you," she said softly. "My lord, I am not sure how my sister feels, but in speaking for myself, mayhap you will accept my apology for my behavior towards you all of these years."

Brandt eyed her. She looked so much like her mother that he was having difficulty overcoming the innate aversion to her.

"What do you hope to gain by telling me that?" he asked an honest question. "You are a woman grown. Do you expect to establish a relationship with me?"

Rosalind shrugged. "If not a relationship, at least a rapport," she replied with equal honesty. "The older I have grown, the more I have become more curious about you. Mother does not care for us, and although you were my father in name only, at least you have done right all of these years to provide for us. That says something for your character no matter what my mother has said. I simply want you to know my thoughts."

Brandt's guard went down another notch, at least where Rosalind was concerned. Margarethe was still standing against the wall, staring at the floor. He wasn't sure about his youngest, but if she was truly like him, then she would be very stubborn about things.

"And so I do," he finally said. He cleared his throat softly, forcing himself to show a measure of compassion. "You may stay here tonight and be on your way in the morning. Remain here and I will send someone to tend to you."

He exited the room and quietly closed the door behind him. Still inside the cold and dark solar with items cluttering the floor, Rosalind turned to her sister, who was still silently staring at the floorboards. The older she and Margarethe grew, the more they seemed to grow apart in thought. Margarethe still very much hated their father, but that was purely based on their mother's teachings. Margarethe wasn't so sure she wanted anything to do with their father, but Rosalind was different. She thought perhaps he might be worth knowing. Age and inherent common sense told her that.

Rolling her eyes at her stubborn sister, she moved to the other side of the chamber to wait for one of her father's servants to come for them.

\*\*\*

"You certainly carry your own storm with you wherever you go," Ellowyn said after hearing Brandt's report on his meeting with his daughters. "Nothing about you is peaceful for very long, is it?"

Brandt smiled wryly. "Apparently not. Except for moments like this with you, most everything around me is at some level of upheaval."

"Including daughters you have not seen in years showing up on your door step."

"Exactly."

Ellowyn grinned at him. "Well," she said, easing up on teasing him. "Mayhap this particular storm will quickly pass. Did either girl mention wanting money or a dowry during the course of the conversation?"

He shook his head. "Never," he replied. "They mostly spoke of the fact that they are outcast here in France because of the de Russe name. Odd how I never considered how my association with the prince would affect them. Even now as I consider it, I do not care."

Ellowyn merely wriggled her eyebrows, perhaps with some regret. "I would think it would be rather sad to be an enemy in the land I grew up in," she ventured, perhaps to force him to think about the young women's position. "I do not find it unreasonable to send them back to England. You have other properties other than Guildford you could send them to, do you not? It would not be any trouble."

He looked at her. "Why would you take their side in this?"

She hastened to reassure him. "I am not taking their side in anything," she said firmly. "I am always on your side, Brandt. I do not have to tell you that."

He eased somewhat, looking away and collecting a cup that was on a sideboard near one of the lancet windows in their bedchamber. He poured himself a measure of tart, red wine.

"I am sorry," he said softly. "I know you are my strongest supporter. I suppose their appearance has me off-guard somewhat."

Ellowyn was sitting on their bed with her enormous knitting project strewn across her legs. She could feel his confusion; in fact, she had some of her own.

"Why did they say their mother wasn't dead?" she finally brought up the subject she had wanted to discuss since the moment he had entered. "Did you ask them?"

Brandt didn't look at her. He poured himself more wine. He didn't want to lie to her, but he still believed it might not be the truth. He didn't know his girls; he didn't know if they were liars or not. He didn't want to upset Ellowyn with something that could very well be a vindictive lie. Until something could be proven, it wasn't worth mentioning.

"I did," he finally said. "They were simply being spiteful. They hate me, which means they hate you as well."

Ellowyn accepted his explanation. There was no reason not to. Brandt said a silent prayer that she did not ask more, instead focusing on her knitting. He sipped his wine, watching her from the corner of his eye.

"They will stay here tonight and be gone in the morning," he told her. "I hope that does not distress you."

Ellowyn shook her head, focused on her project. "It does not," she said. Then, she paused somewhat wistfully. "It seems so sad to me that there are girls who have fathers they do not like and then girls who love fathers they no longer have. It is unfair, really."

He looked at her, waiting to see which way her mood would swing. She was volatile these days, as easy to cry or anger as she was to laugh. She seemed to reflect on her father's passing those months back without bursting into tears for which he was thankful. She still grew teary-eyed when she thought on Deston. Wine in hand, he made his way over to her and sat on the bed next to her.

"How is my son today?" he asked softly, changing the subject.

She forced herself from her bleak thoughts, smiling at him. "He is well," she said, shifting her knitting so he could put a big hand on her belly. "He is very active."

He returned her smile, waiting with anticipation to feel the activity she was describing but the baby was largely still. "I have been thinking on names for him."

She lifted an eyebrow. "I thought we were to name him after my grandfather, Braxton."

He shrugged. "It is a fine name," he agreed, not wanting to offend her, "but I was thinking that I would very much like to name him after my father's brother. He died some years ago but he was often much kinder to me than my father. I suppose he was more a father to me than my own, although that is not saying much."

"You have never mentioned him."
"I have not thought of him in years."
"What was his name?"
"Gaston."

"Gaston de Russe," she repeated softly. "I like it very much."

"Better than Braxton de Russe?"

She smiled. "There will be more children and more opportunities to name our children after every male member of my family." She laughed when he did. "If you wish to name him Gaston, I am agreeable."

He grasped her gently by the arms and pulled her to him for a sweet kiss. "Thank you," he murmured. "That means a good deal to me."

Ellowyn put her knitting aside to touch the man, running her hands over his face, watching him kiss her palm sweetly. Her mind was moving on from the birth of the child to the not so distant future. She was also thinking of her husband and his duties to the prince. He had been home a short while and they hadn't much chance to discuss the way of things, including how long he planned to remain at Melesse.

"I have not yet had the opportunity to ask you how long you will remain with me this time," she said softly. "Will you be leaving again soon?"

He cupped her face with a big hand, stroking her cheek with his thumb. "Too soon for my taste," he told her. "I must return to Edward by the end of the month."

Her face fell a little. "That is only eight days away," she said. "Where must you go?"

"Poitier," he replied, still stroking her cheek. "I can only spend the next three or four days here before I must return. I brought my army back with me, you know. It takes time to move a body of that size to Poitier."

She fell silent a moment, feeling his hand on her face, relishing his touch. She had missed it so. "Magnus...," she started to say, stumbling over the words. "Magnus said that Edward has moved north from Aquitaine, burning and pillaging. He said it is as bad as he has ever seen such things. Is this true?"

Brandt sighed faintly, thinking of the horrors he had caused over the past several weeks. It was his duty and he did not feel guilty for such things, but he couldn't help but think of Deston's accusations of his *chevauchee* warfare. They called it scorched-earth tactics, and it was exactly that. It was devastation on a massive scale, only over the past few months, it had been even worse than that.

"War is never pleasant," he said, unwilling to tell her the truth of it because it was too terrible for her to comprehend. "It has been very bad indeed."

She gazed into his face, seeing the exhaustion in the dark depths. "To what end?" she asked. "What I mean is that where *will* it end? Will the prince simply keep raiding and burning without end or is there a purpose to all of this?"

He shrugged. "Of course there is a purpose," he said. "The purpose is to reach Paris and capture the city, but the army was halted at Tours. We spent a good deal of time there trying to take the city to no avail. Now we have regrouped at Chavigney. The prince has sent a message to the King of France to discuss a resolution to all of this, which is why I must return to Poitier. I must be part of those negotiations."

She felt some hope in that. "Do you think these wars may finally come to an end?"

"Anything is possible."

"Will we return home to England when it is over?"

"You do not want to stay in France?"

She shook her head. "I want to go home."

He understood. With a kiss to her hand, he rose from the bed and took his cup back over to the wine. He was preparing to pour himself another measure when he glanced out of the window and noticed that there was some activity in the bailey. He could see Dylan and Alex chatting with Stefan, who had just come down off the wall. Having been asleep most of the morning and then lingering with womenfolk for the past hour, he thought perhaps it was time to make his presence known and meet with his men. He set the cup down.

"I will return in a while," he told Ellowyn. "I have not seen my castle in several weeks so it is time to make my rounds."

Ellowyn grinned as she continued to knit. "It is falling apart at the seams," she told him saucily. "I have been running it into the ground and taking great delight in ruining your empire."

He scowled, though it was without force. "Naughty wench."

She giggled. Winking at her, Brandt quit the chamber and headed out to the dusty, windy bailey.

It would be the calm before the greatest storm of all.

# CHAPTER TWENTY FIVE

"Patrols returning from the north have reported a large army heading our way," Brennan said. "They are moving in the dead of knight, my lord. That speaks of determination."

Having been woken out of a deep sleep by Brennan, who had the night watch, Brandt stood in the corridor outside of the chamber he shared with Ellowyn. It was close to midnight and the passageway was dim and quiet. Rubbing his eyes, he appeared weary but the mind was sharp. It was already calculating the situation.

"Standards?"

"It was difficult to see beneath the moon glow, but he thought he caught the *fleur de lis.*"

Brandt stopped rubbing his eyes and looked at him. "*Fleur de lis*?" he repeated, somewhat incredulous. "Is it Jean?"

"The army is large enough, my lord. Thousands, at the very least."

"Coming here, did you say?"

"Their path will take them to our doorstep."

Brandt let out a hiss. "Someone told him I had come home," he muttered. "This was planned, don't you see? They knew I had separated myself from Edward. They've come to destroy me or at the very least, weaken me and keep me from joining up with Edward."

"The king has many spies in our camp, just as we have spies in his," Brennan replied quietly. "The king was already heading south towards Poitier. It would not have taken much for him to alter his course and head for Melesse."

Brandt could see the logical tactics taking place. He understood them implicitly. "How much time do we have?"

"They will be here by dawn."

"Which was, no doubt, part of their plan." Brandt was on the move, heading to the spiral stairs that led down to the first level and the keep entry. "Rouse the rest of the knights. Everyone has their assigns posts. I want everything bottled up tightly and if I know Jean, he is particularly fond of flaming projectiles. Make sure the thatched roofs of the stables and trade shakes are thoroughly watered down. He will try to burn us out but we will not allow it. Hurry, Brennan; there is no time to waste."

Brennan ran off as Brandt continued down to the living level of the keep. He continued outside in the dead cold night, heading to the armory and listening to the sounds of the castle as the knights began to rouse it for battle. He could hear men moving and shouting, wagons moving, and servants as they were given orders. Already, the smell of battle was in the air. He could feel the energy rise.

In the armory, he donned his armor with the help of the sleepy squires. Straps were secured, weapons checked. He was very calm, as he usually was before a battle, because he knew only calm heads would survive. He intended to survive.

*Ellowyn.*

He paused in his dressing, thinking of his wife asleep in their chamber and struggling not to feel fear on her behalf. He had time to remove her from Melesse, but the closest trustworthy shelter was at least four or five hours away through the dead of night. He wasn't sure that was a safer option than barricading her up inside of a keep that had withstood many sieges. Melesse was built for battle. After much internal debate, he decided the safer option was to keep her at the castle.

Fully dressed, the Black Angel emerged from the armory and headed towards the keep. By now, the entire castle had been alerted and men were running about in organized chaos. Brandt made his way across the bailey, now lit with hundreds of torches burning brightly into the night, and took the stairs to the keep.

The keep was still fairly quiet although servants were dashing about. He took the wide spiral stairs to the second floor, making a great deal of noise as he traversed the dead-quiet corridor. As he neared the bedchamber door, it suddenly flew open and Ellowyn was standing there.

"What is happening?" she demanded. Then, she noticed his state of dress and her eyes widened. "Why are you dressed to kill?"

He reached out and put his enormous hands on her arms, turning her around and forcibly escorting her back into the room.

"Our patrol has spotted a large army heading our way," he said calmly and quietly as he closed the door. "They will be here at dawn. I suspect we may see a bit of a battle come sunrise."

Ellowyn remained calm because he was. But she seemed confused. "Who on earth would be moving in the dead of night to attack us?"

"Our patrol thinks it might be the king," he said softly.

She cocked her head. "The king? Of England?"

"Of France," he said, chuckling. "France happens to have a king as well."

She made a face, that face her father used to call the pickle puss, which made him laugh harder. He hadn't seen it in months and it always made him laugh, but if he called it what her father had called it, she would become angry. So, he simply laughed. It was a lovely bit of relief in the midst of fearful emotions.

"Well," she said after she was finished twisting up her face. "It would seem that I should be making some kind of preparations for the wounded we will receive."

His humor faded. "Nay," he told her. "I want you to remain here and bolt that door. You will not open it for anyone but me or my knights. Is that clear?"

Her humor faded as well. "Men will need help, Brandt," she said seriously. "I cannot remain bottled in this room, safe and protected, while men are injured or dying."

He sighed; he didn't want to fight with her, not now. "When your father thought to lay siege to Guildford, I told you to stay to the keep and bolt the door. Do you recall?"

"Aye."

"Do you recall what I said would happen if you did not?"

She gave him a droll expression. "You cannot spank me."

"I most certainly can."

She shook her head and patted her big stomach. "You cannot put me over your knee with this belly."

He rolled his eyes. "I do not need to put you over my knee in order to spank that lovely white bottom," he said. Then, he pointed a massive finger at her. "I do not want to have to worry over you, do you understand? I must know that you are safe and locked up. Any other thought will cause me to lose concentration and quite possibly cost me my life. Can I make this any clearer to you?"

She sobered dramatically. "But I only wish to help."

"I know. But you will be the most help to me if you and our son remain safe." He moved towards her, putting his big hands on her shoulders. "I am not relishing the thought of you in a castle under siege. The mere idea eats at me. Will you please help me and stay to your rooms?"

When it put it that way, she could only agree. "Very well," she said, pressing up against him and trying not to get jabbed by sharp objects on his body. "Please take great care, my love. I would have you return to me safe and whole."

He bent over, kissing her with great emotion. "I plan to."

"Thank you."

He kissed her one last time before releasing her. "I will have provisions brought up to you so you will not want for anything. I will also send Annabeth and Bridget to you."

"What about your daughters?"

"I will make sure they are comfortable and safe, but they will remain in their chamber."

She simply nodded, feeling sadder and more despondent by the moment at the thought of him heading in to battle. Certainly, he went to battle all of the time, but she was never witness to it. There was something different about being with him as he risked his life. As he winked at her and left the chamber, she tried not to let her fear overwhelm her. She went to sit on the bed, thinking of the coming battle, struggling not to weep.

When Brandt returned a couple of hours later to see her one last time before the keep was sealed up tight, he found her fast asleep. Kissing her gently, he let her sleep.

\*\*\*

At sunrise, hell was unleashed.

Flying sky blue standards with yellow *fleur de lis*, Jean II of France unleashed his great war machines on the fortress of Melesse and by mid-morning, a horrible battle was underway.

It was as Brandt had feared; they knew very well the Black Angel had separated himself from the Prince of Wales, and they intended to keep de Russe bottled up and away from Edward, who was having some issues of his own with other French nobles. Divide and conquer seemed to be the French battle cry.

Jean traveled with thousands of men; Brandt estimated it was at least four thousand. They had a sea of foot soldiers, mounted cavalry, and archers. Melesse was boxed in very early on, for the massive walls did not have a moat because they were more than twenty feet high and the gatehouse was like a fortress itself. The gates themselves were iron, without wood to burn that would soften the iron, and there were three portcullises to prevent an easy breech. Moreover, the portcullis were aligned so that Brandt could post a legion of archers inside the bailey, shooting out of the gatehouse to all those crowded around the exterior of the gatehouse. It was a very simple thing to pick men off as they tried to breach the gates.

Flaming pots of tar and oil were slung over the walls, some bursting against the keep, others hitting the floor of the bailey and splashing their flaming contents out over men and animals. Stefan, in fact, had been sprayed with burning tar but his armor prevented any serious damage. He had been extremely hot in it, however, until Magnus had rolled him in the dirt to quench the flame.

Most of the knights had taken to mounting the walls with crossbows, picking off those attacking the walls. Because of the terrain surrounding the castle, the sloping mountain, it made it exceptionally difficult for the king's army to gain a good foothold for positioning ladders against the walls, and siege towers were impossible. But the mangonels and ballistas, positioned further down the slope, had adequate footing to hurl their deadly cargo over the walls.

Brandt remained on the walls most of the morning, monitoring the gatehouse and watching the ballistas down below as they were reloaded. He tried to anticipate their trajectory and move men away from the area where they were presumed to hit. He was very good at predicting their targets, saving lives of men. But as the day wore on into night, the kings army would not give up. Realizing the walls were nearly impossible to scale, they focused their numbers on the gatehouse and things began to happen.

At sunset, the first ladders began going up on the gatehouse, which was amply protected. However, there were corbels on the structure that were big enough for men to gain footholds, and there was a window for light and air on the third story of the structure overlooking the road below. Conceiveably, men could mount the ladders and use the corbels to propel themselves up to that window. It was risky but possible, and that was exactly what the French were intent on doing.

Brandt could see their plan, however, and charged up to the third floor of the gatehouse with Brennan, Magnus, Dylan, and Alex along with several heavily armed soldiers to wait for them. As the war machines continued to hurl missiles over the walls, men began climbing the gatehouse with the intent of breeching it. Brandt and his men were waiting. The first soldier that managed to thrust himself through the single window had his head ripped off, courtesy of Brandt. The duke literally grabbed the man by the head, twisted, and yanked.

It was an ugly, bloody fight.

# CHAPTER TWENTY SIX

*It was that dream again, only this time, there was a different dimension to it.*

*Behind her, the castle had melted until it looked like soft butter. Everything was running onto the ground, now blending with the mud and the rain. Standing over the knight leaning against the tree, she could only stare at the crest on the breastplate. She knew it. It was the talons of the de Russe dragon, the Duke of Exeter. It was Brandt; she knew it was Brandt even though she couldn't see his face.*

*God, help me! She cried.*

*The child in her belly was kicking terribly, as if he knew his father was dying. Kicking and kicking until it caused her pain and she gripped her belly, holding it, as stabs of agony ripped through her body. She ceased to see the man at her feet any longer, only concerned with the pain radiating through her torso. The baby's kicking lessened but the pain was still there. The kicking faded until it was virtually no more. She couldn't feel the kicking any longer. As the last embers of life diminished from the father, so perhaps did they diminish from the child. Both of them were dying and she could do nothing to help them.*

Crying out, she awoke in a cold sweat.

\*\*\*

Something was wrong with the child. She knew that the moment she awoke in agony. As the battle raged below, she held her belly and wept, terrified that something was horribly amiss. Annabeth and Bridget, keeping company with her in the barricaded room, were alerted to the sounds of her weeping.

"My lady?" Annabeth was on the bed beside her. "What is amiss?"

Ellowyn wiped her eyes, struggling to calm herself. She was terrified. "I... I will be all right," she assured her frightened ladies. "I am sure it is simply the fear of the battle causing me to...."

"Causing *what?*"

"... well, there is some pain, but I am sure it will go away."

Annabeth's eyes widened but she held her control. Bridget, seated on the other side of the bed, reached out to touch Ellowyn's arm.

"We shall find the midwife," she said. "Do not distress, my lady. We shall find her."

Ellowyn shook her head, reaching over to grasp Bridget before the woman could run off; she was very fast in that respect.

"Nay," she insisted. "It will pass, I am sure. Moreover, the midwife is in town and it would be impossible to get through the closed gates."

"Then I will seek the duke's surgeon," Bridget insisted. "He must be able to help."

Again, Ellowyn shook her head, holding fast to Bridget so she would not run away. "He is tending wounded," she said. "It would be foolish to pull him away from dozens of injured men to come and tend one woman.  Nay, leave him be. You are here. You are all of the help I need."

"But... then I must send for the duke!"

"You will do no such thing. This will pass."

Bridget and Annabeth exchanged fearful glances. "As you say, my lady" Bridget said. "Where is your pain? Do you believe the child is coming now?"

Ellowyn sighed; the pain had subsided somewhat but it was still there. "I do not know," she admitted. "I have never had a child before. I do not know what it feels like other than I was told to expect pain when the child is delivered."

As Bridget went to get water and a rag to wipe over her mistress to comfort her, Annabeth grasped Ellowyn's hand.

"Would you like some wine?" she asked softly. "It might help ease you."

Ellowyn shook her head, feeling exhausted and sleepy, and struggling to put the pain behind her.  She could hear the battle down below, the shouts of men as they tried to kill one another. To know her husband was in that chaos did not help her state. She closed her eyes, trying to block it out.

"Nay," she replied. "I believe I will try to go back to sleep. The pain seems to have lessened."

Annabeth nodded silently, watching Ellowyn close her eyes. The truth was that she was terrified but she didn't want Ellowyn to see it. They were trapped in a room as a battle waged below, and now her mistress was feeling childbirth pains well before the child's due date. Under normal circumstances, either of those individual events would have been reason for panic. Indeed, there was much to be terrified over.

She began to pray.

***

The gatehouse breach had proved to be a disaster for the French. Every man that came through the narrow gatehouse window met his death at the hands of Brandt or one of his knights. Then, the body would be hauled out by soldiers who would throw it over the walls. It had a hugely demoralizing effect on the army of Jean, and eventually, men stopped trying to climb through the hole because it was certain death. No one wanted to commit suicide.

The entire night of the siege saw more projectiles hurled over the wall. Giving up on the gatehouse, the king's army focused their energy on the iron gates and the three successive portcullises, which was a futile endeavor. It only cost Jean more men. Melesse was truly an unbreachable fortress and at dawn on the second day, the king's armies began to retreat.

Watching the pull-out from his post near the gatehouse as the sun began to rise, Brandt was exceptionally relieved as the French collected their dead and began to subside. But he was also leery. He turned to Dylan.

"They will be heading for Edward now," he said with urgency in his voice. "Gather the men. Make sure everyone is fed and moderately rested. We must follow that army and provide Edward with support."

"But I thought that the king wished to negotiate with Edward to avoid a big battle at Poitier?" Dylan said. "Why would he move on to attack him now?"

Brandt cocked an eyebrow at the army retreating in the distance. "His actions in laying siege to my castle tell me that what the man says and what he intends are two different things," he said. "We must hurry if we are going to prevent him from slaughtering Edward. Even after losing soldiers in this battle, he carries many more men than Edward does."

"When do you wish to leave?"

"No more than four hours. See to it."

Dylan nodded and began issuing orders. Brandt remained on the wall, watching the retreat to ensure they did not regroup and attack a second time, before his thoughts turned to his wife. The moment he saw her face in his mind's eye, he could think of nothing else.

Descending the wall, he made his way across the littered and blasted bailey as he headed for the keep. He would spend a few hours with Ellowyn before heading out with the army. He was already relishing the time spent with her, eager to feel her in his arms. The battle with Jean had been a relatively short but particularly brutal one and he was anxious to get his mind off blood and pain and onto something soft and soothing.

The keep door was bolted and it took quite some time for the servants to work the bolts loose. Two big iron bolts liked to stick and Brandt stood impatiently on the doorstep as the big panel was opened. Once it swung loose, he shoved it open the rest of the way and retreated into the cool, musty interior.

As anxious as he was to see his wife, that enthusiasm was quickly doused when Annabeth met him at the door. She motioned for silence and left him standing in the hall as she came out of the room and shut the door softly behind her. As he opened his mouth to question her actions, she put her hands up again to quiet him.

"I must speak with you before you see your wife, my lord," she whispered. "Lady Ellowyn awoke in great pain last evening. She would not let us send for you or the midwife. She has been in pain all night and has only now fallen back asleep. If the battle is indeed over, we must send for the midwife immediately."

Brandt knees went weak. "Something is wrong?"

Annabeth lifted her shoulders. "We do not know," she said. "Only the midwife can tell us. Will you please send for her, my lord?"

Brandt was on the run. He raced down the spiral stairs, through the keep entry, and down to the bailey. The first knight he came across was a lesser knight, helping with some repairs on the keep stairs, and he sent the man on the run into the town for the midwife. Only a command from Brandt was able to open all three portcullises and the gate, and Brandt made sure the knight was well on his way before ordering the gates closed again and retreating back inside the keep.

All the while, his mind was a blank slate of distress. He could not think on Ellowyn or the child at the moment because it would surely cripple him and it was imperative that he keep his head. He had to remain calm and in control, but the truth was that he was feeling more panic than he had ever felt in his life.

Battles and kings and frightening men with weapons could do nothing to threaten his heart. But a lovely slip of a woman that he loved with every fiber of his being could. By the time he reached the second floor chamber, he was wiping the tears from his eyes. He just couldn't fathom anything happening to Ellowyn or their child. He was emotional, exhausted, and distraught.

The chamber was very quiet as he entered. Bridget and Annabeth were sitting by the bed, their eyes big on Brandt as he entered the room. His gaze was riveted to his wife, curled up on her left side and sleeping peacefully. His eyes never left her as he pulled up a chair and sat next to Annabeth and Bridget, staring at Ellowyn as if afraid she was about to disappear. The tears he had been trying so hard to wipe away were back and they coursed down his cheeks as he stared at her.

Annabeth and Bridget watched in shock as the mighty Duke of Exeter crumbled. As Annabeth sat next to him, wondering how on earth she could provide the man with some comfort, Bridget rose to pour him a measure of wine. They were desperate to do something to comfort him. Brandt took the wine gratefully and gulped it down, so Bridget poured him another. She was pouring him a third cup when she noticed a figure in the slightly ajar door.

Brennan stood there, peering into the room. He was dirty and exhausted, his ice-blue eyes lined with circles. He locked gazes with Bridget, so she carefully handed Brandt his third cup of wine and left the room, pushing Brennan back out into the darkened corridor. She shut the door softly behind her.

"What is the matter?" Brennan hissed.

Bridget put her hands on his chest, quieting him. "My question first," she insisted softly. "Are you well?"

His face softened somewhat and he nodded. "I am well," he whispered. "Most everyone is well."

She smiled at him and he took one of her hands and kissed it gently. "What is happening with Lady de Russe?" he asked, her hand still against his lips. "The duke sent someone to fetch the midwife. I came to see if he needed anything else."

She shook her head. "I will ask him," she said. "Lady de Russe has been in pain since yesterday and we do not know what is wrong. He is understandably distraught."

Brennan looked rather distressed himself as he nodded, kissing her hand again as she left him and went back into the room. Bridget left the door cracked as she quietly moved to Brandt.

"My lord," she whispered. "Brennan is here. He wants to know if you require anything at all."

Brandt was still staring at his wife, now fortified by three cups of strong wine, which was loosening him up. He thought a moment on the question.

"Have him see to my daughters," he replied. Then, he glanced up at Bridget, and Annabeth. "Please leave us alone. I would be grateful."

Without another word, the ladies slipped out and closed the door. When Brandt heard the door shut and he was finally alone with Ellowyn in their comfortable chamber, his head sank face-first onto the mattress next to his wife. He could no longer control what he was feeling. He held her hand tightly. It was the worst thing he had ever experienced.

"Please, God," he whispered, the tears flowing. "Please spare her. I shall never ask another thing from you ever again if you will only spare her."

He lay there, face down, praying fervently until his exhaustion swamped him and he fell into a deep and troubled sleep.

\*\*\*

"I cannot tell you what is amiss with the child," the midwife told Brandt. "Your wife is in pain but she is not ready to give birth. Her body is not in preparation."

Brandt was pale, unshaven, and edgy as he listened to the old woman from the village speak of the things he loved most in the world. He expected more of an answer but when she didn't elaborate, he lifted his eyebrows expectantly.

"And?" he demanded. "What do you intend to do about it?"

The old lady was little and wrinkled. She had also been in hiding from the siege along with most of the village when Brandt's knight came looking for her. It had been hours before she had been located and brought back to the castle. Brandt's army was ready and waiting below to pull out and follow the king's army south, but they could do nothing more than mark time. Their liege wasn't ready to leave until the midwife gave him a report.

But it wasn't a report he wanted to hear. After an examination of a miserable Ellowyn, the woman didn't have much to say about the situation and Brandt could feel his frustration mount.

"Only time will decide my course of action," she replied, intimidated by the big warlord. "It could be something within her own body causing her pain and not something to do with the child. The pain seems to be located in her back more than in her belly, but it is difficult to know. We will have to wait and see which course the body takes."

Brandt didn't like that answer at all. "So we just wait?" he repeated. "Wait for what? Wait for her or my son to die?"

The old woman took a step back, fearful to tell him what more she suspected. In fact, she decided against telling him that the child's movements were weak. It might not reflect well on her. She gave one last try in an attempt to give the man some hope.

"I can administer a potion that will cause her to have the child, my lord," she said quietly. "It is early, that is true, but I have seen earlier children survive. Only when we purge the child from her body can we truly hope to discover the reasons behind her pain."

Brandt didn't like that answer, either. He was starting to feel sick. He sighed heavily and seemed to deflate, leaning up against the wall in the corridor outside of the chamber where Ellowyn was. Brennan and Magnus were with him, silent support for the duke with the weight of the world on his shoulders. He had enough to worry over with the King of France, with the Prince of Wales, and with the winds of war that had now turned into more of a tornado. Now, with his wife's illness, it was almost too much for the man to bear, but he had no choice.

"If we do not force her to deliver the child early, what are her chances?" he asked hoarsely.

The midwife didn't want to lie to the man but she didn't want to get her head cut off, either. "It is difficult to say without knowing what is wrong," she said truthfully. "We could force her to deliver and discover that the child was not the issue. Or, we could let nature take its course and discover that the child was indeed the problem. There is just no way of knowing. I have seen your wife regularly over the course of the past few months and never at any time did I see an indication of a problem. I am as concerned as you are."

Brandt stared at the old woman a moment before running a weary hand over his face. He was indecisive and frustrated.

"The babe is not due until October," he muttered.

"I realize that, my lord."

He looked at the woman. "What would you recommend?"

The woman was in a tight spot. Either option could see the death of one or both of her patients, which would more than likely result in her own death at the hands of a distraught father. She knew the duke and knew his reputation; most in France did. He was the Black Angel, the Bringer of Death, and she had no desire to experience his reputation first hand. Still, she knew her job. She trusted her instincts.

"I would recommend we leave the child inside of her and see where it takes us," she said. "The child would be born very early and chances of survival would be difficult. The longer we leave him in the mother, the better. However, if her pain does not subside or grow worse, I can give her a potion that will begin her labor. I am afraid we have limited options, my lord."

As Brandt leaned against the wall and weighed his choices, Dylan came off the stairs and entered the corridor. He was exhausted, just like the rest of them, his gaze fixed on Brandt.

"My lord," he said as politely as he could. "A word, please."

Brandt just looked at the man. He didn't move. There was a deluge of reluctance in his expression, something that made him want to forget everything but his wife and her health. So much of his life had been dedicated to war. Now, all of that seemed to pale by comparison. He didn't want to fight anymore, but he knew he had an entire country depending on him. It was a horrible burden to bear.

Wearily, he pushed himself off the wall and moved towards Dylan as the midwife retreated back inside the chamber. Brennan and Magnus crowded around as well.

"Our patrols have returned from following the king," Dylan said, his voice low and hoarse. "They tell us that terrible weather is occurring to the south and that the king's army has camped for the night south of Rennes. They have been slowed by the wounded they carry and also by the weather. If we leave now, it is possible to catch up to them."

Brandt thought on that a moment. "Our troops are relatively fresh," he said. "Our men were locked up in the fortress dodging arrows while his men were doing everything they could to breach the castle. We could conceivably catch them and weaken them further before they reach Edward."

"That was my thought, my lord."

"Jean carries more men that I do."

"But the beast is weakened. If we strike while it is weak, we have a good chance for victory."

Brandt knew that. "But what of these alleged negotiations to prevent Poitiers from becoming a massive battle? Jean violated that suggestion when he attacked Melesse to keep me away from Edward. Now he rides for Edward himself. We must show him that the Prince of Wales' war machine is not weakened in the least."

Dylan, Brennan, and Magnus nodded. "The men are prepared, my lord," Dylan assured him.

Brandt could feel the familiar excitement of a battle march in his veins but it was tempered by his concern for his wife. He was terribly torn, not wanting to go with his men but by virtue of the fact that they were *his* men, knowing he must. It was his sense of obligation, of honor, that forced him to comply. It was not his heart, which very much remained here at Melesse with his wife. He'd never felt so torn or miserable in his life but he knew what he had to do.

"Ready my charger," he told his men without any enthusiasm whatsoever. "I will be down shortly and we will depart."

His knights left the corridor, noisy armor and mail echoing off the walls, the stairwell, until the sounds of death and warfare faded away. Brandt stood in the corridor, summoning every ounce of courage he had to do what he knew he had to do. Already, it was killing him. He would have to leave his wife.

Quietly, he pushed open the chamber door. The midwife was burning white sage and peppermint because, Brandt suspected, she had a bit of mystic in her so the room smelled strongly as he entered. Ellowyn was lying on her back on the big bed, her eager attention focused on him as he came into the room. He smiled at her as he approached the bed.

"So you are awake?" he asked lightly. "I have not seen those lovely eyes in quite some time."

Ellowyn smiled weakly in return. "How is everything?" she asked. "Did the castle fare well in the siege?"

He hadn't really spoken to her about any of it because she had been sleeping so much.  He sat down on the bed beside her and collected her soft hand, kissing it.

"Well enough," he replied, but he changed the subject right away. He didn't want to speak of the castle or his army just yet. "How are you feeling?"

Her smile faded.  "Well, I suppose," she said. "I want to get up and move about but the midwife will not let me."

Brandt glanced at the midwife, who shook her head at him. He returned his focus to his wife.

"Has the pain in your belly gone away?" he asked.

She turned her head, not looking at him. "Not entirely."

"Then perhaps you should listen to her."

Unhappy with the opinion, Ellowyn simply kept her head turned, bordering on a pout.  Brandt looked over at the midwife again and jerked his head in the direction of the door, silently ordering the woman to leave. Fortunately, she understood his command and slipped from the room.

When they were finally alone, Brandt leaned over Ellowyn, arms braced on either side of her. He studied the shape of her face, seeing perfect beauty in her delicate features. But she was staring off into the room, refusing to meet his eye, so he leaned down and began to gently suckle her jawbone.

"Do you recall when we first met that I said you were pleasing to the eye?" he murmured.

Ellowyn closed her eyes as he kissed her, thinking back to that day of days. "You also said you had no use for me."

"I lied."

Her grin broke through and she looked up at him, seeing how very weary he appeared. Reaching up, she stroked his rough cheeks tenderly.

"What is happening?" she begged softly. "Is there more battle to come?"

The twinkle in his eyes dimmed. "Eventually," he told her. "Jean's army is bivouacked about twelve miles south.  They did not make it very far with all of the wounded they are carrying. Additionally, I am told that there is very bad weather to the south which is also hampering their travel. The king is moving south to attack Edward, I believe, and it is my intention to weaken him seriously before he can accomplish that."

She gazed up at him. "When will you leave?"

He sighed heavily and averted his eyes. "Before the sun sets."

"That does not give us much time to say what needs to be said."

He looked at her again, his expression guarded. "I do not want to go, Wynny."

She nodded patiently. "I know," she said. "But you must. Too many people are depending on you."

"Do you want me to go?"

"Of course not. But if you remain with me, who else can command in your stead? Who else can bring fear to the hearts of men but the Black Angel?"

He grunted with displeasure at her statement, at the situation in general, before stretching out on the bed beside her and wrapping her up in his arms as much as he was able. Armor and a mail coat made it very difficult but he did the best he could. He had to hold her, to feel her in his arms. It gave him such comfort. As he lay there with his mouth on her forehead, tears began to fill his eyes. He simply couldn't help it.

"The midwife says she does not know what is wrong with you," he whispered. "She believes we should wait and see if your pain subsides because it is too early for the child to be born. However, if your pains do not subside, she says there is a potion she can give you to induce the birth. Wynny, if it comes to saving your life over the child's, I will choose your life every time. We can always have another child, but there will never be another you."

She sighed faintly. "The child will be fine," she murmured. "There is nothing to worry over."

"Are you still feeling pain?"

"Not much," she lied.

He wasn't sure if he believed her or not but he let it go. He leaned back, pinching her chin between his thumb and forefinger and forcing her to look at him.

"Do you understand me?" he said softly. "If the choice is between you and the child, I will choose you. Those are my wishes and you will not disobey them."

"I understand."

Gazing into her bottomless eyes, he kissed her tenderly. Then he kissed her again and hugged her tightly, staving off the flood of tears that threatened. Ellowyn sensed his sadness, wrapping her arms around his neck and squeezing him tightly. She sensed his deep reluctance, his unwillingness to do what he had been born and trained to do. His mind was with her and as long as he believed she was in danger, his thoughts would be with her even though his body would be with the army.

*Distraction is deadly.* It was all she could think of. She didn't want her distracted husband taking an arrow to the chest because he wasn't being vigilant. It would absolutely destroy her. She tried not to think on that terrible dream that had plagued her for so long, the one she now determined had something to do with Brandt.

*The de Russe dragon on the breastplate.* Brandt didn't give any stock in her dreams and she would not bring it up. Perhaps this one would not come true, as other had not. Perhaps it was just the musings of her over-active mind. Still, it was difficult to shake off the sense of foreboding she had at Brandt's imminent departure.

But it would be her burden to bear alone. As much as she didn't want him to go to war, she knew she had to be the strong one at this moment. He had to continue Edward's fight and she could not stop it. Brandt had to believe she was well and that everything was going to all right.

"I do not want you to worry," she said, forcing her courage. "I am feeling much better. I am sure everything will be fine. But I must ask you a question."

"What is that?"

"How are *you* feeling?"

He paused, considering the question. "My strength has never been better," he replied. "But my mind...."

"Your mind is sharp and cunning," she insisted. "You must not worry over me, Brandt. The babe and I will be fine and I swear I will send you word if anything changes. But for now, there is a prince who needs you as he has always needed you. You must go."

He knew that. God help him, he knew it. He pulled back to look at her, the sweet lines of her face, tucking it back into his memory for days that were particularly lonely. But he knew the risks, not only to her but to him; she was facing an uncertain pregnancy. He was facing battle. There was every reason to believe he would never see her again but every hope that he would. His throat was tight with emotion as he kissed her gently on the mouth. "Walking through life with you, Madam, has been a very gracious thing," he murmured. "I love you more than words can express."

"And I love you," Ellowyn whispered, struggling against the tears. "I will see you soon."

He nodded slowly, his dark eyes riveted to her. "Aye, you will."

"Be safe, my love."

There was nothing more to say. He kissed her one last time and climbed out of bed. His heart was so heavy he didn't think he could stand it. He knew that if he turned to look at her one last time, all would be lost. He wouldn't leave at all. So he squared his shoulders and quit the room without a hind glance. There was no other way he could accomplish it. By the time he hit the stairwell, he was weeping silent tears.

Back in the bed chamber, the one that smelled of sage and peppermint to ward off the bad spirits, Ellowyn was weeping sorrowful tears of her own. Dear God, she missed him already.

But Brandt had a job to do, one he had no choice but to see through. He had wiped his face and cleaned up by the time he reached the bailey where the army was waiting. It smelled strongly of smoke, men, and animals as he set foot in the dusty bailey and as he glanced overhead, he could see dark and angry storm clouds well off to the south. It must have been the terrible weather the scouts had described. As he made his way towards his big black charger, he noticed a painted white wagon off to his left.

Rosalind and Margarethe were standing next to the wagon. Brandt noticed them, hesitated his forward momentum, and then headed over in their direction. The girls seemed to grow increasingly nervous as he approached.

"Are you leaving?" he asked, indicating the wagon. "It will grow dark soon. Mayhap you should remain here until I return and we can speak more of your return to England at that time."

The young women looked at each other, shocked, before returning their attention to him.

"You... you would have us return to England?" Rosalind was genuinely shocked. "We thought that mayhap... well, you certainly have a good deal on your mind. We thought we should return to Gael and perhaps speak to you again about England another day."

Brandt could see they were nervous, as they seemed to be around him. He was growing soft in his old age, feeling more and more pity for them. He was also reconsidering his harsh stance against him; they had made the effort to come see him, after all. As Rosalind put it, perhaps it was time for a rapport between them. He was coming to hope so.

"Remain here until I return," he said again. "At some point I plan to return to England and mayhap you will go with me. Moreover, I would have you here where you will be better protected than at Gael. Is that acceptable?"

The young women nodded readily. As Margarethe turned back to the wagon, Rosalind took a few timid steps towards Brandt.

"Thank you, my lord," she said genuinely. "We are very appreciative of your offer."

Brandt nodded his head, not having much more to say. As he turned away, Rosalind caught his attention one last time.

"My lord," she called. When he turned to look at her, she grew nervous again. "I... I wanted to wish you luck in battle."

He looked at her, seeing a well-spoken young woman who, much like him, had been without parents for most of her life. Her father had been absent and her mother had run off. Now, she was trying to make an effort to know him, having the opportunity that he himself never had with his own parents. Something about her effort warmed him. He wasn't sure if he trusted her completely, but he was willing to give it a try. Ellowyn had given him the confidence to open himself up emotionally. He was much more sure of himself than he had ever been.

"Thank you," he said quietly. "Should you need anything, please let Mme. Simpelace know. She will provide for you."

"And your lady wife, my lord?" Rosalind asked. "May... may we come to know her?"

He cracked a smile. "I think she would like that."

Rosalind smiled timidly in return and gave him a little wave to bid him farewell. "Thank you, my lord."

"You may call me Father if you wish. I am yours, after all."

With that, he turned away and headed to the area where the bulk of his army was staging.

He had a battle to fight.

# CHAPTER TWENTY SEVEN

*Three weeks later*
*12 September 1356*

Ellowyn sat motionless in a chair, gazing out of the long lancet window over the rainy Brittany landscape. A cold breeze was blowing and she could smell the mist. Although the bed chamber was warm and fragrant with new rushes, the cold breeze made her shiver. She thought she could smell death upon it.

The door to the chamber opened quietly and Annabeth entered. She carried a tray of food with her, laden with all manner of tempting offerings. Her mistress hadn't truly eaten in over a week so she wanted to entice her. Setting the tray on small table against the wall, she approached Ellowyn.

"My lady?" she said timidly. "I have brought you something to eat."

Clad in a dark blue wool surcoat with a heavy knitted sweater over it that flowed all the way to the floor, Ellowyn glanced over her shoulder at Annabeth. Her face was pale, her lips without color, and her blond hair knotted at the nape of her neck.

"I am not hungry," she said quietly. "Please take it away."

Annabeth didn't turn away as she should have. "My lady, please," she begged softly. "You have hardly eaten in days. You must keep up your strength."

Ellowyn was still staring from the window, her eyes glassy and distant. "For what?" she asked, her tone dull. "For the son who will not suckle my breast? For the child now buried in the earth of Melesse's chapel? There is no reason to keep up my strength. That reason died ten days ago, birthed blue and with the cord strangling him. Nay, Annabeth... there is no reason to keep up my strength."

Annabeth sighed heavily. They had been through this subject daily, sometimes hourly. The still birth of the duke's son nearly a week after the duke's departure had done something to Ellowyn; she was dead inside, too. She hadn't even had the strength or the will or the nerve to send her husband word of the child. Reports had come back from Poitiers telling tale of preparations for a massive battle because negotiations between the French and the English had failed. Ellowyn didn't want to distract Brandt in the fight of his life. Or perhaps he was already dead. Instead, she spent every day staring out of the window as if waiting for the man to return to her. Her mind was wandering far, far away and sometimes those around her wondered if she had lost it completely. There was no soul left in her with Brandt's departure and the death of their child.

"It was God's Will, my lady," Annabeth said softly. "We do not know why these things happen, only that they do."

"Do not speak to me of God," Ellowyn snapped softly. "You may speak to me of anything else, but not of God. I will not hear of him within these walls. God has failed me."

Annabeth shushed her. "Dare you speak that way with your husband fighting a vicious battle? Say a prayer of forgiveness, quickly, that God will not abandon him because of your blasphemy!"

Ellowyn merely shook her head. "Say it for me, my pious friend," she murmured. "God and I are not on speaking terms right now."

As Annabeth murmured a prayer for Ellowyn and Brandt, Bridget appeared in the doorway. She looked at Annabeth, who merely shook her head sadly. Bridget summoned a deep breath for courage, understanding the silent implication that the mood of the room was bleak.

"My lady?" she said, entering the room. "Lady Rosalind has asked me if she may come to visit you. Would you receive visitors today?"

Ellowyn sighed. Rosalind and Margarethe had been allowed to remain at Melesse while Brandt was away and they had come to visit her before the birth of the child. Ellowyn had actually enjoyed her time spent with Rosalind, who seemed like as if she genuinely wanted to be friendly. Margarethe, however, was still reserved and uncertain. Ellowyn had enjoyed the brief conversations she and Rosalind had before the event of the birth, but since then, she hadn't felt much like conversing. She still didn't.

"Please tell Lady Rosalind that I am still not well today," she said sadly. "Mayhap tomorrow. We shall see how I feel."

Bridget nodded and prepared to leave the room when Mme. Simpelace was in the doorway, her severe face taut. Her gaze found Ellowyn.

"Madam," she addressed her breathlessly. "A messenger has arrived from Chavigney. He comes from your husband."

Ellowyn felt a bolt of fear and excitement rush through her. It was enough to set her hands to shaking as she moved away from the window.

"Where is he?" she demanded.

"In your solar, madam," the chatelaine told her. "He has come with news for you!"

Ellowyn was moving faster than she had in months. Even though she had birthed a child only ten days before, the truth was that the birth had been rather fast and easy, and she wasn't particularly sore. She felt rather good.

But all thoughts of births and deaths and battles were purged from her mind as she scooted down the spiral stairs with Annabeth, Bridget, and Mme. Simpelace in tow. She could hear Bridget hissing insults at the old woman and being called a rodent in return. It was almost enough to make her smile, but not quite.

It was warm on the lower living area as she gathered her heavy skirt and sweater, and charged into her solar. It was even warmer in that room, as Rosalind and Margarethe had been using it for their sitting room with Ellowyn holed up in her chamber. The young women were there even now, seated before the blazing hearth, as Ellowyn and her entourage rushed in. The messenger, an exhausted cavalry soldier bearing Brandt's crest, was seated near the hearth with a hunk of bread in his hand. He bolted to his feet when Lady de Russe swept in.

"My lady," he said with his mouth full, startled by her swift appearance. "I come with a message from your husband."

"Well?" Ellowyn demanded. "What is it?"

The young soldier swallowed the food in his mouth before continuing, nearly choking on it as he forced it down.

"My lord de Russe says to tell you that he is hopeful that you and the child are of excellent health and that he prays for you by the hour," he began. "On the eve of my departure, there was a terrible battle brewing, my lady. On the fields outside of Poitiers, King Jean of France, Dauphin Charles, and Prince Phillip were aligning their armies against the Prince of Wales and the Duke of Exeter. Thousands and thousands of men, my lady. The duke wanted me to tell you that if he does not return before Christmas, then you must take the remainder of the army he has stationed here at Melesse for your protection and return to England. He begs that you do this for your own safety."

Ellowyn stared at the young messenger, stunned. Her legs suddenly felt weak and she grasped at the nearest chair, lowering herself onto it. Her mind was so much mush at the moment, making it difficult to grasp a single thought.

"Leave?" she repeated, shocked and incredulous. "Leave without him?"

"Aye, my lady."

Ellowyn stared at the messenger before tearing her gaze away, her mind whirling with what she had been told. The more she thought on it, the more despondent she grew.

"He speaks as if...," she began, but quickly recovered. She looked at the messenger. "You said there were thousands of men. How big is the king's army?"

"Several thousand, my lady," he replied quietly.

"And the Prince of Wales' army?"

"Not as many."

Ellowyn thought on that a moment, sickening realization flooding her. "Dear God," she whispered, pressing a hand to her forehead in a weary and disillusioned gesture. "They are out-numbered."

Standing beside her, Annabeth and Bridget could only think of their respective loves, Dylan and Brennan. Just like their mistress, they were fighting off a horrid sense of dread. As Ellowyn hung her head in sorrow, Annabeth addressed the messenger.

"Had the battle started when you left?" she asked. "How long ago was that?"

The messenger looked to the lovely brunette. "The battle had not yet started but the lines were drawn, my lady," he replied. "I left six days ago. I am sure much has happened since then."

Ellowyn couldn't shake the anxiety. The more she tried, the more it clung to her. All she could think about was her husband and his fate. *That dream!* That horrible, horrible dream came crashing down on her and her apprehension exploded. She had no idea why she should suddenly think of that dream she hadn't had in weeks, but it loomed heavy in her mind nonetheless. She couldn't stop herself.

"Tell me," she said, her voice quivering. "Is the weather poor?"

The messenger nodded. "Raining, my lady, the likes of which I have never seen. It has turned everything into a sea of mud."

*Mud!* As in her dream, everything had turned to mud, mud so deep and think that it was nearly impossible to penetrate.

"And... and the field?" she forced herself to ask. "Where is the field where they are fighting?"

The messenger shrugged. "All around Poitiers and Chavigney," he said. "The lines move as one side overwhelms another."

"Is there a castle nearby?"

The messenger thought a moment. "Jaudres Castle is near the lines, my lady," he said. "It is a big beast of a castle, impenetrable. There was already fighting around it when I left."

*A castle. Mud. Rain.* It was her dream come to life. Something inside was screaming at her, telling her that she had to go there. Already, she was feeling the same panic and anxiety that she felt whenever she had the dream, telling her that she had to find Brandt. It was an overwhelming sensation, something she could not control. She'd had the dream for months, a premonition of things to come, and she would not ignore it. She had to go to him, like a moth to a flame, the lure was just too great. She couldn't sit back and ignore the dreams, the messages she had been given. *She had to go!*

"I am going to Poitiers," she said, bolting to her feet. As those around her gasped in shock and horror, she pointed to the messenger. "What is your name?"

The messenger was taken aback. "Sully, my lady."

"You will take me there, Sully," she commanded. Already, she was on the move. "Annabeth, Bridget, you will remain here. I must go to my husband."

They were all following her out of the room, protests seeping from their lips. "My lady!" Annabeth gasped. "You cannot go! You are putting yourself in terrible danger!"

Ellowyn turned to her. "I understand," she said patiently, "but Brandt is in danger. Mayhap he is even dying. Please do not ask me how I know this, but I do. I swear that I do. You must let me go to him."

Annabeth's mouth popped open in horror and she turned to Bridget for support. Bridget was deeply concerned.

"My lady, please," she begged. "It is pure madness to want to go to Poitiers now. There is death and battle everywhere. You will be killed!"

Ellowyn shook her head. "I will not be killed," she assured her. "Please understand me; I must go to my husband and I will risk my life to do it. If anyone gets in my way, I will run them down and if anyone tries to stop me, I will kill them. I must go to my husband *now*."

Annabeth was in tears at this point. They were all following her out into the entry hall, voices of reason pleading with a very determined lady. It was chaotic as the servants took up the call and shouts of the duke's death began to fly. No one understood why Lady de Russe was so agitated but there could only be one explanation.

There was one voice, however, that was not pleading with Ellowyn to reconsider. Rosalind had followed her out into the entry along with the group, listening to the protests.

"My lady," she said. "I know that area well. My mother had relatives near Chavigney and we would travel there often. I will go with you and help you find my father."

Above the objections, Ellowyn gazed into Rosalind's face, seeing that she was indeed sincere. She was also showing her father's strength, something that impressed Ellowyn. She knew she should deny her but it was difficult.

"I appreciate your offer, but Sully will escort me," she said. "You cannot put yourself in such danger."

Rosalind cocked her head and Ellowyn could see Brandt in that gesture. "I know the area better than he does," she said. "If you are looking for my father, I will be able to help you find him better than a messenger. I know every possible place to look, and I will know where to hide. You must take me."

Ellowyn gazed steadily at the young woman. There was truth in what she said, but still, she shook her head.

"I cannot be responsible for your life," she said softly. "I can only be responsible for mine."

"You will not be responsible for me," Rosalind insisted. "I alone am responsible for my life and for my actions, and everyone in this room is witness. You will not be blamed if something happens to me because I am going with or without your permission."

Margarethe tried to talk to her sister but Rosalind gently pushed her away. Her focus was on Ellowyn as the woman locked gazes with her. It was evident that Ellowyn was very reluctant but she did not want to argue with Rosalind. Much like Brandt, the woman was evidently resolute and stubborn. They could all see that trait. Finally, Ellowyn nodded her head.

"Very well," she said. "But we travel light and fast. In this weather, there is no telling how long it will take us to get there. Days if not weeks."

Rosalind nodded firmly. "I will be ready."

As Ellowyn continued to look at the young woman, she began to feel a bond with her, a common goal. Moreover, the woman was of Brandt's blood. Ellowyn would love anything born from Brandt. Rosalind was brave and determined much as her father was.

"Foolishness!" Mme. Simpelace cried. "Stupidity! You must not go!"

Ellowyn turned to the old chatelaine. "I *will* go," she said, jaw ticking. "If you will not help me, then get out of my way."

Mme. Simpelace seemed to go through the throes of fainting without actually accomplishing the act. She was distraught, as were they all, but there was no changing the course that Ellowyn and Rosalind were about to take.

They went their separate ways to prepare for the journey, both women with people trailing after them begging them not to go, but they were determined. Eventually, those same people gave up the battle and began to help. There was no discouraging the inevitable.

With a purpose, with resolve and bravery bred from a love for her husband that ran deeper than the earth itself, Ellowyn was mounted and ready to ride only a few hours later. Astride a leggy warm blood stallion, she was dressed in peasant clothing disguised as a male just as Rosalind was. It was determined that would be the safest way to travel.

With six armed soldiers from the contingent guarding Melesse and with Sully in the lead, Lady de Russe and Lady Rosalind thundered from Chateau Melesse, heading south into the fiery jaws of death and destruction.

# CHAPTER TWENTY EIGHT

*20 September 1356*
*Near the woods of Nouaillè*

Ellowyn on the edge of a meadow, looking at a massive castle in the distance, partially obscured by sheets of driving rain. In spite of the weather, smoke rose in ribbons over the damaged battlements.

Overhead, the sky was the color of pewter with fat, angry clouds, but upon earth, the field was flooded from the unforgiving rain that had been falling for days, perhaps weeks, mayhap even months. It was difficult to know. It seemed as if it had been raining forever.

A great battle had concluded the day before upon the field and there was a sea of bodies strewn about, like pieces of driftwood upon an endless muddy sea. Ellowyn's heart was in her throat as she observed the scene, her breathing coming in panicked little gasps. Something was here for her, something she loved so desperately that she couldn't think of anything else. Even though she couldn't see Brandt, she knew he was here.

"Sweet Jesus," Rosalind breathed at the sight. "Is this possible?"

Ellowyn couldn't even speak. Her eyes were drinking in the horror that she had seen in her mind's eye before. Everything was as it should be down to the color of the sky. The castle towards the northeast was heavily damaged, the top of the walls nearly sheared off from the projectiles flung at it. With the rain and the debris, it gave the illusion that it was melting.

*Melting....*

Ellowyn fought down the panic. She handed her reins over to the nearest soldier. It didn't matter that she was exhausted from over a week of travel in horrible weather and still recovering from birthing a child. All that mattered was that she locate her husband.

She knew was out here, somewhere. She had to find him.

"One of you stay with the horses," she ordered in a trembling voice. "The rest of you fan out and look for the duke's men. Find them!"

The soldier holding Elloywn's horse was designated to stay behind. He collected everyone's reins as the small group began to descend into the pit of hell where men were dead or dying, and a sea of mud was slowly swallowing everything up. Rain, buckets of it, was falling and no matter how tightly Ellowyn pulled close the oiled cloak around her shoulders, she was still wet. She had been wet for days. But that did not deter her. Brandt was here and she had to find him.

She thought back to that terrible dream. She had found him lying beneath a tree. *A tree.* She began to look around frantically for something that seemed recognizable to her, but the landscape was slightly out of place from what her dream had conveyed. Rosalind was next to her, peering at the dead and dying to see if she recognized Brandt's colors and, indeed, she came across several dead men bearing Brandt's standard. There seemed to be quite a lot of them. Rosalind eventually turned to Ellowyn in confusion and horror.

"So many of my father's men are lying here," she hissed. "What does it all mean?"

Ellowyn was struggling to remain calm. God help her, she was. "It means that they were the bravest," she said hoarsely. "It means that they were the first into battle and fought the hardest."

She trudged off with Rosalind hanging on to her and together the two of them slugged through the mud as Ellowyn tried to get her bearings, struggling to separate the dream from reality, looking for her husband with such desperation that her stomach was in horrific knots. Twice they had to pause as she dry-heaved, riddle with nerves, but nothing would deter her. She had to find him.

"My lady!" Rosalind hissed, tugging at her and pointing off to the right. "Is that not one of the duke's knights?"

Ellowyn was electrified with the possibility, straining to see through the rain at what Rosalind was indicating. She began to move in that direction even though she couldn't clearly see, but soon enough, a big man bearing the Duke of Exeter's tunic.

Ellowyn broke into a run, sliding over the slippery mud, getting stuck in it at other times. It was like a nightmare, the ground as it tried to suck her down and prevent her from getting to her husband. As she drew closer to the knight, she could see who it was.

"Stefan!" she screamed. "*Stefan!*"

Le Bec had been tasked with assessing the duke's dead. He was looking down at group of infantry that had been brutally slaughtered when he heard his name. It as a woman's voice and he thought that, quite possibly, he was going mad. But his head came up, seeking the sources of the shout. He could see two small peasants struggling towards him through the mud, but one peasant's hood came free and he recognized Lady de Russe immediately. He went into a panic.

"My lady!" he called, struggling towards her just as she was struggling towards him. "Here, my lady, here!"

"Stefan!" Ellowyn called again.

They came together near a pile of dead French infantry. Stefan reached out to grab her.

"My lady!" he gasped. "What on earth are you doing here?"

"Stefan," Ellowyn breathed, holding on to him for dear life. "Where is my husband?"

Stefan just looked at her, his pale and worn features tightening. "Oh... my lady," he sighed. "Why have you come? Who was stupid enough to let you come to this place of death?"

Ellowyn was very aware that he had not answered her question. Struggling to keep her terror at a manageable level, she fixed him in the eye.

"I will ask you one more time," she said, sounding stronger. "Where is my husband? You will tell me now and you will not delay."

Stefan stared at her. Then, his eyes filled with tears; both Ellowyn and Rosalind could see it.

"He is this way," he said hoarsely. "I will take you."

Ellowyn clung to him as he led her out of the mud, moving away from the castle and the horrific dead. In fact, both Ellowyn and Rosalind were trying not to look down at the many dead at their feet, but it was difficult considering how bad the footing was. They had to look down to make sure they didn't stop on anything. There were men without heads, without limbs, without faces. Ellowyn thought it was even worse than the dream.

"Tell me what has happened," she begged softly.

Stefan had a good grip on her as he pulled her carefully with him. "We met the armies of Jean yesterday," he said quietly. "I will omit the most of the tactical details but in spite of being heavily outnumbered by the French, it was a decisive English victory. The Black Angel was once again victorious."

Ellowyn listened carefully. "Why do I see so many de Russe men among the dead?"

Stefan sighed faintly. "Because we were charged with splitting the French forces in two," he said. "We accomplished a great strategic victory that allowed the Prince of Wales to gain the upper hand. It was very, very costly, however; we lost Dylan in the fight and Magnus was badly injured."

They had come to the end of the sea of mud and stood on more solid ground. Ellowyn gained her footing as she digested Stefan's words. As they stood on firmer soil, she turned to the exhausted knight.

"Dylan is dead?" she asked.

Stefan nodded, his lower lip trembling. "Aye."

Ellowyn was deeply and wholly saddened. She closed her eyes at the thought of the brave, efficient knight now counted among the dead.

"Dear God," she breathed. "Poor Dylan. Poor Annabeth! How badly is Magnus injured?"

"He lost an eye but the physic believes he will recover."

"Thank God for small mercies," she whispered. "And my husband?"

Stefan wouldn't look her in the eye. He began to pull her with him. "I am sorry to say that he was badly injured as well."

Ellowyn's knees buckled and it took both Stefan and Rosalind to steady her. Her calm demeanor shattered, Ellowyn began to gasp, struggling not to scream or weep. She had to keep her head.

"Take me to him now," she gasped. "*Now*, Stefan."

He was already on the move, half-carrying her, half-dragging her. Even though Ellowyn had known what the answer would be, still, it was a shock to hear the truth. Her dream had forewarned her of this moment but she found she was wholly unprepared. *He has been badly injured.* The reality of it was too great.

There was a collection of hastily pitched tents off to the west and Stefan took her in that direction. With the wind blowing and the rain pouring, they moved swiftly through the elements, making way to the large Exeter tent that Ellowyn had become so familiar with during her travels with Brandt. She recognized it immediately.

Breaking free from Stefan, she ran as fast as her shaking legs would carry her and plunged into the de Russe tent. Once inside, she nearly crashed into one of several men standing inside the tent. Recoiling from the strange man, she looked around in a blind panic through the sea of unfamiliar faces until she came to one she recognized. It was Alex de Lara. As she rushed to him, she realized that he was kneeling on the floor next to a supine body. That body happened to be Brandt's.

One look at her husband's ashen face and Ellowyn collapsed beside him. She had no control any longer, only fear and panic.

"What has happened to my husband?" she demanded of anyone who would answer. "Tell me now!"

Gasps of shock went up throughout the room, including Alex; *a woman was here!* Alex grasped Ellowyn to keep her from pitching forward on to Brandt.

"Lady de Russe!" he exclaimed. "How did you get here?"

Ellowyn only had eyes for Brandt. His eyes were closed and he was stripped from the waist up. A massive bandage wound around his muscular torso as his surgeon, squatting on the other side of him, tugged at the wrappings. Ignoring Alex's question, she put her arms around Brandt's head with exquisite gentleness, feeling pain in her heart that was too deep for words. Her tears, warm and soft, pelted his pallid face. The raw ache, the horror, was indescribable.

"Brandt?" she whispered. "I am here, my love. I am here."

"He is badly injured, my lady," Alex said, his voice faint and hoarse. "He was fighting on horseback yesterday when we broke the French lines. You should have seen him, my lady; he was magnificent. He felled man after man with no signs of slowing. He was fighting near Gascon knights that were supposed to be allied with Edward but they turned on him. One knight gored him in the back while a second knight gored him in the gut. My brother saw this occur and went to save him. He managed to kill two of the assassins but he was killed by a third. As my brother fell away, Lord de Russe, severely injured, then killed my brother's assassin before he himself fell to the ground. Magnus saw it all and told us."

"Assassins?" she breathed, horrified.

"Aye, my lady. That was the only way anyone could get close enough to kill him, for he is too great to be felled by ordinary enemy."

Ellowyn closed her eyes at the information, never more appalled or proud. Tears rained on Brandt's face as she knelt low, kissing him tenderly.

"He is a hero," she murmured.

"He is a legend."

Ellowyn couldn't help it; the sobs came and she wept pitifully over Brandt as the man lay dying. Alex, too, gave up the battle against his tears and wept with her. He had lost his brother and his tears were for himself; he didn't know how he was supposed to go on without his other self. It was tragic on so many levels.

Rosalind came up behind Ellowyn, laying gentle hands on her shoulders as she, too, wept. In fact, there wasn't a dry eye in the tent, listening to Lady de Russe weep in sorrow over her dying husband. As Ellowyn lay there with her forehead against Brandt's as if forcibly willing her life into him, she felt a timid hand on her arm. She happened to look up into a face she didn't recognize.

"My lady," the young man said hesitantly. "I am Edward. I want you to know how much I love your husband and how grateful I am to him. No finer warrior has walked this earth and I am greatly diminished without him."

Through her grief, Ellowyn realized that she was looking at the Prince of Wales. Her head came up, her gaze drinking in the sight of the handsome young man with the fair hair. Finally, they were face to face. There was something Ellowyn had to say to him.

"Your Grace," she greeted hoarsely. "I am greatly diminished without him as well, but not for the same reasons. He is my life, my love, and my heart. I hate you for doing this to him, do you hear? I will hate you forever."

Edward wasn't offended. At this moment, he hated himself also. So much death and waste because of him. Before he could reply, however, a weak, deep voice interrupted.

"Wynny," Brandt mumbled. "You will apologize to Edward. It is not his fault."

Hearing Brandt's voice sent Ellowyn into loud and agonizing sobs. He held his head against hers, weeping, as his very weak hand came up to very gently touch her. It was all he could manage.

"Shhhh," he soothed her, so faintly that she could barely hear him. "Do not despair. I will be well again. Have I come home?"

Ellowyn was a mess, wiping at her face and kissing his mouth with her salty lips. "You are not home," she murmured. "I have come to you. I will make you well again, I swear it."

Brandt grunted, that disapproving grunt that he was so capable of making. "Where are we?"

"Still at Poitiers."

"What fool would bring you here? Tell me now so that I may thrash him for allowing you to travel into the midst of hell."

She glanced at Edward, at Alex, before replying. "It does not matter who brought me here," she told him, stroking his face tenderly. "All that matters is that you will get well again. We will return home to Guildford. Perhaps we will even travel to Erith to visit my mother and grandmother. We will live our life, do you hear me? We will live and have a dozen children to surround ourselves with."

Brandt tried to open an eye to look at her but it was extremely difficult. "My son," he murmured. "Where is my son?"

317

Ellowyn froze, looking at him with shock. She could hear Rosalind behind her, still weeping softly. Strangely, her courage seemed to make a return and she wiped at her face, thinking on his question. She already knew that she would not tell him the truth, at least not now. Perhaps if he thought he had something more to live for, it would help him. She had to give him all the ammunition she could to help him. Later, when the storm had passed, she would tell him the truth and pray he would forgive her.

"He is at Melesse," she replied steadily, kissing his cheek with painful tenderness. "His name is Gaston. Brandt, you have always been a warrior but now you are in for the most difficult fight of your life. You must fight your way back from the brink of death so that your son may come to know you. You must live for your wife and child who adore you more than words can express. *Please,* Brandt; you must do this for us."

Brandt sighed faintly, unconsciousness clutching at him. He was so very, very weak, but Ellowyn's words rang about in his hazed mind.

"My son," he whispered. "Does he look... like me?"

Ellowyn smiled, tears pooling in her eyes. "He looks just like me."

It was a tease; even in his current state, Brandt knew that. But Ellowyn had been correct; the knowledge of his son, of his loving wife, gave him the will to fight. He couldn't even think of the fact that she had made a dangerous journey to be with him. The fact that she would risk herself so was not surprising; she was a brave and astonishing woman, and he loved her more with every beat of his heart.

"I love you, my sweet husband," Ellowyn whispered in his ear. "You are my sweet angel. Sleep, now. I will be here when you awaken."

His big fingers found hers and he held her hand tightly as he drifted away. Thoughts of the day they met in London flashed through his mind, thinking on the first time he ever laid eyes on her. She had been so very beautiful and so very angry. The thought of it brought a smile to his lips. He wondered if their children would have the same hair-trigger temper. He hoped he would find out many times over.

The Black Angel had done his duty for king and country. Now, he had his own life to live.

# EPILOGUE

"Die!" The child cried. "Die already! I have killed you!"

A big lad with dark hair and dark eyes pointed the stick in his hand imperiously at a similar looking child slightly younger than he was. But the younger boy shook his head stubbornly.

"You did *not* kill me," he said. "I am the evil black knight and you cannot kill me. I am holding your children hostage! Fight me!"

The big lad with the stick frowned terribly. At six years of age, he was rather large for a boy of his years. He was also good with a sword, or really a stick, during the times his mother didn't know he was using one. She didn't allow them to strike at each other with sticks and she wouldn't let them have real swords. It made it difficult to play battle games if they weren't allowed to be armed.

So they had to plan their play times in secret, for example, during times when they were supposed to be napping. It was easy to slip past their fat nurse, who would fall into a heavy sleep in the afternoons. At this moment, his younger brother by one year was holding their little brother and sister hostage. In reality, the two and three year old children were sitting on top of a hay pile in the stables, but in their minds, it was a great castle. Now the great castle was under siege and the two older boys began smacking each other with their sticks. It was deadly battle.

Next door in the main part of the stable block, Brandt had been inspecting three new chargers purchased in Caen, recently shipped to Guildford when he heard the smacking going on. The horses were nervous enough without the sounds so, lured by the noise, Brandt went in search of the source.

Standing in the entry with his hands on his hips, he watched his older sons whack each other with long sticks. On a pile of fresh hay behind them were the two younger children, a three year old boy with his mother's blond hair and a daughter that looked like her father. Brandt watched the older boys swing away at each other.

"Aramis? Trenton?" he called to them. "What are you doing?"

The boys came to a halt, turning to their father with innocent faces. They lowered their sticks. "Playing, Father," Aramis, the oldest boy, said. "I am fighting Trenton to rescue Edward and Isabeau."

"They need rescuing?"

Trenton nodded emphatically. Younger than Aramis by fourteen months, he was the most aggressive of the four children.

"I am the evil black knight," he told his father. "If Aramis wants to rescue Edward and Isabeau, he must fight me."

"I see," Brandt said, coming into the stable. "Where is your nurse?"

"Sleeping," Trenton said defiantly.

"Aren't you all supposed to be sleeping as well?"

Trenton frowned. "We are not tired," he declared. "Only babies sleep. We are not babies."

Brandt looked over at Edward and Isabeau, who were reclining on the hay pile, yawning. "Look at your brother and sister over there," he said, pointing. "They are babies and they are tired. Let's take them back to the keep where they may have their nap."

He started to move but Trenton turned the stick on him. "If you want them, you must fight me for them."

Brandt came to a halt and put his hands up to show he was unarmed. "I have no weapon, evil black knight. Will you let me pass?"

"Nay," Trenton barked. "You must fight me."

With a shrug, Brandt moved towards Trenton, who started whacking at his father with the stick. Brandt caught the stick easily, and his son, and grabbed the boy around the waist so he was facing away from his father. Thoroughly angry, Trenton started to kick and howl. That brought Aramis running, who began whacking at his father's backside with his stick. Brandt yanked the stick away and tossed it, causing Aramis to plow into the back of his father's legs.

The man lost his balance and fell to his knees. Once down, Aramis began jumping gleefully on him while Trenton managed to wriggle free.

Brandt laughed softly as his boys pounced on him. Behind him, he could hear the babies squealing as the climbed down off the hay pile and joined the fun.  Soon, Brandt had his toddler in his arms, nibbling her fat little cheeks, as his three boys tried to wrest him to the ground.  He ended up laying down just to make it easy for them.

"There you are!"

The cry came from the stable entrance.  Five pairs of eyes turned to see Ellowyn standing there, hands on her hips and accusations written all over her face.  She pointed a finger at Brandt.

"What on earth are you doing?" she asked her husband. "They are supposed to be sleeping. Do you have any idea of the panic I have gone through for the past ten minutes when I went to check on them and found all of my children missing?"

Brandt sat up with the baby still in his arms.  He glanced at his boys, who were looking rather guilty, before looking back at his wife.

"They did not want to sleep," he told her. "We were inspecting horses."

Ellowyn knew better. She scowled at her boys.  "Aramis, Trenton," she snapped softly. "Upstairs, now, or you shall feel my wrath."  As the boys bolted past her, she called after them. "If I do not find you in bed when I get to your chamber, there will be trouble."

The boys yelled something back to her she couldn't quite make out, but they were moving to do her bidding and that was all she cared about.  Her attention the returned to Brandt, still on the ground, with their two youngest children in his arms. Ellowyn shook her head at him as she moved to collect Isabeau from his arms.

Brandt rolled to his knees, slowly reclaiming his feet.  He wasn't as young as he used to be and not nearly as agile since the injuries he sustained at Poitiers. But he was alive, and reasonably healthy, and that was all that mattered.  He picked Edward up.

"Are we all in trouble, Mummy?" he asked.

322

Gazing up at her tall, handsome, and playful husband, Ellowyn shook her head with resignation.

"What am I to do with you, Brandt?" she asked rhetorically. "You know I have enough trouble maintaining control with Aramis and Trenton without you acting as their partner in crime. And now you drag Edward and Isabeau into your escapades?"

Brandt grinned and bent down to kiss her on the cheek. "You are right," he said. "I am sorry. It will not happen again."

Exasperated, Ellowyn turned away and headed out of the stables. "Nay, you are not sorry and it most certainly will happen again."

He simply grinned at her. Out in the sunshine, they headed across Guildford's bailey on their way to the keep, which had a third story added to it a few years ago to accommodate their growing family. Mother and father still had the big chamber on the second level but the new third level was now divided into two chambers for the children. But the de Russe clan wasn't the only family growing within the walls of Guildford.

It seemed that everyone was settling down and getting married. In fact, in the bailey, Brandt had three small cottages built to accommodate his married knights. Brennan and Bridget had married almost three years ago and now had an infant son.

Alex, having spent a good deal of time comforting Annabeth after the passing of Dylan, had married the woman a year ago and they had a child on the way. Lastly, Rosalind and Magnus had married after Rosalind had spent a good deal of time nursing the knight back to health after his injury at Poitiers. They had no children yet but were hopeful that God would soon bless them. Guildford was filling up with children and they wanted to make their contribution.

But that wasn't all that changed; Evan St. Hèver now served the Duke of Exeter, a very young and enormous knight that was easily as skilled and powerful as his brother. He and Stefan had become very good friends and they had shared many single-man adventures together, much to the amusement of the others, and Margarethe had joined a convent shortly after her father returned from Poitiers. With Brandt's connections and money, Margarethe had found a lucrative position at Westminster in London. Never fully comfortable with her father or with the path her sister had chosen, she had decided to join the cloister and Brandt had been happy to finance it.

Lives that had happily moved on, existing in peace, even though the Prince of Wales continued his warring campaign. Because of the severity of Brandt's injuries at Poitiers and because he was getting on in years, Edward had permitted him retirement. After all, the man had spent over ten years of his life fighting in France. He had put his time in. Now, it was his turn to enjoy his life and his family as he had never before had the opportunity. Aramis, Trenton, Edward, Isabeau, and Ellowyn were his very reasons for living and he thanked God daily that he'd been given the opportunity.

And he planned to keep playing with his boys no matter what his wife said. The best things in his life seemed to happen when she was angry with him.

## ABOUT THE AUTHOR

Kathryn Le Veque has been a prolific writer of Medieval Romance Novels for twenty years.

Brandt and Ellowyn's story pulls two major warring families together – the House of de Russe and the House of de Nerra. That means that Gaston de Russe (THE DARK ONE: DARK KNIGHT) can count Brandt de Russe and Braxton de Nerra (THE FALLS OF ERITH) among his ancestors. No wonder he's such a great knight!

Moreover, all of his knights have connections with other Le Veque novels – Dylan and Alex de Lara are the sons of Tate de Lara (DRAGONBLADE), and sweet Brennan St. Hever is the son of Kenneth St. Hever (ISLAND OF GLASS/THE DRAGONBLADE TRILOGY). Magnus de Reyne is the descendent of Creed de Reyne (GUARDIAN OF DARKNESS) and Stefan le Bec is the ancestor of Richmond le Bec (GREAT PROTECTOR). This is a novel that truly tied in many great houses.

Visit Kathryn's website at www.kathrynleveque.com for more information. Kathryn lives in Mission Viejo, California with her husband, two children, three cats, and one dog. It's a full house. When she's not writing, she likes to cook, garden, golf, and travel.

All of Kathryn's novels are available for Kindle at Amazon.com.